LITTLE WHITE LIES

ALSO BY KATIE DALE

Someone Else's Life

LITTLE WHITE LIES

katie dale

DELACORTE PRESS

Text copyright © 2013 by Katie Dale
Jacket art © 2014 Nikki Smith/Arcangel Images

Published in the United States by Delacorte Press, an imprint of Random House Children's Books, a division of Random House LLC, a Penguin Random House Company, New York. Originally published in paperback by Simon and Schuster UK Ltd., a CBS Company, London, in 2013.

Delacorte Press is a registered trademark and the colophon is a trademark of Random House LLC.

Visit us on the Web! randomhouse.com/teens

Educators and librarians, for a variety of teaching tools, visit us at RHTeachersLibrarians.com

Library of Congress Cataloging-in-Publication Data
Dale, Katie.
Little white lies / Katie Dale.—First U.S. edition.
pages cm
"Originally published in paperback by Simon and Schuster UK Ltd., a CBS Company, London, in 2013"—Copyright page.
Summary: "The first time Lou meets mysterious Christian, she knows he is The One. But when Christian's secret is unveiled in front of the whole world, it seems everything he's ever told Lou is a lie, and Lou finds herself ensnared in a web of deceit"—Provided by publisher.
ISBN 978-0-385-74067-8 (hc)—ISBN 978-0-375-89973-7 (ebook)
[1. Dating (Social customs)—Fiction. 2. Secrets—Fiction. 3. Deception—Fiction. 4. Family problems—Fiction.]
I. Title.
PZ7.D15244Li 2014
[Fic]—dc23
2013015479

The text of this book is set in 11-point Garamond.

Printed in the United States of America
10 9 8 7 6 5 4 3 2 1
First U.S. Edition

Dedicated to Chris, and our own
wonderful chance encounter at
Sheffield University

Oh, what a tangled web we weave,
When first we practice to deceive!

—Sir Walter Scott

Prologue

Sweat trickles down the back of my neck as I check the computer clock for the millionth time. *"Hurry up!"*

"Patience, Titch," Kenny chides. "You can't rush genius!" He winks, his eyes the only part of his face visible through his balaclava.

My heart beats madly in the darkness. "This is taking too long," I hiss. "Are you sure you can do it?"

"Piece of cake," Kenny assures me, his gloved fingertips dancing over the office keyboard, illuminated by the unbearably bright computer screen. "Trust me."

A woman laughs loudly outside, and my eyes fly to the unshaded windows.

"Can't you reduce the brightness or something?" I beg. "Someone might see."

"Settle, petal, I'm nearly there." Kenny clicks the mouse as it flickers quickly over the screen.

I glance again at the open blinds, then carefully pad across the dark office to the window. I reach for the cord—then headlights suddenly slice across the room.

I drop to the floor, my pulse racing. "Shit!"

Kenny looks over. "Titch. Seriously. Chill. No one can see us."

I swallow hard and stand up.

"Unless you stand in front of the window, of course," he adds. "Get back here."

I scurry back to his side, but suddenly I freeze. "What's that?"

"What?" Kenny hisses.

"I thought I heard something."

He rolls his eyes. "You're just para—"

A door slams noisily, cutting him off.

Kenny's eyes widen as footsteps echo on the stairs.

"Quick!" He flicks the screen off, grabs me, and ducks beneath the computer desk, just as the fluorescent strips flicker on, flooding the room in glaring white light. I squeeze myself closer to Kenny, his heart thrumming madly against my ear.

"Lucky we had to come back, eh, mate?" a man's voice says. "Old Harris would've had your guts for garters in the morning!"

"I don't understand," a second man says. "I swear I set the alarm when I left."

Kenny's eyes meet mine as we both recognize the voice of Neil, the work experience mentor I've been shadowing for the past week, learning the ropes—including secretly memorizing the codes for the burglar alarm and computers. Turns out my careers advisor was right—work experience *is* invaluable.

"You're going senile!" The first man chuckles.

"Watch it, Trev—you're older than me, remember?" Neil says.

"Older and wiser," Trev laughs. "At least I don't forget stuff! Where'd you leave your phone this time?"

"It must be on my desk."

Shit. Neil's desk. The desk we're hiding beneath!

I hold my breath, my blood pounding deafeningly in my ears as his heavy footsteps thud towards us.

Oh my God, I'm going to jail. I'm going straight to jail. What was I thinking?

2

I fold my knees into my chest, trying to make myself as small as physically possible as I squeeze my eyes shut, praying desperately, madly, hopelessly. . . .

Please don't find us. Please don't find us. Please, please, please . . .

The footsteps get louder, closer . . . then a mobile phone bleeps.

"Hey, Neil!"

The footsteps stop. I hold my breath.

"False alarm. You left it at home, you plank!"

My heart leaps. *No way!*

"What?" Neil says.

"I just got a message from your mobile—your wife's got it. Come on, let's get out of here before you lose *all* your marbles!"

The footsteps move quickly away, and the door slams again.

"Hey." Kenny nudges me after a few moments. "They've gone."

I crack open an eyelid. The room is dark again. "What happened?"

He holds up a mobile phone, a text message shining on the screen.

Sent to TREVOR: Hi Trev, can you tell Neil I've got his phone at home?

"Neil's phone?" I stare at him. "*You* sent the text?"

He grins. "How much do you love me?"

"Kenny, you're a genius!"

"Like, duh." He shrugs. "Should buy us some time to get out of here anyway. Let's go."

My heart sinks. "What about—"

"This?" Kenny winks, his dark eyes sparkling as he holds up a USB stick.

"You got it?" I stare at him. "You actually *got it*?"

"I never break a promise." He grins. "What's it worth?"

I take the precious memory stick and throw my arms around him, adrenaline surging through my veins, unable to believe what I'm actually, finally, holding in my hands.

"It's utterly priceless," I whisper. "Thank you so much, Kenny."

"Thank me later." He smiles. "First we have to get out of here."

ONE

"Run!" I yell over my shoulder as I sprint as fast as I can. "Come *on*!"

I round a corner and send a flock of flustered pigeons flapping into the trees, my heart pounding as hard as my feet on the concrete path as I glance backwards. But the path behind me is empty. I stop running, gasping for breath as I wait for a moment, but there's still no sign of my friend. Hastily I retrace my steps, but it's only when I reach the corner that I see the familiar figure splayed out on the grass.

"I'm dying!" she groans.

"You're such a drama queen." I smile as I jog over.

"And you're a slave driver!" Vix moans.

"It was your idea to come running with me!" I laugh. "Don't you remember last night?"

"No!" she says, blinking up at me. "I was drunk last night. Or crazy. Or both. I didn't mean it, *obviously*."

"So you don't want to shape up to snag a cute fresher?"

"Well, yes," Vix admits grudgingly. "But why do we have to run so *early*?"

"What time *is* it?" I ask, gazing out over the beautiful sunlit park. Other joggers are already bouncing round the perimeter, past families making their way to school and a couple of dog walkers.

But there's still no sign of him.

Vix checks her watch. "Ten past eight."

I frown. He should be here by now.

"Did you hear me? Ten past *eight*!" Vix cries. "And I haven't even had a coffee yet! How am I even *functioning*?"

"Come on, lazybones." I take her hand. "Just a few more meters."

"Can't," she says. "I can't move."

"There's a café just over there."

Vix looks up. "With coffee?"

"Yes," I laugh, helping her up. "There's coffee, and comfy sofas, a great view and—"

Suddenly my heart jumps. *There he is.* Quickly, I bend to retie my shoelaces as he crosses our path.

"Aha!" Vix grins. "So *that's* the real reason you've been running every morning."

I look up sharply. "What?"

She raises an eyebrow. "The tall, dark, and handsome hotty who nearly gave you a heart attack?"

Shit. *Am I that obvious?*

"You're blushing!" she squeals.

"*Shh!*" I hiss, glancing over to check he didn't hear. He heads into the café, the hood of his red jacket pulled over his mess of black hair despite the warm morning sunshine.

"No wonder the cute freshers are crashing and burning with you—you're totally smitten with Mr. McHotty over there!" Vix smirks. "Not that I blame you. He's totally fit. Check out that *arse*! Now, that's a view worth exercising for. What's his name?"

I shrug.

"You haven't even *talked* to him?" Vix stares at me. "Come on!"

"No—Vix!" I protest, grabbing her arm as she heads for the café. "I can't just go up and talk to him—I don't know anything about him!"

6

"Well, how are you ever going to *get* to know him if you never even meet?" she argues.

Cold dread trickles down my spine. Do I have the guts to actually *meet* him?

"Seriously, babe, what's the worst that could happen?"

I shudder. *If only she knew.*

"You don't get on, you say goodbye, you get to lie in in future?" Vix grins. "Anyway, you do know *some* stuff about him," she argues. "You know he's cute, you know he's athletic. . . ."

"I know you're shallow!"

"And *you're* a *chicken!*" Vix cries. "Life's too short—I'm going in!"

"No, Vix!" I grab her arm.

"Then *you* go!"

"But—"

"Bye!" She shakes her arm loose.

"Fine." I hurry past her towards the entrance of the café.

"Atta girl!" Vix cries.

Keeping my head down, I walk through the door, make a beeline for the counter, and order two iced coffees before risking a quick glance round the café.

I spot him almost immediately. He has his back to me as he takes a seat at a corner table with a bottle of orange juice. I watch as he peels his jacket off and drapes it over the back of his chair, revealing toned, tanned arms.

Sweat beads on my forehead and my own hoodie suddenly feels two sizes too small.

I pay for the coffees, pick up my tray, then take a deep breath. *This is it.*

I head towards him, my fingers tightly gripping the tray.

I can do this, I tell myself, forcing my feet to move. *One step, then another. Simple.*

So why does it suddenly seem like the hardest thing I've ever done in my life?

Just talk to him—just words.

Through the window, Vix gives me a thumbs-up. Great. An audience.

Another step. Then another.

The coffee shivers and slops over the sides of the cups. I will myself to keep walking, my eyes fixed on the back of his head.

One more step . . .

My tray slips suddenly from my fingers, the crockery crashing to the floor as coffee splashes everywhere—including straight down the back of the guy, who leaps from his chair, his jacket tumbling to the floor.

"Oh my God, I'm so sorry!" I cry.

He looks up and I freeze as his pale blue eyes meet mine, goose bumps prickling down my arms as I struggle to breathe. I look away quickly, my cheeks burning.

"Oh no—your jacket!" I pick it up, grab a napkin from the table, and hurriedly dab at the coffee stains.

"It's fine, really," he says, smiling down at me.

"No, I'm really sorry. I'll pay for the dry cleaning," I offer.

"Forget about it." He smiles again, taking his jacket and orange juice. "It's fate's way of telling me it's about time I did some laundry."

"I'm so sorry," I say yet again, stupidly, as he hurries out of the café.

"*What* was *that?*" Vix rushes in, her face a mixture of horror and amusement.

"Smooth, huh?" I sigh.

"*Now* I understand why you didn't want to introduce yourself," she laughs. "Lucky it wasn't *hot* coffee—he'd be in hospital!"

"What a disaster!" I sink my head into my hands. "Or then again, maybe not . . ."

"Seriously?" Vix smiles. "Exactly *which* part of the last five minutes wasn't completely catastrophic?"

I reach down and pick something up off the floor.

"The part where Mr. McHotty dropped his wallet . . ."

TWO

"Beautiful!" Vix beams at my reflection. "Ooh, and I've got just the right color blush in my room."

"Vix, I don't want any—"

"Back in a sec!"

I sigh as she disappears into the corridor; then I turn to the mirror and stare at the unfamiliar girl gazing back at me.

Just months ago my hair hung, lank and mousy-brown, round my shoulders. Now it twists and curls, dyed blond a few weeks ago by me, now pinned and styled by Vix, who has also plastered so much makeup over my face that only my black-rimmed eyes are recognizable. Though there's something different lingering behind *them* now too. A flicker of . . . what? Excitement? Fear?

Maybe both.

"Here we go . . ." Vix bounds back into my room. "Smile!"

I grimace as she dabs at my cheeks with a soft brush.

"Yikes! I hope you're gonna do better than that when you see McHotty!" she scolds. "No wonder he ran a mile!"

My heart beats fast at the thought of seeing him again.

"There!" she says finally, stepping back and admiring her handiwork. "What do you think?"

"I don't recognize myself," I tell her honestly.

"Well, duh!" She grins. "That's kind of the point! It's your second week at university—what better time to reinvent yourself?" She smiles. "You're gorgeous, Lou. Believe it. Work it. No more klutzy Louise Shepherd, no more being tongue-tied and awkward around guys. Now you are *Lou*—smart, sophisticated, confident femme fatale." She giggles. "McHotty doesn't stand a chance."

"I hope you're right." I lick my strawberry-glossed lips nervously. "Come on, let's go."

"Just a sec." She grabs the curling iron.

"*Vix!* How much longer?"

"One second! Just the finishing touches . . ."

"You've been saying that for hours!" I protest. "We should have returned his wallet straight away."

"We couldn't!" Vix protests. "We had lectures to get to."

"But we walked past his house on the way back from the park this morning," I remind her. "We could have dropped it off then."

"But *he* doesn't know that." Vix grins. "Besides, you were *not* presentable. This way you get to make a great second impression— God knows you need it after the first!"

"Very reassuring," I groan. "But hurry up—what if Christian's been freaking out all morning about losing his wallet?"

"*Christian* now, is it?" Vix says, a smug smile on her lips.

My cheeks burn. "That's what it says on his driving license, Christian Marcus Webb." I stare down at the little pink card, usefully printed with his name, date of birth, address, and those piercing eyes that seem to stare straight into my soul.

"Well, *Christian* will be so knocked out by your appearance he won't even care about his wallet." Vix grins, setting down the curling iron. "There. Done. We can go."

"Finally." I grab my bag from my bed and usher Vix out of my room, locking the door behind us, then hurry down the two flights of stairs to the bustling reception area of our halls of residence.

"Lou! Vix!" Matt calls over from the group of students hanging out on the sofas. "We're thinking of hitting that new club on Division Street tonight—Lush. Do you guys fancy it?"

"Sounds like a plan!" Vix beams.

"Excellent!" He smiles.

"What about you, Lou?" his mate Dan asks. "Have you done something different with your hair? It looks great."

"Oh. Thanks." I smile.

"Lou will have to let you know later." Vix grins. "She may have a hot date tonight!"

Dan's face falls. "A date? Who with?"

"No one," I tell him, hooking my arm through Vix's. "See you later. Come on, Vix."

"No fair." Vix pouts as I drag her towards the exit. "Why do all the decent guys always fancy *you*?"

"They don't!" I protest.

"Please. So beautiful. So blind."

"Matt likes you," I argue. "And he seems really nice."

"Yeah, but he's a computer science geek." She rolls her eyes. "It doesn't count. Ooh—post!" She slips from my grip and skips over to the pigeonholes to check her mail.

"*Vix!*" I protest. "Come on!"

"Chill, hon—Christian's house is, like, a two-minute drive away!"

"You want to take the car? What happened to getting in shape?"

"I jogged this morning, didn't I?"

"Barely." I smile.

"Besides, jogging in trainers round a nice flat park is *not* the same as trudging up and down Sheffield's bleeding hills. It's bad enough trekking halfway across the city to lectures—I *so* should've gone to a campus uni—but there's no *way* I'm hiking up hills in *heels!*" she says vehemently. "Besides, I thought you were in a hurry to return Christian's wallet. And you don't want to turn up all puffed and sweaty after spending so long getting beautiful, do you . . . ?"

"All right!" I laugh at her swift change of tactics. "We'll take my uncle's car."

"Sweet." She smiles, then frowns as she flicks through the collection of envelopes in her hand. "I still haven't heard from the student loan company, have you? I need to know when my money's coming in."

I sigh, then search the pigeonholes for my own mail.

"Uh, Lou, why are you looking in the *W* box? You're not Mrs. Webb yet, you know!"

"Oh yeah, right." My cheeks burn as I move to the *S* box. I have to stop *doing* that. Louise Shepherd. My name is *Louise Shepherd*. I riffle through the letters, then freeze as I spot the familiar postmark.

"Bills, bills, bills!" Vix moans, opening her mail. "You get anything interesting?"

"Same," I lie quickly, shoving the letter into my bag as she hooks her arm through mine. "I'm gonna have to start looking for a job soon!"

"Seriously!" Vix nods as we head into the car park. "No one ever warns you how expensive uni is! I thought it was all about late nights and lie-ins, booze and bonking, good times and—"

"Good grades?" I raise an eyebrow.

"You sound just like my dad," Vix groans as we slide into the car. " 'University is not about getting drunk all day, Victoria. This is your future on the line.' He's still sore that I didn't get into Cambridge like his beloved *Darius*." She pulls a face. "Dads! It must be easier living with your uncle and aunt, huh? Less pressure?"

I falter. *I wish.* I owe them everything. They had no obligation to adopt me, so when I let them down it's a hundred times worse.

And boy, have I let them down.

"Not that I'm saying it's easy losing your mum and dad," Vix adds quickly. "Just . . . just tell me to shut my big mouth."

"It's okay." I smile as I maneuver the car out of the car park. "I never really knew my parents, but I don't think my aunt and uncle treat me any differently than my cousins. Except, I guess, my uncle's a little more protective of them, but that's probably just because they're younger than me."

I smile as I think of fearless little Millie and her comical take on the world. She'd be into everything, given half a chance.

"Tell me about it," Vix groans. "It's a nightmare being the youngest. Especially with Darius for an older brother—he's like another parent!"

I laugh.

"But you and your cousins get on okay?" she asks.

"Like a house on fire." I smile. "I think of them more like sisters, really. One's only a year younger than me, so we always did everything together—horse-riding lessons, ballet classes, same piano tutor, same swimming coach, same school . . . till sixth form, anyway."

"Why, what happened?"

My heart sinks. *Then everything changed.*

"My uncle always wanted us to go to his old boarding school for our A levels—to make sure we got the best grades. They only take girls in the sixth form, and I was a year older, so . . . it was the first time we'd been separated nearly our whole lives."

And I wish I'd never gone. Never left her side.

"I wish I had sisters," Vix sighs. "All I hear is: 'Victoria, why can't you be more like your brother?' My dad doesn't understand that I don't *want* to be a bloodsucking lawyer, and investigative journalism is an equally valid career choice. He thinks it's all just paparazzi on motorbikes." She sighs. "You know he gave Darius a Porsche for

14

his twenty-first? A *Porsche*? And he won't even let me drive his old *Volvo*. I can't believe your uncle loaned you his car. You're so lucky. And it's an automatic too. So easy to drive."

"Yeah, it is—except when you have to go up and down all these hills!"

"So how come you've got your uncle's car anyway?" Vix asks. "Doesn't he need it?"

I shrug. "Not for a while." *Not where he is.*

"He's away?" Vix asks.

I nod.

"Business or pleasure?"

"Business," I say quickly, focusing on the road in front of me as we drive down a steep hill, hoping Vix will drop the subject.

I think of the envelope in my jacket pocket. *It's certainly not pleasure.*

"Isn't he worried about you damaging his car?" Vix asks. "I'd be totally paranoid about even *scratching* it, if it were me—my dad would go completely mental."

I smile. "My uncle doesn't really go mental about that stuff anymore."

"Anymore?" Vix raises her eyebrow.

I hesitate. I've only known Vix for two weeks, and even though we seem to have clicked straight away, making friends and sharing secrets isn't exactly high on my list of priorities right now. I'm not sure how much I really want her knowing about my life.

"He . . . he used to be a bit of a drinker, and there was this one time—years ago—someone keyed his new car and he went crazy, punched a brick wall, and broke his hand."

"Wow," Vix says.

"But he went on an anger management course and now he's really mellow." I smile, remembering how he laughs when he tells the

15

tale, showing us the scar on his knuckle. "He doesn't drink much anymore either, and the story comes out every time he tries to warn us about the dangers of alcohol."

"Tell me about it!" Vix smiles. "'Alcohol is poison from the devil, Victoria. Do not succumb to its evil temptations.' Thank God my dad didn't see me last night."

I laugh.

"Or the night before, come to that. Or all last week, or— Ooh, we're here!"

She points out of the window and my heart beats fast as I pull over in front of a cottage with a green door.

Twelve Bromley Road.

"Can you believe you've passed his house every morning on your way to the park?" Vix grins at me. "And all this time you had no idea that the man of your dreams lived just inside!"

The man of my dreams. If only she knew.

I look up at the little gray stone cottage, and although I've seen it many times before, goose bumps prickle down my arms. Can I really go through with this?

"Don't worry." Vix squeezes my arm. "I know last time didn't go that well, but this time you're the hero, returning his precious wallet. He can't *not* be glad to see you!" She grins.

I smile tightly, then take a deep breath, step out of the car, and walk through the gate, up the garden path to the door. I swallow hard, then knock tentatively.

Nothing happens.

"Louder!" Vix calls through the open car window.

I hesitate, then knock harder.

Still nothing.

"Oh, for Pete's sake." Vix jumps out of the car, races up the path, and thumps her fist on the door.

16

"Vix!"

"What?"

Still nothing happens. My heart sinks. *He's not in.*

"You looking for Christian?"

Vix and I turn in unison.

"Yes!" Vix beams, skipping towards the lanky red-haired guy who's leaning on the gatepost.

"Then you're in luck." He grins. "Because I know exactly where you can find him."

But I don't feel lucky at all as I stand frozen on the doorstep, unable to believe my eyes.

"How serendipitous!" Vix beams at him. "I'm Vix. This is Louise."

"Lovely to meet you both."

A shiver runs down my spine as his sparkling dark eyes meet mine.

"I'm Kenny."

THREE

"Christian works at The Flying Pig pub down the road," Kenny says. "I'll walk with you."

"Thanks!" Vix smiles.

"No need," I say quickly. "If you could just give us directions, that'd be great. We don't want to put you to any trouble."

"No trouble." Kenny grins. "I'm on my way there now anyway."

"Wonderful!" Vix beams.

Yeah. Wonderful.

"What about your heels, Vix?" I protest.

"Don't be silly!" She shoots me a look. "They're fine! Besides, I could do with some fresh air."

"So are you a student here—*Leigh,* was it?" Kenny asks as I reluctantly follow them down the road.

"Louise." I shoot him a look. "Yes. I'm studying English literature."

"Ah, fiction." He smiles knowingly. "Of course."

Shit. He's going to ruin everything. So much for reinventing myself.

"We're both students. That's how we met," Vix pipes up. "Lou and I are in the same halls, and have some of the same classes too, but I'm doing journalism."

"All hail the power of the press." Kenny bows. "The media have

18

created and destroyed more careers than any other force known to man."

Brilliant. He could tell her *everything*. Vix, the fricking aspiring investigative reporter.

"Oh, I'm only interested in the facts," she says earnestly. "I believe that's the true function of the press."

"Quite right." Kenny smiles. "*Fact* and *fiction*. What an intriguing pair you make."

"Is it far to this pub?" I snap as we turn onto a street filled with more terraced cottages and there's still no sign of it.

"Nope." Kenny grins. "Not far."

"So are you a student too, Kenny?" Vix asks.

"Yep. I'm doing computer science."

"Wow, that must be interesting," she gushes. "I always think it's amazing how computers are programmed by code—it's like a secret language or something!"

What? I shoot her a look. She's changed her tune.

"Ah, it's when you crack the code that it gets interesting." Kenny winks. "Once you've hacked one computer you can hack them all."

My heart beats fast. "So how do you know Christian, Kenny?" I ask, quickly changing the subject.

"A result of my drinking habits, I'm afraid. The pub's just round the corner from my flat—"

"You live in a flat, not halls?" Vix says, impressed.

"Yeah, I had enough of communal living at boarding school." He shudders. "I moved up here a few weeks early to acclimatize, and I met Christian in the first pub I went to. Plus his house is almost opposite my nearest off-license, so I've bumped into him on the street a few times too. How about you two?"

"Oh, we don't know him—yet." Vix smiles.

Kenny raises an eyebrow. "Then why are you looking for him?"

"Well . . . ," Vix starts.

"He dropped his wallet," I say quickly. "We just want to return it."

"Ah! A couple of Good Samaritans, are you?"

I feel sick.

"Hey, you could ask him about a job too, Lou," Vix suggests. "Kill two birds with one stone? Returning his wallet proves you're trustworthy, after all."

Kenny nods. "Trust: you can't put a price on that."

I shiver. *Except when you can . . .*

"You can trust me," Kenny said the day I first approached him, back at Oakwood Grange boarding school. But I didn't believe him, not straight away. Despite the fact that we'd been at the same school for a whole year, I barely knew him—our social spheres were galaxies apart. Until that day. Until I needed him.

I gate-crashed a meeting of the computer club and found Kenny showing a new website he'd created to his geeky mates.

"Impressive," I said, and instantly they all turned, startled. Girls were rare enough at the college—we were outnumbered three to one—but in the ICT room they had long been declared extinct.

"Nice work." I let my Chanel-spritzed hair brush Kenny's shoulder as I leaned towards the screen. "What else can you do?"

He spent the rest of the evening showing off all his codes and tricks, till finally I asked him to walk me back to my boarding house.

"The truth is, Kenny, I need your help," I sighed once we were alone. "I'm in big trouble, and you're the only one who can get me out of it."

I told him I was struggling in biology and had a mock exam coming up that would determine my predicted grade—and consequently which universities I could apply to.

"So I'm guessing you don't want me to tutor you, as I'm not even taking biology?" He raised an eyebrow.

"Not exactly."

"So . . . ?"

I took a deep breath. "The mock paper's on the school computer system. . . ."

"Wait." His eyes widened. "You want me to hack into the system so you can cheat on the exam?" He ran a hand through his thick ginger hair. "Bloody hell."

"Please, Kenny, you're my last hope," I said desperately, grabbing his hand and squeezing tight. "I can't fail it. If I do, I won't have a *chance* of getting offers from the universities I want. Plus my aunt and uncle will *kill* me—they've forked out a fortune for me to come to Oakwood!"

"But you'll still need to get good grades in your actual exams in the summer." Kenny frowned. "Otherwise the universities won't take you anyway."

"I can turn things around by then," I insisted. "I've just been . . . distracted lately. Let me worry about the actual A levels." I gazed up at him pleadingly. "Or are you saying it's too difficult?"

"As if!" he scoffed, looking at me for a long moment. "Okay, I'll do it. Anything for a damsel in distress."

"Thank you!" I cried, throwing my arms around his neck.

"You're welcome, Titch," he laughed, squeezing me tight. "But I'd like a favor in return."

His price was being his date to his cousin's wedding. I agreed—it was a small price to pay if he could really do what I asked—and, more importantly, keep his mouth shut.

And he delivered on both fronts. He never told a soul what we'd done. I passed the test—and he passed mine. As time went by I tested his computer knowledge, his skill, and his loyalty. He seemed

21

to relish the opportunity to show off, and each time he passed with flying colors. Then finally I approached him with the big one.

I shudder as I remember that night in Neil's office. After that, I never thought I'd see Kenny again—we were never *supposed* to see each other again. . . . Yet here he is, hundreds of miles from where we last met. But *why*?

"Are you ready?" Vix suddenly stops in front of me and turns, shaking me from my thoughts.

I blink at her. "For what?"

"For the moment of truth!" Vix cries.

I freeze. Have I missed something? Has Kenny told her?

"Lou, come on, have you got the wallet ready?"

Wallet? Oh, right, *Christian*. Suddenly I realize we're standing outside a pub.

"No," I say, my head spinning as I stare up at the Flying Pig sign, at the people sitting, chatting and laughing at the tables out front. "I just . . . need a minute, okay?"

"Of course." She nods, then glances at Kenny. "Excuse us for a moment while we powder our noses," Vix says to him. "Lou?"

"Hm?" I look up.

"You coming?" Vix raises her eyebrows.

"Um, no thanks." This is my chance to speak to Kenny alone.

"You *sure*?" She frowns, confused.

"Positive. See you in a bit."

Kenny looks from Vix to me, amusement twinkling in his eyes.

"Okay, then! You guys grab a table out here. I'll be right back." Vix glares at me as she disappears inside the pub.

"Uh-oh." Kenny grins, sitting down at a table. "I think you missed her subtle hints."

"I don't care," I hiss. "What the hell's going on, Kenny?"

"Calm down, *Louise*." He winks. "I thought blondes were meant to have more fun? Maybe it's only *natural* blondes."

22

My blood runs cold. "Why are you here?"

He shrugs. "Getting a degree."

"But why *here*?" I demand. "Why *Sheffield*?"

"Same as you." He shrugs. "I got in through clearing."

"But *why* did you go through clearing at all?" I stare at him. "Unlike me, you didn't flunk your exams—you're a genius!"

"Aw, thanks, babe." He grins.

"What I mean is you could've had your pick of universities," I press. "Why choose *here*?"

"Of all the gin joints in all the world, why'd I walk into yours?"

"Exactly!"

"Simple." He shrugs. "You're here."

An icy shiver trickles down my spine as my whole world falls apart in front of me. This was it, this was my chance, and Kenny's ruined it. It's over. It's over before it even began. Unless . . .

"What do you want, Kenny?"

"Settle, petal, I can keep a secret. You know that better than anyone."

"But what's it worth, right?" I nod grimly.

He frowns. "I'm hurt, Titch. I don't want anything. Besides, I was kidding, Ms. Ego. The whole world doesn't revolve around you, you know?"

I look at him uncertainly. "Then . . . ?"

"I just decided Oxford wasn't for me," he sighs. "I've had my fill of quads and spires, and too many stuffy snobs from Oakwood were going there. And then Professor Kentley—one of my heroes— transferred to the faculty here, so . . . Sheffield was the obvious choice."

"So it's just a coincidence?" I say warily.

"It's serendipity!" He beams.

I shuffle my feet. It's hardly a *lucky* accident. . . .

"Now I can help you."

"What?"

"I've been worried about you." Kenny's face softens. "It must be really hard, starting a new life, with a new identity, having to lie to everyone. . . ."

"*Shh,*" I hiss as a group of girls from my halls pass by. "So what was all that crap about fact and fiction?"

"I was just having a little fun. I'm sorry, okay? I won't give you away, I promise."

I search his eyes, trying to work out what's going on inside his head, unsure whether to believe him.

"I understand why you're doing it, you know," he says gently. "If it'd happened to my family, I'd do the same thing." His gaze softens. "How is she?"

My heart sinks. "The same."

He nods. "And your uncle?"

"How do you think he is?" I snap.

"Hey, I'm on your side. I just ask because . . . well, I haven't seen anything in the papers for a while."

"Thank goodness." It was almost impossible to leave the house once the press got hold of the story. And as for school—it was like I'd grown a second head. Everywhere I went, people stared at me. Conversations would stop the minute I entered a room, then bubble up in excited whispers the moment I left. All I wanted was to forget for a while, to be normal, to be like everyone else.

And now I am.

"No one here knows who I am, Kenny—as far as anyone knows I'm just Louise Shepherd, a normal fresher starting at uni."

"Got it," he says earnestly. "Honestly, I'm not here to cause trouble, Titch. I just thought you could use a friendly face. Someone to talk to. Someone you don't have to lie to."

I sigh. It *is* exhausting lying all the time. Vix was right; the great thing about uni, moving into halls with hundreds of other students, is that it's the perfect place to reinvent yourself. No one knows you, your past, your family, your background, so you can be whoever you want to be.

In theory.

But the trouble with pretending to be someone else is that you can't let your guard down for a moment. Especially when you're befriended by an aspiring investigative journalist.

"I'm here for you, Titch," Kenny says softly, taking my hand. "Haven't I kept your secret so far?"

I nod. *The biggest secret of all.*

"You can trust me." He squeezes my hand. "I promise. Let me help you."

I smile weakly. It's not exactly like I have a choice. If Kenny's here to stay, it's safer to keep him onside.

"What've I missed?" Vix says as she emerges from the pub with two pints.

Too late, I drop Kenny's hand.

"Cheers, Vix!" He grins as she sips her pint and passes him the second. "What about Lou?"

"I thought Lou might want to go to the bar herself." Vix's face tightens as she looks at me. "That's why we're here, after all!"

I hesitate.

"Shall I come with you?" she offers.

I falter, torn between the danger of leaving her alone with Kenny and the torture of trying to approach Christian with an audience.

"Come on!" Vix grabs my arm, making my decision for me as she drags me into the pub.

"What are you doing?" She turns on me once we're safely inside. "What?"

"I thought you liked *Christian*."

25

"I do!"

"So why are you trying it on with Kenny, the only guy I've met who's half decent?" she demands.

"I'm not! I'm not interested in Kenny—he's not my type," I tell her.

But I don't want *Vix* getting interested either. . . .

"Besides, he seems a bit . . . weird," I add.

"He's not weird!" Vix protests. "He's quirky. I like quirky. And he's fit."

"Yeah, but . . . there's just something about him that seems a bit . . . shifty," I insist.

"Jeez, Louise! Don't judge a book by its cover—we've only just met the guy!"

I hesitate. It's not like I can tell her about Oakwood . . . "But you hate computer science!" I remind her. "You said it was for geeks!"

"So?"

"So what was all that crap about computer code being an 'amazing secret language'?"

"Lou, it's called *flirting*." Vix laughs. "Find out what a guy's into, then fake an interest so that you seem more attractive. You should do the same with Christian—unless he's done another runner." She frowns as we approach the bar. "He was here a minute ago—he served me. You think he saw you coming?"

Despite her teasing tone, my stomach tightens. *Where's he gone?*

"Can I help you?" A barmaid looks up from wiping a table and Vix nudges me.

"Um, yes, I was just wondering . . ." I hesitate, flustered. "I'm looking for a job," I babble quickly.

Vix raises her eyebrows at me.

"I've got bar experience, and I need some part-time work," I continue. "Are there any shifts going here?"

"Doubtful." She grimaces. "The manager's not in today, but

26

email your CV to him—he does everything online these days." She scribbles down an email address on a napkin and hands it to me.

"Thanks." I smile.

Vix nudges me again.

"Was there anything else?" The barmaid raises an eyebrow.

"Um . . . just . . . is Christian working today?"

"Yep." She nods. "He's just out the back taking a delivery. He should be back any minute." She turns. "Speak of the devil . . ."

I follow her gaze to spot Christian wander in from the beer garden, chatting to a beautiful brunette.

I tense at the sight of them together. "Is that his girlfriend?"

"No." The barmaid smiles knowingly as he heads behind the bar. "So far, so single. Girls ask him out all the time, but he always turns them down."

"Why?" Vix frowns. "Is he gay?"

"No," the barmaid laughs. "He's definitely straight, but he just . . . keeps himself to himself, you know? In the two months I've known him he hasn't been on a single date."

"Two months?" I say.

"Since he moved here." The barmaid nods. "In the summer."

"Where's he from, then?" Vix asks.

"Don't know." She shrugs. "Like I say, he keeps himself to himself. But then, maybe he's just waiting for Miss Right to come along. Good luck!" She smiles at me as she moves away to clear another table.

"Go on, then!" Vix urges. "What are you waiting for? If you don't snag him soon, someone else might!"

She could be right.

"Do you want me to come over with you?" Vix offers.

"No." I shake my head. "Could you just wait here, though?" Far enough away from both Christian and Kenny . . .

"Course." She smiles. "Just call me over if you need moral

27

support. Not that you will. You can do this, Shepherd. Cool, calm, confident femme fatale, right?"

"Right." I nod. *I can do this.*

I take a deep breath, then force myself to turn and walk over to the bar. I climb onto a stool, watching as Christian pours the brunette a glass of wine; then I finally clear my throat.

"Excuse me, Christian Marcus Webb?"

He stiffens. Goose bumps break out over my skin as his pale blue eyes meet mine.

"Sorry, do I know you?" He frowns. "You look familiar. . . ."

"We met this morning," I say nervously.

"We did?" He raises an eyebrow.

I nod. "In the café in the park? I threw coffee all over you? Kinda hard to forget!"

"Oh—yeah, right!" His expression clears. "God, sorry, I've got some kind of face dyslexia, I think—I'm useless at remembering who people are—not great when I'm dealing with customers all day! Now, figures are a different matter—I can remember any number without even trying." He shrugs. "Guess I'm in the wrong job! Anyway, how'd you know my name?"

"Actually, that's why I'm here." I hand him his wallet. "You dropped this."

"You found it!" he cries, his whole face transforming as he smiles, his lips curving gently as those blue eyes shine with warmth. "You're a lifesaver—thank you so much!"

"Well, not exactly," I confess. "It's my fault you dropped it in the first place—I found it in the café after you fled the scene."

He laughs. "Thanks so much for returning it. How did you even find me?"

"I got your address from your driving license." I smile. "Nice picture, by the way."

28

He winces. "Yeah, right."

"Don't worry, everyone looks like a criminal in photo booth pictures."

His smile falters.

"So I called at your house and someone told me you worked here," I continue hastily. "And here I am. Sorry I didn't return it sooner—I had lectures."

"You're a student?"

"Yeah. I'm studying English lit," I explain. "It's mainly reading."

"Ah. Slacker."

"Gratitude!"

He laughs. "Let me buy you a drink."

"That's not necessary—"

"I insist. You came all the way down here to return my wallet, missing valuable sleeping—I mean *reading*—time . . ."

I roll my eyes.

"So it's the least I can do." He grins.

"Well, when you put it like that . . ." I smile. "But only if I buy you one too, to apologize for your jacket—I even promise not to throw it at you this time."

"Deal." He smiles. "So what would you like? Anything but coffee."

"White wine, please—won't stain."

"Good plan!" Christian laughs. "ID?"

My heart beats faster.

"Seriously?" I groan. "My photo's awful."

"*Everyone* looks like a criminal in photo booth pictures," he mimics.

I smile awkwardly. *If only he knew.*

"You've seen mine—it's only fair," he insists. "And a legal obligation—perk of the job." He shrugs.

29

"Fine." I pass him the fake ID Kenny made me.

He winces. "You're right, total mug shot!"

"Hey!" I try to snatch it back.

"Just kidding." He grins, holding it out of my reach. "Louise Charlotte Shepherd," he reads. "What's your date of birth?"

I blink. "What?"

"Need to check it's not a fake." He raises an eyebrow.

I smile confidently. It's not the *date* that's fake . . .

"October eleventh," I tell him. "Libra through and through."

But to my astonishment, he shakes his head and tuts. "Go to jail. Go directly to jail. Do not pass Go. Do not collect two hundred pounds."

Shit. I stare at him. Did Kenny put the wrong date on? I'll kill him!

"Just kidding." Christian winks, passing it back. "You can pass Go, you may drink wine."

Phew. "Funny."

"Sorry." He grins. "You should've seen your face!"

I bet.

I watch him as he pours the wine. "So you're Leo, right?"

The smile drops from his face as wine slops over the edge of the glass. He stares at me. "What?"

My pulse races, wondering if I've gone too far. "Your driving license . . . ," I say hastily. "It said your birthday's in August—that's Leo, right? Or is it Cancer?"

Christian blinks, then smiles quickly. "Right! Yeah. Leo the lion. Sorry, I'm not really into star signs and all that." He grabs a cloth and hurriedly mops up the spilled wine.

"Lucky it wasn't coffee this time!" I babble awkwardly. "Sorry—I should come with hazard lights or something!"

"No, it was my fault—I shouldn't get so distracted by a pretty face." He winks.

I seize the moment. "Well, if you feel like getting distracted later, a bunch of us are heading over to that new club, Lush. It's meant to be really great, and—"

"Sorry, I can't."

"I promise to only have clear drinks. Nothing that will stain!"

He grins. "Sorry. I'm busy tonight."

"Christian!" The brunette taps her empty glass.

"Enjoy your wine." He smiles at me as he moves away.

"Wait!" I say, hating the desperation in my voice. "I still owe you that drink."

"I've got to go—I'm working."

"Christian?" the brunette calls again.

"Thanks again for returning my wallet." Christian smiles, my heart plummeting into my pumps as he turns and walks away.

I blew it.

FOUR

"Jeez, you're a slave driver when you're pissed off," Vix moans as we jog along the road to the park. "I thought you were a fitness freak before, but now . . . you're mental!"

"I'm not pissed off," I fib. "Besides, I let you lie in, as it's Saturday."

"Only to avoid a certain hotty who goes jogging earlier!" Vix raises an eyebrow. "You can't fool me, Shepherd. You should just go back and talk to him. If at first you don't succeed . . ."

"Try again and look really desperate?" I shake my head. "I don't think so. I'm keeping my distance. It's bad enough we still have to pass his house to get to the park." I glance up as we approach the cottage with the green door. "Let's speed up a bit. Then hopefully he won't even see us."

"How fast do you think I can run?" Vix laughs. "I'm invisible!" she mocks. "I am but a blur!"

"Very fu— Oof!" Suddenly I tumble awkwardly to the ground. "*Ow!* Oh shit, bollocks, ouch!"

"Lou!" Vix cries. "Are you okay? What happened?"

"I think I've twisted my ankle." I wince as I try to move it.

"Oh my God!" Vix cries. "It's fate!"

I stare at her. "Fate *wanted* me to twist my ankle?"

"Uh-huh." She beams. "*Right outside Christian's house!* Omigosh, it's just like Willoughby and Marianne in *Sense and Sensibility*. Only without the horse, which is a shame, but look—he's got a motorbike, which is almost as good! It's so romantic," Vix gushes as she races up the garden path.

"Vix—no—wait! *Ouch!*" I wince as she rings the doorbell. When there's no immediate answer she hammers on the door till it finally opens a crack, and Christian peers out cautiously, his hair dripping wet.

"Help!" Vix cries. "Lou's crippled!"

"What?" Christian looks at me, alarmed. The door opens slightly more, revealing the left side of Christian's body, and I realize he's naked except for a towel wrapped round his waist—he must've been having a shower. My gaze strays involuntarily to his chest, where there's a patch of hair the shape of a perfect heart, with a scar running underneath. I can't take my eyes off it.

"Louise?" he says.

"What?" I look up, mortified that he might have caught me staring.

"What happened?" he asks.

"She collapsed in the street!" Vix cries.

"I just stumbled on the curb." I shrug.

"She's twisted her ankle," Vix corrects me.

"Here, I'll—" He moves to step forward, then hesitates. "Please, come on inside, I just have to . . . I'll be back in a sec." He disappears inside the house as Vix helps me hop up the footpath.

"Willoughby carried Marianne," she grumbles.

The front door opens straight into Christian's cramped living room, and as Vix guides me to a chair my eyes quickly drink in my surroundings.

Find out what he's interested in. . . .

It looks more like an old lady's house, with its busy floral wallpaper, brown seventies-style carpet, and tired-looking tasseled three-piece suite. But the bookshelf beside me is lined with CDs, DVDs, and Xbox games, as well as a row of books—mainly on art, music, and Thai cookery—and a couple of sketchbooks. I glance at a calendar on the wall, where Christian's shifts at the pub are scribbled on each day—except Sunday, which also has *St. Augustine's 9:30 a.m.* written in red pen.

"Sorry about that!"

I turn swiftly as Christian rushes into the room, now dressed in jeans and a hooded jacket. *Did he see me staring?*

"Is it okay if I carry you into the bathroom, Louise?" he asks. "All my first-aid stuff's in there."

I nod dumbly, but the instant Christian's strong arms are around me everything inside me freezes. He smells fresh, like forests after the rain, as he carries me effortlessly through to the peachy-pink downstairs bathroom and seats me gently on the toilet lid. He rests my foot on his lap and perches on the side of the bath as Vix follows, hovering anxiously in the doorway.

"Now let's have a look at that ankle." He gently slips off my shoe and I flinch unintentionally as his warm skin touches my foot, sending shivers prickling all the way up my leg. "How did it happen?"

"I'm not sure," I say. "I was running, and I just stumbled. . . . It's probably nothing."

"Can you stretch your toes?"

I wince as I try to flex them backwards.

"No, no, I mean like . . ." He lifts his right leg as if to demonstrate, then quickly changes his mind and tugs his trouser leg back down. "Can you point your foot like a ballerina, I mean—I'm not a good example!"

"Oh, right." Slowly, I extend my toes. "I can, but it hurts." I grimace.

34

"Okay, relax," he instructs. "The good news is I don't think it's broken."

"See?" I tell Vix.

"How do you know?" She frowns.

"I did a first-aid course," he says. "The bad news is we're going to have to chop it off."

"What?" I smile, despite myself.

"No choice, I'm afraid." He sighs. "Total amputation required."

"Which course did you say you took?" Vix raises an eyebrow.

"First aid. Though admittedly it was actually all about CPR and stuff—no ankle injuries—so you might want to get a second opinion on the amputation thing."

"Probably." I grin.

"Anyway, I *do* know that ice helps minimize any swelling—I'll grab some from the freezer."

"Rest is good for swelling too, isn't it?" Vix says, winking at me. "In fact, I don't think she should move at all for the next few hours, do you?"

"I don't think she should walk on it, no." Christian smiles. "But unfortunately you can't stay here as I have to get to work—we can't all read books all day, you know."

I roll my eyes and he grins. "I'll call a taxi for you."

"Thanks," I tell him.

"It was worth a try." Vix shrugs once he's gone. "Nice choice, Shepherd! He's funny, and fit, and sweet—did you see how he got dressed before he let us in? Cute. Shame he covered up those gorgeous abs, though—but probably just as well, the way you were drooling over them!"

"I was not!" I protest.

"Not that I blame you!" She laughs. "Seriously, how can he be shy with a body like *that*? Anyway, I'll give you guys some space."

35

"No!" I hiss, grabbing her sleeve. "Don't leave me alone with him!"

She stares at me. "I thought you liked him?"

"I do—it's just . . ." I think for a moment. "I only just met him, and . . ."

"So? What are you so scared of?" She smiles. "What's the worst that could happen?"

I remain miserably silent. How can I explain?

"Lou," Vix says quietly, her eyes suddenly filled with concern. "Did something happen to you?"

"I . . ." I hesitate. Something, yes. But not what she's thinking. "I . . . don't want to talk about it."

"That's why you don't trust men," she says slowly, her expression clearing. "You don't trust Kenny, and now Christian—is this why you keep turning down the fit guys who ask you out? Because you don't trust them?"

"I don't trust men I've just met, no," I say tightly. "Trust has to be earned."

"Yes, but you have to be open to it too," Vix says gently. "You can't let something that happened in your past stop you moving forward. And Christian seems like a really nice guy."

"Appearances can be deceptive," I mutter darkly.

"True," she concedes.

"Look, I'm sure you're right," I sigh. "I'm sure Christian's wonderful. He's kind, and funny and totally gorgeous . . . but I'm just . . . I'm not ready to be alone in his house with him—not yet. That's all. Do you understand?"

"Of course." She squeezes my hand. "And don't worry. I'm going nowhere."

"Thanks, Vix."

She winks at me, then turns and opens the bathroom cabinet.

"What are you doing?" I hiss.

"Researching," she says, rooting through the bottles and boxes. "You're right, you only just met the guy, you don't know anything about him, and you can find out a lot about someone from their bathroom."

"Like what?" I say skeptically. "Their favorite shampoo?"

"No." Vix grins. "Like their deepest, darkest secrets!" She pulls out a box of black hair dye, her eyes gleaming. "Looks like Christian's hiding something!"

"Really?" Christian says, pushing open the door.

Vix drops the box in surprise. "I . . . er . . . I was looking for aspirin," she lies quickly. "Poor Lou's in pain."

"Second shelf," Christian says wryly. He picks up the hair dye. "And as for my secret," he sighs, "it's really a curse."

"A curse?" Vix's eyes light up.

"Yup." He nods tragically. "We all go gray early in my family. You should see my dad."

"Have you got a picture?" I ask.

"Er, no," Christian says.

"None at all?" Vix frowns.

"Nope. Why?"

"Could've seen what you're gonna look like when you're older." She shrugs. "They say men take after their fathers."

"Uh-oh—that really *is* a curse!" Christian laughs. "Here, Lou, this'll help." He places a bag of frozen peas gently on my ankle.

I shiver, and he frowns.

"You might still be in a bit of shock. You could do with a cuppa," he says. "Vix, could you put the kettle on, please, while I see to Lou's ankle?"

"Um . . ." She looks at me anxiously.

"I'm fine, Christian, really," I protest quickly. "Besides, I'm not sure I can be trusted with hot drinks!"

"Under supervision you'll be okay." He smiles. "A friend of mine

37

once said you can solve anything with TLC—tea, a good listener, and choccie biscuits."

My stomach flips. I've heard that somewhere before. . . .

"Kitchen's second on the left," Christian instructs Vix.

"Uh . . . sure," Vix says, glancing at me apologetically as she leaves the room. "I won't be a sec—and I'll just be in the kitchen."

Great.

Christian shuts the door behind her and immediately the room constricts. There's no air, and I suddenly feel ridiculously self-conscious as he looks at me with those deep blue eyes that make my pulse race. *Get a grip!* I scold myself. *Just stay calm. . . .*

"Have we met before?" Christian says suddenly.

I cough. "What?"

"I mean before yesterday—I'm no good with faces normally, but you just seem really familiar."

"Nope. Never," I say quickly. "I mean, you might've seen me jogging in the park?"

"No." He frowns. "That's not it."

"Probably the trauma," I suggest. "It's ingrained my face on your mind: *Hazardous person, avoid at all costs.*"

"I'm not doing too well with that." He grins. "We've met three times in two days."

I cringe. "Right. You'll be sick of the sight of me—lucky you *didn't* come clubbing last night!"

"Actually, I'm not much of a clubber," he confesses.

"Me neither," I admit. "Give me a curry and an Xbox over a club any day," I add, thinking of the cookbook and games in his living room.

He laughs. "A girl after my own heart."

If only he knew.

"But at uni the whole nightlife scene seems to be sort of expected." I shrug. "If you're a student, you go clubbing, right?"

"Is that the law?" Chistian smiles.

"No, but . . . I dunno. The whole student thing is weird, you know?" I babble. "Suddenly leaving your whole life behind, all your friends and family, and just being plunged into this new life in a new town where you don't know *anyone* . . . It's bizarre."

He nods. "It's tough starting a new life."

"You're not from round here, then?"

"What?" He blinks. "No. I just moved here a few months ago."

"Why?" I push.

"Why not?" He smiles but it doesn't reach his eyes.

"Do you ever get homesick?" I ask.

"Doesn't everyone, at first?" He shrugs. "At least you can always go home." He smiles sadly and I look away.

Home. Home doesn't exist anymore. Not really. Not after what happened.

"I feel like a completely different person here," I say quietly. "Sometimes it's like . . . like I'm wearing a mask or something, pretending to be someone I'm not, just to fit in."

I look up to find his eyes are deep in mine.

"Sorry," I say, my cheeks hot. "You probably think I'm crazy."

"No," he says quietly. "Not at all, actually. I know exactly what you mean."

The silence stretches.

"So anyway, that's why I go clubbing." I shrug finally. "To blend."

He smiles. "Your secret's safe with me."

I search his eyes. "Are you good at keeping secrets?"

A strange expression flickers over his features. "You have no idea."

I shiver again.

"You're freezing. Here, take this." Christian unzips his hoodie, revealing a V-neck T-shirt beneath. My eyes immediately flick back to the scar I noticed earlier.

"What happened to your chest?" I ask quietly.

"What?" He looks up sharply. "Oh, nothing. Birthmark. Here, this'll keep you warm."

"Thanks," I say, my eyes never leaving the scar that is blatantly not a birthmark as he shrugs off the jacket and wraps it round me. It's warm from his body, and is filled with the same foresty smell that's clogging my lungs, and as his blue eyes again meet mine, suddenly I can't breathe.

"I'd better go." I stand up hurriedly—forgetting he's still holding frozen peas on my foot.

"Careful!" Christian catches me as I lose my balance, electricity jolting through me as he pulls me hard against his chest, knocking the breath from my lungs. We stare at each other as he holds me close.

"*Do* I know you?"

My heart thumps hard against my ribs as he gently brushes my hair from my face.

"Honestly, Louise, there's something about you that seems so familiar. . . ."

I swallow hard.

The sharp ringing of the phone makes us both jump. It stops abruptly, and I take a step backwards, hugging my arms as footsteps patter down the corridor.

"Christian!" Vix pokes her head round the door. "Phone call for you. How many jobs do you do?"

"What?" Christian turns.

"Barman, first-aid guru, taxi driver . . ."

He groans.

"Why did you ring for a cab when *you're* a taxi driver?" Vix frowns.

"I'm not," he says grumpily. "Tell them they've got the wrong number. Again!"

"O-kay . . ." Vix walks off, pointedly leaving the door open behind her.

"Again?" I ask.

"I don't know what's going on," he sighs. "Some taxi firm's obviously got a phone number similar to mine, or there's a printing mistake on their cards—for the last week or so I've been getting phone calls all the time from people wanting taxis."

"That must be pretty annoying."

"It's more than annoying!" he groans. "Especially in the middle of the night! And you should hear the abuse I get when I tell them they've got the wrong number!"

"Can't you do anything about it?" I ask.

"Like what? I can't call the taxi company since I don't know their real number, I can't leave my phone off the hook in case there's an emergency—I'll have to change my phone number if it goes on much longer."

"Isn't that expensive?"

"Yeah, but it'd be worth it, I'd give anything for a decent night's sleep. The other day I was so exhausted I slept straight through my alarm and was late for work!"

"How awful. Did you get into trouble with your boss?"

"First strike." He nods miserably. "Three strikes, and I'm out. Speaking of which, I'd better get a move on, or I'll be late again!"

"Sorry, I didn't mean to hold you up."

"It's fine." He smiles. "I'm happy to help. Besides, it's not like you hurt your ankle on purpose, is it?"

I bite my lip.

"Well, everyone, the good news is the tea's ready," Vix says, returning. "But the bad news is the taxi's just arrived too."

"Thanks for the first aid." I smile at Christian. "And for your jacket." I shrug it off and hand it back to him as I make for the door.

41

"Wait," he says. "Cindy—"

"What!" I turn sharply. "What did you call me?"

"Um . . . Cinderella." He looks at me strangely as he holds up my trainer. "Don't forget your shoe."

"Oh. Right." I take it from him, my cheeks burning. "Thanks. Bye."

"We'll see you at the pub later, though." Vix beams. "We're meeting Kenny for lunch, aren't we, Lou?"

I blink. "Are we?"

"Yes, he texted last night inviting me for lunch—didn't I tell you?"

I stare at her. No, she certainly did *not* tell me Kenny asked her out. What is he playing at?

"Anyway, it'd be great if you could come along too, seeing as *I've only just met him*," she mimics pointedly. "Come on, please-please-please-please-please-please-please-please!" She flutters her eyelashes madly.

"Go on, Louise," Christian laughs. "You still owe me that drink, after all."

I smile helplessly. "How can I refuse?"

FIVE

"Wow, it's heaving in here!" Vix gasps as we fight our way into The Flying Pig. "What's going on?"

"No idea." I shrug. I spot Christian in a heated debate with a crowd of guys at the bar.

"Come on," Vix says. "I need caffeine."

"How? We can't even get to the bar it's so busy!"

"Cripple coming through!" she yells. "Make way, people, she's injured!" She forges a path through the mob to the bar, then shouts at a guy till he relinquishes his stool.

"Smooth." I grin wryly as she helps me up. "But my ankle's really not that bad."

"Not the point." She winks. "Nothing should come between a girl and her true love. Or coffee." She stares longingly at the coffee machine as we wait to be served.

Finally the barmaid we spoke to yesterday rushes over, looking flustered. "Hi, girls, back again? Sorry for the wait. What can I get you?"

"A latte, please," I say.

"Double espresso," Vix answers. "I'm all about the caffeine." Her eyes dart around the bar. "Where's Christian gone?"

"He's on the phone to the boss," the barmaid replies. "Is it important?"

"No, I just . . . owe him a drink, that's all." I shrug.

"So it went well with the two of you?" The barmaid smiles as she makes the coffees. "Did you ask him out?"

"Yeah, but he turned me down." I sigh. "Said he was busy."

"Was he working all evening?" Vix asks her hopefully.

"No, Christian doesn't do evening shifts—but like I said, don't take it personally." The barmaid smiles sympathetically.

"He keeps himself to himself." I nod, remembering how he neatly avoided all my questions earlier, about why he moved here, how he got his scar. He did say he was good at keeping secrets. . . .

"Hello, ladies."

Vix and I spin round.

"Kenny!" she cries delightedly as I force a smile.

"Hey, Kenny." The barmaid smiles, passing our coffees across the counter. "The usual?"

"Heidi, you read my mind." He grins.

"Oi, I was here first!" a guy calls from the other side of the bar.

"With you in a sec, love!" Heidi beams at him.

"Actually, make it two," Kenny adds.

"Coming up." She smiles. "But you know the Facebook offer's only on beer, right?"

"Facebook offer?" I ask.

She sighs. "Everyone's claiming there's some buy-one-get-two-free beers offer on our Facebook page, but it's the first we've heard—that's what Christian's calling Mike about now. I wish he'd hurry up—I'm on my own here."

"How strange," I comment.

"One cappuccino." Heidi slides a cup towards Kenny. "The second one'll just be a mo."

"Thanks," Kenny says. "But this one's for you."

Vix's smile slips.

"One sugar, as usual, right?" He opens a packet.

"Perfect! Thanks, Kenny!"

"If only all the staff were so easily impressed," Vix mutters moodily as Heidi turns to make the second cappuccino. "Maybe you should've bought Christian a cappuccino, Lou?"

I raise an eyebrow. "After throwing coffee over him?"

"True," she concedes.

"You threw coffee over him?" Kenny raises an eyebrow. "I'm guessing you didn't get hired, then?"

"Oh, that reminds me." Heidi turns to me as she hands Kenny the second coffee. "I told my boss about you, and he got the CV you emailed, but he doesn't need any more staff at the moment, sorry."

"Are you kidding?" Kenny glances round at the crowded bar. "Even today? It's rammed in here!"

She shrugs. "He doesn't know."

"He does now." Christian appears, looking flustered. "Hi, guys. I finally got hold of Mike. He says we have to honor the beer offer, but he's going mental about it."

"Well, it's his fault! It's a typo—it must be," Heidi says. "Is he at least sending someone to help us out? We're rushed off our feet."

"No," he sighs. "He's tried, but no one's available."

"Lou could help out," Kenny suggests. "She's got bar experience, she's available, and she's emailed in her CV. Demand and opportunity, right?"

"Sorry," Heidi says. "We're not allowed to hire or fire people."

"Only Mike can," Christian adds. "And he's at a christening until later today. How's your ankle?"

"You hurt your ankle?" Kenny turns to me, concerned.

"It's fine," I tell him. "I just went over on it earlier. It's nothing."

"You shouldn't walk on it if it's twisted," he insists.

"It's not twisted, just a bit bruised," I argue.

"Either way, you should rest it."

"I *am* resting it, okay? I'm sitting down, aren't I?" I glare at him.

"Oi!" a guy shouts from the other end of the bar. "Is anyone serving, or what?"

"No rest for the wicked." Christian smiles, turning to go.

"I'll see to them," Heidi insists. "You finish up here." She winks at me.

"I'll get these." Kenny pulls out his wallet.

"No, it's okay," I say hastily, opening my bag. The last thing I need is to be even more indebted to Kenny.

"I insist." He smiles.

"No, *really*." I yank my purse out quickly, sending the contents of my bag scattering over the floor. "Shit!" I jump off my stool.

"Lou, don't—your ankle!" Vix cries.

"Double shit!" I grab the bar for support.

"Here, let me." Vix starts to gather up my things.

"Thanks," I say, cursing myself for feeling so on edge around Kenny, cursing *him* for coming back into my life at all.

"What's this?" Vix holds up an envelope and I freeze.

Shit. I forgot all about the letter since picking it up from my pigeonhole yesterday.

"*HMP Stonegate.*" She reads the postmark. "What's HMP?"

"Her Majesty's Prison." Christian looks at me and my heart sinks.

Vix looks up. "Who do you know in prison, Lou?"

"I . . ." My cheeks burn as I just stare helplessly at the letter. "No one . . ."

She frowns. "What?"

"That must be the letter you were telling me about yesterday, Lou," Kenny cuts in quickly, taking it from Vix.

I stare at him. *This is it. He's going to tell them everything.*

"From the prisoner correspondence program?" Kenny prompts, handing the letter back to me. "Have you replied yet?"

I blink, surprised. "Um . . . no . . ." I shove the envelope deep into my pocket.

"Isn't that weird?" Vix frowns. "Writing to a random criminal?"

"I think it's great," Christian says suddenly, and I look up. "I expect they get really lonely, separated from their family and friends, everyone they've ever known." His eyes meet mine.

"But isn't that the point?" Vix argues. "That's part of their punishment. They're criminals—they broke the law."

"Not everyone in prison has broken the law," Christian counters.

Vix rolls her eyes. "Most people."

"You'd be surprised," he says, a rough edge to his voice.

I stare at him.

"What did the person you're writing to do?" Vix asks me. "Or are they innocent?"

Kenny and Christian both turn to me and I flush under their gaze.

"Um . . . er . . ." I swallow, then shake my head. "He didn't do anything wrong," I tell them. "He shouldn't be in jail."

"Poor guy," Christian says quietly. "It's awful to be wrongly accused."

"Well, that's what they all say." Vix shrugs. "Or else you wouldn't write to them, would you, Lou?"

"I . . ." My head feels like it's going to explode. I have to get away from everyone before I fall apart completely. "Sorry—I'm not feeling very—" I turn and hobble quickly to the toilets, lock the door, and close my eyes.

What am I doing? My blood throbs in my temples, tears stinging my throat. How could I be so *stupid?* So *careless?* I nearly ruined *everything!*

"Lou?" Vix's voice calls gently from outside the cubicle. "Are you okay?"

Get a grip. I swallow hard, trying to steady my breathing.

"I'm fine," I reply shakily. "I just . . . I just feel a little weird. It's probably still the shock of falling over or something."

47

"Right . . . ," she says uncertainly. "Can I get you anything? A glass of water?"

"No, just . . . give me a minute, yeah? I'll be out in a sec."

"Okay," she says reluctantly. "See you in a mo."

I close my eyes and listen till I'm sure she's gone, then take a deep breath and pull the envelope from my pocket.

How could I forget his letter?

The first letter, the first contact in *weeks*, and I just leave it sitting, unopened, in my bag?

I stare at the envelope, at its prison postmark, my heart heavy. Then, carefully, gently, I open the seal and slide out the single sheet of paper, his oh-so-familiar handwriting dancing across the page and tugging at my insides.

Sweetheart,

I hope your first few weeks at uni are going well. It will undoubtedly be hard at first. It's always difficult moving somewhere new, especially where you don't know anyone—believe me, I know.

But I'm sure you'll make good friends. You've been an incredible friend and cousin to my daughters—like another sister—and I'm so proud to view you as a daughter of my own. You're smart and kind, and so, so strong. You've had to cope with so much in your young life, and I'm sorry to have made that even harder for you with my current situation, the notoriety it has incurred, and my enforced absence from your life.

I understand your decision to alter your name for university, and think it a wise one. I hope your new life will be filled with all the happiness you deserve.

All my love, always,

Uncle Jim x

I choke on my tears. *All the happiness I deserve.* I don't deserve any happiness. I *caused* this mess. Guilt floods my veins as I think of him all alone in a prison cell.

It's all so *wrong!* Uncle Jim isn't a criminal. He should be at home with Aunt Grace and his beautiful daughters, living happily ever after. He *would* be if it weren't for me—*this is all my fault!*

Well, not *all* my fault . . . I close my eyes and that face pops into my head, unbidden. The same eyes that have haunted my dreams ever since the trial, boring into my soul.

If it weren't for *him,* none of us would be in this situation.

And it's time I put things right, once and for all. . . .

SIX

"That," Vix sighs, setting down her cutlery, "was delicious."

"Lovely," I lie, forcing a smile. I didn't taste a single bite. The whole meal has been unbearable, with Vix tiptoeing on eggshells around me, and Kenny all secret smiles at being my knight in shining armor.

I suppose I should be grateful—he covered for me, after all—but I would never have dropped the stupid letter if it weren't for him, if he hadn't followed me here, if he didn't make me so tense—he's like a ticking time bomb.

"Glad you both enjoyed it." Kenny beams. "Who'd like another drink? My treat."

"No, *I'll* get these," I insist. "You've done enough."

"You're welcome." He winks.

"I'll come with you," Vix says, looping her arm through mine as I hobble to the bar, which is still rammed. "Is he a catch or what?" She grins.

"What?" I turn.

"Kenny!" she hisses, her eyes sparkling. "Did you know he turned down *Oxford*? Cute, smart, and loaded. A triple threat, huh?"

I glance over at him tapping at his iPhone. He's definitely a threat, but not in the way Vix means.

"He's not really your type, though, is he?" I say quickly.

Her face falls. "Why? Because he's cute and smart?"

"No, just . . . you like sporty guys and Kenny's all . . . lanky, and kind of clingy," I add. "I mean, we only met him yesterday and he just seems a bit full-on."

"You mean because he actually asked me out instead of turning me down flat?" She glances pointedly at Christian.

"No, I just . . . think you could do better," I tell her.

"Because he's not going gray?"

I roll my eyes. "Vix—"

"Kenny's been nothing but nice to you, Lou, trying to get you a job here, buying you drinks—and you nearly snapped his head off when he was worried about your ankle. What's your problem? Why don't you like him?"

"Vix, I . . ." I falter. I can't tell her the truth.

"What?" she demands.

"I just . . . I guess I don't trust him," I tell her honestly. "I don't want you to get hurt."

"You don't trust *any* men," she counters.

"*And* he seems to be flirting with everything that moves," I add for good measure. "It wasn't *me* trying it on with *him* yesterday, and it's obviously not the first time he's bought Heidi a coffee. . . ."

She frowns.

"Just . . . play it cool for a bit, you know?" I suggest. "You've only just met him, after all."

"What would you like?" Christian asks breathlessly as he finally gets to us.

"Three beers, please," I say. "Make it four. I owe you one, and you look like you need it."

"Thanks, but I'm teetotal."

"Teetotal?" Vix stares at him. "How can you trust a barman who doesn't drink?"

He grins. "I'll have a lemonade, if that's all right?"

"Course." I smile. "Are you okay? Where's Heidi?"

"She went to the loo ages ago." He shrugs. "You couldn't check on her, could you? I'm dying out here."

"I'll go," Vix says.

"Why don't you take down the Facebook offer?" I ask.

"I have, but apparently it's on Twitter too, and every other social media site you can think of, but I don't know the passwords, and Mike's turned his phone off again," he explains. "We're just too technologically advanced for our own good."

"Bad news." Vix rushes back into the bar. "Heidi's ill."

"What?" Christian says, looking alarmed.

"She's locked herself in a cubicle and she doesn't sound good at *all.*" Vix pulls a face.

"Does she need some medicine?" Christian asks. "A glass of water?"

"She's well beyond that." Vix shakes her head. "That girl needs to go *home.*"

"Shit!" Christian says. "She can't—I can't cope on my own. We're swamped!"

"She can't work," Vix argues. "She can't even leave the toilet at the moment. It isn't pretty."

"Bollocks!" Christian groans. "I'll have to close the pub. I can't manage alone. Mike won't be happy, but I can't even tell him cos he's turned his bloody phone off."

"I could help out," I offer. "Like I said, I've got bar experience."

"You've also got an injured ankle," Christian reminds me.

"It's fine," I argue. "I might not be able to run around, but I can certainly sit on a stool and pour pints—that's all anyone's ordering anyway."

He sighs. "But Heidi was right—only Mike can hire and fire people."

"Well, it's better than closing the pub," I counter. "Call it a trial.

52

If it doesn't work out, then you can close up and Mike'll never know. But it's worth a try, isn't it?"

He sighs, then nods. "Thanks, Lou."

"Don't thank me yet." I smile. "Let's see how it goes."

It goes remarkably well. I pour a steady stream of pints while Christian handles all other orders, and even though Kenny manages to hack into the social networking sites and close down the beer offer, the punters remain, happily drinking and watching the football. By the time the next shift arrives the pub's still nicely buzzing, but everything's under control.

"What can I get you?" I smile at a middle-aged balding man as he approaches the bar.

"A pair of glasses."

"Wineglasses?" I ask.

"No." He frowns. "Specs. Either my eyes are playing tricks on me, or you're not Heidi."

"No." I smile. "I'm not, I—"

"Then where's Heidi, and who the *hell* are you?"

"Mike!" Christian rushes to my side. "Heidi's ill—she had to go home."

"Then who's this?"

"Louise," Christian says. "She's looking for part-time work."

"I emailed you my CV yesterday," I add.

"So I just thought I'd give her a trial—"

"Someone I've never even laid *eyes* on working behind *my* bar, selling *my* beer, opening *my* till?" Mike interrupts. "*I* decide who to hire." He glares at Christian. "And who to fire."

"She did us a favor," Christian argues. "Heidi was sick and no one else was available. Lou saved our skins today—you should be thanking her."

"Oh really?" I wince as Mike yanks open the cash register.

"Yes," Christian says heatedly. "You turned off your phone, and if Lou hadn't stepped up, the pub would've had to close."

"And who made that decision? Heidi?" Mike demands, rifling through the till. "That's a managerial decision."

"No, I did," Christian confesses. "Heidi had nothing to do with it. She didn't even know."

Mike looks at him. "*You* did, eh?"

Christian nods.

Mike sighs. "S'pose you're due a promotion, then."

I look up sharply as Christian blinks. "What?"

"The pub's not taken this much money in a daytime in months," he says, smiling at the wad of cash he's taken from the till. "The Facebook mix-up's been a blessing in disguise."

I stare at him in disbelief.

"Young man, you kept a cool head in a tough situation. You kept us staffed, kept us open, and kept us afloat. Well done." He closes the till and tosses Christian a set of keys on a Bugs Bunny key ring. "So I'm making you deputy manager, and your first job can be to open up tomorrow."

Christian just stares at him.

"Well, don't just stand there gawking—there's punters waiting, and I've got to stick this lot in the safe."

"Actually, it's the end of my shift. . . ." Christian glances at the clock. "I've got to go—is that okay?"

Mike shrugs. "If Louise can stay."

"What?" I look up.

"What time did you start serving today, young lady?"

"Um, about three-thirty."

"Well, if you can stay and work till closing, and work tomorrow too, you're hired. I could do with an extra pair of hands tonight—who knows when Heidi'll be back on her feet—and we'll need more

54

weekend staff anyway if we're doing more offers. I'll even throw in a free dinner."

I blink. "Sure. Thanks!"

"Great." He winks. "Welcome to the team."

"Congratulations, Lou!" Vix squeals as Mike walks into the back. "You got the job!"

"Knew you would, given half a chance." Kenny winks.

"I can't believe it," Christian says. "I thought I was about to get fired!"

"Me too," I admit.

"You're a lifesaver." He grins. "Thank you."

"Sounds like you owe me a drink." I smile.

"Definitely. Just . . . not tonight."

"Smile, you two busy barpeople!" Vix cries. "This is a moment to remember!"

I turn as she points her camera phone at us. *Flash!*

"*NO!*" Christian jumps backwards like he's been shot, his hands flying to his face.

Vix stares at him. "Sorry . . ."

"No, I'm sorry," he mumbles. "It's just—I'm not . . . very photogenic."

"*Seriously?*" Vix raises an eyebrow.

"It's true—you should see his driving license." I smile uneasily.

"Anyway, I've . . . got to get going," Christian says, heading for the coat hooks.

"You can stay for one drink, surely?" I protest. "At least wait till the rain eases off—it's pissing it down outside."

"It's okay, I've got a jacket," he says, grabbing it from the rack and slipping the pub keys into the pocket.

"How is your poor jacket?" I take it from him. "Wow, there isn't even a mark."

"Good as new." Christian smiles. "It's like it never even happened. No one would ever know."

If only all stains were so easy to remove.

"Thanks again for your help today, guys," Christian says, pulling on his jacket.

"You're welcome, mate." Kenny grabs him in a bear hug. "Any time."

"Whoa, someone's affectionate after a few drinks!" Christian laughs, patting Kenny on the back as he finally releases him. "Have a good night, everyone!"

"Come on, Christian, it's still early!" Vix protests. "What's so important about being home at six-thirty on a Saturday night?"

Christian sighs. "You wouldn't understand."

"Try me," she challenges.

I watch him closely.

"I can't miss *Doctor Who*!"

Vix groans. "Nerd."

"You got me." Christian grins. "Bye!"

"Bye, mate!" Kenny waves.

"Lame," Vix comments when he's gone.

"Totally," I agree miserably.

SEVEN

"You're alive!" Vix cries as I answer my mobile the next morning. "Thank goodness! I was really worried when you didn't answer your door last night—I thought you must've just been asleep—but when there was still no reply this morning I was starting to panic you'd been missing all night!"

"You knocked on my door last *night*?" I frown. "What time?"

"When I got back from clubbing, just after two-thirty."

"*Two-thirty?*" I cry. "Good thing I'm a deep sleeper—I would *not* have been a happy bunny to be woken at that hour!"

"Sorry. I was drunk and I just . . . I wanted to apologize for going clubbing without you. You're my best friend here, and I shouldn't just abandon you when you've got a bad ankle."

"Vix." I smile. "It's fine. Really. Just cos I'm not up to dancing the night away, it shouldn't stop you going out."

"Thanks, Lou. You're the best. Where are you, anyway? What's that *noise*?"

"St. Augustine's church clock." From my bench I crane my neck to see the time. Ten o'clock. "I'm doing research. You know, for our creative writing assignment?"

I've actually been here since nine-thirty, hoping to bump into Christian and get some quality time alone with him, albeit in a public place. It's impossible to talk to him properly when he's

57

working and there are so many people around, and if I invite him for a drink one more time, I'm going to look ridiculous. This way, hopefully we'll get to spend some time together "accidentally."

Even if it is accidentally on purpose.

But there's still no sign of him, so what started as an invented pretext for being here is now actually the truth.

"Research?" Vix says blankly. "What research? We've just got to write a ghost story, right?"

"Based on a real person," I add.

"So, what, you're trawling a graveyard checking out dead people?"

"Pretty much."

"Hon, we live in the *online* age. We can do research without even getting out of bed! I've got my laptop here—I'll *prove* it."

I sigh. "It's not the same."

"Here we go. Online obituaries. Ooh, how about Rita 'Margarita' Chevalier: 'She lived life like her cocktails—bubbly and full to the brim!' Sounds like my kind of lady! Or how about Gemma Fotherington. Born 1998— Shit. She was really young."

I stop still. "How'd she die?"

Vix hesitates. "She was killed."

My skin turns cold. "Killed?"

"Yup. House fire."

"Oh!" I blink. "Oh, I thought you meant—"

"What? *Murdered?*" Vix says. "That'd make a *much* better ghost story—a spirit out for revenge on her killer."

"Who else is there?" I ask quickly.

"Um . . . Harold Booth? Butcher killed by a runaway bull." She laughs. "How ironic!"

"Vix, these are real people!" I snap suddenly, my temper flaring from nowhere. "They're dead. It's not a joke."

"I know—sorry." Vix sounds stricken. "I didn't mean anything, Lou, I just—I'm sorry."

"It's fine. Look, I've got to go, I've got a call waiting," I lie.

"Okay. Well, see you later, then?"

"I'm working till four," I say. "Bye."

I hang up swiftly, shocked by my outburst. I need to get a grip. Vix doesn't know what happened, after all—at least, she doesn't know it happened to my family. I shouldn't be so sensitive. I could ruin everything.

I take deep breaths, trying to calm down as I glance at the gravestones rising like statues around me. My eyes flicker over the dates and names and inscriptions.

This is where we all end up, one way or another.

Some of the stones look new, their edges sharp and clean, almost shiny, while others have ancient dates which are barely visible, worn clean by time's indiscriminate hand. Like everything else.

The gravel crunches behind me and I turn as an old lady walks slowly past. She stops by a headstone and I can just make out the inscription. *John Fielding, beloved husband, father, and grandfather.* Gently, she lays a bunch of flowers on the grave and arranges them carefully, lovingly.

Where are they now, these people who lived and loved? Are their souls up there somewhere, in heaven? Or floating around invisibly on earth?

Are Mum and Dad watching me right now?

I hug my jacket tighter round me, cold suddenly, despite the morning sunshine.

Would they be proud of me? Of the person I've become? Of what I'm doing? Or would they be disappointed?

I shiver as a breeze rustles through the trees; then I pull out my notebook. But instead of a ghost story, a letter pours out:

Dear Uncle Jim,

I miss you so much.

We're writing ghost stories this week, and all I can think about is how we all used to lie out in the back garden together in the summer, the grass soft beneath our heads as we watched the stars prickle the darkening sky, our smiles sticky with ketchup and melted ice cream. Do you remember? You told me that stars were the holes in heaven where the angels look down on us. That Mum and Dad were up there watching over me. It made me feel safe.

But now everything's changed—and I feel like it's all my fault. I'm so sorry.

I wish more than anything I could turn back the clock, that we could all be together again, go back to those summers—I thought they'd last forever. But now I know that nothing does.

What if Mum and Dad aren't watching over me? What if there are no ghosts? Or heaven, or hell, or judgment day or reincarnation or anything else?

What if there's just nothing?

What if this is all we get—a few years to live our lives the best we can, whether young or old, saint or murderer . . .

"Louise?"

I whip round, startled, dropping my notebook in the mud.

"I'm so sorry!" Christian cries, bending to pick it up, but I snatch it hurriedly, brushing the dirt off with my sleeve. *How long has he been there?*

His eyes darken. "Are you okay?"

"Fine—I'm fine." I look away. The old lady who brought the flowers has gone, but people are milling around the church entrance. The service must have ended.

"What are you doing hanging out in a graveyard?" I ask him.

"Oh"—he shrugs—"picking up chicks."

I blink and he nods, straight-faced.

"You'd be surprised how many girls wander through looking for Edward or Stefan or whoever. Total pulling hot spot."

I smile despite myself, and he grins.

"Not really. I play the organ every Sunday morning here."

"Really?" So *that's* what the note on his calendar referred to. "You're religious?"

He looks around at the swarm of people leaving the church, then lowers his voice. "Not particularly, but don't tell anyone," he confides. "But it fits in with my shifts at the pub, it's an extra thirty quid in my pocket each week, and it's such a beautiful instrument—I used to have a piano at home, but . . ." He trails off, shuffles his feet. "So what are you doing here, anyway?"

"We're meant to write a ghost story about a real person," I tell him. "So I came here for research. But I got sidetracked. Sketching."

"You sketch?" His eyes light up as he sits down beside me, taking the bait.

"Oh, they're just doodles, really," I bluff, sliding my notebook swiftly back into my bag and clutching it tightly. "They're not very good."

"They can't be worse than mine." He smiles.

"You sketch too?" I feign surprise.

"It's a bit of an obsession of mine." He grins wryly. "Whenever I see an interesting face I want to draw it, so I carry a sketchbook everywhere I go." He pats his bag.

"How wonderful! Can I see?"

"Well, I'd show you, but then, you know . . ." He shrugs. "I'd have to kill you."

61

I flinch despite myself. "That bad, huh?" I say quickly.

He laughs. "Yup. That bad. I'm no Lucien Freud."

"You like Freud? Really?" I say eagerly—he's one of the painters I researched after spotting his book in Christian's lounge.

He nods. "He's my favorite painter."

"No way—me too!" I cry.

"Really?" Christian looks at me and something flickers in his eyes.

Shit. Have I gone too far? Is he suspicious?

"What's your favorite painting?" he asks.

"Oh, I . . . It's hard to choose. . . ." I panic, racking my brains trying to remember what I read on Wikipedia. "*The Brigadier,* I think. But the paintings of his mother are wonderful—you know he spent four thousand hours painting her?"

He smiles and relief sweeps through me. If that was a test, I think I passed . . .

"I read that," Christian says. "I love them too. He's just so . . . honest, you know? I really admire how he doesn't try to cover anything up or make his art pretty, because he's more interested in stripping away the layers, finding the truth of a person—the wrinkles, the flaws, the humanity. . . ."

I wince. I certainly hope he doesn't succeed in stripping away *my* layers to find the truth.

"Sorry," he says suddenly. "I could prattle on all day. So you came here to write a ghost story?"

"Oh. Yeah." I blink. "It's meant to be about a real person, so I thought I might get inspiration from the gravestones."

"I'm not sure you get the true sense of a person from a gravestone." He frowns. "They're all the same. Dearly beloved so-and-so, fondly remembered, sorely missed etcetera, etcetera. If you love someone, you should say these things to them when they're alive, when they can hear you, when it can make a difference." He sighs. "Before it's too late."

My heart twists. "You're right."

"Do you know anyone who died?" he asks.

I hesitate, unsure how much to tell him.

"Actually, yes. My parents died in a car crash when I was little."

"Shit, I'm sorry." He frowns. "You think your parents will always be there no matter what. You don't realize how much you need them, how much you'll miss them, till they're out of your life forever."

I frown.

"But I'm sure they're still watching over you." He smiles.

"What, as ghosts?" I raise an eyebrow. "I don't think so."

"You don't believe in ghosts?"

I shake my head. "People just make them up to scare each other."

"Ghosts aren't scary," Christian says quietly. "They're sad."

I look up, surprised.

"Their life is over, and yet they're still here, barely existing, doomed to watch over what they once had, knowing they can never go back, however much they want to, and yet they're unable to move forward."

"In stories ghosts have usually done something terrible—that's why they're stuck here," I tell him, my insides tight. "Maybe some things you shouldn't be able to just forget and move on from. Maybe that's the point."

"I don't think they ever do forget," Christian says. "Memories don't just disappear. They haunt you—secrets, regret, guilt. . . ."

As his eyes meet mine they seem to stare straight into my soul, my own secrets, regrets and guilt swimming like bile in my belly.

"We all have to live with the consequences of our actions." He sighs heavily. "You can't change the past, however much you'd like to. That's the biggest tragedy of all."

I close my eyes, unable to stop the tears.

"Hey, Lou. I'm sorry. Are you okay?" Christian places his hand on mine and I snatch it away like I'm scalded.

"Louise?" His wide eyes are filled with concern.

"I-I'm fine, I just . . . I . . ." I'm cut off by a loud and unfamiliar ring tone.

"Sorry." Christian fumbles in his pocket and pulls out a phone. "It's Mike." He flips it open. "Hello?"

Saved by the bell.

"See you later." I hurry back to the car, shut the door behind me, pull out my own mobile, and dial the familiar number.

Christian's right. If you love someone, you should tell them. Before it's too late.

"Hello?" Gran's voice says.

I take a deep breath, try to make my voice sound normal. "Hi, Gran. Where are you?"

"Oh, hello, dear, I'm just visiting Poppy, then I'm off to Grace's for lunch."

Just as I'd hoped. Her Sunday-morning routine runs like clockwork.

"Is everything all right?" Gran asks anxiously.

"Yes—just . . . can I talk to her?"

"Of course." I can hear her smile down the phone. "Just a second, I'll put you on speakerphone."

"Hey, sweetie, how's it going?" I say, tears stinging my eyes as I press the phone hard to my ear, anxious to hear any sound, but of course there's just silence. I wish she could answer. It's so hard being away from her, having one-sided conversations down a phone.

"She can hear you," Gran reassures me. "Carry on."

"I'll be there soon, sweetie, okay? I'll visit soon." I sigh. "I miss you. God, I miss you." I sing her favorite song, Coldplay's "Yellow."

"Sweet dreams, Poppy," I whisper. "See you soon." I hang up slowly and close my eyes, heavy with guilt.

We all have to live with the consequences of our actions.

EIGHT

A tap at the car window nearly makes me jump out of my skin.

"Christian!"

"Sorry!" he says. "I didn't mean to startle you—again. Are you all right?"

"I'm fine," I say quickly, swiping at my eyes. How much did he hear? "What's up?"

"Mike just called. He wants both of us at the pub ASAP."

"Why?" I frown, glancing at my watch. "We're not late, are we?"

"No, we don't open till twelve on Sundays, but he sounded pretty agitated."

He looks pretty agitated too—pacing up and down outside The Flying Pig as we approach, and as I pull into the pub car park I find a police car already there.

"Omigosh!" I gasp, climbing out of the car and hurrying over. "What's happened?"

"Mike?" Christian cries, jumping off his bike and running up to him. "What's going on?"

"We've been robbed." Mike glowers. "Except nothing was taken—thank God I emptied the safe at the end of the night, eh, Lou? So technically it's just a break-in. But there's no sign of forced entry either. Just broken CCTV cameras, an unlocked safe, an open door and"—he glares at Christian—"keys."

"Excuse me?" A police officer emerges from the pub. "You two are?"

"My bar staff," Mike tells him. "Christian Webb's the one I told you about."

I look at Christian.

"I understand you have a set of keys to the pub, Christian?" the policeman says.

Christian nods. "Mike gave them to me yesterday. I was supposed to open up today."

"Where are they now?" the officer asks.

Christian shoves his hand in his jacket pocket, then frowns. "I must've left them at home."

"Are *these* your keys?" The officer holds up a bunch of keys on a Bugs Bunny key ring.

"I . . . I don't understand." Christian stares at them. "I . . . I must've dropped them, or—"

"When was the last time you saw these keys, sir?"

"Last night, when Mike gave them to me. I put them in my jacket pocket before I went home."

"And you hadn't noticed they were missing?"

"No." He frowns. "I didn't—I had no idea."

"Where were you last night at two-fifteen a.m., sir?"

Christian blinks. "Wait, hold on! Surely you don't think I had anything to do with—"

"Answer the question!" Mike snaps. "Where were you at two-fifteen, when my CCTV cameras were smashed in? When someone used *your* keys to open *my* safe?"

I watch, transfixed, as Christian's face drains of color. He looks scared.

"Please, sir," the officer says calmly. "Let me ask the questions. Mr. Webb?"

"At home," Christian replies curtly. "In bed."

"Is there anyone who can verify your whereabouts?"

"I . . . no, but—"

"Miss?"

"What?" I look up sharply. "I *can't* verify that, no!"

"No." The officer smiles slightly. "Where were you last night?"

"Oh. In halls. In bed. Alone," I say quickly, my cheeks burning.

"Don't be daft, she didn't do it!" Mike says. "I told you, she was there at closing when I emptied the safe and took the money to the bank. She knew it was empty."

"Who might've thought the safe was full?"

Christian. I look up at him.

"Anybody in the bar," Mike sighs. "I've got a big mouth, and I was pleased at the day's takings, and I said as much as I transferred the cash from the till to the safe."

"In front of the whole bar?"

Mike nods.

"What time was this?"

"Just before Christian's shift ended, about six-thirty." Mike scowls at Christian. "I only promoted him because the takings had been so high while he'd run the bar."

"So you would have assumed the safe was full, Christian?"

My eyes flick to his.

"What? No! I don't know—I didn't really think about it," Christian protests, his cheeks flushed.

"What did you do after your shift?"

"Nothing—I just went home."

"You just went home?" the officer repeats. "At six-thirty on a Saturday evening?"

"Yes," Christian says defensively.

"You weren't mugged? You didn't go out? You didn't see anyone else at all? No one who could have stolen your keys?"

"No." Christian sighs heavily, his face creased with misery. "I must've dropped them."

"And no one can confirm your whereabouts during the time of the break-in? No deliveries? No phone calls?"

"Yes, actually—loads of phone calls."

I look up quickly. Does he have an alibi?

"Who called you?"

"Well, I—I don't know," Christian admits. He must mean the nuisance taxi calls, I realize.

The policeman sighs. "You had lots of phone calls, but you don't know who from?"

"Well, yes . . ."

"So you can't contact them to prove this?"

I watch a bead of sweat trickle down the side of Christian's face as he falters helplessly.

"Well, no, but—"

"Would you mind coming down to the station, please, sir?" the officer says. "I have a few more questions I'd like to ask you. You might want a lawyer present."

My heart beats fast. *He's going to arrest him!*

"Wait," Christian says suddenly. "That's . . . that's not necessary. Can I have a word?"

"Certainly, sir."

Christian glances at me and Mike. "In private?"

The officer raises an eyebrow. "Very well. Follow me."

I stare after them as they enter the pub. What can Christian tell him that will make any difference? How can he possibly get out of this?

"Shit!" Mike mutters beside me. "That'll teach me."

69

I turn. "You think Christian did it?"

"It had to be, didn't it?" Mike cries. "Everything points to him—his keys were found on the floor, he thought the safe would be full, and his alibi's pretty shoddy."

"The evidence is very compelling." I nod.

"But he seemed like such a nice bloke." Mike sighs.

"I suppose you can never *really* tell what's going on inside someone else's head," I say quietly. "Evidence doesn't lie. I guess that's why justice is portrayed as blind—criminals deserve to be punished, however they look."

"You're right," Mike says suddenly. "I'm such an idiot—I should never have hired him!"

I look at him closely. "What do you mean?"

"Nothing," he says hastily. "Just . . . I think of myself as a fair bloke, y'know? I've had my share of rough times, I know what it's like to be down on your luck, so I like to give people a fair go. And Christian . . . well, he seemed like a decent-enough lad when I took him on." He sighs. "But I've learned my lesson now, all right—I won't be fooled again."

We wait for what seems like forever until the officer finally emerges from the pub.

"What's happening?" Mike asks. "Are you arresting him?"

"No, sir. I'm satisfied that Mr. Webb had nothing to do with the break-in."

I stare at him, gobsmacked.

"What? Why?" Mike asks.

"Mr. Webb has an airtight alibi for his whereabouts last night."

"What?" I ask quickly.

"I can't tell you that, Miss."

"But you mean he lied about being at home?" Mike says.

"So long as he wasn't breaking the law, his whereabouts are his own private concern, sir."

Could he be any more cryptic?

"So what happens now?" Mike asks.

"Nothing," the officer says, climbing into the police car. "By your own admission, anyone in the pub last night could have overheard you say you had a full till, and Mr. Webb could have dropped the keys anywhere on his journey home—so unless you know the names and addresses of all your customers, it would be like looking for a needle in a haystack."

"But—"

"Plus, as nothing was actually stolen, there isn't really a compelling case for spending police time hunting for that needle, especially as the keys are now once more in your possession, sir. Good day."

Mike's jaw hangs open as the police officer drives away. Then he glares at me. "Get to work!"

"How juicy!" Vix's eyes gleam when she and Kenny come into the pub that afternoon. "What do you think Christian could possibly have told them that he didn't want you to hear? That he rang a sex line? That he was on some dodgy Internet site?"

"Perhaps he just wasn't home alone," Kenny says. "Maybe someone vouched for his whereabouts after all—someone he doesn't want anyone to know about."

I look up.

"Like who? A stripper?" Vix laughs.

"Or a secret girlfriend." Kenny raises an eyebrow. "Maybe he's seeing someone else's wife."

"Or maybe he just had a friend over," Vix says quickly, glancing at me.

"Then why would he keep it secret?" Kenny argues.

I frown. Maybe Kenny's right. It would explain why Christian keeps turning me down when I ask him out. . . .

"Or maybe it's not an alibi at all," Vix suggests. "Maybe Christian's got a secret identity."

"A secret identity?" I laugh nervously. "What, like Superman?"

"No, like a spy," Kenny counters. "Perhaps he's leading a double life. People do."

His sparkling eyes meet mine and I glare at him. What is he *doing*?

"Of course!" Vix hisses. "Maybe he's an undercover policeman. Or royalty! Royalty get away with everything, don't they?"

"Do they?" I raise an eyebrow.

"That would explain Christian's black hair dye too!" Vix beams. "*And* why he doesn't like having his photo taken!"

"Vix, *loads* of people dye their hair," I reason.

"Indeed they do." Kenny winks at me. If there wasn't a bar between us, I'd kick him. Hard.

"Besides, Christian told you why he dyes his hair," I add.

"Yeah, cos he's vain." Vix smirks. "Speaking of which, I see you've glammed up again. Pulling out all the stops, eh?"

"Is it too much?" I run my hand over my curled hair anxiously.

"I'm just teasing." Vix grins. "You look great, doesn't she, Kenny?"

He nods. "Bit over the top for bar work, though."

"What are you guys talking about?" Christian asks, walking over to us.

"Nothing," I say quickly.

"Secret identities." Kenny smiles. "What's yours?"

Christian frowns. "What?"

"If you could choose a pseudonym, what would it be?" I bluff hastily. "You know, like Elton John or Michael Caine or . . . Tinie Tempah." I remember the CD I spotted on his bookshelf.

"I'm not sure I could pull off Tinie Tempah." Christian raises an eyebrow.

"Well, no, I think you'd have to be a rapper—and a good one, at that—to pull it off like he does, but anyway, bad example," I babble, my cheeks growing warm as I try to dig myself out of the hole Kenny's dumped me in. "If you could choose your name, what would it be?"

"I dunno, I've never really thought about it." He shrugs. "'What's in a name,' right? Anyway, it's four o'clock. Our shift's over."

"Great." I smile. "And as it's still early, you must have time for a drink today, right?"

"I'm sorry—I can't," he says.

Another rejection. This time I mentally kick *myself*.

"More must-see TV?" Vix raises an eyebrow.

"Not today—I'm meeting a friend." He smiles. "See ya."

We watch him leave.

"We should totally follow him," Vix says, her eyes sparkling as I grab my jacket and we head out to the car park. "There's a story here, I can *smell* it."

"Uh-uh. No way." I shake my head.

"We can't, anyway—we've got salsa, remember?" Kenny smiles.

"Course I remember." Vix beams at him. "I've been looking forward to it all day."

"Wait." I stare at her. *"Salsa?"*

"Yes!" Vix grins. "Kenny knows this great little tapas bar that does Salsa Sundays—with free sangria! Cool, huh?"

"Shame you can't come, Lou, with your bad ankle and all," Kenny says.

"Oh, it's much better—it hardly hurts at all now," I insist.

"Still, dancing's probably not the best thing for it just yet," Vix says. "Better take it easy for a few days."

I grit my teeth. "Well, do you want a lift?" I offer, stalling for time to come up with another obstacle.

"No thanks, I've got my car," Kenny says, nodding at a black Mini Cooper as we step outside.

"But you've been drinking," I protest.

"Actually, I thought we could walk." Vix grins. "It's more romantic. Hi, Heidi!" Vix waves across the car park to where Heidi's chatting to Christian, who's kneeling by his motorbike. "Feeling better?"

"Much!" Heidi beams. "Must've been one of those twenty-four-hour bugs. Christian says you covered for me, Lou—thanks! And welcome to the team!"

"Thanks." I smile. "Something wrong with your bike, Christian?"

"Someone's keyed it!" He frowns, pointing to a deep scratch in the paintwork.

"Oh no!" Vix cries. "Who would do such a thing?"

"I don't know," he says moodily.

"Jealous kids with nothing better to do, I reckon," Heidi says.

"But thanks to whoever smashed the CCTV cameras last night, we'll never know," Christian grumbles.

"It's still gorgeous," Vix sighs. "What I wouldn't give for a motorbike, scratched or not."

"I've got a Ducati," Kenny says quickly. "Maybe we could take it for a spin sometime?"

I roll my eyes.

"Really?" Vix beams at him. "That'd be awesome!"

"No problem." He smiles. "Ready to go?"

"Ready and raring." Vix grins. "Bye, Lou!"

"Wait." I grab Vix's sleeve, pulling her to one side and lowering my voice. "You're right, we should follow Christian."

"What?" She blinks. "You've changed your tune. Why?"

Because I'm desperate. Because I don't trust Kenny. Because this is my last-ditch attempt to stop your date.

I glance at Heidi. "Because if it *is* a girlfriend he's meeting to-night, who provided his alibi, then I just need to know." I sigh. "So I can stop wasting my time."

Vix squeezes my arm sympathetically. "So follow him."

"I can't do it alone!" I protest. "I don't know how to do it discreetly—I can't risk him seeing me and thinking I'm some psycho stalker or something."

She laughs.

"Please, Vix," I beg. "I need you."

"Hang on," she says, and walks over to Kenny. A second later they both come back.

"Vix filled me in." Kenny winks. "Let's go."

Crap. *Not* part of the plan. But I guess it's the best I can hope for.

The motorbike is difficult to follow in the busy stream of traffic, as are Vix's instructions on tailing him.

"You need to keep at least four cars between you and Christian," she says authoritatively. "But don't lose sight of him round the corner! Hurry up—overtake that van! Bugger, we've lost him. No, there he is! Second left! No *second* left! Not too close, he'll see us!"

We weave through the traffic, up and down the hills, past shops and parks and university buildings. . . . By the time Christian finally turns into the hospital car park I'm exhausted.

"The *hospital*?" I stare after him as I pull into a parking space on the street. "What's Christian doing at the hospital?"

"Oh my God, is he sick?" Vix cries. "Is that why he couldn't have broken into the pub? Maybe he's got a debilitating illness!"

"Or maybe he's just visiting a patient," Kenny says. "He did say he was meeting someone."

"That someone *could* be a doctor," Vix argues.

"There's only one way to find out," I say, getting out of the car.

We round the corner into the car park just in time to spot Christian stepping through the sliding doors into the building. But by the time we enter the foyer, with its large waiting area, gift shop, corridors leading in three directions, and two lifts, he's vanished.

"He could be anywhere," I sigh.

"I'll check the toilets," Kenny says, following a sign down a corridor.

I turn and scour the waiting area. There are a few women flicking through magazines, a child glued to the news on the TV, and an old man who looks like he's fallen asleep, but no Christian.

"Louise? Vix?" Christian's voice startles me.

I spin round.

"Hi." He's standing in front of the little gift shop holding a beautiful bouquet of flowers. "What are you doing here?"

"Oh, I . . ."

"She's come about her ankle," Vix lies quickly. "It's still really painful, so we've popped in to see if we can get a doctor to have a quick look at it. What about you?"

"I'm visiting a friend. She's a patient here."

"A friend, huh?" Vix raises an eyebrow. "Nice bouquet."

"Thanks." He smiles. "I hope my landlady likes them too."

"I'm, er . . . I'm sure she will." Vix smiles sheepishly. "Excuse me." She moves off to inspect the magazines.

"We just keep bumping into each other, huh?" he says.

My cheeks grow warm. Does he know we followed him?

"It's like fate keeps pushing us together." He grins.

"Well, you can't resist fate." I smile, encouraged. "I think I saw a pub over the road. . . ."

His face falls. "I'm really sorry, I can't, I—"

"Of course you can't," I interrupt curtly, wishing I could just chop out my tongue and save myself the humiliation. "Don't worry. I'm starting to get the hint." I turn away.

"Don't." He catches my hand. "I'm not hinting. Honest."

I look up at him, at those clear blue eyes I'm trying desperately not to drown in.

"I'd love to get a drink with you," he says gently. "Just . . . some other time?"

I sigh. "I'll believe it when I see it."

"Christian!" A dumpy middle-aged woman rushes out of the lift. "I'm so glad I bumped into you—I just wanted to have a quick word about the party Friday."

"Party?" I raise an eyebrow. "So you do actually socialize sometimes?"

"Sorry." The woman hesitates awkwardly. "I didn't mean to interrupt anything. I just wanted to check you can still come? Did you manage to swap shifts at the pub?"

"Yes." He smiles. "I'll be there."

"Wonderful! And are you bringing anyone? Perhaps a date?" She smiles at me.

"Oh . . ." Christian hesitates. "I think Louise is busy next Friday."

"No, I'm not," I argue. "I've only got morning lectures on Fridays and no plans for the rest of the day."

He falters. "And I'm not sure it's really her scene. . . ."

My heart plummets. So much for "some other time."

"It's a party!" the woman protests. "There's music, alcohol, cake—what's not to like?"

"It sounds lovely." I smile at her. "But I don't want to intrude." I glare at Christian as I walk away.

"Louise, wait!" He rushes after me, blocking my path. "I'd be thrilled if you'd come with me to the party next Friday. As my date," he adds, those eyes deep in mine. "Will you?"

He smiles, and somehow I can't help but beam back at him. "I'd love to."

NINE

I glance at the clock for the fiftieth time.

Ten o'clock a.m.

I groan inwardly. Still half an hour of the world's most boring lecture to go, and I don't even have Vix to keep me company. I wish I were still in bed, like her. I mean, I can sympathize with Hamlet—if your uncle kills your dad and then marries your mum, you're not exactly going to sit back and ignore it, are you? You might even feign madness to get to the truth. But Ophelia? Please. Who'd really top themselves because they think their boyfriend's gone mad? Pathetic. Poor Hamlet. That's collateral damage he could never have foreseen.

"Now," the lecturer, who looks eerily like Ophelia back from the grave, says. "Who can tell me how Ophelia died?"

As if on cue the theme tune for *CSI Las Vegas* bursts on, and everyone laughs.

Except me.

"Very funny, Miss . . . ?" The lecturer pins me with a scowl as I scrabble in my bag, trying frantically to locate my phone and turn it off. So much for keeping a low profile!

"Shepherd," I tell her, my cheeks burning as I finally find my mobile, spotting Aunt Grace's name on the caller ID as I switch it off. I look up to find everyone in the lecture theater staring at me, and suddenly I *do* empathize with Ophelia after all. *Oh God, kill me now.*

"Not a very good start to the day, Miss Shepherd." My heart sinks as the lecturer makes a note on her register.

"And the next time anyone's phone disrupts one of my lectures it'll be *them* in a body bag!" she warns everyone.

It's official. This is the worst birthday ever. Not that anyone here even knows it's my birthday.

Still, as we're finally released from the dark lecture theater onto the sunny campus, my heart lifts. Things can only get better. It's the weekend at last, today I'm *finally* going out with Christian, and tomorrow I'll see Gran, Aunt Grace, and little Millie.

I head out of the soaring Arts Tower and across the bustling campus, past the library and the imposing orange turrets of the administration building, through the rumbling underpass, and buy myself a comforting chocolate muffin from the union shop before returning to the car park. It's only once I'm safely inside the car that I pull my phone out of my pocket to call Aunt Grace back and realize it's still turned off. As it flickers back to life I find the missed call from Aunt Grace and a text from Kenny:

Happy birthday Titch xx

I smile. Of course *he* knows it's my birthday. It's sweet of him to text, but I don't want him telling Vix, don't want a fuss, so I quickly send a reply:

Thanks Kenny :) But please keep it quiet. Lx

Then I call Aunt Grace.

"Happy birthday, sweetheart!" she cries. "I've got someone who wants to sing to you!"

"Happy burfday to you!" I smile as my four-year-old cousin sings down the phone.

"You live in the zoo!"

"Millie!" Aunt Grace chides.

"You look like a monkey, and you smell like one too!" I laugh as Millie bursts into giggles and Aunt Grace takes the phone off her.

"Sorry about that. I don't know where she gets these things!"

"It was lovely," I laugh.

"So what exciting things are you up to today?" she asks.

"Oh, you know, lectures, seminars . . ."

"Come on, I was a student once, you know. It's all party, party, party!"

I smile. "Actually, there is a party later, and I just had my last lecture of the week, so I'm heading back to halls to tidy my room before you guys get here tomorrow—I *cannot* let Gran see the state it's in! What time do you think you'll arrive?"

"Actually . . ." Aunt Grace falters. "You know Millie's ballet exam got canceled because the examiner was ill?"

"Yes."

"Well, they've rescheduled it . . . for this weekend."

"Oh." My heart sinks, but to be honest, part of me is relieved—I've been worrying about how to keep them away from Vix and Christian all weekend, and the last thing I need is little Millie accidentally spilling the beans about who I really am. But I miss them terribly.

"I'm so sorry, sweetheart," Aunt Grace continues. "And I'm sorry it's such short notice—I only just found the note crumpled up in her ballet bag. Can you come home for the weekend instead?"

"I'd love to," I tell her. "But unfortunately I'm working."

"Of course you are," she sighs. "I forgot you'd got a job now."

"It's not long till reading week, though," I tell her. "I'll be home then. I miss you."

"I miss you too," Aunt Grace sighs.

"Me too!" Millie cries in the background.

81

"We all do, don't we, Poppy?" Aunt Grace says.

"Can I talk to her?"

"Of course. I'll put her on."

I wait for a moment until I hear the soft sound of Poppy's breath.

"Hey, Popsicle, snoring again?" I say. "Lazy, huh? Wait till you get to uni—you'll love it. Loads of long lie-ins . . . though maybe you'll have had enough beauty sleep by then." My throat tightens. "You're beautiful enough. You're perfect. I miss you."

"The doctor's here." Aunt Grace comes back on the line. "I'd better go."

"Okay," I tell her. "Speak soon. Love you."

"Love you more," she says. "Happy birthday."

My heart sinks as I hang up the phone. *Is it?* I don't really feel like celebrating. That's why I haven't even told anyone here it's my birthday, especially Vix. Knowing her, she'd want to throw a big party or something, and that's the last thing I feel like with Uncle Jim and Poppy the way they are.

Birthdays used to be such happy, joyful events. Aunt Grace and Uncle Jim always went all out: homemade birthday cake, balloons, jelly and ice cream—the works. But most importantly, we were always all together. Whatever our plans or commitments, we always made sure we never, *ever* missed a birthday. It was our family tradition.

But now . . .

Now everyone's scattered. I'm here, Uncle Jim's in prison, and Poppy . . . she can't even wish me a happy birthday.

I close my eyes as I remember the last time she did.

"*Happy birthday!*" she cried, almost the moment I'd logged on to Skype at boarding school. "I've just bought your present and you are going to *love* it!"

"Uh . . . Poppy, you know my birthday's not for six months, right?" I laughed.

"I know!" she squealed. "But this present's special—you have to get it early because it only happens in the summer."

"Intriguing . . ."

"And it was meant to be a surprise, but I wanted to make sure you save the date—you're always so busy. I can't believe you're not even coming home for the Easter holidays! Wish I could afford to go skiing."

"I'd rather have my mum and dad than their inheritance money," I said quietly.

"Of course you would." Poppy looked chastened. "I'm sorry, I just miss you so much. I was even beginning to forget what you looked like!"

"Drama queen," I teased.

"Seriously, Lulu, we haven't talked in ages."

"We're talking now!"

She frowned. "It's not the same on Skype."

"You're right," I admitted. "It's just—"

"I know, the social whirl of boarding school. I can't wait to finally join you there in September! Midnight feasts every night—it must be like one long slumber party!"

I laughed. "You've read too much Harry Potter."

"But best of all, no parentals! The atmosphere at home's been terrible since you left—they're doing my head in. Mum's always at her cookery class, and Dad's working too hard, and when they're at home they just—"

"Make your life hell?" I smiled, remembering how they'd nagged me about revision through my own exams. "Don't worry, it'll be summer soon."

"Not soon enough." She sighed. "I can't wait for you to come home. But anyway, back to your present! All you have to do is keep the last weekend in June free, okay?"

"What?" My heart sank.

"Because . . ." Poppy pounded a drum roll on her desk. "We're going to . . . *Glastonbury!*"

I stared at her.

"I know, right?" She beamed excitedly. "Is that the best birthday present ever, or what?"

We'd dreamed about it for years—going to a proper music festival, camping out, the works, but . . . "Pops—"

"I decided that life's too short," she interrupted. "It's time for us to stop talking about it and actually do it—and this year's perfect, cos I'll have finished my exams, and your term finishes early, and we haven't spent any proper time together in *ages,* so—"

"Pops, wait."

She stopped, startled.

"Poppy . . . I'm really sorry," I faltered. "I'm going to be in Mexico that weekend."

She looked at me blankly. "Mexico?"

"Didn't Aunt Grace tell you? A group of us have planned a trip—we're flying out straight from school," I told her, feeling terrible. "We've already booked our flights."

She just stared at me for a moment. "Oh."

"The thing is," I said hastily, trying to explain, "it's Juanita's eighteenth birthday and she's throwing this big party at her parents' beach house—it's been organized for ages—and let's face it, when else am I going to get to Mexico?"

Truth was, a guy I liked was going on the trip. Brad Glade. Brad Glade, who I'd had a crush on for six whole months. Brad Glade, who Juanita had deliberately invited because she knew I liked him. Brad Glade, who I couldn't wait to spend three long weeks getting hot and sweaty with under the Mexican sun. Brad Glade, who spent those entire three weeks getting hot and sweaty with my (ex) BFF, Emma.

"But I'll be back in July, so we'll still have weeks of summer left together—we can go away somewhere then, okay? Just the two of us. My treat?" I'd said hopefully.

She nodded slowly. "Sure."

"And we'll go to Glastonbury next year, okay? Write it in your diary in big font." I pointed at the maple-leaf USB necklace hanging, as always, round her neck. "We'll be there come hell or high water—literally!" I laughed. "Rain check?"

"Definitely." She nodded.

"Great." I smiled back, deliberately ignoring the disappointment in her voice, the slump of her shoulders.

But we never got to Glastonbury.

Because that weekend in June, when we should both have been at the festival, Poppy was at home instead.

Because I was off chasing stupid waste-of-space Brad Glade, Poppy was in the wrong place at the wrong time.

Because when I got back from Mexico, my cousin was in a coma.

And she still hasn't woken up.

TEN

The theme tune from *CSI* jolts me from my memories.

I wipe my eyes quickly and glance at the phone: Kenny.

"Hi, Kenny, thanks for my birthday text," I tell him as the call connects. "You didn't tell anyone, did you?"

"No," he says agitatedly. "But someone knows."

"What?" I sit up straight. "What do you mean?"

"You have to come back to your halls, like right now," he says anxiously. "There are two cards on display in reception with your names on them."

"Oh crap." I frown. "Wait—*names*?"

"Yep," he says grimly. "One of each."

Oh *shit*!

I speed back to halls, cursing myself for forgetting that cards and parcels aren't put in the pigeonholes I religiously check every morning, but kept in the office for safekeeping—where they're also prominently displayed behind the window for everyone to see.

I park my car; then, as I enter the foyer, Kenny rushes over to me.

"There you are!" he cries. "I didn't know what to do—I've been hovering in front of the window, trying to block everyone's view, but the girl behind the desk keeps giving me dirty looks."

"Thanks, Kenny." I hurry to the counter. Sure enough, there, stuck to the inside of the glass, are two brightly colored envelopes with my names on them.

Purple: Miss L. Shepherd.

Pink: Miss L. Willoughby-White.

I glare at the pink envelope and recognize Gran's distinctive swirly handwriting. *How could she forget my pseudonym?*

"Hi!" I smile at the girl through the window. "Can I collect my card, please?"

She looks up from her magazine. "ID?"

"Actually, one's for a friend of mine too," I say quickly. "Can I collect both?"

"Sorry," she says. "You can only pick up your own post."

My heart sinks. Whichever card I collect, either everyone will know it's my birthday, or everyone will know L. Willoughby-White lives here. . . .

I dig out my driving license.

"Just a sec." Kenny drags me back outside.

"What are you doing?" I demand, snatching my arm free. "I need to get that card down, now!"

"You can't show her your real ID!" he hisses, glancing at the other students milling around the reception area. "You'll blow your cover!"

"But I can't just leave the envelope there," I protest. "Anyone could see it."

"But they won't know it's you," he argues.

"No," I admit. "But it's like *advertising* L. Willoughby-White's here—it's too dangerous. What if Vix sees it? Or *Christian*?" I shake my head. "It has to come down."

I hurry back into reception, leaving Kenny outside.

"Hi again." I smile at the girl. "Sorry about that."

"ID?" she repeats impatiently.

"Lou!"

I freeze as Vix bounds down the stairs towards me.

"So." She beams at me as I quickly shove my driving license back into my purse. "Today's the day, huh?"

"What?" I stare at her.

"Your hot date with Christian!" she cries. "What time's he coming? Is he taking you on his bike?"

"No way I'm getting on that death trap!" I say, turning to try to block her view of the cards. "He's meeting me here at noon, then we'll take my car."

"Noon's kind of early for a party," Vix comments. "It's a good sign, though—maybe he wants to take you for lunch first? Ooh, you should go to that little Italian on West Street—Kenny and I went yesterday and it makes the best cannelloni I've ever tasted."

Another date? She kept that quiet. They both did.

"Anyway, what are you doing now?" Vix asks, her gaze straying to the girl at the counter.

"Oh, nothing. Actually, can I borrow some of your makeup again?" I try to steer her away from the desk.

"*Excuse* me, do you want your card or not?" The girl behind the counter glares at me and I feel like glaring straight back at her.

"Card?" Vix's eyes flick to the envelopes tacked to the window. "Omigosh, it's your *birthday*? Why didn't you say anything? Happy birthday!" Vix throws her arms round me.

"ID?" the girl snaps.

I dig out my student ID and pass it to her. "It's the purple envelope."

"Looks like it's someone else's birthday too." Vix peers at the other card in the window. "*Miss L. Willoughby-White . . .* very posh."

I cross my fingers, praying she doesn't recognize the name.

"Hey, wasn't that the surname of the guy who was in that big trial last year?"

My heart plummets.

"You know," she says. "The one whose daughter's in a coma?"

"Dunno." I shrug quickly. "I don't think so. No, that was Wilson something—"

"No, it wasn't!" Vix says excitedly. "I remember the newspaper headline: *Black Day for Willoughby-White*! I wonder if they're related." Her eyes gleam. "What a scoop that'd be. Do you know what she looks like?" she asks the girl behind the counter, who shrugs as she passes me the purple envelope.

"Vix!" Kenny rushes through the door towards us. "Good morning! Hi, Lou."

"Hi!" Vix beams, surprised. "What are you doing here?"

"I wondered if you ladies fancied grabbing some brunch? Unless you've got lectures to get to?" he says. "My treat."

"Great. I've got nothing on till this afternoon. Just a sec." Vix turns back to the girl. "Listen, I'll give you twenty quid if you call me when L. Willoughby-White comes to collect her mail. Deal?"

"Deal!" the girl says.

"Vix!" I stare at her, horrified. "The girl deserves some privacy, you know?"

"Then she should have changed her name." Vix winks as she scribbles down her mobile number. I glance at Kenny helplessly.

"Relax, Lou." Vix smiles. "A good reporter is always on the look-out for a story, that's all—I haven't had one juicy assignment since I started at the uni paper!" She moans. "But I wouldn't print anything she didn't want me to—I do have ethics—it'd just be really fascinating to talk to her if she is related to that guy. Plus a story like this could really kick-start my career!"

Terrific.

"Anyway, give me two secs to grab my stuff from my room, then let's go get some food!" Vix turns and disappears up the stairs.

"Are you okay?" Kenny asks as we move away from the counter.

"Yes. No. I don't know. Bloody Gran!" I run my hands through my hair. "I can't believe she forgot my name. She was meant to come and visit this weekend too—can you imagine?"

"You've dodged a bullet then, eh?" He smiles.

"Twice!" I agree. "If Vix had come down ten seconds later—"

"But she didn't," Kenny soothes. "And when someone else is on reception duty later you can come and retrieve . . . the rest of your mail," he says, lowering his voice as he eyes the groups of students milling around the foyer. "Lucky it's still so close to the beginning of term that not everybody knows each other yet."

"And lucky you spotted it," I add. "Thanks for the heads-up, Kenny. I guess it's lucky you were here for your *date*, huh?" I say grudgingly.

"Actually, I wasn't," he says. "I just invented that as a diversion."

I look up. "What?"

"I came to see you." He pulls a gift box from his jacket pocket. "Happy birthday, Titch."

I blink, surprised.

"Kenny, I . . . Thank you." I open it to find a beautiful silver digital watch. "Wow," I say, taken aback. "You shouldn't have—it's too much."

"It's nothing," he says. "I just wanted you to have a little reminder that I'm here for you. Any time," he says softly, taking my hand.

I shift uncomfortably. "Kenny . . . I can't . . . I don't . . ." I falter. "I can't accept it—it must have cost a fortune." *Far more than you'd spend on a present for a friend . . . unless maybe he thinks we're more than that . . . ?*

"What's money for?" He shrugs. "I'm loaded. Plus now you can literally have two faces." He points to the face of the watch. "Get it, *Shepherd*?"

"Very funny." I smile, relieved at his change of tone. This is probably the kind of present he gives all his friends. He *is* minted, after all.

"There's that beautiful smile—it *is* your birthday, you know!" He beams, and as he fastens my new watch onto my wrist I suddenly feel really bad for ever distrusting him. He's helped me out of a couple of tricky spots now, without expecting anything in return. I guess that's what friends do. Maybe it *is* lucky he ended up coming to Sheffield, after all.

"And what better way to celebrate than with a big birthday fry-up?" Kenny adds. "My treat."

"Actually, I can't come." I head for the stairs. "I've got to get ready to go out with Christian."

"What?" The smile drops from Kenny's face as he rushes after me. "What do you mean, like a date? You're *dating* Christian now? Are you *insane*?"

"*Settle, petal,*" I mimic, rolling my eyes. "It's not a date."

"Then what is it?"

"He . . . invited me to a party, that's all," I say. "He owed me a drink."

"You work in a *bar*," Kenny reminds me. "You can have a drink any time."

I roll my eyes again.

"*Lou,*" Kenny hisses. "It's one thing changing your name, and lying about everything to your new friends—"

"*Shh!*" I hiss as a group of students pass us on the stairs. Silently, he follows me to my room; then, as soon as the door's closed behind us, he explodes.

"You can't be serious, Lou! You can't *date* this guy! It's too close. It's too dangerous. *One* mistake, *one* slipup, and it's all over—you'll blow your whole cover!"

"Hypocrite!" I retort. "So, what? I can't date Christian, but you can date Vix? What's *that* about?"

"It's about keeping a very inquisitive investigative reporter off your case," Kenny counters. "A girl *you* chose to befriend. Plus I like Vix—she's cool—so what's the harm? She's having fun, I'm having fun. But at the same time I'm also looking out for you, Lou, because we're a *team.*"

"No," I argue, suddenly finding his concern for me oppressive. "We're *not* a team. I came here alone, I'm doing it *my* way."

"Lou, you can't—"

"Kenny," I interrupt. "I'm grateful for your help and your support, really I am, but you do *not* get to tell me what to do. Got it?"

"Look—"

"It's *my* life," I tell him. "It's *my* decision."

"No, Lou—*look!*" He points out the window.

I spin round to see a man climbing out of a police car and immediately my blood runs ice cold.

"Neil?"

ELEVEN

"What the hell is *Neil* doing here?" Kenny stares at me. "Does he know what we did? Does he know it was us?"

"No." Goose bumps prickle down my back. "He can't know—there's no way."

"Then why's he come all the way up to Sheffield?"

"I don't know! To visit?"

"Then why's he rocked up in a bloody *police* car?"

"I don't know!"

"He knows it was us who hacked the system," Kenny panics. "He must have found some evidence. He's figured it out. We're going to jail!"

"Calm down!" I tell him firmly. "Panicking won't help anything. I'll handle Neil. You take Vix out like you planned. Just keep her well away."

He nods, pale-faced, as he follows me out of the room. "What about Christian? Shame you'll have to cancel your date," he remarks snidely.

"Shit. He'll be here any minute." I grab my phone from my pocket and call Christian's mobile, but it goes to voice mail.

"Christian, hi, it's Lou," I say quickly. "I'm really sorry, but there's been an emergency . . ."

Kenny smiles as we head down the corridor.

". . . so don't come and meet me, but if you text me the address of the party, I'll meet you there as soon as I can, okay? Really sorry. Bye."

Kenny shakes his head. "You're crazy."

"Lou!" Vix bounds up the stairs. "Look who I found in reception—your godfather!"

"Surprise!" Neil beams behind her.

"Neil!" I force a smile as I hurry to hug him. "What are you doing here?"

"And what are *you* doing up here, Kenny?" asks Vix. "I thought we were meeting downstairs?"

"I was trying to convince Lou to come for that fry-up, but it's a lost cause," Kenny says, grabbing Vix's hand. "Let's go!"

"Lovely to meet you, Neil!" Vix calls as she's dragged away.

"Nice to meet you too!" Neil watches them go, then turns to me. "Hope I didn't scare them away?"

"Don't be silly!" I smile brightly as I lead him quickly back to my room. "What brings you all this way?"

"Aren't you pleased to see me?"

"Of course!" I say, hastily picking up an empty coffee mug and stack of books and clothes so he can sit down on the only chair. "Sorry about the mess—if I'd known you were coming, I'd have tidied up a bit!"

"You're a student." He shrugs. "It's expected." He glances at the posters and photos on my walls. "Nice room you've got here."

"Thanks . . . but how did you know I'd be in?"

"I have my sources." He raises an eyebrow. "Grace tipped me off that you were heading back to halls."

I nod. "Right."

"Anyway, can't a guy visit his favorite goddaughter without an inquisition?" Neil protests.

I smile weakly. "I'm your *only* goddaughter."

He shrugs. "Semantics."

"So you came all this way just to say hi?" I ask nervously.

"Well, no . . . ," he confesses.

Shit.

"Actually, do you fancy going for a coffee or lunch or something?" I say quickly. Whatever he's here for, it'll be better if Christian doesn't suddenly turn up. "I'm sick of the sight of these four walls—it's like a cell!"

I wince. Bad choice of words.

"First things first," he says gravely. "Some information has come to light that I seriously hope you can refute, despite the compelling proof."

I swallow hard. This is it. Kenny was right. We must have left some evidence. . . .

"I just can't believe it's true," Neil says, his eyes pained as he looks at me. "But I have to ask."

He takes a deep breath and my skin prickles.

"Are you, young lady—my goddaughter—guilty of turning *nineteen* years old today?"

"What?" I freeze.

"*Please* tell me it's not true—it can't be. That would make me *old*!" He cringes.

I smile tentatively. "'Fraid so."

"Ugh," he groans. "Then I guess lunch is on me, eh?"

"Definitely." I smile. "But I'll drive."

"On your birthday? Wouldn't hear of it. We'll get a cab." He jabs at his mobile.

"No need," I insist, "my car's just downstairs." And Christian could arrive any second if he hasn't got my message. . . .

"But you can't have a drink if you're driving," Neil argues. I start to protest, but he holds up a hand. "Yes, mate, can you give me the number for a taxi company in Sheffield, please?"

I keep an anxious eye on the car park while he orders the cab. I can't risk Neil meeting Christian—meeting anyone else. Kenny was right—*one* mistake, *one* slipup, one *mention* of my real name . . . and it's over.

I stare miserably at my mobile. There's still no reply from Christian, so I text him as well, just in case.

"Cab'll be here in five minutes." Neil smiles. "So how are you finding Sheffield?"

"Oh, hilly."

He laughs. "That's what Steve says."

"Steve?"

"I'm staying with an old mate who joined the Sheffield force last year," he explains. "He's the one who dropped me off here."

I nod, relieved. "Hence the police car."

He winces. "Sorry, kiddo. I know you're trying to keep a low profile. I did remember your pseudonym, though."

Phew. At least that's something.

"So how's life as Louise Shepherd?"

"It's . . . tricky," I confess.

"I can imagine." He nods. "You need to be pretty good at lying."

My skin prickles. Maybe I'm not out of the woods yet.

"Like I said, it's tricky. But it's better than everyone knowing I'm the niece of the most famous inmate in Britain."

He sighs. "Have you heard from Jim recently?"

I nod. "I got a letter."

"Me too. I've been thinking a lot about what happened. I can't think of anything else. I can't stand the thought of him in jail. It's not right. It's not justice."

I nod. "I know."

"I know you do." He looks at me. "Jim didn't do anything wrong. You know that, I know that."

I nod again.

"If you're innocent, you should go free, if you break the law, you should pay the price, end of," he says, his eyes deep in mine. "But the justice system . . . it makes so many mistakes." He shakes his head. "It makes me sick that innocent, decent, *good* people like Jim rot in jail, ripped from their loving families, while the guilty live it up, walk free, *get new identities* . . . It's not right. *Ever.*"

My blood pounds in my veins. *He knows.* He knows I stole the burglar alarm code, that I'm the one who broke into the building, who hacked the computers. Why I'm really here . . .

"And we should do everything in our power to make things right, whatever it takes." He looks at me, hard. "*That's* why I'm really here."

Shit. Kenny was right. I'm going to jail. We're going to jail. It's over.

"So anything you need—anything at all—call me, okay?"

I blink.

"It's killing Jim that he can't be here for you," Neil sighs. "But I can. I am."

I stare at him as he takes my hand.

"You've already lost one father. I can't imagine how tough it's been with Jim gone too. Especially like this."

I look away.

"So I want you to know I'm here for you, kiddo. Not just today. Just call and I'll be straight here. I promise. Day or night. Twenty-four seven."

"Thank you," I whisper, overwhelmed by his kindness, by his generosity, by guilt.

"No sweat." He pulls me close and ruffles my hair. "You deserve to be happy. You are my favorite goddaughter, after all."

A horn beeps outside and I nearly jump out of my skin.

"Taxi's here." Neil smiles, peering through the window.

Thank God! I hurry downstairs as fast as I can.

"Someone's hungry!" Neil laughs as I fling myself into the cab just as Christian's motorbike roars into the car park.

"Famished!" I agree, slamming the door behind me. "Let's get out of here."

TWELVE

"Are you sure I can't drop you off somewhere?" Neil offers as I walk him to a taxi stand after lunch. "We can go past your halls?"

"No, thank you." I smile. "My friend texted—we're meeting for a drink just round the corner."

It's not a complete lie. Christian did finally text me the address, and we *are* meeting for a drink.

Just got ur message. Phone on silent. Hope everything's OK. See you later hopefully: Cedar Court, Tanglewood Lane, Castleton his text had read.

Admittedly, it's not just round the corner. I've never even *heard* of Castleton.

"Oh, to be a student again." Neil grins. "Drinking all day long. Well, enjoy, and happy birthday, kiddo."

"Thanks." I beam. "And thanks for lunch."

"Any time." He winks. "Remember what I said. Just call me if you need anything. Bye!"

I wave till his taxi disappears round the next corner, then hurry to the next cab in the line and give the driver the address, hoping I've got enough cash to get me there.

We drive past the sights of Sheffield—the cathedral, City Hall, past the university—then we keep on going, till all that surrounds us are gently rolling hills, grassy fields, trees, sheep, and the

99

occasional farmhouse. Gradually the hills get steeper, gorsier, more rugged, as rocky cliffs begin to shoot up from nowhere, ripping through and scarring their grassy coats. It's beautiful, like something out of Middle Earth.

"Where are we?" I ask.

"Peak District, love."

"Derbyshire?"

He nods.

"Are you sure this is the right way?"

"Yep, nearly there."

I hope so, I think, checking my new watch. It's two-thirty. I'm not sure there'll be much point me turning up at this party at all if it takes much longer—we've been driving for half an hour already.

Finally the taxi pulls into the gravelly drive of a huge redbrick manor house and stops by the front door.

"Are you sure this is the right place?" I stare up at the building doubtfully.

"Yep." He points to a sign. "Cedar Court Care Home."

"Care home?" I stare at him. "There must be some mistake." I try to call Christian.

"You'll not get signal here, love. The hills get in the way."

He's right. I get out of the car and try again, holding my phone high in the air.

"Are you coming or going?" the driver asks impatiently. "I can't wait all day."

"I . . ." I falter.

"Louise?"

"Yes?" I turn as the woman we bumped into at the hospital hurries out of the front door.

"Oh good! You made it!" She beams. "Sorry, we've not been properly introduced—I'm Shirley, one of the carers here. Christian asked me to keep an eye out for you. Happy birthday, by the way!"

"What? How did you . . . ?"

"Christian told us." She smiles. "But don't worry, he didn't divulge your age—he's a gentleman."

I stare at her. How did he . . . ? *My driving license,* I realize. He must've remembered my birthday from when he checked my ID in the pub.

"He's just in the garden—I'll take you round, shall I?"

The taxi driver clears his throat. "That'll be thirty quid, then, love."

I spin round. "Thirty!"

He nods. "Many happy returns."

I empty my purse and hand him the money grudgingly. If Neil hadn't given me a tenner for my birthday, I'd be stuck. I hope there's a cash machine round here somewhere—I've not got enough left for the return fare.

"Follow me." Shirley smiles, leading me round the side of the building to a vast sprawling garden. A large patio hugs the side of the building, stretching tiled pathways snaking in several directions across the pristine lawns, which are studded with benches, trimmed with immaculate flower beds, surrounded by colorful bushes and evergreens, and filled with old people, happily chattering and mingling.

This is the party Christian couldn't miss . . . ?

"Ladies and gentlemen, your attention, please!" I look round as a guy in a suit appears at the patio doors.

I blink. *Christian?*

"Doesn't he scrub up nicely?" Shirley beams. She's not kidding. He looks incredible, his dark hair tied back in a neat ponytail, the crisp suit fitting him like a glove.

He winks at me. "It is time for the birthday girl to take to the dance floor."

I freeze. What is he doing? I can't dance! I open my mouth to

101

protest when a tiny wizened old lady in an emerald dress emerges from the house, her smile radiant as everybody claps.

"Edna scrubs up well too, doesn't she?" Shirley says. "If I look that good on my ninetieth birthday, I'll be a happy lady."

I feel myself relax. *Edna's* the birthday girl.

"Maestro, music, please!" Christian cries, nodding at an old man next to a stereo, and the waltz from *Sleeping Beauty* starts playing.

Christian bows to Edna. "May I have this dance?"

"I'd be delighted." She beams.

He takes her in his arms and I watch incredulously as Christian gently, slowly, impossibly gracefully, dances Edna around the patio until the music finally comes to an end.

"Oh, I feel like a princess!" she laughs.

"You look like a princess." Christian smiles, kissing her hand as he leads her to a chair. "Your throne, Your Highness."

He bows again, and as he disappears into the building I move to follow him.

"Young lady!" I stop in my tracks as Edna beckons to me. "I don't think we've been introduced."

"H-happy birthday," I stammer, panicking as I move closer. "I'm really sorry—I'm not gate-crashing your party—Christian invited me."

"Oh, then you must be Louise! Christian told me it's your birthday today too—please, have a seat." She pats the bench beside her. "Happy birthday!"

"Thank you." I smile, sitting down. "Happy birthday to you too!"

"I'm so thrilled Christian's found himself a nice young lady." Edna beams.

"Oh, we're not—I—I haven't known him long," I stutter.

"Neither have I!" Edna smiles. "He just blew in with the summer breeze a couple of months ago like a migrating bird, but some people you can just read like a book, can't you?"

I smile tightly. I hope not.

"Sometimes I feel like I've known him his whole life." Edna smiles.

"*I* have!" another old lady interrupts, wielding a wrapped present. "He's such a lovely boy, my nephew."

I look up, surprised. "You're his aunt?"

"No, she's not," Edna whispers. "Thank you for my present, Daisy, you're so kind."

"So's my Tommy," Daisy says. "Such a dear boy." She moves away.

"Daisy's got dementia," Edna whispers to me. "She gets confused. They all love Christian, though."

"How did you meet him?" I ask her.

"Oh, I'm his landlady, dear." She smiles. "Although he's been much more than a tenant to me, especially since I moved in here. I don't have any family of my own anymore, but Christian visits me every week, you know? Even when I was in hospital after my little dizzy spell."

"Are you all right?" I ask.

"Oh yes, yes, they've changed my tablets and now I'm stronger than ever, but that hasn't stopped him spoiling me rotten with chocolates and the most beautiful bouquets of flowers." She beams. "And when I told him how I used to dance that waltz on my birthday every year with my late husband, well, Christian promised he'd dance it with me instead." She blinks quickly. "He's an absolute angel. You'll not find anyone sweeter or kinder. Why aren't you two together?" she asks suddenly. "What have you got to lose?"

Far too much.

"Oh, I know he didn't move here under the *best* of circumstances."

I frown. What does she know?

"But everyone deserves a second chance, don't they?" She smiles. "Life's too short. Give him a shot, love."

"Edna, what do you—"

"Speaking of shots . . . Bartender!" Edna cries. "Mine's a cosmopolitan!"

"Coming right up, m'lady!" Christian appears with a silver tray.

"Your Majesty." He hands Edna a glass, then offers me a blue cocktail. "I promised you a drink." He grins. "I keep my promises."

"What's in it?" I ask warily.

"I'd tell you . . . but then I'd have to kill you." He winks. "Trade secret. You'll love it."

"It looks disgusting!" I wince.

"Don't be fooled," he chides, handing me the glass. "Appearances can be deceptive. If you don't try it, you'll never know. . . ." He swoops off with his tray.

"Edna—" I turn back to the old lady, but she's gone, tottering off to join a game of croquet on the lawn.

I sniff the blue concoction suspiciously, then decide to risk the smallest sip. It's utterly delicious.

My head spins as I watch Christian deliver more canapés and cocktails to the delighted old ladies, laughing and flirting and teasing and comforting them in turn, revealing a side to him I'd never imagined in my wildest dreams. Is this the real him? Or is he playing a part? If so, who is he trying to impress? The lovely old ladies? Or me?

"So how was it?" Christian asks, finally flopping onto the bench beside me. "The cocktail?"

"Oh." I smile. "Repulsive."

"I can tell." He eyes my empty glass.

"I had to throw it away." I shrug.

"So why've you got blue lips?"

My hand flies to my mouth.

"Gotcha." He grins. "Was everything okay earlier? I was worried when I got your message about an emergency."

"Oh no, everything's fine," I tell him. "It turned out to be a false alarm."

"I'm glad." He smiles. "And I'm glad you made it in the end."

"Me too." As my eyes meet his a warm feeling tingles through my body. When it reaches my cheeks I blink quickly and look away. That cocktail must have been stronger than it tasted.

"It's really lovely what you're doing for Edna," I say, watching her cheer as she knocks a ball through a hoop.

"I owe her." Christian shrugs. "She's been really good to me. She reminds me of my nan." He smiles wistfully. "Plus it's hard, suddenly leaving all your friends and family behind and being plunged into a new life where you don't know anyone. . . ." He smiles. "A wise person told me that."

I shrug and look away.

"So I thought a party might help."

"Seems to be working," I agree. "Though I have to admit, this isn't *exactly* what I was expecting when you said 'party.'"

"Whatever do you mean?" he protests. "There's music, alcohol, cake. . . ."

"It's great," I laugh. "I was just surprised, that's all."

"I'm full of surprises, me."

"No kidding," I say, looking at him closely. "Barman, butler, dancer . . . What else have you been hiding?"

"We've all got our secrets." He glances around at the old ladies. "Mrs. Groves over there was Miss Cleethorpes 1951, Ms. Williams with the walker used to play professional golf, and Mrs. Harris with the head scarf did time for robbing a bank."

I giggle. "You're kidding."

"Everyone's got a past." He shrugs. "Some like to remember, some prefer to forget."

No kidding.

"What about you?" I ask.

He turns.

"Why did you really come to Sheffield?"

He meets my gaze. "What did Edna tell you?"

"Just that you didn't move here under the best of circumstances." I watch him closely.

"She's right." He sighs. "To be honest, I didn't have a choice—I *had* to move. I lost my job and my home where I used to live."

"I'm so sorry," I say. "What happened?"

He shakes his head. "There was a . . . misunderstanding. I was in the wrong place at the wrong time."

A *misunderstanding* . . . ?

"Anyway, it's a long story." He shrugs. "I needed to make a fresh start—here's as good a place as any."

"To reinvent yourself?" I say.

He nods. "In a way, I think we all do it, to different degrees. But in the end it doesn't work, you know?" He looks straight at me in the piercing way I find so disconcerting. "Wherever you go, however hard you try to reinvent yourself, there's always one person you can't fool. One person who's too close, who sees through the web of lies, who knows the real you."

His eyes stare deep into mine and I feel totally exposed.

Christian sighs. "You."

I blink. "What?"

"No one can hide from themselves, from their memories."

"Right." I nod, relieved.

"Unless you're like some of these ladies." He glances around at the pensioners.

"What do you mean?"

"A lot of them have dementia," he says. "They can't remember who I am from week to week. Some of them can't even remember who *they* are." He sighs. "I'm a bit jealous, to be honest."

"Jealous?"

"Sometimes I think it would be nice to forget, to start each day totally afresh like that—a clean slate—no baggage, no bad memories, no regrets."

"Regrets?" I ask gently, not wanting to push him too far now he's finally started to open up to me.

He sighs heavily. "I—"

"Tommy!" Daisy calls. "Hurry up, dear, you'll miss the cake!"

"I'm right behind you, Aunt Daisy!" Christian replies, waving as she blows him a kiss.

"Sorry." He smiles at me. "She's convinced I'm her nephew."

"I know." I smile. "We met earlier. Why don't you tell her the truth?"

"I tried to the first day I came here, but she got really upset." Christian frowns. "Then a care worker told me her real nephew died in Afghanistan."

"How awful."

He nods. "I felt terrible the next time I visited—but she was thrilled to see me. She'd completely forgotten our conversation, and still thought I was her nephew, so now I just go with it."

"You don't feel bad, lying to her?"

"Is not telling the truth the same as lying?" he asks. "Is a white lie still a lie?"

I frown.

"If it's not hurting anyone, and makes someone happy, surely it's okay?" he says. "Sometimes telling little white lies is the only way to protect the people you care about from ugly truths."

"I guess so," I say uncertainly. "But it means you're pretending to be someone you're not."

"Don't we all do that?" He looks at me. "Even if it's just to fit in?"

My cheeks burn. Does he remember everything I say?

"So who are you really, Louise Shepherd?" He smiles. "What's your story?"

"Oh." I shrug and look down at my hands. "I don't really have one. My life's pretty boring."

"Don't lie."

"What?" I look up sharply.

"You can't fool me," he says.

I stare at him. Has he finally recognized me? His eyes glitter in the sunlight.

"If you don't want to tell me, that's cool," he says. "But don't lie. You're far from boring. I bet the person you write to in prison doesn't think so either."

"What? What do you mean?" Why would he mention that now? Does he know it's Uncle Jim?

"Just that I think it's really cool. Most people's compassion wouldn't stretch that far—not for people they don't know. I just don't know why you're pretending to be someone you're not, because the real you seems pretty cool to me."

I shrug. "We've only just met. You don't even know me."

"You don't have to know someone's life history to know them," he counters. "It's what we *do* that defines us. I know you're honest—you went out of your way to return my wallet when I dropped it," he says. "And I know you're slightly insecure, and go clubbing just to fit in with your friends, even though you secretly have much better taste."

I smile.

"I know you're generous—you helped out at the bar when I really needed you, despite having a twisted ankle. You're a bit of a klutz, and shouldn't be trusted with hot drinks. . . ."

I grin.

"But most importantly, I know you're a Libra, which of course tells me *everything* I need to know." He grins, pulling a piece of paper from his pocket.

"You didn't!" I laugh as he unfolds a horoscope page.

"'Libras, represented by a pair of scales, endeavour to be fair and even-handed in all aspects of life, although this sometimes leads to difficulty in taking sides,'" he reads. "'They can be very bossy.'"

"Hey!"

"'They dislike noise, confusion, dirt, pressured decisions, and being rushed. . . .'"

"True," I relent.

"'They always plan ahead, and have a meticulous eye for detail.'"

I bite my lip.

"'They also love attention, admiration, *credit cards* . . .'"

I laugh.

"'And gifts.'" He pulls a small square present from his pocket. "Happy birthday."

"Christian!" I stare at in surprise. "You shouldn't have."

"Actually, I didn't," he confesses. "I've had it for ages. I'm a complete skinflint."

I laugh as I unwrap a scratched CD case.

"Tinie Tempah?"

"I remember you saying you liked him."

Wow, he really *does* remember everything I say.

"Thank you." I smile. "It's great."

He grins. "Turn it over."

I do as he says, then stare at the inlay.

"Oh my God, Christian, it's signed!" I gasp. "I can't accept this!"

"Course you can." He shrugs. "I don't even like him."

"What?"

"I bought it from a charity shop by mistake."

I raise an eyebrow. "By mistake?"

"Uh-huh. Anyway, I was going to chuck it the other day, but it seemed easier to give it to you. Less effort. Save the landfill, and all that."

"Well, in that case"—I grin—"I'm all for recycling. Thank you."

"Happy birthday." He smiles.

"Christian!" someone shouts suddenly, startling me. "Christian! Come quick!" Shirley runs onto the lawn. "We're about to bring out the birthday cakes!"

"We'd better go." Christian grins. "After all, one of them's for you!"

THIRTEEN

"Ugh!" I groan as I stagger out of the party. "I have eaten *far* too much cake!"

"No such thing," Christian argues. "There's *always* room for birthday cake. After all, it has no calories."

I laugh. "If only!"

"It's true," Christian says, deadpan. "In fact, you *have* to eat it all on your birthday, otherwise it's bad luck."

"Oh, bugger, I need an ATM," I remember suddenly. "I haven't got enough cash for a taxi. And I need to call a taxi too!"

"There's an ATM in the middle of the village, but there aren't any local taxi firms," Christian says. "You could try a Sheffield cab, but it will take half an hour to get here."

"Crap!" I moan.

"See, it's bad luck—you should've eaten more cake!"

"What am I going to do?" I glance at my watch. Five-thirty. "It'll be starting to get dark soon too."

"The answer," Christian says with a grin, "is staring you in the face." He nods at his motorbike.

"No. Way," I say firmly.

"See you later, alligator!" He climbs on.

"Wait—you're just going to leave me here?" I protest. "On my birthday?"

"No, I'm offering you a ride." He pats the seat behind him. I hesitate.

"Come on," he says, those blue eyes dancing at me. "You're not scared of falling, are you?"

But I am. Suddenly I'm terrified of falling. And it has absolutely nothing to do with the bike.

"There's nothing to be scared of." He smiles. "I've got a spare crash helmet, and I'll even let you wear my special protective leather jacket. Then, if you do fall, you won't feel a thing."

"Very reassuring," I say nervously. If only there was another way back . . .

"Come on!" he laughs. "You might even enjoy it—you never know till you try, remember? And I'll look after you," he says. "I promise."

I don't have much of a choice. Reluctantly, I take the big leather jacket and helmet and pull them on.

"Suits you." Christian winks, putting on his own helmet. "Now, the important thing is to hold on *really* tight."

"Yeah, right," I say, climbing on and wrapping my arms around him as loosely as possible, the familiar foresty scent already making me feel dizzy. *Calm down,* I tell myself. *It's just the cocktail messing with your head. It's just a way to get home. It's okay . . . Oh God, he smells so good . . .*

"Tighter," he insists, tugging my arms closer around him, and a shiver tingles down my spine as I feel the warmth of his body through his jacket. "That's better."

It's too close. It's too dangerous. Kenny's words echo in my head.

"Ready?"

Hell, no. *One mistake, one slipup, and it's all over. . . .*

"Steady?"

I've never been more unsteady in my life—what am I *doing*?

112

"Go!"

My body lurches backwards as we set off, and I shriek, instantly clinging tighter to Christian as we swing out of the car park in an explosion of gravel.

The road rushes beneath us like a concrete river as we roar along the country lanes, trees flashing past, the evening sunlight flickering like a strobe as we race beneath the dappled canopy of the trees, lazy cows and horses glancing up as we disturb the peace.

My heart beats madly, my whole body trembling as the engine roars like an untamed beast between my legs, Christian's body jammed against mine as the wind rushes past like a tornado, so intense, so fast, so dangerous.

Every corner takes my breath away as we dip and lean and turn, one way, then another, more like we're flying than driving, till finally we swing to a stop outside my halls of residence, and the bike's roar dulls to a contented purr, then judders to silence.

Christian pulls off his helmet. "Are you okay?"

"That," I gasp, "was *amazing!*"

"See!" He grins. "I knew you'd love it once you tried it."

"It was incredible!" I beam, climbing off the bike and shaking my hair free from the helmet. "Thank you."

"Any time." He smiles.

"And thank you for today, for my cake, my present—everything."

"You had a good time?"

I nod. "A surprisingly good time."

"A *surprisingly* good time?" He raises his eyebrows. "As in you weren't *expecting* to have a good time with me?"

I giggle giddily. "There was a lot I wasn't expecting—a care home, riding a motorbike, blue cocktails. . . ."

"Point taken." He grins. "But despite all those things, you still had a good time?"

"Yeah." I smile. "I did."

"Me too." He beams, his gaze deep in mine. "Happy birthday."

I beam back at him, drowning in those eyes, my whole body warm and tingling.

"HAPPY BIRTHDAY!"

I turn, startled, as Vix races out of the building, a cake tin clutched in her arms.

"Happy birthday, Lou," she says, presenting the tin to me as Kenny appears behind her. "You can't have a birthday without a cake!"

"Vix! You shouldn't have!" I smile, opening the tin. Inside lies a singed lump with *Happy Birthday* scrawled over it in pink icing.

"Wow!" I gasp.

"She's been slaving over a hot oven all afternoon," Kenny says, glancing from me to Christian.

"Well, I wasn't given any notice!" Vix nudges me. "Hope it tastes as good as it looks!"

"Mm." I nod enthusiastically.

"Well, go on, then—try it!" Kenny urges.

"Oh, I don't have a knife," I say.

"Use your fingers—it's your birthday!" Vix winks.

"I just ate," I tell her. "I'm stuffed!"

"Just a tiny piece—just to taste," Vix insists.

Here goes! I break off a piece of cake—black on the inside as well—and start to pop it in my mouth.

"Stop!" Vix squeals with laughter as she grabs my arm. "I can't believe you were really going to *eat* that—it's terrible!"

"She set off all the halls' smoke detectors and everything," Kenny adds. "The whole wing had to be evacuated!"

"What can I say? I'm not a cook!" Vix shrugs. "So, unfortu-

114

nately, no birthday cake. But I *do* know how to party." She winks. "I've managed to reserve the VIP room for all of us at that new club in the city center!" She beams at me, and Christian and I force a smile.

Great. More clubbing.

"Sorry, Vix . . . ," Christian starts, and my heart sinks. Just as I thought things were going well between us . . . "But unfortunately I sort of already promised I'd cook Louise a birthday curry," he lies, glancing at me.

I stare at him in surprise, then smile.

"I'd put it off, of course, but I've already put the chicken into marinade, and I'm not sure it'll keep till tomorrow."

"Oh right. Of course." Vix's face falls.

"Sorry," Christian says. "I didn't know you had plans—you can go clubbing instead, Lou, if you want?"

"Oh no—I couldn't," I say quickly. "Not after you've gone to so much trouble."

"Well, we can go out afterwards," Kenny says, an edge to his voice.

"Actually, then we've got an Xbox tournament lined up—I got Lou the new *Halo* for her birthday, and she naively challenged me to a dual." Christian smiles at me. "There's money and honor at stake."

"Xbox?" Kenny blinks.

Curry and Xbox. I smile. He remembered.

"Besides, I can't really dance much with my ankle," I add.

"Oh yeah." Vix frowns.

"So is eight o'clock okay for you guys?" Christian asks.

"What?" Vix looks up, surprised. "Oh, I thought you meant just—"

"It's not a party without you, Vix."

115

She beams.

"And should I get red or white wine? Or both? We are celebrating, after all."

"Well, in that case." Vix grins. "Make mine a bottle of vodka."

Christian winks at me. "Vodka it is."

FOURTEEN

"I hate this game!" Vix tosses her Xbox controller onto Christian's sofa in disgust as her character is blown to smithereens yet again. "It's boring!"

"Only cos you're losing!" I laugh.

"Can't we do something else?" Vix asks. "*Anything* else!"

"Not yet—one more round. A decider," Kenny says. "After I've been to the loo—*nothing's* coming between me and victory this time, Shepherd!"

"In your dreams!" I scoff.

"I need a drink!" Vix frowns at her empty glass. "Do you have any more wine, Christian?" she yells.

"Yep, white's in the fridge, red's in my bag by the sofa!" he shouts from the kitchen. I spot it by my feet. "Can you help yourselves?" he calls. "Sorry, can't leave the stove!"

"No worries! I can have bigger glassfuls that way!" Vix winks at me. "You want white wine?"

"Nope, I'm on red, thanks." She bounces out of the room while I open Christian's bag to retrieve the bottle and my fingers brush against his sketchbook.

I'd show you, but then, you know, I'd have to kill you. . . .

I lean closer. What could be so secret . . . ?

I glance at the doorway; then carefully I pull the sketchbook from his bag, open it up, flick through the pages . . . then I freeze.

117

Now I understand.

"Oh my God!" Vix cries, coming in behind me. "What's *that*?"

"Shh!" I hiss. "It's Christian's sketchbook."

"Lou!" She stares at me, her eyes wide. "This *proves* it!"

"What's going on?" Kenny asks, returning.

Vix grins. "Christian's in *lurve*!"

"What?" he frowns.

"Look!" She points at the sketchbook. "Why else would he draw Lou so beautifully?"

We all stare at the picture.

"It's not a bad likeness either." Vix takes it from me and holds it next to my face. "He's got your eyes, definitely, and your nose—but the shape of your chin's not quite right, and your hair's all wrong—he obviously doesn't see enough of you!"

Kenny looks at me, his face pale. Then the doorbell rings, making us all jump.

"Could someone get that, please?" Christian calls. "I'm kind of tied up."

"Ooh, *kinky*!" Vix winks at me as she jumps up to answer the door. I close the sketchbook quickly and slide it back into Christian's bag, my heart beating fast.

"Lou," Kenny says quietly, his eyes serious. "The sketch—"

"Pizza!" Vix cries suddenly, cutting him off. We both look up to see a delivery guy at the front door, holding a stack of six boxes. "Guess we're not having curry after all!" She laughs, showing him in. "Just pop them on the coffee table, hon. Now, *that's* what you call a leaning tower of pizza, huh?" She grins. "You can stop hiding in the kitchen, Christian! Your secret's out—the pizza guy's here!"

"*What?*" Christian hurries into the room.

"Guess you're not much of a cook either, huh?" Vix jokes.

"Nice contingency plan, mate," Kenny says. "Everyone loves pizza!"

"That's fifty-nine pounds seventy, please," the delivery guy says.

"No. There's been a mistake," Christian says agitatedly. "I didn't order these!"

"This *is* Twelve Bromley Road?" The guy folds his arms.

"Yes, but I didn't call you!" Christian protests.

"Well, someone did."

"Not us," Christian insists.

"Then we've got a problem."

"No, *you've* got a problem," Christian argues. "It's not our problem. We didn't order any pizza."

Everyone looks at each other awkwardly as Christian and the delivery guy glare at each other.

"Listen, mate, all I know is I've got six pizzas getting cold here and *someone's* got to pay for them," the guy says gruffly.

"Well, that's your mistake, not ours. *Mate,*" Christian says hotly, squaring up to him. "Maybe *you* should pay for them?"

I stare at him. I've never seen Christian so aggressive.

"Is that right?" The guy takes a step closer.

"Yeah," Christian says, stepping closer still, his face flushed with anger. "It is."

Every hair on my body stands on end. What's he going to do? Hit the guy?

"All right, calm down, boys!" Vix says quickly, stepping between them and pulling out her purse.

"Vix, don't," Christian says. "It's his mistake."

"It's fine!" she insists. "I love pizza, and I've got . . . well, I've got enough for a couple, anyway." She pulls out two ten-pound notes and glances at me.

119

"I don't," I say. "Sorry, I used the last of my cash on the taxi."

"I've only got twenty quid too," Christian sighs, fumbling in his wallet.

"Kenny?" Vix says pointedly.

"Sorry." He shrugs. "I don't really carry cash."

"What about the money you withdrew from the ATM when we went to buy ingredients for Lou's cake?" she reminds him.

"Oh yeah." He glances at me apologetically as he reluctantly pulls out his wallet. "I forgot about that." Vix takes it from him and pulls out a twenty-pound note.

"Here." She gives the cash to the delivery guy. "Keep the change." He takes the money, glares at us all, then leaves, slamming the door behind him.

"I'm so sorry, guys," Christian says miserably, sinking into a chair. "I don't know what got into me. It just . . . it just seems to be one thing after another at the moment. First taxi calls all day and night, then I lose the pub keys and there's a break-in and Mike *still* thinks I was involved—he's been giving me dirty looks all week—then my bike gets scratched, and now a fricking stack of unwanted pizzas arrives at the door! I don't know what's going on!"

"Maybe you've pissed someone off," Kenny says.

"Or maybe it's just bad karma," I suggest. "Maybe you did something terrible in a past life?"

I watch as a frown flickers across Christian's face.

"By the way, did you sort out your taxi problem?" Vix asks. "The phone hasn't rung since we got here."

"I had to unplug it in the end," Christian sighs. "I only use my mobile now."

"Who needs a landline anyway?" Vix shrugs. "And as for pizzas? They're *never* unwanted."

"But what about my curry?" He frowns. "It's all done, it just has to simmer for another forty minutes."

"And it smells delicious." Vix smiles at him. "So let's all eat the curry tonight, then take the pizza home for breakfast—problem solved!"

A smile tugs at his lips. "Breakfast?"

"Course!" She grins. "Cold pizza's my favorite."

"Seriously?" I cringe at the thought.

"Don't knock it till you've tried it, Shepherd. Besides, you've got some odd eating habits yourself, Miss Marmalade Sandwiches— ugh!" She shudders.

"They're delicious!" I protest.

"All the secrets are coming out now!" Kenny laughs. "Hey, why don't we play Never Have I Ever? Then we'll *really* get to know each other."

"Ooh *yes!*" Vix squeals.

"No way!" I glare at him. The last thing I want is anyone discovering my secrets, and Kenny knows it. What is he playing at?

"What's Never Have I Ever?" Christian asks.

"A drinking game." Kenny grins. "Everyone has to say something they've never done, and if anyone else *has* done it, they have to drink. We'll be nice," Kenny promises me. "Nothing too rude or embarrassing." He winks. "Trust me."

"Okay . . ." I relent. I can always lie if someone asks something tricky, after all.

"Er . . . one problem," Christian says. "I don't drink."

"Come on!" Vix protests. "Make an exception—it's a party!"

"Um, it's *my* party," I remind her. "And it's Christian's house, so he doesn't have to drink."

Christian smiles at me.

"Killjoy!" Vix groans.

"We can still play," Kenny insists. "Christian, you just have to down three fingers' worth of juice for every finger of wine we drink—deal?"

121

"Why not?" Christian shrugs. "I think I'll need a bit more juice, though."

"I'll get it," Kenny offers, leaping to his feet. "Wine okay for everyone else?"

"Fine." I nod.

"Vodka shots for me!" Vix cries, rushing after him.

"Thank you." I smile at Christian once we're alone. "You didn't have to do this. The curry, the Xbox game."

"It's nothing." He shrugs. "Anything to save you from the evil clutches of clubbing on your birthday!"

I laugh. "My hero."

"Let's get this party *started*!" Vix cries, rushing back into the room with bottles of wine and vodka as Kenny follows, carrying a *huge* pitcher of what looks like orange juice for Christian.

"Is *this* enough?" Kenny grins.

"I hope so—otherwise you'll have uncovered *all* my secrets!" Christian laughs. "I didn't know I *had* that much orange juice!"

"You don't," Kenny says. "Orange, apple, pineapple—it's all in there. Might taste a bit odd, but we couldn't make it *too* easy for you, mate!"

"Cheers!"

"Enough chitchat, let's *start*!" Vix cries. "Me first. *Never* have I *ever* drunk alcohol!"

"You're meant to *actually never* have done it, Vix!" I laugh as we all chink glasses.

"But then I wouldn't get to drink!" she protests. "Where's the fun in that?"

"Never have I ever shaved my legs." Kenny grins as Vix and I drink.

"Never have I ever shaved my *face*," I retort.

"Never have I ever worn a dress," Christian counters.

122

"Kenny!" Vix laughs as he drinks.

"Boarding-school prank," he mutters. "Don't ask." Everyone laughs.

"Never have I ever ridden a motorbike," Vix sighs, and Christian smiles at me as the rest of us drink.

"Never have I ever gone jogging!"

"Pulled a pint!"

"Watched *Doctor Who*!"

"Just as well this is only fruit juice!" Christian grins. "I seem to be drinking all the time!"

As the game continues I start to relax. The questions are surprisingly tame, everyone's having a good time, and I feel the wine loosening me up.

"Never have I ever enjoyed clubbing." Christian smiles at me when it's his turn.

"Never have I ever known someone who died," Vix says.

"Morbid, Vix!" I frown as I take a shot.

"I have my reasons." She shrugs.

Christian hesitates, then takes a swig of his juice.

Vix turns to him. "You know someone?"

His eyes cloud as he nods. "A guy I knew died in front of me."

My stomach tightens. "What happened?" I ask, watching him closely.

"A drunk guy stabbed him," Christian says quietly. "That's why I don't drink."

I frown.

"Shit!" Vix gasps. "Can I use him for my ghost story?"

"Tactful, Vix!" Kenny comments.

"What? A vengeful spirit out to punish those who killed him—it's great!—just like *Hamlet*!" she protests. "Revenge always makes a good story."

123

"But they're usually tragedies too," Christian comments. "Revenge just makes people bitter or miserable. It's not worth it. By the end of *Hamlet* everyone's dead."

"So what are you saying?" I frown. "That criminals should just get away with it?"

"No, just . . . that there are already systems in place to govern justice."

"But the justice system doesn't always work," I argue.

"I know," Christian sighs. "Believe me, I know."

"Did they catch the person who killed your friend?" Vix asks.

"Yes." Christian nods. "He went to jail."

"Good." She smiles. "The story's got a happy ending, then."

If only it were that simple, I think.

"Well, that killed the party!" Kenny says. "So to speak!"

"Sorry," Vix laughs. "Okay. Never have I ever . . . shagged a policeman!"

"Been to Disneyland!"

"Been skinny-dipping!"

"Got a tattoo!"

"Smoked a cigarette!"

"Smoked weed!"

"Never have I ever used a fake ID!" Kenny says.

I look up sharply. What is he doing?

But to my surprise, both Vix and Christian take a drink too.

"Never have I ever dyed my hair," Kenny continues.

Christian cheers and drinks again.

"Lou?" Kenny's eyes sparkle at me. "Drink up."

"No way!" Christian cries. "You're not a natural blonde?"

"You got me." I smile tightly.

He laughs loudly and I look at him in surprise. It's not that funny.

"How did you know?" Vix asks Kenny, who shrugs. "What color is it really?"

"Uh-uh, that's not how the game works," I say, glancing at Christian.

"She's right," Kenny says. "You have to start 'Never Have I Ever,' remember?" I flash him a smile.

"Like, never have I ever . . . lied to the police," Kenny says.

My smile evaporates as he winks at me, and my blood runs cold. Is he planning to expose me in front of everyone?

My pulse races as I hesitate. If they see me drink, it'll give me away. But if I don't, Kenny could call me on it like the hair dye, making it worse. Maybe if I drink really quickly, they won't see. . . .

"I *knew* it!" Vix squeals delightedly. I turn, startled, to see Christian draining his drink.

"Got me again!" he laughs, slamming his empty glass back down on the table. "I need a refill."

I stare at him. Why would he admit it?

"So?" Vix prompts, her eyes gleaming. "Where *did* you tell the police you were during the break-in last Saturday night?"

"What?" Christian frowns, reaching for the now almost-empty jug. "Here."

"But you weren't really?"

"What?" Christian looks really confused now.

"You weren't really here that night?"

"No, I was," he says.

Vix frowns. "So you didn't lie to them?"

"Nope."

She blinks. "I don't understand . . . if you didn't lie to them about that, what *have* you lied to the police about?"

"About taking th'bag," Christian says, picking up the jug to pour himself more juice.

"What bag?" I frown.

"Th'bag in th'house!"

"What?" He's not making any sense. . . .

125

Suddenly he tips the jug, completely misses his glass, and juice sloshes all over the coffee table. We all spring to our feet out of the way. Except Christian.

"Oh shit." He stares at the mess, then bursts out laughing.

I stare at him. "Are you *okay?*"

"Um, no." His face turns pale. "Actually, I feel really . . . Excuse me. . . ." Christian lurches out through the door.

"Never have I ever spiked a drink!" Vix says, sniggering as Kenny downs another shot.

I round on him. "You spiked Christian's drink?"

"Moi?" he says innocently. Vix snorts with laughter.

"It's not funny." I glare at her. "Christian's teetotal. Did Kenny spike the juice?"

"No comment, Officer."

"Vix!"

"Come on, you can't play Never Have I Ever sober!" she argues. "It's not fair!"

"In vino veritas!" Kenny adds.

"Or vodka, in this case!" Vix giggles.

"So Christian's been gulping down shots while we're sipping wine?" I glare at Kenny. "You're an idiot."

"Lighten up, Lou!" Vix cries. "It's a party!"

"No, it's a farce," I snap. "I'm going home."

"No!" Vix protests as I stand up. "Lou, don't go! It's your birthday!"

"Good night!" I storm out of the room.

"No, Lou, wait!" Vix calls after me.

"I'll go," I hear Kenny tell her as I open the front door. "It's my fault."

Damn right. I move faster as I hear him follow me down the dark street.

126

"Lou, wait—" He catches up with me. "I'm sorry. I didn't mean to upset you."

"Like hell," I hiss, not slowing down. "What were you *thinking,* telling everyone my secrets!"

"Come on, Lou, *what* secrets?" he protests. "That you've dyed your hair and used a fake ID—so have most teenage girls!"

"And lying to the police?" I say. "Have most teenage girls done that too?"

"That was aimed at Christian, not you," Kenny says. "Besides, you didn't lie to them—you just broke into their offices."

I bite my lip, remembering what Christian said: *Is not telling the truth the same as lying?*

"Don't you want to know what he told them?" Kenny asks, "What his alibi was?"

I hesitate. "Yes."

"Well, *that's* why I spiked his drink, and *that's* why I asked the question," he says. "I wanted to make sure you really know what you're getting into. And surely you have some burning questions of your own for Mr. Mysterious, now he's feeling more . . . chatty?"

"Of course I do," I admit. "But not in front of *Vix!* The last thing I need is for Miss Investigative Reporter to uncover any secrets—about any of us. You saw how desperate she is for a story. She could ruin everything."

"You're right. I'm sorry," he sighs. "I didn't think it through. I was just trying to help."

"Well, don't!" I retort.

"Well, you obviously need it!" he counters. "*And* I've given it. I covered for you when you dropped your uncle's letter, and when your birthday card arrived, *and* I got you the job at the bar—"

"You *what?*" I stare at him.

"Titch," he sighs. "You think Heidi just *happened* to get ill when the bar was super-busy?"

My jaw drops. "What did you do?"

He shrugs. "Nothing much."

"Kenny, what did you *do*?"

"Nothing! I just bought her a drink, that's all."

I stare at him incredulously. "You mean you *poisoned* Heidi's drink?"

"She's *fine*," Kenny argues. "She just had a dodgy stomach for a day."

"Oh my God, what were you *thinking*?"

"I was thinking that you needed that job as part of your cover, and that I could help—I didn't think you'd start *dating* Christian!"

I stiffen. "I told you, it wasn't a date."

"You looked pretty cozy together."

"Whatever."

"But it wasn't a date?"

"Jeez, Kenny, what if it was? You're not my boyfriend. It has nothing to do with you!"

"It has *everything* to do with me!" he argues. "Even if you don't want to admit it, we're in this together, Lou—I can't just stand by and watch you throw it all away! Not after everything we've been through. There's too much at stake!"

Far too much.

"So don't shut me out, don't tell me I don't matter, that I'm not involved. I mattered that night in the office, didn't I?"

I sigh.

"*Didn't* I?"

"Yes," I admit.

"Oh my *God*!"

We both swivel to see Vix standing behind us on the pavement, her eyes wide.

Shit. How long has she been there?

She stares at me. "You and *Kenny*?"

I stare back at her, trying to figure out what she heard. *Me and Kenny . . . what?*

"*Now* I know why you tried to warn me off him," she says bitterly. "So you could have him all to yourself!"

"No!" I cry, relieved that she's misunderstood the situation. "No, Vix, it's not what you—"

"No?" she says. "Just what exactly happened *that night in the office* then?"

I look at Kenny anxiously.

"And when exactly *was* that night?" she demands. "How long has this been going on?"

"I . . ." I falter.

"Oh my *God.*" Vix steps backwards suddenly. "*Boarding school . . .*"

"What?" I blink.

"You both went to boarding school—did you go to *the same one*?"

"No!" I cry, panicking.

"It'll be easy enough to check." Vix's eyes darken. "You can find anything online these days, can't you, Kenny? Like, say, yearbook photos."

Shit. There weren't exactly many girls in our year at school, so if Vix looks up our yearbook, she'll spot my photo and find my real name, my true identity.

"*That's* how you knew Lou dyes her hair!" Vix turns to Kenny. "You knew each other before you even got here—you've been lying to me this whole time—*both* of you!"

"Vix—"

"And not just to me. I bet Christian doesn't know either, does he?" she says. "Not yet, anyway." She turns on her heel.

"No—Vix—you can't tell him!" I grab her arm desperately.

"Why not?" She shakes me off. "He deserves to know what's going on!"

"*Nothing's* going on!" I protest.

"*Seriously?*" She glares at me. "Do you think I'm *stupid,* Lou?"

"No!"

"Then by all means, explain!" she cries. "If I've got it all so wrong, tell me what Kenny meant—what happened *that night?*"

"I . . ." I falter, my mind spinning painfully. I can't tell her the truth, but I can't let her look me up either.

"Just as I thought."

I watch helplessly as Vix marches back to Christian's house.

"Wait, Vix—you're right," Kenny says quickly.

She turns.

"Lou and I . . ." He glances at me. "We did know each other at boarding school."

"I knew it!" She shoots me a dirty look.

"And one night . . . something happened. We broke into an office."

"Kenny, don't—please," I beg.

"I'm sorry, Lou," he says, not looking at me. "But Vix deserves the truth."

I close my eyes. *Shit.*

"And the truth is . . . we broke into this office because it was the only place in the school we could be alone, unsupervised."

My eyes fly open to find Vix glaring at me.

"You slept together?" she asks tightly. I glance at Kenny nervously, wondering where he's going with this lie.

"No." He shakes his head. "No, we just kissed. We were both drunk—it was the end-of-year dance and I'd smuggled in a hip flask of vodka. But as soon as we started kissing, Lou seemed to sober up and change her mind, and she left. But the damage was done." He shrugs. "I'd liked her for ages. More than liked her, actually. And that kiss . . . it sparked something inside me, a ray of hope that won't go out. That's why I followed her here. Because . . . because I'm still in love with her."

I stare at him. Where does he come up with this stuff? He's so convincing!

"I thought we had a future, I thought if I followed her here, I could rekindle that spark . . . that I could persuade her to give us a chance." His eyes meet mine and a tingle runs down my spine. If I didn't know he was lying . . .

"But it's useless," he sighs. "She's not interested. I'm not even on her radar."

"But . . . why did you pretend not to know each other?" Vix asks.

I look at Kenny, praying he's thought this through.

"I thought it would help us start again," Kenny says. "That we could have a fresh start if we acted like we were meeting each other for the first time. But it didn't work."

"But why did *you* go along with it, Lou?" Vix asks. "Why didn't you tell me what was going on?"

I shrug. "I . . . I didn't want to prejudice you against Kenny," I lie. "You liked him, and he's a nice guy. Just because I don't want to go out with him doesn't mean he shouldn't be with someone else, someone great like you. He deserved a fresh start too."

Vix frowns. "Then why did you try to put me off him?"

I hesitate, glance at Kenny. "I . . . didn't realize how hard it would be, being around him so much, and having to lie all the time," I say. "But once you tell one lie it just snowballs. And then it was too late to tell you the truth—"

"It's never too late," Vix interrupts, looking me straight in the eye. "Not for the truth."

My cheeks burn. "You're right. I'm sorry, Vix."

She looks away.

"You won't tell Christian?" I beg.

"I can't, anyway." She sighs. "He was asleep when I left, snoring on the bathroom floor."

Thank goodness.

"I'm going home," Vix sighs, turning away.

"I'll come with you," I offer.

"Don't," she snaps, her eyes cold. "I just . . . I need to be on my own for a bit."

I swallow, then nod, feeling unbearably sad as I watch her walk away.

"Sorry," Kenny whispers beside me.

But I've only got myself to blame, really. I caused this mess. I've known Vix for such a short time, but I feel terrible deceiving her, letting her down. But even as guilt weighs heavily on my shoulders, I know I'll still keep lying to her.

After all, I have no choice.

FIFTEEN

The next morning, Vix doesn't answer her phone or her dorm room door. I don't blame her. But when I get to the pub for my Saturday shift to find Christian's not there either, I start to worry.

Did Vix tell him about Kenny? Did she ruin my chances just as I'm starting to get close to him . . . ?

Anxiety niggles in my gut as Mike glares at the clock for the umpteenth time.

Did we do the right thing, lying to Vix again? Maybe we should have told her the truth—or at least part of it—that Uncle Jim's in prison, and I've changed my name to avoid notoriety. Perhaps she wouldn't feel so betrayed, so humiliated, if she knew that there really is nothing between me and Kenny, that he's just here to support me—as a friend. Part of me thinks she'd keep my secret, that she'd understand. But I can't take that chance. She is an aspiring journalist, after all. So the price of keeping my secret is to lose my only new friend here.

I glance at the clock. Eleven-thirty.

And now it seems I've lost Christian too.

Suddenly the pub door bursts open.

"Sorry, sorry! My alarm didn't go off, I just woke up." Christian staggers into the pub in his motorbike gear.

"You're an *hour and a half* late!" Mike yells. "Take that helmet off!"

"Sorry!" Christian removes it to reveal puffy, bloodshot eyes and cheeks that are still creased from his pillow.

"You look like shit," Mike tells him. "Go home."

"Okay." Christian turns. "I don't feel great, actually."

"And don't bother coming back," Mike adds. "You're fired."

"What?" Christian spins round. "You can't fire me for being ill!"

"You're not ill!" Mike argues. "You think I can't spot a hangover a mile off? I run a pub!"

"I'm not hungover!" Christian protests. "I don't even drink!"

Oh shit.

"Liar!" Mike scowls. "*And* you're late. Again. I've been waiting for a reason to get rid of you ever since the break-in, and now you've given me two."

Christian stares at him. "What?"

"Don't give me that butter-wouldn't-melt act. I know you were behind it," Mike spits. "And after I gave you a chance too. Gave you a job—a bloody *promotion*! And that's how you repay me?"

I glance at Christian, not daring to breathe.

He looks gobsmacked. "What? Mike, no, I—"

"Oh, I know *you* didn't break in—you're far too smart for that— you had your mysterious *alibi*," Mike sneers. "But that wouldn't have stopped you giving the keys to one of your dodgy mates, would it, eh? Well, I'm not as dumb as I look, so get out."

"But, Mike, I—"

"I said *get out*!" Mike yells.

Christian glares at him, his eyes blazing, then pulls on his helmet and storms out of the pub.

"Christian, wait!" I hurry after him. *He can't drive—after all that vodka, he'll be over the limit!*

"Where d'you think you're going, young lady?" Mike growls. "You walk out of this pub, you're out of a job too!"

134

"Fine!" I rush out of the pub to find Christian already revving his motorbike.

"No!" I yell as he roars out of the car park. "Christian! *Stop!*"

Shit!

I hurry to my car, hoping I can catch him before it's too late. As soon as I leave the car park, I spot him at the bottom of the hill and I hit the accelerator, not caring if he sees me following this time.

Keeping up with him is another matter. He streaks wildly along the busy road, wobbling as he weaves in and out of the traffic like a maniac, leaving a trail of blaring horns.

Oh my God. Panic rises inside me. *He's going to crash, he's going to die.*

Images of my parents' crash flash into my mind—the car reduced to twisted hunks of chewed-up metal that crushed them in its jagged jaws.

I blink the picture away, forcing myself to focus on the speeding motorbike, determined not to lose sight of him.

Finally—thank God!—we're out of the city streets and Christian turns off the main road onto a country lane, heading up into the Peak District. Sheep scatter like snooker balls as he roars past the stone-walled fields, the gray-green hills rolling away around us.

I glance at my speedometer.

Thirty miles an hour.

Forty.

Fifty.

I have to do something.

I punch my horn and he twists round.

"Stop!" I wave out of my window. "Christian, it's me! Slow down!"

Gradually his speed drops.

Thirty.

Twenty.

"Pull over!" I yell.

He twists again, then wobbles wildly. Suddenly he's veering all over the road as the bike skids out of control.

"Christian!" I scream as he crashes onto the grassy verge. He tumbles into a bush as the bike slides out from underneath him and smashes into a nearby hedge.

I swerve to the side of the road, jump out of the car, and rush to his side.

"Christian? Oh my God! Are you okay?"

He groans.

Carefully, I slide up the visor of his helmet. "Are you hurt?" I ask anxiously. "What do I do? I don't know any first aid."

"Mouth to mouth," he moans. "It's the only way."

I laugh with relief. "You're okay. Does it hurt anywhere?"

"Just my pride," he groans, sitting up and removing his helmet. "And my poor bike! Is it rideable?"

"I think it's okay, but you probably shouldn't ride it," I tell him firmly. "Not at the moment."

"Why not?" He frowns.

"Because . . ." I hesitate. How do I explain that he's hungover without telling him his drink was spiked? "Because you've just had an accident," I say, pulling out my mobile. "You're in shock. I'll get Kenny to pick it up—he's got a motorbike license." *And it's his fault, after all.*

I call Kenny and curtly explain what happened, then hang up. "He's on his way."

"You're so clever." Christian smiles. "And so pretty."

I frown. "Did you hit your head?"

"What? Yeah, a bit. Why?"

"I think you might be a little concussed."

136

"No, I'm *not*! You *are* beautiful!" he says so indignantly I smile. "And clever and kind and generous—"

"Well, *you're* a bit delusional, mister, so I think I should take you to hospital, get you checked over properly," I tell him. "Come on."

"Wait—shouldn't you be at work?" He frowns suddenly. "Mike'll be really mad."

"I quit."

"Why?"

"I wanted to make sure you were okay." I shrug. "I was worried about you."

"Wow." He stares at me, wide-eyed. "I think that's the nicest thing anyone's ever done for me."

Guilt swims in my veins. "Plus I wanted to see the look on Mike's face," I add quickly. "You should've seen him—I thought he was going to burst a blood vessel or something!"

Christian laughs loudly, then sighs heavily. "Shit. I can't believe he fired me. Why did he fire me?"

"You were late."

"Oh yeah."

"Twice," I add.

"Shit, yeah."

"And you lost the pub keys."

He sighs.

"And whoever found them broke into the bar."

"Oh crap, I'm having a really bad week!" He bursts into laughter.

I stare at him. "Why are you laughing?"

"I don't know!" he chuckles. "I'm unemployed, I crashed my bike, and I'm sitting in a muddy puddle! What else could go wrong?"

As if in answer, a van suddenly roars round the corner and splashes straight through a large puddle, drenching us from head to toe. We stare at each other for a moment, then collapse in hysterics.

"You had to ask, didn't you!" I laugh.

"Come on!" he yells at the sky. "Is that the best you can do?"

"No! Don't tempt fate!" I cry. "We'll get struck by lightning or something!"

"Bring it on!" he shouts. "Do your worst!"

"Don't!" I flick some mud at him and accidentally splatter his face. His eyes widen.

"I'm sorry!" I giggle. "I didn't mean—" A lump of cold mud hits me square on the ear and I shriek. Suddenly it becomes all-out war, as we flick and splash mud at each other mercilessly, till finally I hold my hands up in surrender.

"Truce!" I squeal. "I give in!"

"You're such a chicken." Christian laughs, trying to wipe the mud from his face, but ending up smearing more on.

"Well, you look like a pig in muck!" I laugh.

"Why, thank you." He grins. "Pigs are very intelligent creatures—and they say mud's good for the skin." He rubs it into his cheek like moisturizer. "Mud," he says, pouting. *"Because I'm worth it."*

I double over in stitches, laughing till I can't breathe.

"Wait, wait—you missed a spot!" I lean forward and smear mud over his forehead. "There. Perfect. You'd be right at home at The Flying Pig now, huh?" I giggle.

"Typical!" Christian cries. "I'm *always* in the wrong place at the wrong time!"

I smile as he brushes a piece of mud from my cheek.

"Well," he concedes, his voice softer as he gently cups my face. "Maybe not always."

My heart beats madly as he leans forward, his clear blue eyes deep in mine as his lips finally meet my own, smooth and warm and soft.

Suddenly I jerk away from him like I've been shot, stumbling over backwards into the mud.

"Louise?"

What am I *thinking*? I screw my eyes shut. What the hell am I doing? Shit! Shit! *Shit!*

"Lou, are you okay? Lou?"

I open my eyes. "I've got to go."

"Lou, wait—" He catches my arm as I scramble to my feet.

"Let go!" I say, my pulse racing.

"Please, don't leave," he begs. "I'm sorry."

"Let me go!" I scream, and instantly he releases me, his face stricken.

"I'm so sorry." His eyes fill with regret. "Please. I didn't mean—"

"Kenny's here," I interrupt, spotting the approaching taxi as I hurry to my car. "Take the cab back. Go to the hospital. I've got to go."

"Wait—Lou!"

I get in my car and slam the door shut behind me, my heart beating wildly as I quickly drive away.

Nothing happened, I tell myself over and over as I watch Christian shrink in the rearview mirror. Nothing happened. *But it nearly did.*

I punch the steering wheel. What was I *thinking*?

Kenny was right. This was a mistake. An epic mistake. I can't *date* Christian. It's too close, too risky, too . . . *wrong*.

Bile rises in my throat and I swerve onto the grass verge just in time to puke my guts out over a stone wall.

I screw my eyes shut, flooded with tears as Poppy's face fills my mind, her comatose cheeks so pale against her hospital pillow— while I'm out laughing, joking and *dating Christian*?

I spit out the vomit, the bile, the taste of Christian's lips, but the bitter guilt remains, sour and familiar.

How could I forget? Even for a minute? How *could* I? I've let

139

everyone down. Uncle Jim, Vix, Poppy, and now Christian will think I'm a complete nutcase too.

My mobile buzzes angrily in my pocket, and I pull it out.

Gran.

I ring off. I can't face talking to her, not right now. Besides, she'll think I'm at work.

It rings again.

Vix.

My heart leaps as I answer quickly. "Hi! I'm so glad you rang, I'm so sorry—"

"Where are you?" Vix says tightly. "You're not at the pub?"

"No," I sigh. "It's a long story. I'm in the middle of nowhere right now."

"Well, come back."

"I'm on my way," I tell her, hurrying back to the car. "Do you want to go for a coffee, or—"

"You've got a visitor, Shepherd," Vix says curtly. "Or should I say *Willoughby-White*?"

I freeze. *"What?"*

"Hello, sweetheart!" a familiar voice sings down the phone.

Shit.

Gran.

SIXTEEN

Shit, shit, *shit*!

I speed down the country lanes back to halls. What is Gran *doing* here? I thought they couldn't come up? What does she want? *How much has she told Vix?* Forgetting my new name on a birthday card was bad enough, but turning up here and spilling the beans? *She could ruin everything.* If she hasn't already.

I park quickly and paint on a smile as I hurry up to Vix's room.

"Gran! Hi!" I rush in and give her a hug. "What are you doing here?"

"It's your birthday weekend—you knew I was coming to visit!" she laughs. "I've been looking forward to it for weeks!"

"But . . . Aunt Grace said you guys couldn't make it," I tell her.

"Oh, just because *they* can't come doesn't mean I'm going to miss my trip! I'm perfectly capable of getting on a train, you know! Besides, you can't have a birthday without one of my cakes—it's tradition!" Gran smiles. "Though Victoria was telling me that she made you one yesterday—and nearly burned down the building!"

I glance at Vix. "You've been having a nice chat?"

She looks away.

"Oh yes." Gran smiles; then her face falls as she grabs my hand. "But I'm so sorry, sweetheart, I'm afraid I may have let the cat out

141

of the bag. When I was knocking on your room door Victoria found me and I asked for you by your real name. I keep forgetting you've changed it—my memory's just terrible these days! I had to bring your letter with me to remember which hall you're in!"

"I thought she'd just got the wrong room, till she showed me your letter, mentioning me," Vix says. "Then I put two and two together."

"I'm so sorry, darling." Gran frowns.

"It's fine, Gran," I tell her. "I'm sure Vix can keep a secret." I look at her pleadingly.

"Course." She smiles at Gran.

"Thanks, Vix."

"And how's your ankle, dear?" Gran frowns. "Victoria said you fell over?"

"Oh, I did," I say, "but it's much better now. Shall we go and grab some lunch, Gran?"

"That sounds lovely!" She beams. "I'll just pop to the loo first."

"You can use mine, Mrs. Brown," Vix says, indicating her en suite.

"Thanks, dear."

I wait till Gran closes the door.

"Vix—"

"Don't." She holds up her hand. "Your gran told me everything."

Crap. What will she do now she knows? Miserably, I remember how she bribed the girl in reception for news of L. Willoughby-White: *A story like this could really kick-start my career!*

"You lied to me," Vix says. "This whole time you were pretending to be someone you're not."

I close my eyes. "I'm so sorry, Vix."

She sighs. "It's okay. I get it."

I look up, surprised.

"I understand why you didn't want anyone to know the truth, especially as I was ranting on about needing a scoop!" She squeezes my hand. "But I'm your friend, Lou. You *can* trust me."

"I'm sorry," I tell her. "I just . . . wanted to be normal, you know?"

She smiles. "Your secret's safe with me."

"Thank you." I hug her and she squeezes me back.

"So that's why you were really trying to put me off Kenny?" she says tentatively. "Because he knew your identity and might spill the beans?"

I hesitate, then nod. *That's part of it. . . .*

"You know what would've put me off more than anything? Telling me he's in love with *you*. All that energy I spent chasing Kenny when there are thousands of other fit students around? What a waste!" Vix cries. "I can't believe he followed you here after one kiss—I'm actually not sure if that's incredibly romantic or just really creepy!"

I smile uneasily. There was no kiss, of course, but I can't tell her that without explaining what *really* happened *that night*. And though I hate lying to her, that's just not an option.

"I am sorry, Vix."

"It's okay." She shrugs. "I've only known him a week, after all. Plenty more fish, eh? Speaking of which, Matt's playing football later, so I might go and watch."

"He's sporty?" I say, surprised.

"Who knew, right?" Vix grins. "Anyway, have a good time with your gran. Maybe take her out for the afternoon—as in, well away from everyone you know—she's a bit of a loose cannon!"

"I know." I smile. "You should see her when she's had a couple of brandies!"

Vix laughs.

"They're purely medicinal!" Gran protests as she emerges from the bathroom.

"Nothing wrong with your hearing, eh, Gran?" I smile. "Come on, let's go."

"I can see why they call it Meadow*hell*!" Gran laughs as, after a long afternoon driving through the countryside and shopping in the mall, we finally tuck into dinner in front of an open fire at a cozy little country pub. "It's like death by shopping!"

"You grabbed yourself some bargains, though, Gran." I smile, thinking of all the shopping bags in the trunk of the car.

"I've got an eagle eye, me." She winks. "But my feet are about ready to drop off! Though maybe that's because of the fish pedicure?"

I laugh. "I can't believe you talked me into that!"

"It was fun! You mustn't be afraid to try new things, sweetheart—it keeps you young," she says. "I haven't had a good girly shopping spree in *ages*! Not since . . ." She hesitates. "Well, certainly not since you started uni, anyway. We used to go all the time, didn't we?"

"I'm sorry I've not been home to visit yet, Gran."

"Nonsense. It's only been a few weeks, and you've been busy settling in, making friends. Besides, it's a long way back to London."

I nod.

"But then, that was the point, wasn't it?" she says gently. "The further the better?"

I look away. "I don't know what you mean."

"I may be old, but I'm not daft." She smiles. "I know it's not easy, being at home. Not now."

I sigh. "It's like when I'm not there I can almost pretend it never happened. That everything's just as it always used to be."

144

Gran squeezes my hand and I blink against the tears.

"But they feel like dreams now, not memories. So much has changed."

"So much is still the same," Gran insists gently. "Family is still family, even if we can't always all be together."

"We'll never all be together," I say quietly. "Not with Uncle Jim in prison, and Poppy . . ." My voice cracks as Gran wraps her arm round my shoulders.

"We will get through this," she promises. "One day at a time. Together. Everything will be okay." She kisses my forehead, and as she holds me tight for the first time in ages I feel like it might be true.

"I can't believe I left your birthday cake in Victoria's room!" Gran tuts as we drive back to my halls after dinner. "We'll have to hope she hasn't eaten it all!"

I laugh. "We should be okay. She's on a diet. What flavor is it?"

"Chocolate, of course!"

"Uh-oh," I say. "Then we might be in trouble."

Gran chuckles. "Ooh, I shouldn't laugh after that big dinner—I'm stuffed! I hope you've still got *room* for birthday cake!"

"There's *always* room for birthday cake." I smile, Christian's words popping into my head unbidden, and as we turn onto his road I feel a twinge of guilt. I've ignored so many of his calls today that in the end I turned my phone off just so Gran would stop raising her eyebrows at me. But I shouldn't have just left him in the middle of nowhere after he fell off his bike—especially with a concussion.

"Candles!" Gran cries suddenly. "I haven't got any birthday candles! Honestly, I'd forget my own head if it wasn't screwed on!"

"Never mind," I say.

"No, sweetheart—we have to get some. Look, there's a corner shop, they might have them." She points to the off-license.

"There's nowhere to park," I say quickly. I can't risk bumping into Christian with Gran. She's already spilled the beans to Vix—he can't find out too.

"No, look, there's a space just there, outside the cottage with the green door." Gran points to Christian's house. "Pull over."

"No, Gran, it's fine—"

"You *cannot* have a birthday cake without candles," she insists. "Otherwise it's just cake! How will you make a wish?"

I wish I had a wish right now.

"Fine." I pull into the space. "You stay in the car, *I'll* pop to the shop."

"Okay, sweetheart."

I climb out of the car and almost immediately Christian's front door flies open.

"Lou!"

I freeze.

"Lou, I'm so glad you're here, I'm so sorry—"

"Christian," I interrupt swiftly, thankful that it's dark. "I can't talk now. I'll call you later, okay?"

"Lou, please!"

"Sweetheart!" Gran calls through the car window. "Who's that?"

Shit. "No one, Gran." I lower my voice as I peer back into the car. "Just a friend."

"Shall we invite him round for cake too?"

I can't think of anything worse.

"No—no, that's okay." I smile hastily. "Christian's busy tonight."

"Are you sure?" She glances over my shoulder. "He's very hand-some. In fact, have I met him before? He looks familiar. . . ."

146

"Nope," I say quickly, blocking her view. "He's a local. He does look a bit like that guy from *Mamma Mia!*, though."

"Yes . . . yes, he does a bit," Gran says thoughtfully. "Perhaps that's it."

"Lou, please, talk to me!" Christian calls.

"He seems to be keen to see you," Gran comments. "Why don't *I* pop to the shop while you two have a little chat?"

"No, I . . ." I hesitate. If I go to the shop alone, Gran might start talking to Christian. If I take Gran to the shop, Christian might follow us. This might be the only way to keep them apart. "Okay. Thanks, Gran. I won't be long."

I hurry up the path to Christian, pushing him inside the house quickly and closing the front door, trying to keep him as far away from Gran as possible.

"Okay," I sigh. "Let's talk."

"Lou, I'm so sorry about this morning—I was a complete moron," he says. "I didn't know what I was doing, I misread the situation—I didn't mean to upset you."

"No, I'm sorry," I tell him. "I completely overreacted, and I should never have left you on your own like that. Did you go to the hospital?"

"Yes." He nods. "They said I was slightly concussed—but also that there was a high level of alcohol in my blood."

"What do you mean?" I say carefully. "I thought you were teetotal?"

"I am! That's why I couldn't understand it—and why I thought Mike was crazy when he fired me for being hungover—until I got home, picked up my mobile, and checked my voice mail." He looks at me. "I had a message from Vix."

Oh shit. My heart beats fast. *What did she say? When did she call him?*

147

"She told me that Kenny's infatuated with you—that you knew each other at sixth form and he followed you here," Christian says. "Is it true?"

I nod helplessly.

"Then she said that Kenny spiked my drink last night." Christian pales. "*That's* why I was late for work, *that's* why I got fired, and *that's* why I crashed my bike—I could've been killed! And all because he's trying to turn you against me!"

I blink. "What?"

"Don't you see? He's jealous," Christian says. "I've worked it out. Everything that's happened—*everything* that's gone wrong for me lately—it all started around the time I met you!"

I freeze.

"It was all *Kenny*!" Christian cries. "It's obvious! *He* spiked my drink, *he* ordered the pizzas, *he* scratched my bike, maybe *he* even set up the bogus Facebook offer at the pub—he's studying computer science, for God's sake!"

"But . . ." I hesitate. "Why would he do all that?"

"To make my life a misery. To get you the job you wanted. To be your hero," Christian explains. "*Demand and opportunity*, right? On the day of the Facebook offer he made sure you were there—he invited you and Vix for lunch. Jeez, he even bought Heidi a drink—he could've poisoned her!"

I hug my arms tightly.

"But then he must have got jealous of us working together, so he tried to get me *fired*! I've been thinking about it all day. What if he was the one who stole my keys and broke into the pub to make it look like it was me? Remember how he hugged me before I left that night? He could've nicked them from my pocket!"

My mind whirls madly as the walls close in.

"He's crazy, Lou. You need to get a restraining order—you need to call the police!" He hands me his mobile.

"I . . ." I stare at the phone. "I can't—This is too much—I need a minute." I slump onto the sofa.

"You need to do something, Lou," Christian insists.

"Just . . . let me talk to Kenny first, okay?" I say, thinking fast. "It could all be a huge misunderstanding. These are serious charges, Christian."

"It *is* serious." He nods. "I could've been killed today."

"But Kenny couldn't have known that you would ride your bike drunk!" I protest. "It was an accident!"

"And poisoning Heidi?" Christian asks. "Was that an accident too?"

I bite my lip.

"Who knows what he'll do next? What he's capable of?" Christian says. "You need to call the police, Louise."

"I will." I nod, gripping the phone tightly. "Just . . . just give me tonight, okay? My gran's visiting—I don't want to upset her, she's got a weak heart. I'll call them tomorrow."

He nods. "Okay."

"Actually, I'd better get back to her, check she's all right," I say, putting his phone down and opening the front door.

"Lou?" Christian says as I walk away. "Just . . . be careful, okay?"

I nod. "Good night, Christian."

As he closes the door behind me I spot Gran lit by a streetlight halfway down the street, her mobile pressed to her ear.

I hurry up to her.

"Sorry about that, Gran, Christian just—"

"Oh my God!" She stares at me, her eyes shining with tears. "*That's* who—"

"Gran?" I freeze. "Gran, what's the matter? Are you all right?"

149

Suddenly she gasps and clutches her chest, her mobile phone dropping heavily to the ground. I rush forward as she topples headfirst into my arms.

"Oh my God! *Gran!*" She goes limp and heavy and I can't hold her, so I lay her down gently on the cold, hard pavement, panic rising inside me like steam, bubbling, blinding, suffocating. "Gran, can you hear me?" She doesn't move. *"Gran!"*

I stare at her helplessly, trying to focus, concentrate. *Think.* What should I do? CPR? Put her on her side? Every episode of *ER* I've ever seen streams through my mind, but I don't know what I'm doing—*what if I do the wrong thing?*

My eyes fall on Gran's dropped mobile and I pounce on it, my fingers fumbling in their rush to call 999, my eyes glued to her unmoving body.

"An ambulance is on its way," the man says calmly after I give him the address. "It'll be about twenty minutes."

"Twenty minutes?" I cry. "What if she doesn't have that long?"

"Is she breathing?" he asks. "Has she got a pulse?"

"I don't know! I don't think so!" But what if I'm doing it wrong? My own pulse races madly.

"Okay, then you'll have to perform CPR."

"What?"

I wedge the phone against my shoulder as he tells me what to do, but it's impossible to focus. I position my hands on Gran's chest as he instructs and tentatively begin to push, but as I feel her fragile bones beneath my palms, my blood rushes in my ears.

"Oh God, what if I'm not doing it right? What if I'm doing it too hard—or not hard enough?" I can barely breathe myself, with the tears gushing down my face.

"It's okay," he says. "Just—"

Then the line goes dead.

"Hello?" I say quickly. "*Hello?*" I stare at the phone. No battery. *Shit!*

And now I've lost count! I can't do this! I've no idea what to do—I've never even done first aid!

But Christian has.

The thought flashes into my mind, and in an instant I'm on my feet and racing towards his house. Why didn't I think of him *sooner?*

I shove his garden gate open, sprint up the path, and batter on his door until it finally opens and I fall inside.

"Louise!" Christian catches me in his arms, his eyes wide in surprise. "What's wrong? Is it Kenny?"

I shake my head furiously, fighting for breath. "It's my gran! She's hurt—you have to come!" I pull on his arm, but he hesitates.

"You need to call an ambulance," he says. "Use my phone."

"I *have*!" I cry. "They're coming, but they're twenty minutes away. The man on the phone told me to do CPR, but I can't, I don't know what I'm doing and she's not . . . she's not moving!"

"Lou." He swallows, his eyes troubled. "Calm down—I'll tell you what to do."

"There isn't *time*! You have to come now!" I wail, tears streaking down my cheeks. "Please, Christian," I beg, my insides crumpling. "Please! She might die!"

He nods. "Okay, let's go."

Within seconds we're both kneeling by Gran's side.

She hasn't moved.

"What's her name?"

I hesitate. "Cynthia Brown."

"Mrs. Brown?" Christian kneels beside her. "Cynthia, can you hear me?" He checks her breathing and pulse, then quickly, calmly, starts pumping at her chest, counting under his breath.

I watch helplessly, each thump of Christian's palms pounding painfully in my own chest. I'd never have been able to press so hard, too scared of hurting Gran, but what if it's too late? I hug my arms, each second feeling more and more hopeless.

She's gone, I know it.

Suddenly there's a gasp of air and Gran coughs. I jolt upright, hopeful, fearful.

"Is she—"

"She's breathing." Christian smiles. "Her pulse is weak, though."

He gently rolls her onto her side, and I can hear her breathing—faint rasps from deep within her throat.

"Will she be okay?" I whisper.

"I hope so," he says quietly, brushing Gran's hair from her face. "Now all we can do is wait for the ambulance." He looks at me. "Will you be all right? Only I—I really need to get back."

"Don't leave!" I panic. "Don't leave me alone. What if she stops breathing again? What if the ambulance doesn't get here in time? What if . . ." Fear and shame flood my head, and suddenly I'm sobbing uncontrollably.

"Hey." Christian wraps me in his arms. "Shh, it's okay. Here, you're freezing." He gives me his red hoodie, but it doesn't stop my shivering.

"If you hadn't been here . . ." I sniff. "She'd have—"

"But I *was* here," Christian soothes, holding me close. "She'll be okay."

He strokes my hair, his arms warm around me as we rock gently, my eyes glued to Gran. I hold her hand tightly as Christian calls Vix, tells her what happened.

"Listen," he says finally. "I've really got to go, but Vix is on her way and the ambulance will be here any minute."

"Please stay. Just till they get here." My voice cracks as I look up at him, his face tinted yellow in the glow of the streetlight. "I'm so scared."

He strokes a hair gently from my face, tracing the line of my cheekbone.

"Please?"

"Of course," he whispers, his lips so soft as he gently kisses my forehead. "Of course I will."

He holds me tighter and I burrow myself deeper into his chest, trying to lose myself in him, his warmth, his scent, his comfort, my mind tangling in knots.

"Shh," he whispers. "It's all right."

But it's not all right. None of it is. I owe him so much. I need him so much. Christian, of all people.

Suddenly shrill sirens pierce the silence like banshees wailing wildly through the night; then finally an ambulance speeds into view, lights flashing like a disco, the spectacle drawing curious neighbors and shoppers flocking to the scene.

"You did well." A paramedic smiles at me as they carry Gran into the ambulance on a stretcher. "By performing CPR you might well have saved your gran's life."

"Oh, I didn't—it wasn't me," I stammer. "It was Christian."

"Well done, mate," the paramedic says.

"Will she be okay?" Christian asks.

"We'll know more once we've checked her over at the hospital. Do you want to come with her?"

I nod quickly and climb into the ambulance as more sirens begin to howl through the night, getting increasingly louder.

"How many ambulances did you call?" Christian smiles.

Suddenly a police car rounds the corner and his face falls.

"You didn't call the police too, did you, love?" the paramedic says, climbing into the ambulance beside me.

"No, I—I don't know what they're doing here."

"I'll go and find out," Christian says quietly. "Take care, Lou."

"Christian . . ."

He looks back over his shoulder.

"Thank you," I tell him sincerely. "For everything."

He smiles briefly; then the ambulance door slams shut, blocking my view as we drive away.

SEVENTEEN

"You're awake!"

I stop pacing and turn to see Vix hurrying down the hospital corridor towards me with two Styrofoam cups. "Do you want some coffee?"

"Thanks," I say gratefully, perching on one of the uncomfortable plastic chairs outside Gran's room.

Vix plops down beside me and hands me a cup. "Is there any news?"

"Gran still hasn't woken up," I sigh. "But the doctor came by a few minutes ago to tell me she's stable."

"Well, that's good, right?" Vix says brightly.

"I hope so." *It could be worse.* I rub my eyes. "I can't believe I slept."

"You needed to," Vix says kindly. "It must've been awful, your poor gran collapsing in the street like that. Thank God Christian was there, huh?" She beams. "What a hero."

I smile weakly.

"Good fashion taste too." She nods approvingly.

"What?"

"Suits you." She smiles, and I realize I'm still wearing Christian's red hoodie from last night. "Have you heard from him this morning?"

"No." I shake my head. "My phone's been off, and I haven't seen him since I got into the ambulance with Gran and he went off to deal with the police."

"Yeah . . . ," Vix says thoughtfully. "About that."

"What?"

"Well, doesn't it seem *odd* to you? The police turning up, sirens blaring, when you didn't even *call* them?"

I shrug. "I assumed it was a mix-up."

"But what if it *wasn't?*" Vix says, her eyes sparkling. "Listen, when I arrived at Christian's, after you'd gone, the police were still there and I overheard one of the officers saying—get this—that Christian had "broken his curfew," but it was a false alarm as he was just down the street saving an old lady's life! What do you think that *means?*"

I swallow hard. "Maybe you misheard?"

"That's what I thought at first," Vix admits. "That's why I didn't mention it last night. But I couldn't stop thinking about it, and then suddenly it started to make sense. Don't you think it's strange that Christian *never* wants to stay out late, and he *never* does the evening shift at the pub, plus he *always* turned you down when you asked him for a drink after work, even though he *obviously* likes you?"

I stare at her numbly, my breath caught in my throat. She's right.

"The only question is, *why* would he have a curfew?" Vix frowns thoughtfully as I desperately rack my brains.

"Oh my God!" I say suddenly. "He must be in witness protection!"

"What?"

"I saw a film once where, in order to safeguard a witness, the police kept tabs on them—and at night there was an alarm that went off if they weren't at home!" I say, thinking quickly. "Don't

156

you see?" I count off on my fingers: "*That's* why he dyes his hair, *that's* why he doesn't want his photo taken, and *that's* why the police rushed round last night—they thought he was in danger because he wasn't at home!"

Vix's eyes gleam excitedly. *"Witness protection?"*

"It makes sense!" I insist. "Christian even told us that his friend was stabbed *in front of him* last year, and that the killer went to jail. He must have testified against his friend's murderer, and now they're out for revenge!"

"Bloody hell!" Vix cries. "You're right. It all fits! How did I miss it?"

"He did a good job of hiding his secret," I say somberly. "And now we have to keep it too—we mustn't let on we know, Vix."

"Course not," she says gravely. "Poor Christian. How could you live like that? Changing your whole identity, lying to everyone you meet?" She looks up suddenly. "I mean . . . well, I suppose you two are more alike than you knew, huh?"

I smile weakly.

"But for Christian . . . knowing your secret could be revealed at any moment, that your whole life is on the line if the wrong people find you, having to hide away, to be home early every night—except last night." She looks up at me, her eyes wide. "Last night he broke his curfew and put his cover in danger. For you." She sighs dramatically. "It must be love."

A cold feeling lodges in my gut as I remember how reluctant Christian was to leave his house last night. But when I begged him to help me he did. He came. He stayed. He put himself at risk. He *broke his curfew.*

For me?

"And then, as if Christian's life wasn't hard enough, along comes jealous Kenny with his petty vendetta!" Vix says.

I look up. "Christian told you about his theory?"

She nods. "I can really pick 'em, huh? Not only is the guy I fancy *besotted* with my best friend, he's also a complete psycho! Spiking Christian's drinks, scratching his bike, ordering pizzas, poisoning Heidi, conjuring up bogus Facebook offers—even framing him for the pub break-in!"

I bite my lip.

"Except . . . he didn't . . . ," Vix says slowly.

I look up. "What?"

"Lou, Kenny *didn't* break into the bar—he couldn't have—I've just remembered he was with *me* that night. We went clubbing."

"What?" I stare at her. "You didn't tell me you went clubbing with Kenny."

"Well, no—you'd been so down on him that day at the pub, and it wasn't as if you could exactly come with us on your bad ankle—but that's not the point! There's no *way* Kenny could've broken into the bar. The police said the CCTV cameras got smashed at two-fifteen, and Kenny was still in the taxi when it dropped me off at two-thirty!" Suddenly Vix's eyes flash. "Lou, what if Kenny wasn't behind *any* of it?"

"What do you mean?" I say uneasily.

"What if *someone else* has been harassing Christian all along? Someone involved in the murder, who's figured out who Christian is—*where* he is—someone who wants to . . . to silence him!" Vix cries, her eyes wider than I've ever seen them. "Lou, Christian's in danger—we have to warn him!"

"Can't you go any *faster*?" Vix yells at the taxi driver as we hurry back to Christian's house. "This is a matter of life and death!"

10 Missed Calls my phone screen reminds me as it flickers to life. Guiltily, I remember how I ignored Christian's calls yesterday—the whole reason I switched my phone off in the first place.

158

I scroll down the list. Five from Christian and five from Aunt Grace—probably worried because she can't get hold of Gran. I meant to ring her last night to tell her what happened, but she's got enough to worry about with Poppy in a coma, so I didn't want to upset her needlessly, and it's not as if she could come rushing all the way up from London in the middle of the night with Millie, so I kept putting it off, hoping that there would be better news to report . . . and then it just got too late to call. But now Gran's stable.

"I need to call my aunt," I tell Vix, dialing Grace's number. "Tell her about Gran—"

"Later!" Vix insists, grabbing my phone and scrolling through my contacts. "We need to reach Christian *now!*"

"But—"

"What if we're too late?" Vix cries, handing it back to me as it rings. "It's my fault! I should've remembered I was with Kenny during the break-in when Christian told me he thought Kenny was behind it all—I could've figured it all out then, and Christian would know he's in danger!"

"But we don't *know* Christian's in danger," I reason. "If he dropped his pub keys on the way home, *anyone* could have found them and broken into the pub. We don't know anyone's discovered who he really is, and if his identity's safe, we really shouldn't let on we know—it'll just freak him out."

Vix thinks for a moment, then shakes her head. "We can't take that risk, Lou—Christian deserves to be warned that the bad guys might be on to him."

"But Vix, if the 'bad guys' *have* discovered Christian's location, why haven't they confronted him?" I counter. "Why would they just faff around on Facebook and break into an empty pub? It doesn't make sense."

"It makes perfect sense!" Vix protests. "It's too easy, too *risky* to attack Christian directly—the police would just move him

159

somewhere else, right? They'd have to find him all over again! Much better to be subtle, to make his life a living hell without being obvious about it."

"Well . . . okay, but by *that* reasoning Christian's safe, then, isn't he?" I argue. "If they're all about being subtle?"

She shakes her head. "That was before Christian broke his curfew," she says. "If they're monitoring Christian, if they're nearby, they probably saw the police car last night, and now they might panic, thinking he's about to be moved. They could do something rash."

"Rash?"

"Like attack him or confront him, or . . . oh my God, *burn his house down*!"

"Vix, calm down. No one's going to burn down any houses!"

"No, Lou, *look*!"

She points out the window and my heart leaps into my throat. A cloud of thick black smoke billows into the sky from a nearby road.

"Oh my God!" I stare at it, horrified. *It can't be. . . .*

"Hurry up!" Vix yells at the driver.

"All right!" he grumbles. "Keep your hair on!"

But I can't. Christian's still not answering his phone and my pulse pounds deafeningly in my ears as we get closer, closer. Then, as we round the corner onto his road, my heart stops completely.

Flames twelve meters high reach for the sky and smoke surges from the broken lounge window, engulfing Christian's house and motorbike.

"Christian!" I scream, jumping out of the taxi as it pulls over. I barge through the small crowd of onlookers, past a man trying hopelessly to quench the roaring fire with a flimsy garden hose, and get as far as the doorstep before I start coughing.

"Christian!" I shout. *"Christian!"*

"Lou!" Vix screams behind me. "Lou—stop!"

"Has someone called the fire brigade?" I yell. "CHRISTIAN!" My eyes sting as I push against the door, smoke flooding my lungs.

"Lou!" Vix grabs my arm. "Get back!"

"No!" I protest.

"Wait, girls! Stop!" the man with the hose yells. "The fire brigade's on its way and there's no one in there!"

"What?" I say hopefully. "Are you sure?"

He nods. "I saw the lad who lives here leave over an hour ago, before the attack."

I stare at him. "Attack?"

He nods. "Two men drove up in a blue car and threw a petrol bomb straight through the window! Can you believe it?"

"Petrol bomb?" My blood runs cold. Vix is right; someone's out to hurt Christian—even kill him. He's in serious danger—wherever he is.

I check my watch. Ten-thirty. Of course—it's *Sunday!*

"Lou, wait!" Vix cries as I wrench myself from her grasp, fly through the gate, and fling myself into my car, still parked on the road after last night. "I'll come with you!"

"No!" I tell her. "Stay here—call me if Christian comes back, if you hear anything at all!"

I slam the door and drive quickly to St. Augustine's church, just praying I find him before those men do.

The service must have just ended, because the churchyard is busy, buzzing with dozens of people who aren't Christian. I scan them all, searching desperately for his face, his wild black hair.

I pull out my phone and try his number again, crossing my fingers tightly as it rings. And rings and rings and rings. Finally I reach his voice mail.

"Christian! It's Lou. Call me!" I beg. "Something's happened at your house. If you're all right, please call me." I hang up miserably. *Please, please, please be okay.*

I rush up to an old couple. "Have you seen Christian?"

They shake their heads.

"Have you seen the guy who plays the organ?" I ask a young mum.

"Sorry, love."

I run from person to person, asking everyone I meet, but no one's seen him.

What if he didn't play the organ today? What if he'd just nipped to the corner shop instead and was back in his house when the fire started? *What if he's still in there now?* The wail of a fire engine in the distance fills me with dread.

"Louise?"

I spin around. *"Christian!"*

I fly at him in a tight hug, relief flooding through me like a tidal wave. "Thank *God*!"

"Hi yourself." He smiles. "How's your gran?"

"I'll tell you in the car," I say, dragging him out of the church-yard. "Come on."

"What's going on, Lou?" He frowns as we climb in. "Are you okay?"

"No," I say, gunning the engine and swinging swiftly out of the car park. "Your house is on fire."

"What?"

"Someone's found out where you are—*who* you are," I babble quickly. "And they set fire to your house, so we have to get out of here. Now. Okay?"

He stares at me, his face pale. "*Who* I am?" he asks quietly.

"Vix and I worked it out," I say hastily, shooting him a glance. "That you're in witness protection, I mean."

There's silence for a moment.

"She overheard the police say something about a curfew—that's why they rushed over last night, right?" I add. "And that's why someone's burned down your house—why they're after you? Because you witnessed your friend get stabbed?"

More silence.

"Don't worry," I say. "I can keep a secret. Believe me."

Can I ever.

"So where should we go?" I ask as I weave through the traffic, trying to put as much distance between us and Christian's house as possible.

"Wait—" Panic flashes across his face. *"We?"*

I nod. "You're in trouble, you need to get out of here quickly, your bike's burnt to a crisp along with everything else you own, and I have a car."

"No!" he protests. "Lou, pull over. I can't let you do this."

"You *need* a car!" I argue. "How else will you escape?"

"Then let me *borrow* it!" he begs. "I'll get it back to you, I promise."

"Nope." I shake my head firmly. "I'm coming with you."

There's *no way* I'm losing him—not now. I might never find him again.

"What about your gran?" Christian says. "She needs you!"

I hesitate. "When I left the hospital she was doing okay. The doctor said she was stable."

"Lou, you can't come with me, you don't understand! The people who are after me are violent, dangerous—you saw what they did to my house! I can't put you at risk!"

"They're looking for *you,* not me," I counter. "So you shouldn't be seen driving. Climb into the back and pull that blanket over you."

"Lou—"

163

"Christian," I interrupt. "I'm not stopping, I'm not getting out. The longer we drive around aimlessly arguing, the more likely they'll find us, and then we'll *both* be in trouble."

He hesitates, then sighs. "Okay, but only till we're a safe distance away. Agreed?"

I don't answer.

"Agreed?" Christian presses.

"Okay!" I cross my fingers. "Just till you're safe. Whatever."

I'll say whatever I have to to get him to accept I'm going with him. But there's absolutely no way he's going *anywhere* without me.

"Can I borrow your phone?" he asks.

"Course." I hand it to him.

"Your *phone,* Lou. This is some random cassette tape."

"It *is* my phone." I turn it over to show him my mobile inside. "That's just a retro cover."

He stares at it for a moment, then tosses it out the window.

"What the— *Christian!*"

"I'm sorry, but it's too dangerous. They can trace it."

I stare at him. *"Seriously?"*

"Seriously." He nods. "You need to know what you're getting yourself into, Lou. If I were you, I'd pull over now, pick up your phone, and get on with your life."

"No," I tell him. "I've made up my mind. Now get in the back before someone sees you."

"Fine!" He hauls himself onto the backseat and I glance in the rearview mirror as he covers himself with the blanket.

"Who's after you?" I ask quietly.

He sighs. "Some people who think I did something I didn't do," he says, his voice muffled under the blanket.

I frown. Something he *didn't* do?

"Why would they think that?" I ask.

"I . . . I guess I was in the wrong place at the wrong time."

"Meaning?"

He sighs. "It's a misunderstanding."

"Seems like a pretty big misunderstanding!"

"Yes," he admits. "It is. That's why I had to leave. Vanish. It wasn't safe. It *isn't* safe," he corrects himself.

"Christian—"

"I'm sorry, Lou," he interrupts. "I'd tell you everything, but—"

"But then you'd have to kill me?" I say lightly.

"Something like that," he agrees. "It's too risky. You're in enough danger as it is."

A shiver runs down my spine.

"So where should I take you, anyway?" I ask. "The police?"

"No!" Christian says quickly.

I swallow. "Why not?"

"How do you think they found me, Lou? The police are the only ones who knew where I was."

I bite my lip.

"I can't trust them. Not anymore."

I stare at the road as I try to take it all in.

"So where *do* you want to go?" I ask as we stop at traffic lights.

"Just head for the M1 South for now."

"South." I nod. "Got it."

"Lou—"

"Shh!" I hiss as a dark blue Ford pulls up beside us. Two heavyset men sit in the front, grim expressions on their faces. Could they be the ones after Christian?

Calm down, I tell myself. What are the chances of that, really? Just cos they're in a blue car? I'm being paranoid.

Even so, I glance in my mirrors. We're the only two cars on the road. I risk another look at the car and find one of the men staring straight at me. He runs a hand through his dirty blond hair, then nudges his buddy. I sweat under their gaze, my heart pattering in my chest like a hamster on a wheel. Slowly, he winds down his window and I flash him what I hope is a dazzling smile.

"What's up?" I grin.

"You turning left, sweetheart?" he grunts.

"Um, y-yeah," I stammer, trying to keep my voice steady. "Why?"

"Because your light turned green about twenty seconds ago."

"Oh!" Blood rushes to my face. "Oh, right—thanks! Bye!" I pull away swiftly, just as the lights change back.

"What was all that about?" Christian whispers from the backseat.

"Nothing," I hiss, keeping a close eye on my rearview mirror to make sure they don't follow us.

Finally they pull off, heading straight over the junction, and I breathe a sigh of relief. "Everything's fine."

For now.

As we reach the motorway we lapse into a heavy silence. I don't know if Christian's fallen asleep beneath the blanket, or if he just doesn't feel like talking. He must be so scared. I can't believe someone *torched* his house. How did they find him, anyway? I can't believe the police leaked his location. But then again . . . My stomach lurches uneasily. They were the only ones who knew where he was. . . .

My mind whirs wildly, wondering what's going to happen next, when they'll realize Christian wasn't inside the house, whether they'll catch up with us any moment, whoever they are. I check my rearview mirror every few seconds as we drive, but I don't even know what I'm looking for. Finally the petrol light begins to flash.

"What are you doing?" Christian asks anxiously as I pull up at a service station.

"We need petrol," I tell him. "And food. I'm starving!"

"Where are we?" he mumbles. "What time is it?"

"Somewhere on the M1." I check my watch. "And it's one o'clock."

"Shit," he mutters. "Why didn't you wake me up? You were only supposed to drive me a safe distance away."

"I didn't know you were asleep." I shrug. "You want to come in? Get a burger?"

"No," he says quickly. "No, I can't."

"Christian, come on, we're miles away from Sheffield now."

"It's not safe," he says. "I'll stay here."

"Okay." I sigh. "Well, do you want me to bring you some food?"

"No thanks, I'm not hungry," he says. "But could you see if they've got any hair dye?"

Randomly, the service station does sell hair dye, but I kick myself for not asking what color Christian wanted.

Not that the range is incredibly inspiring. Most of them are varying shades of brown, with one ginger and one black, and they've all got Cheryl Cole on the box. As Christian's hair's dyed black already and bright orange isn't exactly great camouflage, I pick a brown at random, grab a sandwich, and head back to the car.

I pause as I reach a pay phone. I could call the police right now—tell them where he is . . . but something stops me. The look on Christian's face when I suggested it earlier, how adamant he was that it's the police who betrayed him, and something about his story has got me thinking . . . *They think I did something I didn't do.* What did he mean by that?

I turn away from the phone and head back to the car. He trusts me, after all.

167

"I hope 'cappuccino' dye's okay—they didn't have much choice,"
I say, tossing the box onto the backseat as I start the engine and pull
away. "I got a BLT. Though I'm not sure what that stands for in this
case. Burnt Leftover Tomatoes?" I eye the sandwich suspiciously.
"Sure you don't want half?" I glance in the rearview mirror.

But Christian has gone.

EIGHTEEN

"Christian!" I screech to a halt and scan the car park quickly, but there's no sign of him.

Goose bumps break out down my neck. He *told* me it wasn't safe. What if they found him—what if they've got him now? I look around anxiously, but he's nowhere to be seen.

Shit! I hit the steering wheel in frustration.

Suddenly another thought flashes across my mind. *What if he's just done a runner?* He *said* it was too dangerous, that he wouldn't take me with him, that I should just drive him somewhere safe and then go back. . . .

Crap. He's gone. He's buggered off. *He could be anywhere!*

But then, *why* ask for hair dye? I reason. I was going inside for food anyway—he didn't have to find a way to get rid of me . . . and why would he leave me *here,* at a service station in the middle of nowhere? How would he get away without a car?

It doesn't make sense. Where *is* he?

Slowly, I coast round the car park, searching everywhere. I have to find him—I *have* to. Otherwise . . . it's all been for nothing. *Think!*

He'd have to hitchhike, get a lift with a lorry driver, perhaps. I crane my neck as a lorry pulls out, but I can't see him in the cab. Even if I could, what then?

169

It's hopeless. I've lost him. *Shit!*

Suddenly the back door of the car flies open and a man hurls himself inside. I scream.

"*Lou!* Shh!"

"Shit—*Christian!*" I cry incredulously, slamming on the brakes. "What the hell? You nearly gave me a heart attack!"

"*I* nearly gave *you* a heart attack?" he gasps. "You're the one who drove off and left me!"

"Why did you even get out of the car?" I counter, twisting in my seat.

"I . . ." He hesitates. "I needed the loo."

"What? Well, why didn't you just come into the services with me?"

"I couldn't go *inside,* but you parked near those trees—I thought I could make it before you got back."

"You should've come in," I tell him. "It was really quiet in there—you'd have been fine."

"Yeah, but there's still CCTV."

"*CCTV?* " I raise an eyebrow. "Paranoid much?"

"No," he says evenly. "Not paranoid, *cautious.* If I get caught on CCTV, if anyone recognizes me . . . they'll find me again."

I look at him for a long moment.

"I'm serious, Lou. This isn't a game. It's not safe—for either of us." He sighs. "I'm putting you in danger."

"No, I'm putting myself in danger," I argue. "And sitting here isn't exactly the safest place to be either."

"Okay." He hesitates. "Well, maybe if you could just drive me a bit further—to London . . ."

"Of course," I say immediately.

"But then you have to leave—go back to Sheffield. Okay?"

"Okay." I shrug. *Yeah, right.* "What's in London?"

"It's my home. I've got mates there who'll help me, hide me."

"But if you're from London, don't you think it's the first place they'll look for you?" I frown. "You can't go back there."

"I have to," he says sadly. "I've got nowhere else to go."

"But—"

"And it's time I put a stop to this. Once and for all."

I look at him, trying to work out what he's planning.

"I can't live in hiding anymore, Lou. I've tried, and it doesn't work. I've given up everything, and for what? They still found me."

I stare at him. "What're you going to do?"

"First of all"—he swallows—"I need to find my mate Joe."

But fate isn't on our side. We haven't been back on the motorway for more than ten minutes when the overhead hazard warning lights come on and I spot a queue of slow-moving vehicles ahead; then, eventually, the traffic comes to a complete standstill.

"What's going on?" Christian asks from the back.

"Dunno. Roadworks or an accident," I say, gazing miserably at the line of cars stretching into the distance. We share the BLT sandwich as we inch along for mile after mile until we reach the mangled wreckage of a car and my blood runs cold. I'll never get used to seeing the debris of other people's lives. Every accident, every crash fills me with dread, as it reminds me of that terrible day. The day my parents were snatched from my life forever.

After what seems like days, the traffic starts to flow more quickly, and finally, just before half past three, Christian directs me off the motorway and into the outskirts of London, but it's difficult to follow his instructions through the maze of side streets—especially as he's still hiding beneath the blanket, so he can't actually see where we're going.

"This is impossible!" I cry as we end up at our third dead end.

"No, it's not—you just have to turn right at the kebab shop."

"*Which* kebab shop?" I ask. "I can see three from here!"

"Um . . . I think it's called something like Tikka Tikka? No—Marsala Marsala?"

"Marsala Marceau?"

"That's it! Bexley's only French kebab house."

"Great! We passed that twenty minutes ago!" I groan. "So it's right at Marsala Marceau. . . ."

I spin the car around and follow Christian's directions till finally we arrive at a tall bleak-looking block of council flats identifying themselves as Jonas Towers.

"Okay, Joe of Jonas Towers," I sigh. "We've found you at last!"

"Let's just hope he's in," Christian mutters.

I nod. "I'll go check it out."

"No, I'll go."

"Stay put," I order. "There's no point risking your neck to knock at an empty flat, is there? And if you need the loo, hold it. Got it?"

"Got it." He grins sheepishly. "Third floor. Flat thirty-nine."

"See you in a mo."

"Lou—"

I turn.

"Tell him . . . Leo's here." He looks at me awkwardly. "That's my real name."

"Leo?" A shiver runs down the back of my neck.

"Like the star sign." He nods. "And take care. This can be a rough neighborhood."

Great.

I lock the car and walk towards the tower block. It's a gloomy, gray afternoon, and I shiver as the wind whips past, sending dead leaves and litter scuttling across my path.

In the courtyard a group of tall black guys are passing a basketball between them, bouncing it off the walls and shooting hoops. They look up as I pass and I glue my gaze to the ground, hugging Christian's hoodie closer around me. Finally I reach the relative privacy of the concrete stairwell. I punch the button for the lift, but nothing happens. I sigh, then head up the stairs, ignoring the graffiti scrawled all over the walls and holding my nose against the stench of urine. I walk quickly along the concrete balcony and am filled with relief as I reach the last door: number thirty-nine.

Down in the courtyard I can still see the group of guys slamming that ball around, and I'm not sure whether to feel comforted or threatened by their closeness. I take a deep breath, knock at the faded red door, and cross my fingers that this isn't a complete waste of time.

Nothing.

I knock again, then hear a noise inside, and something moves behind the frosted glass panel in the door. The third time I knock, there's a rattle, like a series of bolts being unlocked; then suddenly the door opens but catches on a security chain.

"Hello?" A skinny guy in his late twenties peers out suspiciously, his face covered with volcanic acne.

"Hi—Joe?" I smile tentatively.

"Who're you?" he demands.

"I have a message. From a friend of yours."

The guy's expression hardens and he pulls the door closed a few centimeters.

"What friend?"

I glance around, then drop my voice to a whisper. "Christian."

His eyes narrow. "Who?"

I blink. "Christi— Leo. I mean Leo."

"Leo?" The guy's eyes bulge.

I nod, glance around again, then drop my voice even more. "He's downstairs."

"Shit." His eyes widen even more. "Leo's *here*?"

I nod. "Can he come up?"

"Yes! Yes, bring him up, I'll just—clean up a bit." He slams the door in my face.

Charming.

When I return with Christian, Joe's door opens on the first knock. He pulls us quickly into a small living room, shuts the door, then grabs Christian in a bear hug.

"Mate!" Joe cries. "Bloody hell, you're a sight for sore eyes!"

"It's good to see you, Joe." Christian beams.

"How *are* you?" Joe asks. "I haven't seen you since—"

"Forever," Christian finishes for him quickly, glancing at me. "Tell me about it."

"See you haven't wasted much time, though!" Joe grins at me. "Girlfriend already? Better luck with this one, eh?"

I look up sharply as Christian stiffens, and immediately Joe's smile disappears.

"Jesus, sorry, man—I didn't mean—I didn't mean anything." He turns to me. "I'm Joe, Joe Macdonald. Pleased to meet you." He shakes my hand.

"Louise," I reply, my eyes locked on Christian, who looks incredibly tense suddenly.

"Lou just gave me a lift," Christian says quickly. "She has to get going."

"You've got time for a cuppa, surely?" Joe offers. "Tea? Coffee?"

"Coffee'd be lovely, thanks," I say swiftly.

"Milk? Sugar?"

"Actually, Lou really has to—"

"Watch her sugar intake," I interrupt. "Just milk, thanks." I smile at Joe, avoiding Christian's gaze.

"Leo?" Joe asks. "Wait—tea, two sugars, right? Or have you gone all hard-core since being inside?"

Christian's eyes dart to mine.

"Come on, let's have a real drink!" Joe rubs his hands eagerly as he hurries over to a cabinet by the TV. "Let's see, what've I got? Whisky? Vodka? I know, how about a JD and Coke—your favorite!"

"Just Coke for me," Christian says. "I don't drink anymore."

"Go on—it's a special occasion! It's not every day I get to see my best mate, after all! Wasn't sure I'd ever see you again, to be honest."

"Me either," Christian sighs.

"And I didn't expect it to be so soon!" Joe beams, pouring a glass of Coke. "Sure I can't tempt you with a cheeky shot in here?"

"Sure." Christian smiles.

"Your loss." Joe shrugs, passing him the drink and putting the bottle away. "So you just passing through, or what? They moving you somewhere else?"

Christian's face darkens. "Not exactly."

"What do you mean?"

Christian hesitates. "They found me, Joe."

Joe freezes. "They *found* you?"

Christian nods. "They set fire to my house this morning."

"Shit, man!" Joe's hands fly to his hair as he starts pacing the room. "*Shit!* But . . . the whole point of changing your name and moving hundreds of miles away was so they *wouldn't* find you—so this wouldn't happen again!"

I look up sharply. *Again?*

"I know." Christian sighs. "At least it's me they're intimidating this time, not Mum and Dad."

I stare at him. They threatened Christian's mum and dad?

"So why've you come back, then?" Joe asks anxiously, hugging his arms.

"I've got nowhere else to go," Christian says helplessly. "If I

175

check into a hotel I'll need to give my name and the police would find me, and after the fire . . . I can't trust them to keep me safe anymore. I just need a place to lie low for a couple of days while I work out what to do. I figured they don't know about you, so . . . ?"

"Course, man! Of course you can stay here!" Joe cries. "What are friends for?"

"Thanks." Christian smiles, sinking onto the lumpy sofa. "You're a mate."

"Forget about it. Host with the most, that's me!" His eyes flick nervously to the locks on the door; then he smiles brightly as he notices me watching.

"So how do you two know each other?" I ask Joe. He's forgotten about my coffee, but that works for me—the longer I can put off leaving, the better.

"Oh, we go way back." Joe smiles, moving to the window and glancing outside as he picks up a photo frame from the windowsill. "I used to live next door to Leo, and his parents would always take me on outings with them, and in return I babysat for this pipsqueak." He shows me the photo. It's a family at a fairground—a kind-looking man with a pretty woman, a skinny teenage boy who looks vaguely like Joe, and a chubby blond younger boy proudly clutching a huge teddy bear.

"It took him six tries to shoot that target and win that bear, but he finally did it—all by himself." Joe smiles. "He was only seven. Your first time with a rifle too, wasn't it, mate? You should have seen him, Louise—he was so proud of that teddy. And his mum and dad were so proud of him."

Christian sighs. "Were."

Joe sighs. "They still are, mate. They miss you heaps."

Christian turns. "You've seen them recently?"

Joe nods. "I like to keep an eye on them, you know. Make sure they're all right."

"And are they?" Christian asks quietly.

"They're . . . okay." Joe nods, perching on the arm of the sofa.

I slide silently into a chair in the corner, my gaze on Christian. He looks broken suddenly, and so young. Every time I think I've got him figured out, something else happens to make me think again.

"Your mum's taken up knitting—you never see her without her needles now," Joe says. "And your dad's quit the pub quiz team— spends most of his time cooped up with his crosswords instead. It's like . . . Never mind."

"What?" Christian says. "What's it like?"

Joe sighs. "It's like they're grieving. Which I suppose they kind of are."

Christian looks away.

Joe shifts uncomfortably. "And you know your grandad—"

"Died, yes," Christian sighs. "Three months ago." His face darkens with sadness.

"It's been hard, mate, I won't lie." Joe sighs. "But they'll be made up to see you—have you told them you're back?"

"No." Christian looks up quickly. "They can't know. No one can know, Joe. It's too dangerous."

"Course. Of course. Sorry." Joe frowns. His gaze flicks to the door again; then he glances at me and springs to his feet. "Coffee! You wanted coffee, Louise, sorry! Just milk, right?"

"That'd be lovely, thanks." I smile.

"Actually, I'm all out of milk," he says suddenly, grabbing a set of keys from the coffee table. "I'll just nip to the corner shop. Have you guys eaten?"

"Yes," Christian says quickly.

"Half a sandwich since breakfast," I argue. "I'm starving."

"I'll get a takeaway too, then," Joe says. "Do you like Indian, Louise?"

"If I could live on korma, I would." I smile. "Thanks, Joe."

"Actually, Lou, shouldn't you be going so you can get back while it's still light?" Christian prompts.

"It's half past four, it's too late for that anyway," I reason. "Besides, I can't drive on an empty stomach, and I'll need a coffee to keep me awake."

Christian meets my gaze. *Stalemate.*

"Okay, well, I'll be back in a flash." Joe grabs his jacket and flicks the TV on. "Make yourselves at home."

"Actually, do you mind if I grab a shower?" Christian asks, jumping to his feet. "I'm really grubby."

"Of course!" Joe grins, disappearing through the front door. "Help yourself."

"Christian, wait—" I start, but he hurries from the room before I can stop him. I sigh; then my eyes flit back to the photograph and I pick it up.

Christian's parents look so nice, so kind. His dad has graying hair at his temples and crinkly, smiling eyes. One arm is wrapped round his beaming wife's waist, while the other rests proudly on his son's shoulder as she ruffles his hair.

I try to imagine them now, attempting to come to terms with the fact that their child has been ripped from their lives, never to be seen or heard from again. As good as dead. They don't deserve that. No one deserves that—I know what losing a child can do to people.

Beside me, the theme for the news fanfares.

"Good evening," the newsreader begins. "Police are hunting for convicted criminal Leo Niles."

Joe's photo smashes on the floor as the face of a blank-expressioned teenage boy stares out from the TV screen. His hair is blond and cut short, his face slightly on the chubby side, but those blue, blue eyes are exactly the same.

It's Christian.

NINETEEN

My blood runs cold as the newsreader continues.

"The case hit headlines last year when the now infamous 'burglary gone wrong' left a teenage girl fighting for her life while her father was convicted for killing her attacker," she says somberly. "But this morning Niles, who was released nearly three months ago, broke the conditions of his parole and is thought to have gone on the run—just hours after the girl tragically died."

Something like a sledgehammer hits me straight in the gut.

It can't be true—it can't be!

I can't think.

Can't move.

If I move it's real, if I move it's really true. . . .

As the red-haired schoolgirl's smiling face fills the screen the ground trembles beneath me and the room begins to spin.

In the bathroom Christian begins to sing. The sound makes my skin crawl, and suddenly I snap to my senses. I flick off the TV, race to the front door, and yank the handle.

It's locked. Frantically, my fingers fumble over the array of bolts on the door, but still it doesn't budge. It's locked from the outside!

Shit!

I glance at the frosted glass pane in the door, but it's too small for me to fit through, so I rush to the large living-room window instead—but we're three floors up and it's a straight drop.

I'm trapped!

The blood rushes in my head as the running water gushes in the shower.

I have to get out of here before Christian discovers his cover's blown—that his face is all over the news and I know who he really is. There'll be no need to pretend now. No "witness protection" cover story, no "nice guy" persona to hide behind or keep up. The whole mask has been ripped off, and there's nowhere to hide.

For either of us.

Desperately, I scan the pavement below, the courtyard, the car park, but the basketball players have gone and the area around the tower block is deserted. I stare round the flat helplessly.

Think!

Phone! Joe must have a phone somewhere. I scan the surfaces frantically, shoving aside papers and post and leaflets and litter, but there's nothing.

Where would he keep his phone?

Finally my brain kicks in. A phone needs a phone *line*! I dash to the wall, searching every centimeter of it till finally I find a socket. I grab the wire and follow it till at last I find the base unit . . .

But no handset.

Sweat beads on my forehead and I want to scream. I glance at the bathroom—the water's still running—but panic bubbles inside me, making it impossible to think. I search behind the TV, under the coffee table, down the manky sofa cushions—still nothing.

My eyes fly desperately round the room; then I spot the kitchen doorway. I rush inside, scanning the counters, shoving aside takeaway menus and dirty dishes, till finally a shiny black phone tumbles to the floor. My heart jumps in relief as I snatch it up.

Then I spot a large pair of kitchen scissors on the counter. Light flashes on the long silver blades as I pick them up, fear throbbing in my temples as I stare at the sharp edges, imagine stabbing those blades into Christian's stomach, tearing his flesh, blood gushing out. . . .

My stomach convulses, vomit threatening in my throat as the room begins to spin.

Could I really do it?

Sweat trickles down the back of my neck as I slide the scissors inside my hoodie pocket, praying I won't have to.

My fingers fumble as I dial 999, then press the phone to my ear. It's only then that I'm suddenly aware of the complete silence in the flat. The sound of the shower has stopped.

"Lou?"

The handset clatters to the floor as I spin round to find Christian staring at me. Then the phone. His eyes widen.

"What are you—who were you calling?" He strides towards me and I snatch the phone and hang up quickly before he can see who I rang.

"Jeez, Lou, what were you *thinking*?" he cries. "You know we can't call anyone. It's too dangerous!"

"I—I was just calling the hospital!" I lie hastily. "I wanted to see how Gran's doing."

His face immediately softens. "Shit. I'm sorry, Lou. How is she?"

I stare at my feet. "No change."

"I'm so sorry." He sighs. "And I'm sorry I yelled. It's just this is the only place I feel safe at the moment, and if anyone finds out I'm here, it's over."

I nod. That's what I'm counting on.

182

"I don't know what I'd have done without you today," he says gently. "I wouldn't be safe, I know that much."

I force a smile.

"So thank you." He steps closer. "For everything."

He tries to hug me and I flinch, scared he'll feel the scissors in my pocket.

"What's wrong?" he asks.

"Nothing!" I shrug, managing a tight smile.

He shakes his head. "You're such a bad liar."

I look up sharply. "What?"

"It's written all over your face. Plus you've barely said two words since I came in."

My skin prickles and I take half a step backwards.

"It's your own fault, you know," he sighs. "You made me this way."

"What?" I stare at him.

He shrugs. "You chose the dye."

"*I didn't choose to*—what?" I frown at him.

"*Cappuccino,* my arse." He gestures at his hair, which is the color of a dog turd.

"Oh. No, it's . . . great." I smile in relief. I hadn't even noticed he'd dyed his hair in the shower. "It looks lovely. Really. You done in the bathroom?" I duck past.

The moment the door's bolted, my legs turn to jelly, my breath coming in great shuddering gulps as the tears that have been threatening finally burst from me and I dissolve to the floor.

She's dead!

I can't believe she's *dead*!

I crumple over, the pain in my stomach sharp, unbearable, her beaming school photo torturing my mind.

She'll never smile again. . . .

Never laugh. . . .
Never breathe. . . .
Never *hug* me ever again. . . .
My heart twists painfully.
Because of Christian, my beloved Poppy is dead.

TWENTY

Tears burn my eyes as a million memories crowd my head—Poppy racing me to the park swings to see who could fly the highest; starting ballet class together like a pair of twirling sugarplum fairies; giggling and gossiping in the department store changing rooms while Uncle Jim waited patiently for us to *finally* come out; big picnic parties in the park playing hide-and-seek with Millie; shrieking and squealing as we skipped through the sprinklers . . . coming back from Mexico to find her thin and pale and broken in a hospital bed.

The number of tubes and wires spaghettiing around her took my breath away.

"She must be very, *very* tired," Millie sighed, slumping in my lap. "She's been sleeping for *ages*."

"She's just getting her beauty sleep," I told her.

"Like Sleeping Beauty?"

"Sort of." I smiled. "Just think how pretty she's going to be when she wakes up."

"But I want her to wake up *now!*" Millie moaned.

"We all do, sweetheart." Aunt Grace smiled weakly. "We all do."

"I know!" Millie whispered suddenly, her huge brown eyes lighting up. Quickly, she leaned towards her sister and, ever so gently, kissed her cheek. She looked up at Poppy expectantly for a moment; then her face fell and broke my heart.

How I despised the two guys who had broken into our house, who'd attacked Poppy when she startled them, who'd shattered my family to pieces when they left her in a coma and made Uncle Jim a criminal—sentenced to five years in prison for manslaughter just for trying to protect her—for killing the thug who hurt her.

I wanted to *scream* at the injustice of it. Uncle Jim should never have gone to jail—he was a hero! A police officer, for God's sake! It was like the whole world had gone stark raving mad, especially when the guy who fled the scene—Christian—was given a shorter sentence than Uncle Jim. How crazy was that? They charged him with burglary—*burglary!* If it was a burglary, why did they hurt Poppy? Why was nothing stolen except Poppy's bag, and why didn't they run away when they discovered she was home, instead of beating her up?

Or maybe attacking Poppy was the plan all along? She was a teenage girl alone in the house, after all—in her bedroom. What would have happened if Uncle Jim hadn't come home when he did?

I feel sick at the thoughts that have been swarming round my head for the last year.

Was the burglary just an excuse? A way to avoid being charged with something much, much worse? Was *that* the lie Christian admitted to telling the police when we played Never Have I Ever? He said he'd lied about taking a bag—did he mean he lied about being a *burglar*?

Hate surges in my veins as the tears flow faster.

Either way, burglar or not, he killed Poppy. He might not have struck the fatal blow—or who knows, maybe he did, then blamed his dead accomplice?—but he was there, he did nothing to stop the attack on my cousin. And they let him go before serving even *half* his sentence—after just over a *year*?

How could he be allowed a new beginning, a fresh start, while Poppy was still dangerously hovering between life and death? How was that justice? How was that *right*?

The newspapers had the right idea:

CONVICTED CRIMINAL RELEASED AS HERO DAD ROTS IN JAIL
KILLER ACCOMPLICE GETS NEW IDENTITY!
CRIME PAYS—AND TAXPAYER FOOTS BILL!

They decried the fact that public money was being spent giving him a new home, a new identity. Why should *he* get a new life when he'd wrecked ours forever? Why should he get to walk away scot-free? Forget what he'd done? Pretend he was *normal*? That he was innocent, ordinary Christian Marcus Webb?

So I decided to do something about it. If the justice system wouldn't hold him accountable, it was up to me to make sure "Christian" didn't—*couldn't*—forget what he'd done. To make his new life as unbearable as possible. I just had to find out where they were sending him.

My skin prickles as I remember the night Kenny and I broke into the police headquarters—how close we'd come to getting caught by Neil—the utter thrill when Kenny gave me the memory stick containing Christian's new address in Sheffield. It was like the stars had finally aligned.

Like it was fate, I think, remembering Christian's words when we'd met.

If only he knew.

It was ridiculously easy—getting the place at Sheffield University through clearing, putting Christian's phone number on fake taxi cards, jogging past his house every day to discover his routine, bumping into him in the café and "accidentally" spilling coffee on his jacket so I could nick his wallet, giving me an excuse to see him again and him a reason to trust me. It was so simple, pretending to twist my ankle to get into his house, then pinching Christian's keys from his jacket as he left the pub that night, to frame him for *my* break-in, hoping he'd be sent straight back to jail. Of course, I didn't know about his curfew then. . . .

And even though it was annoying at first when Kenny showed up, and I don't approve of all his methods, he turned out to be a great asset. He orchestrated the Facebook offer which, along with poisoning Heidi, got me the job at the bar, giving me the perfect opportunity to "bond" with Christian. Scratching his bike and ordering the unwanted pizzas were lovely touches too—I really thought Christian was going to punch that pizza guy! Then when Kenny spiked his juice at my party, causing Christian to turn up at work late and hungover—along with the suspicions I'd already planted in Mike's mind that Christian was behind the break-in—we got Christian fired.

Between us, Christian didn't stand a chance. We made him lose his job, and he'd have lost his mind too within a few months if everything had gone to plan—if Vix hadn't overheard us the night of my birthday, if Christian hadn't decided to ride his bike while unwittingly over the limit, if I hadn't panicked he might get killed and raced after him, then completely lost my head when he kissed me. . . .

The taste of Christian's lips on mine flashes into my mind and I feel sick to my gut for my moment of weakness, for letting myself forget who he really was, what he did. . . . My blood runs cold as I remember the last time I saw Poppy—the last time I'll *ever* see her alive—how I promised her I'd get justice, that everything would be okay if she'd only wake up. . . . But now things will never be okay. I choke as fresh tears flow down my cheeks.

Poppy's gone. She's never coming back. She's dead.

And if Christian discovers who I really am, I could be too. Who knows what he's really capable of . . .

"Lou?" I jump as Christian knocks on the door. "Are you okay?"

"Fine! Just having a shower!" I call, hurriedly turning on the taps, my pulse spiking in my veins as I look around the bathroom. I'm trapped. There's no window, and one glance at the flimsy lock tells me it won't last long against any kind of force.

"Only I need to wash out the hair dye—the longer it stays in, the worse it'll get!"

I know the feeling.

"I'll be out in a minute!" I tell him, buying time.

"Okay."

Okay. I take a deep breath, sliding my hand into my hoodie pocket, feeling for the scissors. At least I've still got a weapon.

But to my surprise, my fingers close around something smooth and hard instead. *Gran's phone.* I stare at it incredulously. I completely forgot I had it.

Quickly, I try to dial 999, but of course it's off—it died on me last night. I press the power button anyway, hoping against hope it'll last for one more call. *Come on, come on. . . .* The screen lights up; then the phone beeps loudly.

Shit! I fumble with the buttons, trying desperately to find mute.

"Lou?" Christian knocks again. "What was that?"

"It was just my . . . watch!" I lie quickly. "I forgot I'd set an alarm."

"You have an alarm on your watch?"

"Yup—it was a present from Kenny. The gadget king."

I stare at the phone helplessly. Should I risk calling 999 again? After two close shaves, if Christian hears me talking to anyone in here, I'm screwed. And that lock won't keep him out.

The screen flashes silently as a text message arrives from Aunt Grace:

Mum, please call. Really worried after we got cut off last night—are you all right? Can't get hold of Lulu either. I really need you both. Please call me back asap.

My heart aches as every part of me itches to call her back. What must she be going through? I reread her message.

Really worried after we got cut off last night

So *that's* who Gran was on the phone to when she collapsed. *That's* why she was so upset—Aunt Grace must've just told her about Poppy.

My breath catches as I remember Gran's last words: "Oh my God! *That's* who—"

That's who Christian looks like, I realize suddenly. *That's* what she was going to say—she must have recognized him. Within ten minutes she'd discovered her granddaughter was dead, and that she'd come face to face with the man who was responsible. No wonder she had a heart attack. *It's all my fault!*

If I'd never hunted Christian down, never followed him to Sheffield, she'd never have come anywhere near him, never have had her heart attack, and I wouldn't be trapped in this flat with a violent criminal, not even able to call for help.

I stare miserably at the text; then suddenly my heart leaps.

I can't *call* anyone . . . but there might just be enough battery for a *text*!

Quickly, I message Kenny.

Help! Call police! Trapped in flat with Christian—39 Jonas Towers, Bexley—he's on news! Hurry!

Suddenly the screen fades as the battery finally dies.

Did it send? I press the power button again, desperately trying to resuscitate it, but it's no use. I shove it back into my pocket miserably.

Now all I can do is wait. I just have to hold out till either the police or Joe get here. As long as Christian doesn't know I know who he really is, I'm safe. I close my eyes as I remember how close we've come to blowing it before. First when Kenny spiked Christian's drink and started asking him probing questions—if Christian had let slip who he really was, it would have been curtains then and there, as once he realized what he'd done he'd have moved away for sure, and I'd have lost him for good. Then when Vix overheard the police mention his curfew I knew it wouldn't be long before she realized he was on parole—so thank goodness I came up with the witness protection story. It was meant to throw her off the scent and stop her confronting him about it, but it's proved invaluable to me too, allowing me to tell Christian that I know he has a secret identity and that people are after him, and come with him to keep tabs on him—all without revealing that I know the truth. That I've known all along.

Then I hear it. Canned laughter. The TV.

Shit! I flick the lock and wrench the bathroom door open just as he changes channels. To the twenty-four-hour news.

"Do you mind if we turn back?" I say, hurrying into the living room. "I love that show!" I reach for the remote, but Christian snatches it away.

"Just a minute—I'm watching this."

"What about your hair dye?" I remind him desperately.

"I'll go in a sec—look, there's been a terrible earthquake in San Francisco." His eyes flick back to the news. Sweat trickles down my back and I glance hopelessly at the door. Where the hell is Joe?

"Actually, you know what, let's not watch TV," I suggest quickly.

He looks at me like I've got two heads.

"I mean"—I think fast—"if this is the last time I'll ever see you, I don't want to waste our last moments together." I sit down on the coffee table in front of him, trying to block his view of the screen as I take his hand. "We could've been so great together," I add for good measure.

His expression softens. "You're right." He flicks the TV to mute and pulls me onto the saggy blue sofa beside him. "Lou," he sighs. "It's not that I don't *want* to see you again—it's just . . . it's too dangerous." He tucks my hair behind my ear and my pulse races.

Definitely too dangerous. My eyes dart to the TV, which shows the wreckage of a skyscraper.

"You know," Christian says. "You're the best thing that's happened to me in a really, *really* long time."

I force a smile; then the screen flashes and my eyes flick back to the TV as a photo of Poppy fills the screen.

Shit!

"Lou?" He turns to see what I'm looking at.

Quickly, I cup his face and kiss him. He seems surprised for a moment; then he closes his eyes and kisses me back.

My mind races as fast as my pulse as I try to decide what to do. Checking his eyes are still shut, I carefully reach past him for the remote control. He presses closer and my heart beats madly as my fingertips grasp the remote. He pushes me deep into the sofa, the fruity smell of his hair dye making my head spin as my fingers fumble blindly on the buttons. *Change channel—off—anything!*

"Tonight, police are hunting for convicted criminal Leo Niles!"

My heart stops dead as the volume bursts on and Christian's lips freeze against mine.

It's over.

TWENTY-ONE

I can't breathe.

Christian's lips break from mine, his expression a complete blank as he stares at the TV.

"Leo Niles has broken his parole conditions, just hours after his victim, Poppy Willoughby-White, tragically died."

Christian gasps. The photo of Poppy in her school uniform fills the screen again, but this time my eyes are glued to Christian as his face drains of all color.

"Convicted burglar Leo Niles ignited public outrage last year when he and his accomplice, nineteen-year-old Tariq Khan, broke into a policeman's home and assaulted his teenage daughter."

My pulse races as I carefully edge away from Christian, who sits transfixed by the screen.

"When Sergeant Willoughby-White returned home he startled the youths and tried to defend his daughter, killing Khan, while Niles escaped with stolen goods," the reporter continues. "On his release, nearly three months ago, Niles was given a new identity to protect him from vigilantism, much to many taxpayers' disgust, but today he broke his probation after his house was set on fire in what is thought to be a reaction to Poppy's tragic death. The police are calling for anyone with information on his whereabouts to report it."

Christian flicks off the TV and I freeze. I've only made it to the edge of the sofa. The revelation hangs in the air between us, filling the room.

No more secrets.

No more fake identity.

The truth is out there for the world to see.

My heart hammers painfully, panic rushing in my veins as I look around desperately, feeling trapped, helpless and unbelievably stupid.

Why did I come with him? What was I *thinking*?

I blink quickly, trying to stop the tears prickling at my eyes. I should've just delivered him to the police when I had the chance—but what would they have done? Put him back inside for a few months, then released him under another secret identity somewhere else? I couldn't have followed him again because he knows me now—I'd have lost my only chance for vengeance. *Keep your enemies close,* isn't that what they say? But now he's far too close for comfort . . .

Suddenly he turns—my hand flies instinctively to the scissors in my pocket—but I am shocked to see tears streaming down his face. He screws his eyes shut tight and a low moan escapes from somewhere deep inside him, growing louder and louder till it reaches a roar; then he crumples into the sofa, his body shaking violently as he buries his head in his arms and sobs.

I stare at him.

Why is he crying? Because he's been found out? Because he's scared of what's going to happen to him? Or because he's remorseful?

I swallow hard. "Christian?"

He doesn't respond. Tentatively I lean forward, keeping the scissors gripped tightly in my hand.

195

"Are you okay?" I touch his shoulder lightly and his head snaps up, his eyes red and watery.

I stare back, a deer caught in headlights.

"Louise . . . ," he says finally. "Oh God, Louise." He covers his face with his hands. "I'm so sorry."

Sorry he didn't tell me? Sorry for what he's done? Or sorry for what he's about to do?

"I should've told you—I'm sorry." He sniffs. "God, what must you think?"

He looks up and my face must make it pretty clear what I think.

"It's not true!" he insists. "Lou, I swear—it's not!"

I narrow my eyes. "You're not Leo Niles?"

"No—I mean, yes, but—"

"What? You're not a convicted criminal?" I ask, anger hardening in my veins. "The police aren't looking for you?!"

"Yes, yes!" he moans wretchedly. "But, Lou, I'm not—I didn't do that—I can't believe . . ." Tears wash away his words.

"What?"

"I can't believe Poppy's dead!"

"Really?" I say. "You didn't think that if you break a girl's skull, leaving her in a coma, death might someday be on the cards?" Tears scorch my words.

"I didn't hurt her!" he protests.

"Right, you were just a thief," I amend, the scissors giving me courage. "A burglar who stood by and watched his mate kill an innocent girl?"

"No! I didn't, I wasn't—Poppy was my *friend*!"

I don't move. "Your—your *friend*?"

"Yeah—I mean, I didn't know her that well, but—"

"You burgled your *friend*?" I interrupt scathingly.

"No! I . . . I just went to pick her up. I mean, I was meant to pick

196

her up." His face crumples. "But I was too late and—and now—now she's dead!"

I stare at him as more tears streak down his face, my thoughts whirling wildly.

"If I'd been on time, she'd be okay," he sobs. "She'd still be alive."

I swallow hard, trying to think, focus.

"What do you mean?" I say quietly. "What do you mean, you were going to pick her up?"

"That was the plan—that's the whole reason we were there," he says. "Tariq offered to give us a lift to the train station—we were going away for the weekend, but I was running late. I texted Tariq and Poppy to tell them I was on my way, but when I arrived . . ." He shakes his head miserably and I hold my breath.

"Tariq's car was outside and the front door was wide open. Poppy's bag was there, packed and ready in the hallway, so I picked it up and called out to her. But there was no reply. I could hear noises upstairs, so I went up." He presses his eyes closed tight and tears seep out beneath.

"There was so much blood," he gasps. "I've never seen so much blood."

My throat constricts.

"Poppy's dad had Tariq handcuffed to the bed, but Tariq wasn't moving, just—just bleeding." Christian swallows. "I tried to stop her dad—I grabbed his arm—but then he turned on me with a pair of scissors."

He runs his fingers gently over the scar on his chest and I immediately let go of the scissors in my pocket as a chill trickles through me.

"He swung at me with the blades, but he was clumsy—drunk."

I look up. That's the second time Christian's said Uncle Jim was drunk that night, but as I told Vix, Uncle Jim hardly drinks at all

197

now—just a pint after work on a Friday, or a glass of wine with a fancy meal. I frown. That's why I always thought the prosecution was exaggerating when they too claimed Uncle Jim was drunk that day. I assumed they'd found alcohol in his blood from a drink after work and then blown it out of proportion to support their case. But then why would *Christian* lie? It doesn't affect his burglary conviction, after all.

"I managed to duck out of his reach and ran down the stairs and away," he continues. "All I could think about was escaping. I didn't look back. Not once. I didn't even *see* Poppy—I had no idea she was hurt." He covers his face and groans, a terrible, painful sound that sends shivers down my spine.

"It's my fault they're both dead! It's my fault Tariq was there in the first place. I barely even knew him!"

"Why did you ask him for a ride if you didn't know him?" I ask.

"I knew his girlfriend—Sabina. She said he'd be happy to drive us." He clasps his head in his hands. "If only I hadn't been late, none of this would have happened!"

I hug my arms tightly, trying to take it all in, hideous pictures flooding my head.

"But if you were innocent, why didn't you go to the police? Or did you?" I ask, knowing full well he didn't—that the police tracked him down after they found his fingerprints on our bannister.

"No," he sighs. "I should've done, but I was too scared—the attack was all over the news—and I . . . I was in shock, I suppose."

"But then when they found you why didn't you tell the police what really happened?"

"I tried." He shakes his head miserably. "I even gave them my phone with the sent texts to prove I knew Poppy, that she was expecting me, but it got smashed—I dropped it down the stairs in my hurry to get away from her dad, and the SIM card was too damaged."

"Couldn't they trace it from the phone company records?" I say, trying to mask the suspicion in my voice. He's good at thinking on his feet, I'll give him that, but then I guess he's used to lying after three months with a fake identity.

"They tried, but the messages get deleted from the system after a few days, and they didn't find me for over a week. It was too late."

How convenient.

"What about Sabina? Couldn't she verify your story?"

"She did! But they didn't believe her either. They thought we'd concocted the whole story together in the week before I got arrested. I'd never met Poppy's dad before, I'd never met any of her family, so he didn't recognize me. Didn't believe me. He thought because I turned up just after . . ." He swallows. "He assumed I was involved."

"But how come you'd never met her dad?" I ask. "Why didn't she tell them about you?" *Why wouldn't she have told me?*

"I don't know," Christian says. "We didn't know each other that well, I suppose. We'd only met a few times—in the art gallery."

I blink. "The art gallery?"

He nods. "I used to go there to sketch passersby and one day Poppy caught me sketching her, so we got talking."

Sketch . . . I remember the portrait in Christian's sketchpad that Vix had assumed was of me.

"I thought it was odd that she'd spend her holidays sitting in the same gallery day after day," Christian continues. "But she said it was the only place she could get any peace, that she was having a hard time with her parents and had to get out of the house."

I frown again, trying to connect the Poppy I knew with the Poppy he's describing.

"After that we kept meeting up. We got to talking about music, and she told me she was going to go to Glastonbury."

I freeze. *"Glastonbury?"*

He nods. "She'd bought tickets and everything—but the person she was going with had pulled out."

The world spins before my eyes.

Me. *I* pulled out. Poppy was desperate to go to Glastonbury—and thanks to me, she did have a spare ticket: the one she bought for me for my birthday. *How could he know that?* Unless . . . *Unless he's telling the truth . . . ?*

My head pounds painfully and I stare at him as if I'm only just seeing him properly for the first time.

He's innocent.

"She didn't want to go by herself, so she asked me to go with her," Christian continues. "She seemed cool, so I thought why not? I had no idea her parents didn't know." He rubs his hand roughly over his face. "Or why she never told them about me."

I have. There's no way Uncle Jim would let Poppy go away with a guy she'd just met. He always insisted on meeting all our boyfriends before he'd even let us go on a first date! He was always really charming and funny, but it still freaked them out, getting the third degree from a policeman, so Poppy and I sometimes "forgot" to tell him about boys, in order to bypass the inquisition.

Now I wish we hadn't.

"They had no idea who I was," Christian sighs. "They thought I was lying about the whole thing, trying to cover my own back. All they knew was that Tariq had attacked Poppy, I'd turned up just after, and then they found my text on his phone saying I was on my way, linking me to him."

I nod grimly.

200

"It did prove that I wasn't at the house at the time Poppy was attacked, though. So the police charged me with burglary."

"But why did they think it was a *burglary*?" I frown.

"I didn't notice it at the time, but apparently one of the little windowpanes by the front door was smashed in—Tariq must've done it to reach inside and unlock the door. They found his fingerprints and blood on the broken glass. And . . . and some of Poppy's stuff was missing," Christian says. "I didn't realize her bag was still on my back when I ran away."

So that's the bag he lied about in Never Have I Ever.

"But why didn't you hand it in to the police?" I ask. "You could've explained."

"I couldn't," Christian argues. "Poppy's bag was filled with money and jewelry and stuff. The police were already trying to charge me with burglary, and if they'd found it, I just—I panicked that it would've looked like I *had* nicked it. So I hid it." He sighs. "Not that it made any difference in the end. Tariq was dead and Poppy was in a coma, so they couldn't tell them the truth. I kept hoping, kept *praying* that she'd wake up. . . ." His face crumples again. "But now she never will."

My heart constricts.

"My lawyer advised me to plead guilty to burglary—he said there wasn't any evidence to prove my story, that I'd get a much shorter sentence if I did, that otherwise I could go down for years and years." He looks away. "So the police concluded that it was a burglary gone wrong. They said that Tariq and I had planned it together, but he had become impatient and broken in without me. Then, when Poppy had surprised him, he'd panicked and attacked her. And the jury bought it." He shakes his head. "It's crazy. Tariq *knew* she was there. That's the whole reason we'd gone round—to pick her up!"

"So why *did* he attack her?" I ask quietly.

"I don't know." Christian looks at me for a long moment, his eyes pained. "I can only assume the worst. They were in her bedroom, after all."

I hug my arms tighter, look away.

"If only I hadn't been late—if I'd got there sooner." He sighs miserably. "I'll never forgive myself."

"What about your text to Poppy, *saying* you'd be late?" I say suddenly. "Your phone was smashed, and the records expired, but didn't they find it on Poppy's phone? Wouldn't that prove you were friends?"

"The police said they didn't find it, so I assumed she'd deleted it." Christian frowns. "Until today. Until I saw your phone cover in the car."

"What do you mean?"

"Poppy had a cassette tape in her bag—I saw it when I hid the bag and thought nothing of it, except it was a bit odd, old-fashioned—who has cassettes these days, right? But what if it *wasn't*? What if it was a retro phone case like yours?"

I stare at him. It could well have been. She gave me mine, after all—what if she'd bought one for herself too?

"Then the police might've *lied* about having Poppy's phone . . . ?" I frown.

"I told you," Christian says. "I can't trust them. If they can leak my location to vigilantes, who knows what else they're capable of?"

"Vigilantes?" I ask quietly.

He sighs. "I got death threats all the time in prison. People who thought I'd got off lightly, who wanted to take justice into their own hands."

I look away guiltily.

"And now Poppy . . ." He rubs his hands over his face. "Now

that it's all over the news again, they'll be more determined than ever. I can't believe they found me so quickly—it can't be a coincidence."

My stomach tightens. I can't believe it either. The thought that there are other vigilantes around, hunting him down, ready to go to such extreme measures, gives even *me* the creeps.

"I can't trust the police to keep me safe anymore. I can't trust anyone." He shrugs. "Except you." His eyes pierce mine and I look away. "And Joe, of course. Wherever he's got to."

Just then there's the sound of footsteps running along the balcony outside.

"That'll be him now." Christian wanders to the window. Then suddenly he rushes to the door.

"It's locked," I tell him. "Joe locked it."

His head whips round. "Joe *locked* it?"

I shrug. "But he's back, right?"

"No. Not Joe." He hurriedly slides all the bolts across the door, then grabs my arm and drags me off the sofa. "We've got to go."

"Christian, wait!"

"We've got to get out of here." He hustles me into the bathroom. "Shit. No window."

"And we're on the third floor!" I add.

"We could lock ourselves in." He bolts the door.

"That won't keep anyone out for long."

"Shit!" He opens the bathroom door and looks around hopelessly, the footsteps just outside now. "Shit!"

"Maybe it's for the best, Christian." I hesitate. "Maybe you should turn yourself in."

"Lou!" He stares at me. "It's not the police!"

"What?" I stare at him, goose bumps prickling down my arms. "What do you mean? Who is it then?"

There's a sudden thud at the front door.

"We know you're in there, Niles!" a man's voice yells angrily. "And this time there's nowhere to run!"

I shriek as a cricket bat smashes through the frosted window in an explosion of glass.

Definitely not the police.

TWENTY-TWO

Christian grabs my hand and races to the bedroom, slamming the door behind us, but there's no lock. He looks around desperately. Amid the debris of dirty clothes, crockery, and papers, there's a disheveled double bed by the window, a desk, and a wardrobe.

"Quick," he cries. "The wardrobe!" Together, we push and shove, but it doesn't budge.

"It's too heavy!" I cry.

Outside the room there's the sound of splintering wood as they break through the front door. We have to do something—fast!

"Desk!" I cry. We shove it onto its side, sending more papers and cups and cans tumbling to the floor, and quickly push it across the doorway—just as the handle turns and the door smashes into the desk, making me jump.

It opens an inch, then a hand snakes through. Quickly, Christian hurls himself against the door. There's a crunch and a yell; then the hand disappears, followed by loud swearing. Christian dives to the floor, wedging himself against the desk, his feet braced against the heavy wardrobe, and I do the same.

"Thanks," he pants.

Suddenly a force like a car crash slams into the door, snatching my breath away.

"Are you okay?" Christian whispers.

I nod. "How many are there?" I hiss through clenched teeth.

"I don't know. At least—*Shit!*"

This time it's a tank that strikes my back. Pain ripples through my whole body and my knees begin to tremble.

"Lou—go and sit on the bed," Christian says.

"No," I argue, my spine throbbing. "You can't hold them by yourself."

"I don't think we can hold them for long anyway, and you're going to get really hurt when they burst through."

I don't move. I told Kenny to call the police, and suddenly a mob of bloodthirsty thugs are at the door? It *can't* be a coincidence! This is my fault, but Christian doesn't deserve this. This isn't justice. Even if he is guilty, and everything he's just told me is a lie, he doesn't deserve this—I wanted to *scare* him, not kill him!

"Please, Lou," Christian begs, just as another battering ram smacks against the door, pushing it open a centimeter. His eyes stream as we shove it closed again. "It's me they want. They won't hurt you."

What should I do? He's right—even with both of us pushing we can't keep them out for long. My heart racing, I scuttle over to the bed.

"Thank you." He sighs, his eyes defeated as he braces himself to cover the whole door.

But I don't sit down. I grab the end of the bed, its legs screeching against the wooden floor as I push it towards the door. Despite everything, I'd rather take my chances with Christian than a violent mob.

"Move!" I yell at Christian, shoving the bed as hard as I can, wedging it between the desk and the wardrobe. There's no way the door can open now. As if to prove it the door shudders again but doesn't budge.

Christian stares at me. "Nice one!"

"Thanks," I pant. "But now we're trapped."

"Trapped is better than caught," he says grimly.

"So what now?" I whisper, flinching each time the door rattles. "We just wait till they go away?"

Christian shakes his head. He crosses to the window and peers outside.

"We're three floors up," I remind him. "It's impossible!"

"Not impossible." His gaze darts around the room. "Difficult, but not impossible."

He grabs two pairs of jeans and starts knotting the legs together.

"Are you serious?" I whisper. "It's at least a ten-meter drop outside!"

"Look around," he says. "There must be enough material here to reach the ground."

He's right. I fly to the bed and start stripping it. "They always used sheets in Enid Blyton!"

"Brilliant." Christian smiles at me.

I pull the scissors from my pocket and cut the sheets in half for extra length.

"Where'd you get those?" Christian eyes them warily.

"The kitchen," I say hesitantly. "I thought they might . . . come in handy." I look away quickly and hack at another sheet. It rips easily between the sharp blades, and I try not to think about what they could have done to Christian's flesh, had things gone differently.

We work swiftly, my fingers fumbling with the knots, my heart racing with every thud against the door.

Then suddenly there's a splintering sound.

207

My head whips round. "They're breaking the door down!"

"Quick!" Christian lunges for the window with the makeshift rope we've cobbled together. "Throw it out!"

But the end dangles hopelessly a few meters above the concrete pavement.

"It's not long enough!" I panic.

"Shit!" Christian hisses as the door splinters again. Shards of light begin to stream through. "We don't have much time. . . . We'll just have to jump from the bottom of the rope."

"Jump?" I stare at him. "Are you crazy?"

"Ladies first," Christian says, tying the end of the sheets to the radiator pipe.

"Are you kidding? They're after *you*. They won't hurt me, re-member?"

"I can't take that chance," he argues, pushing me towards the window. "Besides, you have to go first."

"Why?"

"I need to check it's safe." He grins.

Large shards of wood spatter onto the bed.

"Lou, go—before they see what we're doing," he pleads. "Other-wise it's over. They'll be down before us."

"Okay." I climb gingerly onto the narrow window ledge, my legs trembling. The ground rushes beneath me, the makeshift rope in my hands wafting flimsily in the breeze.

What if it snaps? What if the knots aren't tight enough? What if I can't hold on?

"Lou, you have to *go*!" Christian urges. "Take a deep breath, take it steady, and don't look down. I'll be right behind you."

"Okay!" Clutching the sheet tightly, I step backwards off the window ledge, holding my breath as my arms suddenly take all my weight—but the sheet doesn't break. I lean back impossibly, terrifyingly, dizzyingly far, till I'm sure I'm going to fall—then finally my foot meets the wall. Slowly, carefully, hand over hand, I inch my way down, the cold air whispering in my ears as I concentrate on holding on, my hands slick with sweat, the knotted sheets threatening to slip straight through my fingers at any moment.

"You're doing great," Christian hisses. "But can you speed up a bit?"

I try. I take bigger steps, faster, till it feels like I must be nearly at the bottom.

Then I pass a window—I'm only at the second floor! Christian's anxious face stares down at me and my blood pumps as I take quicker, longer steps, then— Shit!

My foot slips completely and my face rockets towards the brickwork.

"*Lou!*" Christian calls.

I twist quickly and my shoulder takes the impact, grazing painfully against the rough wall as I twirl helplessly, my arms burning as I hang on to the rope for dear life.

"Lou!" Christian calls. "Jump!"

I stare up at him. "Are you crazy?"

"Just do it!" he hisses. "Trust me!"

Trust him? The guy who lied to everyone about everything?

"On three," he hisses. "One, two—"

I take a deep breath.

"Three!"

I let go, feeling completely weightless for a second before I crash into a hedge below.

In a second, Christian is out of the window, rapelling like a pro—and not a moment too soon. When he's halfway down a man with dirty blond hair peers out.

I stare at him in horror. It's one of the guys from the blue Ford in Sheffield. They *were* after Christian!

"He's gone out the window!" he yells back to someone in the flat. "Go down and cut him off!" He grins grimly. "While I *cut* him off."

"Christian!" I squeal as the man disappears. "Hurry!"

He bounds faster and faster—but he's not fast enough. Suddenly the rope slackens and he drops like a stone, crumpling to the ground.

"Take that, *murderer*!" the man yells as his head disappears back inside.

"Christian!" I rush to his side. He's clutching his left leg. "Oh my God, are you okay?"

"Car!" he gasps. "Get the car!"

I scramble to my feet and sprint to Uncle Jim's car, slamming on the accelerator as I screech into the road running behind the flats, praying the men haven't got to him first.

I round the corner and spot the gang up ahead, just where Christian landed. My heart plummets. I'm too late!

Suddenly a dark shape hurls itself out of the bushes next to me and I immediately hit the brakes. The gang's heads turn as one, and my heart flips as they shout and start racing towards me.

Christian yanks open the back door and crawls inside. "Go!"

I spin the car around and speed off down the road.

"You . . . ," I pant, ". . . have got to stop *doing* that!"

"Sorry!" he gasps.

I scan the rearview mirror. The gang is sprinting after us, but they're not fast enough. One by one they disappear from sight; then I round a few corners swiftly, till I'm sure we've lost them.

"Are you okay?" I glance round.

His trousers are covered in blood.

"Shit, Christian—you need to get to a hospital!"

"No!" he says firmly. "No hospitals. It's too dangerous."

"But—"

"I'm fine," he insists.

"Fine?" I question.

He doesn't answer.

"Fine," I say reluctantly. "Then where?"

"Anywhere," Christian sighs. "Nowhere's safe anymore."

TWENTY-THREE

I drive fast along the city streets, trying to get as far away as possible from Joe's flat and the crazy thugs who attacked us. Finally the welcoming neon sign of a Travelodge comes into view and I pull into the car park.

"What're you doing?" Christian frowns.

"Checking us into a hotel. Come on."

He shakes his head. "I'll stay in the car."

"Christian, it's not safe in the car—and you'll freeze!"

"It's not safe to go inside," he argues. "They'll have CCTV."

"Here, have your hoodie back." I unzip the oversized sweatshirt and hand it to him. "That gash needs cleaning, and to do that you need to come inside!"

"Lou—"

"Otherwise your wound will get infected and we'll have to chop it off," I say. "Total amputation."

A smile tugs at his lips.

"It's up to you. Hospital, crippled, or hotel." I shrug.

"You're such a drama queen."

"Says the guy who's made up his whole life," I counter.

"Good point." He sighs. "All right, let's go."

He pulls on the hoodie and slings his arm over my shoulders as I help him inside.

"Is he okay?" the receptionist asks, eyeing Christian warily as we hobble across the carpeted foyer towards her. His hood flops over his face, masking him from the tiny camera winking on the ceiling.

"He's fine." I smile. "Just had a few too many ciders."

On cue, Christian starts singing loudly and off-key. I dig him in the ribs.

"Could we get a twin room, please?"

The room is basic—two beds, a bathroom, TV, and a kettle with two cups—but it's all we need. I help Christian to the bathroom, where he collapses on the white tiles, clutching his leg and groaning.

I kneel beside him and carefully peel the leg of his trouser back to reveal a deep red gash up his shin. I wince.

"Okay," I say, trying to remain calm. Think. *Breathe.* "You should let it soak for a bit in the bath"—I turn the taps on—"and I'll nip out and get some antiseptic wipes and bandages and stuff, and then . . . then you can tell me what to do with them." I smile weakly. "I haven't a clue."

"You're doing great." Christian smiles. "Thank you."

"You hurt your other leg too?" I say, noticing jagged red lines just above his right ankle.

"Oh, that's nothing," Christian says, pulling his trouser leg back down. "It's just . . . it's where I had the ankle tag. I was in a bit of a hurry when I hacked it off at Joe's flat, got a bit careless."

"Ankle tag?" I stare at him.

"It was one of the conditions of being let out of prison three months before my automatic release date," he sighs. "I was supposed to stay at home between seven p.m. and seven a.m., or the tag would alert the police."

I suddenly remember how he'd quickly tugged down his trouser

213

leg when he was going to show me how to flex my ankle like a ballerina—because he didn't want me to see the tag.

"That's why the police rushed round after your gran collapsed," Christian continues. "They knew I'd missed my curfew. That's why I hesitated about coming out to help in the first place—I'm so sorry." He takes my hand and I squeeze his gently.

"But you still did," I say quietly. "You saved her life."

He got himself in trouble with the police . . . he risked being sent back to prison . . . for Gran. For me.

"When I explained what had happened they were really understanding, said these were exceptional circumstances and that it wouldn't count against me. But now . . ." Christian hangs his head. "Now I've well and truly broken the rules. I'm officially "at large," and if the police find me, they'll send me straight back to prison." He laughs bitterly. "A few more days and it wouldn't have even mattered!"

"What do you mean?"

"My curfew period was due to finish on Tuesday." He sighs. "You can't imagine how much I've been looking forward to it."

"I thought you were sentenced to nearly three years?" I frown.

"I was, but at the halfway point you're automatically released. I'd still have to have meetings with my probation officer for another few months, but there'd be no more ankle tag, no more having to stay indoors—I'd finally be free to go out in the evenings, wear shorts without people staring at my tag, actually have a life!"

Just yesterday I'd have been furious to hear he'd be let off so soon, but now . . . now the whole world's upside down. So much has changed so quickly, I feel light-headed.

Suddenly Christian sighs heavily. "You should go."

"What?"

"The police are looking for me—you're harboring a fugitive,

Lou. You're breaking the law just being here with me. Plus you've seen what the vigilantes are like. I can't risk you being here if they find me again—you could get hurt. You should go. Now."

I shake my head. "I can't."

"You have to."

"I *can't!*" I insist.

"Why not?" he asks. "Seriously, Lou, *why* are you helping me? Why would you put yourself in danger—for me? You hardly know me."

I falter. I couldn't leave him earlier because I thought he was guilty and I couldn't let him escape, and I wanted to make him pay. And I can't leave him now because he's innocent and he's injured and it's my fault the vigilantes found him, and he could be in danger. . . .

But I can't tell him either of those things.

"Because I . . . I care about you," I tell him, and suddenly realize it's true. I do care about him, and I don't have to feel guilty about it anymore. All the feelings I've been trying to ignore, to convince myself I don't have, suddenly rush to the surface now that I know he's innocent.

"I care about you," I say again, leaning closer and stroking his hair from his face, looking unashamedly into those clear blue eyes. "We're in this together now."

"I care about you too." He catches my hand. "That's why I can't let you—"

"I'm not going to leave you when you're in danger," I tell him firmly. "Not when it's my fault you're in this state."

He smiles. "How d'you figure that?"

"You name it," I say, looking at his angry wound. "I took too long getting down the rope, and I—I called . . ."

"Lou, I don't think calling your gran caused any of this, do you?"

Christian smiles. "None of this is your fault," he says softly, kissing my hand.

"It is." I press my eyes closed, guilt and shame stinging my eyes. "You're hurt because of me."

They found him because of me.

"No." Christian cups my face. "I'm hurt because of Joe."

I open my eyes.

"He was the only one who knew I was at the flat," he says sadly. "He must've turned me in."

I look away.

"Not that I blame him." He sighs.

"What?"

"He's my best friend, Lou—he wouldn't have betrayed me without good reason. Did you see all the locks on his door? They're new."

I remember how nervous Joe was when I knocked on his door, the fear in his eyes.

"They must've been threatening him, those thugs, hassling him for my location." Christian shakes his head sadly. "It wouldn't be the first time. I was meant to go home when I left prison—live with my mum and dad. It was all arranged. But when the vigilantes found out, they threatened my parents, threw a brick through their window one night, made it clear I wouldn't be safe if I came back to this neck of the woods—and nor would the people I love." Tears fill his eyes. "I've been fooling myself, thinking that someday it would all blow over, that things could go back to normal—that I'd get my life back, see my parents . . . but I can never go back. It's worse than prison. At least there they could still visit, keep in touch. But now . . ." He sighs heavily. "Joe's right. It's like I've died, like I'm one of your ghosts—I don't even exist. Leo Niles no longer exists, and I have to lie about *everything*—can you imagine how *exhausting* that is?"

If only he knew. I shiver.

"Sorry, Lou—have my jumper back." Christian pulls off his hoodie, and as he tosses it to me the scissors fall out of the pocket—and so does Gran's phone.

I freeze.

"What's this?" Christian frowns, picking it up. "I threw your mobile out of the car back in Sheffield."

"It's Gran's!" I say quickly. "I honestly forgot I had it, and the battery's dead anyway—'

"The sound I heard in the bathroom," he says slowly. "It wasn't your watch, was it?"

I falter, every hair on my body standing on end.

"You called the police." He nods as if it all makes sense now. "*They* could've tipped off the vigilantes."

"I'm so sorry!" I cry. "I saw the news headlines when you were in the shower—I thought you were a criminal," I tell him desperately. "Joe had locked the door and I couldn't get out and—and I'm so sorry!"

"*You're* sorry?" He shakes his head incredulously. "I'm the one who should apologize!"

"What?" I stare at him.

"Of *course* you called the police—Jeez, Lou, you must've been terrified! You were trapped, you had no idea I was innocent, and I'd lied to you about *everything*! If only I'd been honest—but I couldn't! The police *made* me lie—to everyone! I didn't do anything wrong that day, but they've *made* me dishonest. How can I have a real relationship with anyone if it's based on lies?"

Guilt twists inside me and I look away as I reach to turn off the taps, avoiding his gaze. I've not exactly been truthful myself.

He sighs. "I'm *so* sorry, Lou. For not telling you about all this, for pretending to be someone I'm not."

"It's okay."

"It's not," he argues, taking both my hands and looking me in the eye. "You don't know the real me at all."

I shift uncomfortably. He doesn't know the real me either.

"Okay, here goes." He takes a deep breath. "I was born in London, only child of Sarah and Albert Niles, and though we never had much money, I was drowned with affection. I had a pet hamster, innovatively named Hamster, when I was three, and cried for a month when it died when I was eight—"

I blink. A five-year-old hamster?

"—not realizing Mum had already replaced it three times so I didn't get upset."

I smile.

"My grandad lived round the corner and taught me the dirtiest jokes I know. My best mate, Joe, taught me magic tricks to impress girls, and my dad made me watch Villa play in the vain hope I'd fulfill his lifelong dream of becoming a footballer, but Mum ruined all that when she bought me my first sketchpad when I was seven. From that moment I wanted to be an artist. I even sketched people's portraits at weekends and school holidays—I was going to go to art school." His smile fades. "But then I met a pretty girl in an art gallery, made a rash decision, let her down, and everything changed." He sighs. "My whole life. And here we are."

I nod slowly.

"It's such a relief to finally tell you the truth, Lou," Christian says earnestly. "I promise I'll never lie to you again. You can trust me," he vows. "Go on, ask me anything. You must have a million questions."

Try a billion. My mind's whirling with them—questions about his past, about what happened that night, but somehow one question burns above all the others.

"Why did you break your curfew last night?" I whisper. "Why did you leave your house when you knew you'd get into trouble?"

Christian looks at my hand, his thumb tracing tiny circles around my knuckles.

"You needed me." He shrugs, then smiles. "Of course I came."

I bite my lip.

"I already let down one friend when they needed me most." He swallows hard. "I'll never make that mistake again. And today you were there when I needed you." He squeezes my hand. "I knew it was fate meeting you, Lou. Some things are just meant to be."

His eyes are so full of warmth, they burn into mine till I can't bear it. I pull him into a hug, anything to avoid his trusting gaze, and he wraps his arms tightly around me.

A perfect fit.

Some things are just meant to be. . . .

But Christian was meant to be mean and tough—a criminal. He was meant to deserve everything that was coming to him. He wasn't meant to be kind, or funny, or charming, or attractive. . . .

His fingers tangle in my hair like the thoughts in my head and my pulse races as I press against him, screwing my eyes shut against the world, the past, my lies. He was never meant to be sweet or sexy or *innocent.*

A sharp pain spears my heart.

Till today, it never occurred to me—never once crossed my mind—that Christian could be innocent. I've been so scared, so angry, so *determined* that he should suffer. Convinced from the moment that we met that every word he said was a lie, that his kindness, his sweetness, his generosity was all just a really good act.

But I was so wrong. He's the real deal. Tears prickle my eyes as I break away.

"I'll—I'll go and get those wipes," I mutter, clearing my throat as I scramble to my feet.

"Okay." He smiles. "You'd better get some more hair dye too—if I have any hair left by the time I finally rinse this one out."

"Right." I nod. "What color?"

"Anything's better than this!" He shrugs. "Ginger, I guess. They've seen me with blond, black, and brown hair. What color are you going for?"

I look up. "What?"

"Lou, they've seen you now too. You need to keep a low profile as much as I do. Actually, you'd better wait until it gets dark," he says. "It'll be safer."

I nod silently, a shiver trickling down my spine.

"I'm so sorry, Lou." Christian's eyes cloud over. "I wish you'd left when I asked you to. I wish you'd leave me now."

"Don't be silly." I smile. "I'm going nowhere. Except to make a cuppa—two sugars, right?"

I turn to go, but he catches my hand.

"Thank you, Lou," he says, those blue eyes so clear, so trusting. "Thank you for everything. So many people have let me down—the justice system, the police, even Joe, maybe." He sighs. "You're the only one I can trust now."

I force a smile, squeeze his hand, then turn away, guilty of the worst betrayal of all.

TWENTY-FOUR

At six-thirty we decide it's dark enough for me to risk going out. *At last!*

I hurry out of the hotel and, checking Christian can't see me from our window, duck into a nearby phone box before I finally allow myself to cry.

You're the only one I can trust, he said.

Hot tears sting my eyes. If only he knew the truth . . . that it's not fate that brought us together, that I tracked him down *deliberately* to make his life miserable, that *I'm* the one who's been harassing him—the girl he broke his curfew for because she begged him to save her gran—*Gran!*

I pick up the phone and quickly dial the hospital, praying that she's recovered, that she's not worried about me, that she'll know what to do.

But the nurse just tells me there's no change. She's still unconscious, but her vitals are stable. At least she's not any worse.

I lift the receiver and dial again, holding my breath until finally Aunt Grace picks up, her voice faint, hesitant.

"Hello?"

"Aunt Grace, it's me."

"Lulu! At last! I've been trying to call you since yesterday!" she cries. "Are you all right?"

"I'm so sorry, I lost my phone," I tell her. "I only just saw the news. . . ."

"Oh, sweetheart, I'm so sorry—I didn't want you to find out that way! Isn't Mum there? Didn't she tell you what happened? She's not been answering her phone either."

"No, she . . ." I take a deep breath. "She's in hospital—but she's fine."

"What!" Aunt Grace's voice rises in panic. "What happened?"

"She had a mild heart attack, but she's okay," I assure her. "She's unconscious but stable."

"Oh my goodness, how awful!" Her voice splinters with tears. "First Poppy, now Mum . . . what's going on?"

I wish I knew. I can't believe only yesterday everything was normal—Gran was well, Poppy was still alive, and Christian hadn't broken his parole. How can so much change in just twenty-four short hours?

"I wish I could come straight up there, but oh, Lulu, everything's in chaos with the funeral tomorrow!"

"Tomorrow?" I say, surprised. "How come it's so soon?"

"Because the media's going crazy again!" she cries miserably. "You should see the house—we're mobbed! I can't take weeks of this. Fortunately your aunt Harriet's friends with a local under-taker, so they've managed to slot us in quickly. We're registering the death tomorrow morning, and Reverend Foster has been very help-ful. Everyone's been so kind in rushing things through. We just need to be left alone to grieve, as a family." Her voice cracks. "Poor Millie's in pieces—she won't leave the house with the press outside. Your uncle Doug's been spoiling her rotten, giving her sweets and chocolate, but she hasn't eaten a single one. She misses you. We both do."

My arms ache to hug her. She sounds so lost.

"I'll be there as soon as I can," I promise.

"Tonight?"

"I . . ." I hesitate.

"No, you're right, it's late, it's a long way to travel from Sheffield, and you should stay with Mum, but . . . will you do a tribute?" she asks quietly. "At the funeral? It's at three o'clock, St. Matthew's."

"Of course," I tell her.

"Oh, Lulu, I can't believe Poppy's gone—can't believe I'm arranging her *funeral*!" Tears gush through her words. "I never stopped hoping, you know? I really thought that one day she might wake up."

"Me too," I say, tears streaking my cheeks. "What happened?"

"She just suddenly took a turn for the worse," Aunt Grace sobs. "I held her hand as they tried to stabilize her, but then her—her heart just gave up beating. It all happened so fast. . . ."

My throat swells.

"Oh, and now that wretched man's on the loose—did you hear?" Her voice catches.

I swallow. "Yes."

"I hope they catch him soon and throw away the key!"

I hesitate. Should I tell her the truth—that he's innocent?

"Actually, Aunt Grace, I—"

"Oh, sweetheart, I'm so sorry—the vicar's just arrived. I've got to go and confirm the funeral arrangements. Can I call you back? Do you have a number I can reach you on?"

"Not right now. I'm just using a pay phone. I'll call you, though, okay?"

"Yes, please do—and let me know the minute anything changes with Mum, won't you? Oh, Lulu, I should be there with you both!" Aunt Grace frets. "I'll come up as soon as I can, but—"

"I'll call you as soon as I know anything," I promise. "And I'll see you tomorrow."

"Okay," she sighs. "I love you."

"Love you more," I say. "Bye." I hang up, feeling more guilty than ever.

I should be there—I should be home with Aunt Grace and Millie—they need me. And I *can't* call Aunt Grace the minute anything changes, because Gran's in Sheffield, I'm in London, and I don't even have a mobile phone anymore. And what about Gran? If she wakes up, she'll be all alone. . . .

But I can't abandon Christian with an injured leg and both the vigilantes and police hot on his trail . . . not when I'm the one who led them to his door.

Miserably, I wander down the dark street and into a twenty-four-hour convenience store. I grab anything that looks vaguely useful from the medical shelf, then add some food, tea bags, milk, and hair dye to my basket. But as I join the queue my eyes fall on the row of newspapers by the counter.

Each front page shows the same pictures: Christian's and Uncle Jim's mug shots . . . and Poppy's school photograph. I pick one up, my eyes glued to her bright smile and kind eyes, the maple-leaf necklace I bought her for her fourteenth birthday glittering round her neck. She looks so young, so happy. So alive. I can't believe she's really gone.

"Miss?"

I look up sharply. The man behind me clears his throat as the shopkeeper raises his eyebrows. "Can I help you?"

I blink quickly, add the newspaper to my basket, then pay for everything before hurrying outside. I try to read the front page of the paper as I walk along, but it's a dark night and the streetlights are few and far between, their orange glow casting strange shadows over the pavement as I pass.

Suddenly a shadow catches the corner of my eye, and my heart races as I hear footsteps behind me. The streets are practically empty and most of the shops are shut, so I shove the paper in my bag and quicken my pace. The footsteps speed up too.

Shit! Vigilantes! My mind races as I start to panic. I hurry down the first street I come to, then another, and another. As the streets get dingier and more desolate I have no idea where I'm going, or who's following me, but there's no way I'm leading them to Christian.

The footsteps echo behind me as I hurry around yet another corner, then quickly duck down behind a bin and wait. Sure enough, my stalker follows, and as he comes into view I leap out and punch him hard in the stomach, stamp on his foot, then aim a kick at his groin, before running for my life.

I sprint blindly, choosing street after street, trying to find my way back to the main road—then suddenly I hit a dead end! My blood runs cold as the hurried footsteps grow louder behind me—it's too late to turn back. I'm cornered.

I look around desperately for a place to hide, but there's nothing but a tall brick wall blocking my escape.

I spin round just as the man turns the corner and walks slowly towards me.

TWENTY-FIVE

I watch helplessly as the dark figure slowly approaches.

"What do you want?" I demand, trying to sound braver than I feel.

"*Jeez,* Titch," a familiar voice gasps. "Where'd you learn those moves? They're *brutal*!"

I blink in surprise as he steps into the light.

"*Kenny?*" I stare at him. "Bloody hell! What are you *doing* here?"

"Besides getting beaten up?" he asks wryly. "Rescuing you!"

"What?"

"Your text message asked for help—so here I am."

"But . . . how did you find me?"

"Ah." He smiles. "That's the clever bit. I told you I'd be there for you *any time,* didn't I?" He nods at my wrist.

My jaw drops. "You put a tracker in my *watch*?"

"Bingo." He beams.

I stare at him. "I don't know whether to kiss you or kill you!"

He grins. "Do I get to choose?"

"Kenny!" I glare at him. "Why didn't you *tell* me?"

"Cos I didn't think you'd wear it if you knew," he sighs. "And I wanted you to be safe."

"Then why did you chase me down a dark alley?" I demand. "Why didn't you call out?"

"Because I had to make sure you were alone!" he explains. "I didn't want Leo to suddenly pop up round a street corner or something."

Just then there's the sound of running footsteps.

Kenny freezes. "That's not him, is it?"

"It can't be . . . ," I say. "He's back at the Travelodge, he's got a bad leg."

We both stare at the corner as a figure races into view.

"*There* you are!" she cries.

"*Vix?*" I stare at her in disbelief.

"I told you to stay in the car!" Kenny scolds.

"Yeah, right," Vix says, rushing at me in a hug. "*Lou!* Kenny told me about Christian—are you *okay?*"

"I'm fine." I hug her tightly.

Suddenly she punches me on the arm.

"Ow!" I cry. "What was that for?"

"For not telling me what was really going on with Christian, for fobbing me off with half truths and white lies, and pretending Christian was in witness protection when you knew all along he was Leo Niles! I'm your *friend,* Lou Willoughby-White. You can trust me! When are you going to get that through your thick skull?"

"It wasn't about not trusting you, Vix," I protest. "I'm sorry. I just thought as long as Christian didn't know anyone knew his identity he wouldn't be dangerous, but—"

"So you let me befriend him instead?" Vix interrupts. "A convicted criminal?"

"I . . ." I sigh. "Yes. I'm sorry."

"Just promise me now—no more lies," she says sternly.

"I promise," I tell her. My gaze flicks to Kenny. "And there's something else you should know."

"What?" Vix says apprehensively.

"I never kissed Kenny."

She blinks.

"It was just a story he made up because you overheard us talking about that night in the office—the night Kenny and I hacked into the police system and found Christian's address. It was a lie," I tell her. "Kenny was never in love with me. He just helped me find Christian."

A strange expression flits over Vix's face. "Lou—"

"And he might find *us* if we hang around much longer," Kenny interrupts, grabbing my arm. "Come on, let's get out of here!"

"No, I can't!" I protest, shaking him off. "I can't leave him—he's innocent!"

They both stare at me like I've gone crazy, so I quickly tell them what happened at Joe's flat.

"So you see, it's all a misunderstanding!" I conclude. "Christian's innocent—he was Poppy's *friend*!"

Vix and Kenny look at each other.

"You can't trust him." Kenny shakes his head. "He's a liar."

"What?" I stare at him. "But it all makes sense!"

"What Kenny means," Vix says carefully, "is that Christian's been in trouble with the police before."

My heart stops. "What?"

Kenny nods. "For *fraud*."

"*What?*" I stare at them, gobsmacked. "How come we didn't find this out before?"

"It was wiped from his record when he turned eighteen." Kenny sighs. "It didn't show up."

"But I asked around about Chri—Leo on a news forum," Vix says. "And one of the local reporters had it on file."

"That's why his prints were already on record, and *that's* why it was so easy for him to start afresh, to play a part and pretend to be someone else," Kenny says. "He's a con man, Lou. He tricked you. He's not innocent."

"No." I shake my head. "No—what about the *Glastonbury* ticket?" I protest. "How would he *know* about that unless he's Poppy's friend?"

Kenny looks at me pityingly. "You said yourself that he took her bag, Lou. Couldn't the tickets have been inside?"

My heart sinks like a brick as all my doubts come flitting back in a shoal of shadows.

"Was there anything else?" Vix asks gently. "Any other evidence that he's telling the truth?"

I rack my brains desperately . . . but it was the Glastonbury ticket that had convinced me—the ticket Poppy bought me for my birthday, that Christian said she gave him because her friend turned her down. I thought that was proof—that he did know Poppy, that he was telling the truth. . . .

But was that just wishful thinking on my part? Did my own feelings—my own incredible relief that he was innocent, combined with my guilt for letting Poppy down so terribly—skew my judgment? My head spins painfully. *What if he's not innocent after all?* How can I have feelings for the guy who was involved in killing Poppy? But how can I just turn them off? My heart clings desperately to the hope that his story's true, that Christian is innocent, but my head realizes that Kenny's right. It could easily just be another lie—a convenient excuse concocted by a con man once he found the Glastonbury tickets. The tickets that would've been in Poppy's bag . . . with her phone.

"Poppy's phone!" I say desperately. "Christian said he texted Poppy to say he was running late, but the police never found his text on her phone. But Christian thinks they lied—that he saw Poppy's phone in her bag."

"Which is where?" Vix says eagerly.

"I don't know," I admit. "He just said he'd hidden it."

"Leo thinks the police *lied* about having Poppy's phone?" Kenny raises an eyebrow. "And that they're tipping off the vigilantes?"

"Lou, your *uncle's* a policeman," Vix says quietly.

"Exactly!" I cry. "I'm not saying they're all corrupt, but perhaps some of his colleagues think the courts were too lenient on Christian and decided to seek their own form of justice—or just stepped back and allowed it to happen? How else did the vigilantes find Christian—*twice!* Once straight after he broke his curfew, and then immediately after Kenny called the police with Joe's address. It can't be a coincidence. I might have orchestrated the other stuff that happened to Christian, but I didn't get involved with any mobs—I never wanted to *hurt* him!"

"But Leo thinks *Joe* might have tipped off the mob," Kenny argues.

"Well, yes," I concede. "But—"

"However they found him," Vix interrupts, "the important thing is to determine if Christian's innocent or not. And prove it."

I nod. "We need to find Poppy's bag. I'll ask Christian where it's hidden." I turn to go.

"No," Kenny argues, grabbing my arm. "Lou, you can't go back to him. Whatever he's said, he's still a convicted criminal—he could be dangerous."

"And he could be *innocent*," I argue. "Besides, if I don't go back soon, he'll know something's wrong and he'll flee—if he hasn't already. We might never find him again!"

Kenny frowns. "Where are your car keys?"

"What? I left them in the hotel room, why?"

He nods. "He's probably long gone, then."

I stare at him. Christian wouldn't take my car . . . would he?

But I remember how reluctant he was for me to come with him this morning, how he begged to take the car then, but I wouldn't let him. . . .

"Well, if you're right, and Christian has fled, there's no danger, is there?" I pull free from Kenny's grip. "And if he hasn't . . . maybe he is telling the truth."

Kenny hesitates, his expression troubled.

"I'll be fine," I say more gently. "And you can track me, right? So you'll always know where I am."

Vix's gaze flicks from me to Kenny anxiously.

"Okay," he sighs finally. "But give me your room number—the tracker's not so great with multistory buildings."

"Two hundred seventy-three."

"And we'll be just round the corner," Vix says. "We're booked into that big Premier Inn, so we can be with you in an instant if you need us. So just call if you're in trouble, or worried about anything—call us anyway to let us know you're all right, okay?"

I nod. "There's a phone box near the Travelodge. I'll tell Christian I need to ring the hospital tomorrow morning and let you know what I've found out—I need to think of an excuse to go to Poppy's funeral too."

"But what if you can't get to the phone box?" Vix frets. "What if you're in trouble? Where's your mobile?"

"Christian made me get rid of it," I confess. "That's why I texted Kenny on Gran's phone, but it's out of battery now."

"Well then, borrow mine," Vix offers, pulling out her mobile.

"I can't—how would I explain it to Christian if he found it?" I argue. "He already caught me with Gran's, he knows I alerted the police. I can't do anything else to make him suspicious."

"But what if something happens? You need a phone!" Vix insists.

"No, you don't," Kenny says. "Lou, you see the yellow button on the side of your watch? If you hold it down for three seconds, it'll send a distress signal to my phone and we'll know you need help."

"Great." I smile, relieved. "If only I'd known that at Joe's!"

"Sorry," he says. "Mea culpa."

"So you'll call us tomorrow?" Vix says, grabbing me in a hug.

"Promise," I say, squeezing her back.

"And don't forget your car keys whenever you leave the room," Kenny reminds me.

"I won't," I tell him.

"You know you don't have to do this," he says gently, his eyes filled with concern. "You could walk away now, come back with us."

"I can't." I shake my head. "I have to know. I have to know the truth."

I have to know how to feel.

He hugs me tightly. "Be careful, Titch."

"I'll be fine." I smile. "Don't forget my 'brutal moves.'"

Kenny rubs his sore stomach. "As if I could!"

They walk me back to the main road, but as I leave them and return to the Travelodge I don't feel quite so brave, or so sure.

My head spins. Christian's a *con man*? I koew he was lying to me about everything before Joe's flat . . . but is he *still* lying? Maybe it's another misunderstanding—perhaps he can explain. But then how could I believe him? It could just be another lie.

I hold my breath as the hotel door swings open, half expecting to find an empty room. But there he is, sitting on the nearest bed, wearing nothing but a towel. I look away quickly.

"Everything okay?" Christian asks anxiously. "You've been ages. I was worried."

"I got a bit lost," I tell him, taking the widest possible path around the bed. "I bought supplies, though." I dump the shopping

232

bag and cross the blue diamond-patterned carpet to the far side of the room to put the kettle on.

"You sure you're okay?" Christian says quietly.

"Yep." I yawn. "Just really tired. It's been a long day."

"I know." He sighs. "Come and sit down." He pats the bed.

"In a minute." I smile quickly. "I'm dying for a cuppa first. Want one?" I busy myself making the world's most complicated cup of tea, buying space and time to think.

"No thanks." He rummages in the bag. "Wow! Did you buy the whole shop?"

I shrug. "I didn't know what you'd need."

The boxes of hair dye tumble to the floor and I snatch mine up, seizing my chance.

"Actually, I'd better make a start with this, get it over with." I make a beeline for the bathroom.

"Lou—"

"What?" I snap.

He looks at me, his eyes wide. "Don't forget your tea."

"Right." I pick up the cup, hurry into the bathroom, and lock the door behind me. Then I take a deep breath. *Calm down.*

I glance at the yellow button on my watch. *We can be with you in an instant if you need us.*

I can do this. *Don't blow it now.*

I rip open the box of hair dye, the contents spilling everywhere. Irritably, I snatch them up, then spot the scissors from Joe's flat lying next to Christian's torn trousers. My heart beats fast as I reach for them, the metal cold and hard in my fist.

I still have these. Still have a weapon. Just in case . . . I tilt them so the blades glint and flash in the light, then suddenly see my own eyes looking straight back at me. I barely recognize myself.

What am I doing? I look away quickly—unable to face myself—

and start hacking at my hair instead. *May as well cut it too,* I reason as great chunks tumble to the floor and tears streak my cheeks.

I don't want to be me anymore. I'm out of my depth and now I don't know what to think, what to believe, what to feel. I don't know what the truth is, what I *want* the truth to be. . . .

Do I *want* Christian to be guilty, so I can make him pay for everything he's done to me and my family? So I can finally get the justice I've worked so hard for? So I can feel less guilty for everything I've done to *him*?

Or do I want him to be innocent so I don't have to be ashamed of the way I feel? For I can't deny that my feelings for him have changed. Christian isn't at all how I expected him to be, and when I think of his arms around me . . .

My stomach churns uneasily. Either I'm a horrible person for persecuting an innocent guy and putting his life in danger . . . or I'm a terrible cousin for developing feelings for the guy who left Poppy in a coma.

My head hurts, my thoughts tangling together like spaghetti, loose ends dangling everywhere.

Why didn't Christian tell me about his other conviction? If he's a con man, how can I believe a word he says?

But if he's innocent, why did Poppy never mention him to me— or any of my family? Why would she keep him secret?

But why bother to make it all up if he's guilty? Just so I wouldn't call the police? He could've escaped any time—why lie?

I lay my head on my arms and instantly that foresty smell fills my lungs and my heart aches as I realize how desperately I want him to be innocent, to trust everything he's said, to believe he really is the kind, gentle, caring guy I've come to know, to like . . . to *more* than like.

I sigh.

Guilty or innocent—whatever the consequences, I have to know the truth. If I can find Poppy's phone, I'll know if he's lying. If it's in Poppy's bag, if it has his text on it, then it's proof he's telling the truth.

If not . . . I swallow hard.

Then at least I'll know.

TWENTY-SIX

"Oh my God!" Christian gasps as I step out of the bathroom. "You look . . ."

"Hideous. I know. I'm not a born hairdresser." I sigh, scrutinizing my jagged ends in the dressing-table mirror.

"No, that's not—" Christian swallows, his reflected face pale beside mine. "It's just you look . . . for a second you looked just like her. Like Poppy."

I freeze.

"That's who you reminded me of before, and now that you've changed your hair . . . it's uncanny." I stare at myself in the mirror, my heart racing as I realize he's right.

Idiot! I curse myself. What a stupid, *stupid* error!

There hadn't been much choice of dyes in the store, so I just grabbed two boxes of red—I didn't even *think*—and now with short hair . . . I glance anxiously at Christian. Has he worked it out?

"You mean she had a really crappy hairdresser too?" I raise an eyebrow, trying to defuse the situation.

He stares at me for another second, then grins. "Sorry. Didn't mean to freak you out."

"I'm the one looking freaky!" I moan, glad to change the subject. "I look like a rag doll."

"Note to self: don't leave you alone with scissors," Christian laughs. "Come here, I'll straighten you out." He reaches for the scissors.

I hesitate, then reluctantly hand them over.

"Sit."

I do as he says, perching on the edge of the bed, all the hairs on my body standing on end as he maneuvers himself behind me, his legs on either side of mine.

"So . . . ," Christian whispers, his warm breath tickling the back of my neck. "Who's the *real* Louise Shepherd?"

I stiffen. "What?"

Snip. The sound of the blades makes me jump.

"Your hair was dyed blond, right?" he says. "So what color is it naturally?"

"Oh—mousy brown," I mumble, my skin tingling at his closeness.

Why does he want to know? Has he figured out who I am? Could Poppy have shown him a photo of me? Or is it just an innocent question? Will it always be this way with him? I wonder. Half terrified, half attracted, all my senses heightened whenever he's near?

Snip. I shiver.

No, I reason. Not once I know the truth. Then I'll know how to feel.

"Head down," he instructs, and I obey, wishing all my choices were so simple.

"So what's your story, Louise?"

Snip.

"What do you mean?"

"Come on, I bored you with my life history, now it's your turn," he says. "Where are you from?"

"Oh, I was born in Brighton," I say truthfully. *But I live in London.*

"Cool. I love the sea. Who do you live with?"

Snip.

"What?"

"You said your parents died when you were little—so who do you live with now? When you're not at uni. Or boarding school."

Boarding school? I flinch as the cold metal skims the back of my neck, my heart beating fast. I never told him I went to boarding school. . . .

"Are you okay?" Christian asks. "I didn't nick you, did I?"

"No, I'm fine," I lie.

Snip.

"So were you, like, adopted?" he asks. "Or do you live with family?"

Snip. The blades slice close to my ear.

I swallow hard. "Adopted." *By my family.*

I sit helplessly as my hair scatters all around me, feeling like I'm falling apart. This is it. He knows who I am. He must know . . . doesn't he? How else would he know I went to boarding school?

"And do they have any other kids or adopted kids?" he says.

"No," I lie again, cold dread filling my veins.

"I always wanted a sister," Christian says. "A younger sister I could teach magic tricks to and take to ballet class and music festivals."

Snip.

Ballet class and music festivals? He's practically describing Poppy! My fingers play with my watch, dancing hesitantly around the yellow button . . . but something stops me pressing it, still hoping I'm wrong.

"Have you been to many music festivals?" I ask lightly, trying to change the subject.

"Only once—to Glastonbury. That's why Poppy asked me to go

with her. She wanted me to show her the ropes—she was so excited."

"So *she* bought the tickets?" I ask. "They were in her bag? With her phone?"

"Yes," Christian says. "I guess so."

"And where's her bag now?"

"My grandad's allotment," he tells me. "It seemed the safest place. I buried it under his shed."

I nod. An allotment should be easy enough to get into.

"My grandad always tried to get me interested in gardening. He used to take me down there after school sometimes—even let me paint a big sunflower on the roof of his shed—but I was hopeless with plants. Everything I grew died. So I gave up. Now I wish I hadn't—that I'd spent more time with him, and with my parents before . . . before that day." He sighs. "Was it really hard for you, being away?"

"What?" He knows I was away when Poppy was attacked?

"For school, I mean. You must've missed your adoptive parents when you were at boarding school?" he says. "Vix told me you and Kenny both went?"

"Oh, right," I say, letting go of my watch, dizzy with relief. *Vix* told him about boarding school! "Yes, we did. It was fine. How's your leg?" I ask quickly, glancing down at his bandaged shin beside me.

"I can barely feel it," he says. "It's okay, honest."

I nod.

"Are you?" he frowns.

"What?" *Honest?*

"Okay?"

I look up as he takes my hand.

"I'm sorry, Lou."

"What for?" I say as he pulls me closer, tucking me under his arm.

He shrugs. "Everything," he sighs. "I shouldn't have dragged you into this mess." He kisses my forehead. "You know you can leave any time, right? You don't have to stay with me."

"Don't be silly," I say, hiding my face against his chest. "We're in this together, right?"

"Right." He holds me tight, like a bird in a trap. A trap I've willingly walked straight into.

TWENTY-SEVEN

I wake suddenly, my heart pounding as I glance round the unfamiliar room. The unfamiliar *empty* room. I sit up swiftly, scouring the floor, the desk, the bed. There's no sign of Christian's clothes anywhere. He's gone.

Slowly, I lie back on my pillow. It's over.

Relief streams through my body but pools in my stomach, mixing with frustration, anger, disappointment. I close my eyes and a tear slides unbidden down my face, leaving my cheek cold, numb.

He's left me behind. It was all a lie.

Suddenly the toilet flushes and my eyes fly open as Christian hobbles out of the bathroom, fully dressed. He smiles when he sees I'm awake.

"Coffee? Milk, no sugar, right?"

I nod numbly as I stare at him, trying to remember what to feel. Fear? Guilt? Affection? All of the above, I decide miserably.

"The supplies you got are great." Christian smiles, handing me my coffee and sitting down next to me on the bed. "They should easily keep us going till tonight."

I look up. "Tonight?"

"It's safer not to stay in one place for too long," he sighs. "And it's safest to move at night. When it's dark."

"Actually"—I jump out of bed—"I'm going out."

241

He looks up. "What?"

"I'm going to find Poppy's bag." *And go to her funeral.* "I'm going to prove your innocence."

"What? Lou . . ." He falters.

I watch him closely as I slip on my shoes. If he's guilty, he'll try to stop me.

"You can't." He shakes his head. "It's too dangerous."

"Dangerous? It's in an *allotment*!" I smile. "Besides, this is the answer to everything," I insist. "If I retrieve Poppy's bag and find her phone, then your text will be on there, proving you were friends—proving you're innocent!" I look at him. "Right?"

Please. I beg silently. Please be innocent. Please let me go out and prove it.

He takes a deep breath and I cross my fingers.

"No," he says finally. "You can't go."

My heart sinks. It's not there. He knows it's not there. Because it doesn't exist.

"I'll go." He climbs off the bed.

"What?" I stare at him. "Christian, that's crazy!"

"I can't let you put yourself in danger, Lou." He grabs his coat. "Not for me."

"I won't be in danger!" I argue. "No one will connect me to you—especially with my new hair. But, Christian, if you go out there, you won't last two minutes! *Everyone* knows what you look like—your face is all over TV, and the papers! You can't go outside—especially with your injured leg."

He looks at me, his eyes troubled, torn.

"But *I* can," I say quietly, stepping closer. "Let me do this for you. For us."

His eyes soften. "Us?"

I nod.

If I can find Poppy's phone, it'll prove that I can trust him, that he didn't hurt Poppy, that he's innocent. And if I can prove that he's innocent, justice will be served. I'll have what I always came for, and he'll be free.

And . . . we can actually be together. The thought hits me, and I realize suddenly that that's what I want. I take his hand, and this time when he kisses me I don't flinch, don't pull away. Instead, I lean into him, surrendering to the moment, to his lips, his kiss gentle, deep, passionate as he pulls me closer to him, banishing every single thought in my head. When his lips finally break away I feel dizzy, weak, bereft.

"Okay," he whispers, his breath sweet in my mouth, our lips barely millimeters apart, his eyes deep in mine. "For us."

I nod slowly as he traces the line of my face with his fingers, my eyes never leaving his, never wanting to, my heart aching as I pray with every fiber of my being that I'll find Poppy's phone, that it's all really true, that there's hope for us, a future . . .

Unable to imagine the alternative.

As soon as I leave the Travelodge I nip to the phone box to check on Gran—still no change—before calling Aunt Grace to update her, then Vix and Kenny to tell them the plan and beg a lift. The allotments aren't far from Joe's flat, so I can't risk taking my car just in case the vigilantes are nearby and recognize it, and taking the bus could be risky too—though that's what Christian thinks I'm doing—so Vix picks me up a few blocks away, out of sight of the Travelodge windows.

"Nice hair!" Vix comments as I slide into the passenger seat of Kenny's Mini Cooper. "I almost didn't recognize you!"

"That's kind of the point." I smile. "Where's Kenny?"

"Keeping an eye on Christian," Vix explains. "He's hacked into the Travelodge CCTV because he doesn't trust him not to do a runner while you're gone. Have you got your car keys?"

I nod, patting my jeans pocket. I don't believe Christian's guilty, don't believe he'll disappear on me, but there's no point taking any chances, just in case.

I give Vix the directions Christian's scribbled on the back of last night's till receipt, while I keep my eyes glued on the rearview mirror.

When I'm absolutely sure we haven't been followed we park in a residential street near the allotments, and even then I watch every car and every pedestrian that passes for a few minutes, till I'm positive it's safe before I risk getting out of the car.

So far, so good.

I glance at my watch. Nine-thirty. Aunt Grace said the funeral's not till three, and it's pretty nearby, so I should have plenty of time to find Poppy's bag and phone before I head to the house.

If the phone's really there.

I duck my head as I climb out of the car and follow Vix, trying not to look like too much of a psycho as I keep glancing behind me, paranoid after last night despite my new sunglasses, haircut, and hair color. The vigilantes could be nearby, and though my house isn't far away either, I don't know this neighborhood at all. At least it's daylight now, and there are people around if we need them—a woman hanging out her washing, a couple of kids playing in a garden, a man walking his dog—

My breath catches in my throat. *I know him!*

He was at a family barbeque one year—I'm sure of it! I turn away as he passes. I don't want to be recognized by anyone, gang member or neighbor.

I take a last careful look over my shoulder before we slip down a narrow alleyway, following the wooden fence for a few meters until we reach a blue gate, just as Christian described it, and Vix turns the handle.

"Shit." She tries again. "It's locked."

I glance both ways down the alley, then take a run up and leap at the fence, doing my best to scramble up it—only to graze my palms as I tumble painfully back to the ground, unable to get a grip.

Double shit.

"Need a hand?" Vix asks, linking her fingers into a stirrup.

"Thanks." Resting one foot on her hands, I finally manage to reach the top of the fence and lift myself up.

"Just what do you think you're doing?" a man's voice yells.

Startled, I lose my grip and crash into Vix, who swears as we tumble to the ground. There's a rattling sound at the gate, and before we can scramble to our feet, it creaks open. An old man with a spade stares down at us.

"And what do we have here?" he says sternly.

"H-hi!" I stammer. "Sorry, we were just—"

"Breaking and entering?" He raises an eyebrow.

"No, we were—"

"Vandalizing? Stealing?" He looks us up and down.

"No . . . I . . . my uncle left something in his shed and we've come to get it," I bluff. "He said it's got a sunflower on the roof."

His eyes widen. "You're *Bertie's* niece?"

"That's me!" I smile quickly. "Nice to meet you."

"Gordon." The old man shakes my hand. "A pleasure to meet you, my dear. That's Bertie's over there." He points to an old dilapidated shed. "Can't miss it with that bloody flower on top. Cheerio!"

"Thanks!"

"Was Christian's grandad called Bertie?" Vix asks me as we hurry across the allotment, past the neatly dug plots filled with rows of

245

vegetables and beanstalks and gooseberry bushes, towards the musty old shed.

"I don't know," I admit. "I hope so. If not—"

"If not, then Bertie must be the new owner of the shed," Vix finishes for me. "Christian's grandad died, after all."

"Oh God, Vix, then what if the new owner's found Poppy's bag?" I cry, panic rising in my chest. "What if it's not even here anymore?"

"There's only one way to find out," she says, trying the door.

Suddenly it flies open, startling me and sending Vix reeling backwards. An old man stares out at us, puzzle book in hand, looking even more surprised than we are.

He must be Bertie.

"Can I help you?" he grunts.

"I'm . . . I'm sorry, I'm, er, looking for my uncle's shed," I stammer, the lie tumbling out again automatically—may as well be consistent. "I'm his niece." *Obviously.*

"It must be that one instead." Vix quickly points to a shed on the other side of the allotment. "That's got a red door too."

The man nods brusquely. "Wrong shed." As he blinks I notice his eyes are red and watery.

"I'm so sorry we disturbed you," I tell him. "Goodbye."

"Wait," he says. "You're Ted's niece?"

"Um, yes," I lie, wondering what hole we've dug ourselves into this time.

"I'm so sorry," he says. "Ted was a good bloke, God rest his soul."

Shit.

"Yes, we . . . we all miss him terribly." I stare at my shoes in what I hope is a mournful way as guilt swells in my throat. I can't believe I'm lying to this old man.

246

"We've come to clear out his shed a bit," Vix says. "Pick up some of his stuff, you know."

He shakes his head. "I didn't even know he had a niece."

"No—I—we hadn't seen each other in years," I bluff.

"That's a shame." He frowns. "Family should never be kept apart. It's the most painful thing."

I nod, thinking of Poppy and suddenly, I realize I don't have to pretend to be grieving. I'm hurting for real. "I guess you never realize how much you'll miss someone till they're gone."

Bertie shakes his head, his voice strained. "And then it's too late."

I look up. The wrinkles seem to crack his face into pieces and somehow I know he's not talking about Ted.

"You lost someone too?" I ask quietly.

He nods heavily. "My son."

My heart plummets like a rock. "I'm so sorry."

"Not your fault," he says, clearing his throat.

"How old was he?" Vix asks gently.

Bertie closes his eyes. "Nineteen."

"So young." My heart constricts. Just two years older than Poppy.

He nods, swallows. "Too young. I'd hardly begun to know him."

I nod, memories of Poppy filling my head. I knew her so well, and yet there was so much I didn't know. Like if she'd been hanging around art galleries before she was attacked, or if she'd met anyone new, or was planning to take someone else to Glastonbury in my place. Things it would've taken only moments to ask, but I never took the time, never made the effort. I didn't realize how much we'd grown apart before she died. How little attention I'd given her.

And now it's too late.

Bertie takes a ragged breath and I look up as a tear slips down his face, streaking a path through the wrinkles. He wipes his eyes quickly with his sleeve.

247

"Sorry," he says gruffly. "You'd think it'd get easier—with time. But it's always there. Always with you. Well, you know."

I nod. "How long's it been?"

"Three months he's been gone. But he's still everywhere. Everything's a reminder." He closes his eyes, sighs. "That in itself is a mixed blessing. It's wonderful to remember—but you're always reminded of what you've lost."

"How did he die?" I ask quietly.

Bertie smiles weakly. "He didn't." He sniffs. "He didn't, but he may as well have."

Vix frowns. "What do you mean?"

He shakes his head. "It doesn't matter. It makes no difference. He's gone." He sighs heavily. "He's gone, and I don't know when, if ever, I'll see him again."

"But . . . but if he's still alive . . ." I hesitate. "There must be some hope—there must be a way?"

"That's the worst part," he sighs. "The hope. The hopeless hope. That's what's destroying my wife. No matter what she does, she just can't let Leo go."

I freeze. *Leo?*

Vix and I glance at each other. *This man is Christian's father?*

Suddenly I realize he's not nearly as old as he looks. He must only be in his fifties, but his eyes are so drawn, so sad and tired-looking, it makes him look much older. I'd never have recognized him from the photograph in Joe's flat.

"Anyway." Bertie clears his throat. "I'd better get home. My wife—it's a worrying time at the moment. She frets if I'm out too long."

I bet. They must be terrified now Christian's on the run.

"Well, it was lovely to meet you both." He tucks his puzzle book under his arm and locks the shed. "And please accept my deepest condolences for your uncle." He lays a heavy hand on my shoulder. "He was a good man."

"Thank you," I say. "And I hope you see your son again soon."

"Me too." He smiles sadly. "Well, goodbye."

"Goodbye," I say, watching him slowly trudge away, my heart dragging after him.

"Poor guy," Vix says quietly.

I nod. I've never seen a man so broken, so lost.

"It's not just Christian who's suffering," I say sadly. "It's his whole family. Joe's right, they're grieving for someone who's not even dead."

"What's the difference?" Vix sighs. "He doesn't know if he'll ever see him again."

"Unless we find Poppy's phone and prove his innocence," I say, glancing at the locked shed. "We should tell him why we're here— that we want to help prove his son's innocence. He could help us look." I move to follow Bertie.

"Wait." Vix catches my arm. "What if Poppy's phone *isn't* here?"

I look at her.

" 'That's the worst part,' Bertie said. 'The hopeless hope,' " Vix reminds me. "We can't get his hopes up—I'm not sure he could take another huge disappointment."

I watch as he lumbers slowly through the gate. She's right. He looks so fragile, so terribly weary.

"What must they have gone through—especially now that Christian's face is splashed all over the TV and papers again?" I sigh. "At least in prison they knew he was safe, but now . . ." Now they have no idea where he is, if he's safe, if he's even alive. . . . I think of the violent mob at Joe's flat. "They must be worried to death."

We watch as he shuts the gate behind him.

"But now we can put a stop to that," I tell Vix. "Or we can at least try."

We give it five more minutes, just to make sure Bertie doesn't come back and there's no one else around; then Vix yanks the shed door. It doesn't budge. I look around for a spade or tool to break the padlock with, but there's nothing, only crumbling flowerpots.

Before I can stop her, Vix picks up a flowerpot and smashes it through the shed window.

I stare at her. "Subtle, Vix! The moment anyone enters the allotment they'll see the broken window. They might even call the police!"

"Then we'd better hurry!" she says, knocking away the remaining shards of glass and scrambling inside.

I glance around once more, then follow. The shattered glass crunches under my feet and my heart pounds loudly in the darkness.

"So where's the bag?" Vix asks, flicking on the torch on her phone.

"Christian said it's under a loose floorboard beneath the table."

She sweeps the tiny light around the musty room. We're standing beside a garden chair on a tatty-looking mat. A cluster of rakes, hoes, and shovels lean lazily in the corner, and a table stands to my right, stacked with flowerpots, damp cardboard boxes, and a roll of kitchen paper. Beside it, I spot a cardboard box full to the brim with screwed-up tissues, and my heart aches.

This is Christian's dad's private hideaway—how will he feel when he sees the broken window, the shattered glass all over the floor? Guilt swims icily in my veins, but I try to ignore it. This is the only way to help him, after all. To help them all.

Vix kicks the glittering glass off the mat and it sparkles like stars as a cloud of dust flurries in my face, making me cough. I wave it

250

away quickly as Vix folds up the chair; then I push the table aside and slowly, carefully, we roll up the mat to reveal the gnarled wooden planks beneath.

Cautiously, I run my fingers over the splintery surface, searching for a loose floorboard. Nothing.

I try knocking against each plank instead, listening carefully, but they all sound the same—and not hollow at all. Panicking, I grab at the rough edges, tugging and pulling, but they all stay firmly in place.

"This is impossible!"

"Move," Vix says, picking up a spade.

"What are you doing?"

"I'm going to pry up every single floorboard till I find the bloody thing, that's what," she says, lifting the spade. "We haven't got time to mess about—you've got a funeral to get to. Move!"

"Wait!" I cry suddenly, pointing to the floorboards beneath the window. "Look! That patch of floor is a different color to the rest."

The darker wood stands out in a clear rectangle beneath the window—the exact size and shape of the table. It must have been moved! Instantly, we set to work on the darker planks, clawing at the edges till at last one gives way. Carefully, we pry it out, and I reach into the dark damp hole beneath.

The hole extends beneath the bottom of the shed, and gradually my whole arm disappears as I reach inside.

"Anything?" Vix asks anxiously. I shake my head, my fingers fumbling blindly, desperately, but finding only damp dirt and stones and weeds.

"What if it's not here?" I say anxiously.

I reach further, my cheek pressed hard against the rough grain of the wooden floor, my fingers grasping, clutching—till finally they touch something solid, soft.

Quickly, I tug it out, and tears spring to my eyes as I stare at the dirty pink backpack in my hands. Poppy's bag.

"Oh, Lou!" Vix cries. "Christian was telling the truth!"

I beam at her. "I just hope he's right about Poppy's phone too," I say, hurriedly unzipping it. Makeup spills out, jewelry, then two tickets. . . . My stomach tightens.

"Kenny was right," I say quietly. "The Glastonbury tickets were in here. Christian could easily have found them—he could have made the whole story up."

"We don't know that," Vix argues gently. "Let's keep looking—the phone will prove it one way or another."

Jeans, socks, T-shirts . . . I freeze. One of the T-shirts has a huge dark stain.

I stare at it. "Is that—"

"Blood." Vix nods grimly. A chill scuttles down my spine as I stretch it out. It's big. A guy's T-shirt.

"Christian's," I gasp. "It must be." I run my fingers slowly over the mark, my heart aching as I think of his scar. "He must have been in so much pain, been so terrified."

I swallow hard, then continue emptying the bag. iPod, purse, hairbrush, but no phone.

"There's nothing left!" I stare at Vix, panic surging inside me as I turn the bag upside down. *"It's not here!"*

"Pass it here." She scrabbles quickly through the belongings again.

"Maybe Christian didn't see the mobile like he thought," I fret. "But then there would be a cassette tape in here, wouldn't there?"

Or maybe he lied. Maybe there was no text message in the first place, no phone to find. The police *said* they had Poppy's phone, after all, *and* that Christian took her bag—finding it here doesn't prove anything. They said he was a thief. A thief and a liar.

"Wait!" Vix cries, shaking the bag. "There's something here—it's in a different compartment!" I watch anxiously as she searches for another zip, opens it, and pulls out what looks for all the world like a cassette tape.

"Poppy's phone!" I cry, dizzy with relief. "Christian *was* telling the truth!"

"Now we just need to find his text." Vix smiles as she presses the power button. "Then we can take it to the police and *prove* Christian's innocence." I lean closer as we both stare expectantly at the screen. But nothing happens.

Vix presses the power button again.

Nothing.

"It's out of battery," I sigh. "It's been over a year, after all."

"Bollocks!" Vix groans.

"Still." I cradle the phone, gleaming like treasure in my hands. *"Now we have proof."*

She nods. "All we have to do is charge it up."

Suddenly there's a snuffling noise at the shed door and I whip round just as a dog begins to bark loudly.

Vix and I stare at each other in panic, then quickly shove everything back into the bag. I swing it over my shoulders as Vix scrambles to the broken window.

"Shit!" She leaps backwards as a large Labrador jumps up at the window frame, all black gums and teeth and drool. Vix tumbles to the floor, knocking over a pile of boxes, and the contents spill everywhere noisily.

Beyond the dog I spot an old man with a stick hurrying towards us, a mobile phone pressed to his ear.

I look around desperately for an escape route, but the door's padlocked from the outside and the only way out is the window—but the crazy dog is just below.

Vix grabs the spade, wielding it like a spear and jabbing it through the window, but immediately drops it as the dog jumps up again. I look around the shed desperately: seeds, bulbs, flowers—and a tennis ball.

I grab it and, never expecting it to work, hurl it out of the window. To my amazement, the dog immediately bounds after it, tail wagging madly. I laugh incredulously, then follow Vix as she scrambles out of the shed—till the backpack snags on the broken glass, pinning me in place.

"Hey!" the old man yells. "Hey, you!"

"Come *on*!" Vix urges. "Hurry!"

"I can't—I'm stuck!" I pull at the strap.

"Lucifer!" the man yells. "Lucifer—kill!" The dog immediately turns and heads for us.

"Leave the bag, Lou—come on!" Vix cries. "There's no time!"

"I can't!" I cry, pulling and tugging, desperate to get free—then suddenly the strap rips and I land flat on my face in the mud, the backpack still strapped to one shoulder—with the vicious dog bounding straight at me.

I jump to my feet and we race across the allotments, straight past the old man, and I hurl myself at the gate, praying it's open, but—*shit!*—it's locked. We both leap at the fence, but while Vix starts to scramble over it, I can't get a grip! I try again, managing to hook my fingertips over the top, then scrabble desperately with my legs, finally managing to get my arm over—just as the dog's jaws close around my shoe, yanking me backwards.

Shit!

"Lou!" Vix cries from the other side of the fence.

I cling on for dear life as the dog wrestles with my foot. I shake my leg, kick at him, and yell for all I'm worth, but it's useless. This is one determined dog. I change tack and start kicking at my shoe

254

instead, pushing and wriggling—till finally it drops to the ground, where the dog pounces on it. Hastily I pull myself over the fence and we leg it back to Kenny's car.

I hurl myself inside, adrenaline pumping wildly in my veins, a stupid smile plastered across my face.

"We did it!" I cry. "I can't believe we've got Poppy's phone—I can't wait to show Christian!"

"Now?" Vix asks, swinging the car into the road. "What about the funeral?"

I look at my watch: 10:20. "That's over four and a half hours away—I've got time." I beam at her. "Christian could be cleared by then!"

She drops me off near the Travelodge and I run inside, up the stairs and all the way down the corridor, fumbling with the lock in my haste to tell Christian the good news. Then suddenly the door swings open on its own.

I freeze. The room is totally trashed.

The lamp lies smashed on the floor, shattered cups and saucers are scattered like broken eggshells, bedding is strewn everywhere, and the mirror has a huge crooked crack like a spider's web threading through it, sending my splintered reflection staring back at me.

My eyes flick quickly around the room, panicking. Tentatively, I tiptoe inside.

"Christian?"

Suddenly someone grabs me from behind, their hand covering my mouth, stifling my screams.

TWENTY-EIGHT

I scream and struggle and kick, but he's just too strong.

"Shh, Lou—stop! It's me!"

The hand disappears from my mouth and I whip round to face Christian.

"What the—"

"*Shh!*" he hisses. "They found us."

"What? Are you okay?"

"I'm fine," he says. "I was in the bathroom when they burst in, and I managed to scramble onto the fire escape and get away. Are *you* okay? What happened to your shoe?"

"Dog. Long story. But look!" I beam, holding up the backpack.

His face lights up. "You found Poppy's bag!"

"And her phone!" I grin. "But it's dead, Christian—we need to charge it up."

He nods. "First we need to get out of here."

We hurry down the fire escape, but when we get to the car I can't find the keys anywhere.

"Shit!" I curse. "They must've fallen out of my pocket when that bloody dog chased me! What are we going to do?"

"Give me the hoodie."

"What?" I shrug it off and pass it to him. "Why?"

Christian scans the car park quickly, then wraps his hoodie round his fist and smashes the car window.

"Christian!"

"We need to get out of here *now*, Lou. These guys don't muck about. They could be back any moment."

"Then why are you still here?"

"I couldn't leave you," he says. "I was afraid they'd hurt you to try to find me."

I swallow.

Christian swiftly brushes the glass off the seat and begins tampering with some wires beneath the steering wheel.

"Where'd you learn that?" I ask incredulously as the engine bursts into life and I jump into the passenger seat.

"You go to prison, you pick up stuff," he says with a shrug as we swing out of the car park onto the road.

Which time? I wonder, shrugging the hoodie back on, a shiver skipping down my spine as I remember his fraud conviction.

"What?" Christian frowns.

Shit. Did I say that out loud?

"How did you even—' He sighs heavily. "The papers."

I don't correct him.

"Lou . . ." Christian looks at me for a long moment. "I didn't go to prison for that—I got a reprimand. And it was all a misunderstanding."

"Another one?" I ask curtly.

He sighs. "Yes."

"Right."

"You don't believe me?"

"Believe a con man?" I counter, then sigh. "I just wish you'd tell me everything," I mutter. "Otherwise I don't know what to believe."

"Lou." Christian takes my hand, but I pull it away. "Lou, please."

My hand closes around Poppy's phone in my jeans pocket as we speed away, but just because it was there doesn't mean Christian's text will be on it. It doesn't prove anything. I close my eyes, my head spinning as doubt creeps back into my mind.

Suddenly he swings the car into a narrow side street and pulls over. My eyes fly open. "What are you doing?"

"Telling you everything." Christian takes my hands in his, looks me straight in the eye. "When I was sixteen I did some busking. I told you I used to sketch people's portraits and sometimes I'd do some magic tricks as well—card tricks, that sort of thing, using my knack for remembering numbers—and sometimes punters would bet that they knew which card would come out and sometimes, usually, they'd lose. But it was a magic trick—they knew that—they were paying for a show."

I frown, unsure where this is going.

"But then this one guy didn't like losing his money, so he called the police, and I got a reprimand."

I look at him. "That's it?"

"I swear, that's it." He crosses his heart. "I wouldn't lie to you, Lou, I promise. I'm done with that. That's no life, it's just . . . fake. It's not real. It's not worth it."

I search his eyes, so clear, so blue. Then I smile. "Okay." I lean over and hug him close, feeling awful for doubting him—and for keeping so many secrets of my own. "I'm sorry."

"No," he sighs. "No, I'm just . . . Shit."

"What?" I laugh, but his body tenses around me.

"We're being followed."

"*What?*"

Christian glares at the rearview mirror. "That car parked behind us. It was in the hotel car park." As I turn to look my blood runs cold.

"It's the blue Ford I saw in Sheffield!" I pull my hood up quickly as Christian swings the car into the road.

"But why didn't they get out?" I ask anxiously. "What are they waiting for?"

"Backup," Christian replies darkly.

Sure enough, at the junction ahead, a red BMW screeches into view, blocking the end of the road as the blue car pulls out behind us and seals our exit.

"We're trapped!"

All the doors on the car in front fly open and four huge men climb out. Behind us, three more get out of the Ford, and they all close in on us.

My hand moves to the door handle. Maybe we can run for it.

"Hold on," Christian whispers, his hand still on the steering wheel, his expression tense. "Just a few more seconds . . ."

The men are almost at our car, their faces stern, their hands balled into fists. I nearly jump out of my skin as the first guy punches the bonnet; then Christian slams his foot on the accelerator and swerves around them, heading straight for the empty BMW.

I grip my seat tightly, wincing as we slam into the car, sending it spinning wildly into the main road. Christian veers hard to the left, tires screeching as he speeds away from the side street.

I twist round to see the four big guys racing to the BMW, horns blaring angrily around them as they jump inside. It's badly dented, but unfortunately still drivable. The car spins a full 180 degrees; then the Ford pulls out behind it, in hot pursuit.

Suddenly I'm thrown against the window as Christian swerves to the right.

"Where are we going?" I ask frantically.

"Anywhere they aren't." He spins the steering wheel to the left and I'm slammed towards him as we turn down another side street.

I stare at the wing mirror. "Have we lost them?"

"Not yet," Christian says grimly, and sure enough, moments later, the red BMW squeals round the corner behind us.

Shit!

Ahead of us, the traffic lights change to amber and a group of pedestrians get ready to cross.

"Christian—" I begin, but he keeps going, his eyes focused intently on the road ahead. "Christian!"

The light flicks to red.

"Christian!" I scream as a woman steps off the pavement.

He swerves hard, missing her by a meter. She leaps back onto the pavement, her hair blowing like a banshee's as we zip through the crossing, the BMW roaring behind us.

Christian grits his teeth as we race on towards a T-junction. Cars on the main road speed past in both directions, but Christian doesn't slow down. My heart pounds as we zoom towards the junction; then suddenly Christian spins the steering wheel and we swing to the left onto the main road—just centimeters from a white truck. The driver blares his horn angrily, but as I stare out the back windscreen I spot the red BMW screech to a halt just as a long car transporter charges past.

Phew.

But suddenly the blue Ford swings out of another side street, right on our tail. Christian swears. He weaves quickly away through the traffic, but the Ford's still gaining on us. Then the lights change to red.

"Shit!" Christian slams on his brakes, and we skid to a stop just centimeters from the car in front.

Behind us, the doors on the blue Ford fly open and two burly guys jump out of the backseat.

I stare at the lights, praying, wishing, *willing* them to change, while Christian squirms in his seat, trying to find a way through the traffic, but it's too busy—there's nowhere to run, nowhere to go.

260

Except the verge.

"Hold on!" Christian cries, swinging the car up the steep grassy slope. I grab the door handle to keep from falling out of my seat, then turn to look behind.

The blue Ford swerves swiftly out of the traffic, pausing only briefly as the two men dive back inside before racing after us. I hold on tight, my knuckles white as we drive along at a crazy angle, the other drivers staring at us as we race past.

Suddenly the grass verge ahead abruptly ends, sloping steeply down to meet the traffic lights, still glaring red at us—as straight ahead two lanes of cars speed around a busy roundabout.

I expect Christian to swerve again, to turn left and join the traffic, or follow the verge, but instead, he watches the stream of cars intently, then suddenly slams his foot on the accelerator, the vehicle jolting wildly as it flies down the hill, speeds straight across the line of traffic and onto the grassy roundabout. The blue Ford follows suit, narrowly missing a double-decker bus.

We judder over the roundabout, then fly down the other side, traffic whizzing past in front of us. I brace myself as we crash back down onto the road, cars swerving wildly to avoid us.

I glance behind, watching as the blue Ford finally slams to a stop to avoid colliding with the medley of vehicles tangled together in Christian's wake. I keep my eyes fixed on it as it shrinks, then finally disappears behind us. Then I take a deep breath and suddenly realize I'm shaking.

"Are you okay?" Christian turns.

I nod numbly, my hand still glued, white-knuckled, to the door. "Where'd you learn to drive like that?"

"My grandad." Christian grins. "Gardening wasn't his only hobby. He was a bit of an adrenaline junkie too, and he took me go-karting a few times.

"Go-karting?" I laugh.

261

Suddenly a siren begins to wail, wiping the smiles from both our faces. I turn in my seat, my heart sinking as I spot the flashing blue lights of the police car.

The traffic behind us peels away as the police car slices through like a lightsaber. But as the cars in front do the same, Christian charges through the gap, forcing Uncle Jim's Toyota up to its top speed as the police car quickly gains on us. Then suddenly another one joins it.

Christian races through an amber light, then turns sharply to the left, leaving the divided highway and heading down an exit ramp towards a street lined with shops. Ahead of us the lights of a railroad crossing flash warningly as the barrier begins to lower.

"Christian, stop!" I shriek. "It's the police—they won't hurt you—it's not worth *dying* for!"

He doesn't answer. His eyes just flick back and forth between the rearview mirror and the road; then suddenly he slams on the brakes and the car screeches to a stop just in front of the barrier.

"You're right," he says. "It's not worth getting you killed."

Behind us, the police cars swerve, blocking our only exit.

I stare at Christian, my pulse throbbing. "You're handing yourself in?"

"Not exactly." He takes my hand. "Lou, I need a favor."

"Anything," I promise, my voice jittery.

"I need you to pretend to be my hostage," he says. "That way you won't be in trouble and it'll buy me some time—to get away."

"No, Christian—it's too dangerous!" I argue. "We'll just show the police Poppy's phone. It proves you're innocent!"

"But it's out of battery," he reminds me.

"I—I know," I falter. "But as soon as we charge it up—"

He sighs. "We don't even know that my text's on there—if it's even going to do any good. I can't take the risk, Lou. I broke my curfew—they'll lock me up again. Please, do this for me."

"No!" I cling to him. "We're in this together, remember? If you go now, I might never see you again."

He hugs me close.

"We'll be together again. I know it. We're meant to be. It's fate, remember?"

I close my eyes miserably. None of it's been fate.

"Please, Lou? Trust me?"

I hug him tight, screwing up my eyes as I breathe him in. "Okay."

"Okay." He grabs Poppy's bag. "Let's go."

He kicks open the car door and drags me out with him.

"Stay back!" he yells at the gathered police officers. "I have a hostage!"

"Let her go, Niles! You're only making it worse for yourself!" a policeman cries, slowly stepping closer.

"Back off!" Christian warns. "I'll let her go if you let me go. If not . . ."

Suddenly I gasp as I feel something cold against my neck. The scissors from Joe's flat.

"You don't want to do this, Niles," the policeman says, inching closer.

"You're right," Christian agrees. "I don't. But if you leave me no choice."

I cry out as the scissors nick my flesh.

The policeman halts in his tracks.

"I'm warning you," Christian growls.

I screw my eyes shut tight, my pulse racing, afraid to even breathe with the edge of the blade pressing against my throat, Christian's arm gripping me so tightly it hurts. But I guess he has to make it seem real.

"Okay, stand down!" the policeman calls to the other officers. "Back away."

I open my eyes as they all slowly retreat to their cars.

"Now keep your word, Niles," he says sternly. "Release the girl."

Christian hesitates for a moment, looks around, then leans his mouth close to my ear and whispers, "I love you."

He shoves me forward roughly, sending me tumbling to the ground.

Within seconds, a policewoman is at my side. I turn quickly, but there's no sign of Christian as a train rushes past.

He's vanished. The officers scramble past each other in a flurry.

"He crossed the barrier! Possible fatality!" a policeman calls into his walkie-talkie. "Ambulance required!"

What? I stare at the train in horror as it slows into the station, my blood running cold as realization dawns.

Oh my God—Christian jumped in front of a train!

TWENTY-NINE

"So let me get this straight, Cinderella." Detective Inspector Gold-smith glances at my still-shoeless foot as he leans back in his chair and smooths his ginger comb-over. "You're saying that Leo Niles, a guy who's convicted for burglary, who left a teenager in a coma, who broke his curfew, kidnapped you, and held you hostage in or-der to escape from the police, has somehow convinced you he's ac-tually innocent?" He smiles at me like a primary-school teacher.

"He *is* innocent." I glare at him. His face is the same shade as the dirty gray walls but even more pitted.

"I've heard of Stockholm syndrome, of course, but I've never understood it."

"Maybe you're not smart enough?" I suggest.

His smile hardens. "If Niles is innocent, then why did he run?" He leans forward. "Why did he cut your throat?"

My hand flies to the plaster on my neck.

"And why did he break his curfew in the first place?"

"Because you put him in danger," I counter angrily.

"*I* did?" He raises his eyebrows so high they'd almost meet his hairline, if he had one.

"You were the only ones who knew where he was living, ex-cept, oh yeah, the mob of violent thugs who torched his house. Funny, that."

"The *only* ones?" He arches an eyebrow and my stomach lurches. *Does he know?*

"Young lady, there are any number of ways Niles could have inadvertently disclosed his location—people get careless."

"Yeah, especially police," I mutter.

He narrows his eyes, now in headmaster mode. "I'm sorry?"

"Lose something, did you? Like a crucial piece of evidence?"

He frowns. "What?"

"Poppy's mobile. With a text that Christian told you would prove his innocence. A text *you* said wasn't there."

"His name"—the detective smiles grimly—"is Leo Niles. And he lies. He's a con man."

"Only you *didn't* have the phone, did you?" I continue, my eyes not leaving his for a second. "You never had it. *You* lied. Because I've seen it."

His smile disappears. "Now, listen—"

"And now it will prove he's innocent."

He looks at me for a moment. "You mean you have this phone?"

I hesitate, my hand clutching the mobile in my pocket.

He looks at me over his glasses. "If what you say is true, then technically it's evidence."

"Evidence you *technically* already have," I counter. "If what *you* said was true."

"Perverting the course of justice is a serious offense, young lady," he warns.

"I don't have it." I shove the phone deep into my pocket. I don't trust him not to wipe the text the minute he sees it.

"Look." He leans forward. "Heaven knows what Niles has told you, and he's obviously been quite, shall we say, *persuasive?*" He raises that eyebrow again and I want to pluck it straight off his forehead. "But I led the original investigation, and I have the case file here, and there's nothing that suggests we ever had Poppy's mobile phone, or that Niles ever mentioned it to us."

I stare at him, my jaw set, trying to read his expression. He's lying. He's lying to cover his own back. *Isn't he?*

"If you really want to help Leo, to protect him, to give him a chance to prove his innocence, then quite honestly the best way to do that is to convince him to come in."

"You mean he's alive?" I say hopefully.

"We haven't found a body. But sometimes with train accidents there's not much of a body left to find." The detective sighs heavily. "Even if Niles escaped, he's clearly not safe out there—there are people who want to punish him for Poppy's death, and they're willing to take the law into their own hands to do so. That is not justice."

He's right. Even if Christian got away, where would he go? He's got an injured leg, he's wanted by the police, hunted by violent vigilantes . . . what chance does he have?

Just Poppy's phone, I remember, gripping it tightly. It's his only chance. The only way to prove he's innocent—the only way he can ever really be safe.

"Help us help him," DI Goldsmith says, all "concerned father" now. "We can protect him. And if he truly has new evidence, then we will investigate that. Fairly. Justly. Now," he says gently, "do you know where he might be?"

"No," I sigh miserably. "I have no idea."

"Looks like we're going to be here for a while, then." He sighs. "I hope you haven't got any plans for the rest of the day."

"What?" I glance at the clock. It's five past two. Poppy's funeral's in less than an hour—I've been at this stupid police station for over two hours!

"I've got all the time in the world." DI Goldsmith smiles smugly.

"We could chat all day, as far as I'm concerned. Or—if you decide to be more cooperative—you can go. It's up to you."

I stare at the clock, torn. I can't give him Poppy's phone, can't risk the only possible piece of evidence that Christian's innocent getting "lost" in the system.

But I can't miss Poppy's funeral either. I owe it to Poppy, and Aunt Grace and Millie. I can't let them down, can't miss my chance to say goodbye.

"I'm not hiding anything!" I protest.

"Really? Let's start with your name, shall we, Cinderella?"

"Louise Shepherd," I say. "You've seen my ID."

"Your *fake* ID, yes. But there's no Louise Shepherd with your date of birth on the electoral roll, which tells me you're *lying*."

My pulse races. I can't tell them who I *really* am—can't risk him contacting Neil, or upsetting Aunt Grace, today of all days. But today of all days, I can't be stuck *here* all afternoon either. . . . I glance at the clock again anxiously.

Just then, an officer knocks on the door. "Excuse me, sir, this just came through."

DI Goldsmith takes the sheet of paper and reads it; then his eyebrows shoot through the roof.

"Well, Cindy," he says. "You're just full of surprises, aren't you?"

"Would you like a ride home, love?" a policewoman asks when they finally let me go.

I hesitate. I need to get home as quickly as possible—Aunt Grace will be wondering where on earth I've got to—but it won't help anyone if I show up in a police car. How would I explain?

"No thanks," I tell her. "I'm fine."

I step out of the police station and gaze at the busy streets, the bland row of shops, and realize I'm totally lost. And without Christian by my side I feel completely alone.

Where is he?

I head into a phone box, pull some coins from my purse, and call Kenny.

"Lou!" he cries as soon as the call connects. "Are you all right?"

"Yes— No!" I wail miserably. "I've got less than an hour to get to Poppy's funeral and I have no idea where I am, I can't even see a tube station, and—"

"You're on Florence Street," Kenny interrupts. "Cross the road away from the police station, turn left, and take the first road on the right. Vix is waiting for you."

"What? How did you—"

"Your watch," he reminds me. "We're here for you, Titch. Now hurry!"

I find Vix exactly where Kenny said.

"Lou! Thank goodness!" She jumps out of the car to hug me. "It's twenty past two—I thought you were going to miss the funeral!"

"So did I," I admit, opening the passenger door.

"No, get in the back," she tells me. "It'll be easier to change."

"Change?" I climb in and gasp to find a black dress hanging up, and a shoe box, a black clutch bag, and a packet of sandwiches on the seat.

"Well, you can't wear a T-shirt and jeans to a funeral!" She shrugs.

"Vix, you are incredible!" I tell her.

"You'd better believe it." She grins as we pull off. "Kenny's at your house already, making your excuses. I think the latest is a huge jam on the M1."

I grin as I tug off Christian's hoodie. "What would I do without you guys?"

"Um . . . you'd be late, and grubby, and you'd have been eaten by a dog." Vix laughs as we swing round a corner. "Luckily you're never without us—thanks to your watch, we can find you anywhere. Speaking of which, do you know what happened to Christian?

They said on the radio that he ran across a railway crossing—did he get away?"

"I don't know." My heart flips as I pull the dress over my head. "I think so. They haven't found a body, and the detective was grilling me pretty hard . . . that's a good sign, right?"

"Definitely," Vix says.

"I hope so, anyway." I can't afford to think of the alternative.

"Do you have any way of getting in touch with him?" Vix asks. "Do you know where he'd go?"

"Nope. This time I've well and truly lost him," I sigh. "But it doesn't matter."

"What?"

"The only thing that matters is proving his innocence—actually, can we make a quick stop?" I say quickly as we drive past a mobile phone shop. "I need to get a charger for Poppy's mobile."

"Pass it here," Vix says. "Kenny said there's a universal phone charger in the glove compartment."

"*What?*"

"You're in his gadgetmobile, remember?" she says. "It's got *everything.*"

"That's incredible!" I scramble into the front passenger seat as we wait at traffic lights, watching as Vix plugs Poppy's phone into the charger, then connects it to the car's cigarette lighter socket.

Please work, please . . .

Finally the screen flickers to life.

"*Yes!*"

Quickly I press the message icon, but it takes forever to load up. I stare at it, waiting, waiting, as it gradually—*agonizingly slowly*—hums back to life, my fingers tightly crossed, praying that Christian's text is on there.

Suddenly a list of phone numbers springs up before me, and I scroll down them swiftly, searching, searching. . . . There're texts from me, from Aunt Grace and Uncle Jim, from other people I don't know.

"Christian's number's not there," I say, a cold chill shivering down my back.

"What?" Vix says. "Are you sure?"

"Yes—I memorized his number as soon as he gave it to me—it's not here!"

"Calm down," Vix says. "Check again."

I scroll down desperately, further, further, till I'm back months before the assault. Then I check again, more slowly this time, scouring the digits as they pass. But it's still not there.

I stare numbly at the screen. "Poppy must have deleted it."

Vix looks at me and I know we're thinking the same thing. *If it was ever there.* Ignoring the pricking pain in my eyes, I scroll back to the beginning and read all the texts sent the day of Poppy's attack, in reverse order.

Darling Poppy, we're all thinking of you. Hope you recover soon xx

I click the next.

You're in our prayers, dearest Poppy. We love you so much

I open the third text and my heart leaps into my throat.

Hi Popsicle! Hope you're having a great summer! Mexico is fantastico! I've got you a sombrero! See you soon! Lxx

I screw my eyes shut. It's from me. I hadn't heard what had happened yet—Aunt Grace decided to wait till I was home, as she didn't want to ruin my holiday. My stupid, *stupid* holiday.

271

I click miserably through the rest of the texts—messages Poppy will never read—filled with love and sympathy and get well soons. Then I'm back to before the attack:

Poppy, why aren't you answering your phone? I have to talk to you. Please let me explain. Call me on my mobile or at Gran's asap—it's urgent. Mum xx

I frown. I wonder what that was about? But when I click the next message I forget all about Aunt Grace's.

I'm coming 2 get U

I stare at it.

"I'm coming to get you?" I read.

"What?" Vix glances across. "Is that from . . ."

"It must be—it *has* to be." My heart beats fast and my thumb fumbles on the screen, trying to scroll down, check the sender. "But there's no name, only a number I don't recognize. . . . *Of course!*" I cry suddenly. "Of *course* I wouldn't recognize his number—his old phone got broken!"

"Plus he'd have bought a new one when he got out of prison, wouldn't he?" Vix says. "If he didn't want to be traced?"

"Yes! Why didn't I think of that sooner?" I beam. "*This* is the text—just like Christian said—telling Poppy he was coming to pick her up! He *is* innocent!" My heart swells so much I can hardly breathe. "And this *proves* it!"

Vix grins at me. "So what now?"

"I don't know," I say. "I have to tell him, but how? I have no idea where he is—or even if he's still safe—and then there's the funeral. . . ." I glance at my watch as we stop at yet another red light.

272

Two-twenty-six. It's going to be touch and go whether I make it.

Suddenly Poppy's phone shudders in my hand, and I drop it instinctively. It shivers around the floor, buzzing and playing a tinny version of "Yellow Submarine." I pick it up and a landline number I don't recognize flashes on the screen.

"Answer it!" Vix urges.

"But I don't know who it is!"

She snatches the mobile, puts it on speakerphone, then slams on the brakes to avoid crashing into the car in front as it stops at a zebra crossing.

"Jesus!" I gasp, my heart jolting out of my chest as we stop just in time.

"Hello?" a voice says on the phone.

"Sorry!" Vix mouths, thrusting Poppy's mobile back at me.

"Hello?" the voice says again. "Hello? Lou?"

"*Christian!*" I cry, dizzy with relief. "You're *alive*! Are you all right? Where are you? How did you know—"

"You've got the phone! Thank God!" Christian cries. "I've been calling it for hours! I nearly went nuts when it wasn't in Poppy's bag—I thought I'd lost it!"

"Sorry! I've just charged it up! I can't believe you remembered her number!"

"Thank goodness I did—told you I was good with figures!"

"Are you okay?" I ask nervously. "I was so worried."

"I'm fine. You can't get rid of me that easily."

I smile.

"So is it there?" he asks anxiously. "The text?"

"Yes!" Vix and I exchange grins. "It's here, just like you said. It says 'I'm coming to get you.' The police will have to believe you now—it's proof!"

"Wait," Christian says, his voice strange. "*What* does it say?"

273

"That you're coming to pick Poppy up," I tell him. " 'I'm coming to get you.' "

There's silence on the other end of the line.

"Christian? You there?"

"Shit."

I frown. "What's wrong?"

He continues to swear, getting louder and louder.

Vix looks at me, wide-eyed. I've never heard him so angry, so volatile. Suddenly there's a loud crash.

"*Christian!*" I cry. "Christian, what's happening? Are you okay?"

"No!" he cries bitterly. "No, I'm completely screwed!"

"What! Why?"

"Lou—don't you see? There's no way that text's going to prove my innocence."

"What do you mean?"

"Think about it. *I'm coming to get you*—it sounds just like a threat!"

"But it wasn't," I protest. "You were going to pick her up!"

"*I* know that, *you* know that. But which way do you think the *police* are going to take it? Especially as, just minutes later, Poppy was attacked! You have to delete the message, Lou—if anyone finds it, they'll take it the wrong way."

"But if we explain—"

"They won't believe us." He sighs, his voice filled with despair. "It's hopeless. It's over."

"No—no, it can't be!" I protest, watching our future swirl down a big fat drainpipe. "There must be something—*something* else we can use, some other proof."

"Like what?" he sighs. "That was it. That message was my only hope."

I slump in my seat, my heart aching as I listen to him break down.

Vix taps my arm, mouthing something at me I can't make out. I

274

shrug. *What?* She tries again. It looks like . . . *Diarrhea?* Is she feeling ill? I rub my stomach questioningly and she rolls her eyes.

"Diary!" she hisses. "Did Poppy keep a diary?"

"Of course! Poppy's diary!" I cry.

"Diary?" Christian says, sounding startled.

"Um, yeah," I reply, trying to sound less excited than I feel. "Is there a diary or anything in her bag?"

I'm such an *idiot*! I was so busy searching Poppy's bag for her phone it never even *occurred* to me to check if her USB necklace with her diary on it was in there. If she really was friends with Christian, she'd have mentioned him in it for sure!

"I can't see a notebook or anything," Christian says.

That's because it'd be a *necklace*, not a notebook, but I can't tell him that. I bite my lip in frustration. If only I'd checked when *I* had the bag! "Well, what *is* there? Tell me everything," I urge, praying madly.

"There's a hairbrush, some clothes, an iPod . . ."

I close my eyes, trying desperately to remember if I saw the maple-leaf necklace in her bag in the shed. Poppy never went anywhere without it—it's where she always kept everything most vitally important to her ever since I gave it to her on her fourteenth birthday. And it wasn't on her when they found her—I haven't seen it since—so it *must* be in her bag. . . .

Otherwise it's all over. Christian will go back to jail—or on the run with God knows how many people after him. We'll never be together.

"A washbag, some makeup, some jewelry . . ."

"What sort of jewelry?" I ask, crossing my fingers tightly.

"Um, there's some earrings, a charm bracelet, some necklaces . . ."

"I thought I noticed a . . . locket or something when I was looking for the phone," I bluff. "I think it was shaped like a leaf. . . ."

"Uh . . . nope. No lockets."

Shit.

"Wait, there's a weird maple-leaf necklace with something on the back. . . ." My heart leaps. *That's it!*

"It kind of looks like a USB stick," he says, and I want to kiss him.

"Where are you?" I ask. "If it's a USB stick, we need to find a computer and see what's on it."

Vix nudges me, then points to the dashboard clock. *Shit.* It's 2:35. There's no time to go and meet him, wherever he is.

"Actually, there's an Internet café over the road from my phone box," Christian says. "I'll try it now."

"Great!" I cry, relieved. "Wait—won't you be recognized?"

"No, I don't think so. It's a dingy little place. I doubt there'll be anyone in there on a Monday afternoon. I'm actually probably safer in there than on the streets."

"Okay—if you're sure."

"I'll call you back if I find anything."

"Good luck!"

I close my eyes as I hang up, praying madly.

Please let him find Poppy's diary on the USB. Please let there be a mention of him, of Glastonbury. Please, please, please let it prove he's innocent.

THIRTY

There are cars parked all along the curb as we finally pull into my road—I've never seen it so busy—so Vix drops me off outside my house before going to find somewhere to park. But just as I hurry up the driveway, Poppy's phone rings in my bag.

"You found something?" I say excitedly, ducking down the side path to answer it.

"Not yet." Christian sighs. "I'm on Skype at the Internet café, but the USB's passcode-protected. Four digits."

Shit. I could try all sorts of possible meaningful combinations, but how would I explain it to Christian if I got it right on the first guess? Unless I try some wrong ones first.

"Okay, how about one-two-three-four?" I suggest.

He sighs heavily. "Nope."

"Zero-zero-zero-zero?"

"Nope."

"Do you know when her birthday is?"

"No."

We try several more numbers, but still the files remain stubbornly locked, and I'm almost out of ideas. Plus I'm running more and more late for the funeral.

What number would Poppy choose?

"It could be anything!" Christian sighs heavily. "It's hopeless!"

277

"Unless . . ." A seed of an idea plants itself in my mind.

"Unless what?"

"Well . . ." I hesitate. "The paper said it's Poppy's funeral this afternoon—I could go."

Christian falters. "Go to her *house*?"

I nod, then realize he can't see me. "Yes. I could have a look around her room, see if I could find any clues—or any other evidence?"

"You'd do that?" he says incredulously. "Go to a stranger's funeral? For me?"

I cross my fingers. "Yes."

He pauses, and I panic. *Has he guessed?* Then he sighs heavily, his voice filled with gratitude.

"You're amazing. Thank you."

"No worries," I say, suddenly overwhelmingly glad he can't see me, where I am, and the lies written all over my face. "Call me later." I hang up, then hurry inside.

"Lulu!" Uncle Doug rushes up to me with Kenny in tow. "Crumbs, I could've sworn you were Poppy's ghost for a sec—nice hair! Thank goodness you made it—traffic's a bitch, eh? Your friend here was just telling me how bad the queues are on the motorway."

Kenny winks at me.

"A nightmare," I agree.

"So how come you two didn't travel down together, then?" Uncle Doug asks.

"Oh, I . . . we . . . ," I stammer.

"We go to different universities now," Kenny lies quickly. "I know Lou from boarding school, but I only had to travel down from Warwick today, so I think I missed the worst of the jam, luckily."

I could kiss him.

"Where's Aunt Grace?" I ask Uncle Doug.

"Trying to get Millie out of the bathroom," he sighs. "She's locked herself in."

My heart aches as I rush upstairs. *Poor Millie.*

I spot Aunt Grace hovering outside the bathroom door with an Asian man I don't recognize. She looks thin and ghostlike in a simple black dress.

"Millie!" she calls desperately. "Please come out, darling, it's nearly time to go."

"I've brought some jalebi just for you, Millie," the man adds. "I know it's your favorite. It's waiting for you downstairs."

"*You* should be downstairs," Aunt Grace hisses agitatedly. "You shouldn't even be here, today of all days. I don't want any trouble, Amir."

"Nor do I," he protests, his eyes wide. "Grace, I'm just trying to help—" He spots me. "Hello?"

Aunt Grace turns, then gasps, her hands flying to her mouth. *"Poppy?"*

"Aunt Grace." I rush up to her. "It's me, Lulu. Are you okay?"

"Lulu!" She wraps her arms around me. "Oh, sweetheart, for a moment I thought . . . your hair."

"I'm so sorry," I say quickly. "I never meant—I just dyed it, then the hairdresser cut it too short, and—"

"It looks lovely." She smiles, her eyes tired. "It's so good to see you." She hugs me fiercely.

"I'm so sorry I couldn't get here sooner."

"You're here now." She squeezes me tight. "That's all that matters."

"I'll leave you in peace," Amir says.

"Lulu, this is Amir, my cookery instructor," Aunt Grace tells me. "Lulu's my niece."

"Nice to meet you," I say.

"You too." Amir smiles. "I'm just sorry it's not in happier circumstances." He looks sadly at Aunt Grace, then turns away.

"Oh, I'm so glad you're here," Aunt Grace says. "Millie won't come out of the bathroom."

"Millie?" I call gently. "Are you okay?"

"Lulu?" a tiny voice whimpers.

"It's me, munchkin." I smile. "And I've got this great big hug waiting for you, and it's so big, it's so heavy, I'm worried I might drop it!"

"Don't drop it!" she cries.

"You'd better come out and get it, then—quick!"

The handle moves, but the door doesn't open.

"I can't." She sighs miserably.

"Why not, munchkin?"

"I'm ugly."

"What?" I say, surprised. "Impossible!"

"I am," she snuffles. "My dress is yucky!" I stifle a smile.

"She hates black," Aunt Grace whispers. "She says only bad guys wear black."

"Well, maybe you could wear a dress the same color as mine?" I suggest. "Then we can be twins."

"Yes!" she cries.

"Well, I'm wearing a beautiful black dress," I tell her. "Have you got anything black you can wear?"

She hesitates. "But . . . my dress *is* black!"

"No *way!*" I say, winking at Aunt Grace. "I don't believe you. Show me."

She opens the door and peers out, her face pale against the somber outfit, but her eyes light up as she sees my dress. "We're twins!"

"Well, fancy that!" I beam, grabbing her in a tight hug. "Great minds think alike, eh?"

*　*　*

Millie holds my hand all the way to the church, squeezing hard as I shield her from the assembled paparazzi outside the gates, suddenly glad for my new sunglasses. The reporters flock like vultures around the mourners, calling out to Aunt Grace as we pass, but she just picks Millie up silently and quickens her pace as we make a beeline through the graveyard to the sanctuary of the cool stone church.

The moment we step through the door, peace descends and the sweet perfume of lilies fills my lungs. I've never seen so many flowers—dozens of beautiful bouquets tied to the pews with silky pink ribbons, arranged in stands, and adorning every available surface—creamy carnations, velvety roses, sprigs of gypsophila, trumpeting lilies, and, of course, dozens of scarlet poppies. Lovely, delicate blooms that will dazzle for a while but then die all too soon, their lives cut short. Just like Poppy.

And there, nestled in a beautiful wreath of poppies at the front of the church, is her photo.

I step closer, drawn by her sparkling eyes and her easy smile, and my heart swells. This is how she was. How I remember her. I reach forward, stroking her cheek with my fingers.

Poppy.

"That's my favorite photo of her," Aunt Grace whispers, appearing at my side. "She looks like she's laughing at something, doesn't she? She was always laughing, always smiling. . . ." She falters, her eyes fixed on Poppy's photo, and suddenly I notice she's shaking.

I take her arm quickly, and she looks up at me, her eyes so sad, so broken, like she's about to fall apart. Then Millie tugs at her dress, and she takes a deep breath, straightens her shoulders, and calmly smiles down at her.

"Yes, sweetheart?"

"Can we sit at the front?" Millie asks. "So I can see?"

"Of course, darling."

"You can even sit on my knee if you like, munchkin," I offer, holding her hand as we head to the pews. "Then you'll see better than anyone."

"Okay." She smiles.

As we take our seats a sea of black figures trickles in, filling the pews around us. Poppy's old teachers, school friends, neighbors, Aunt Grace's work friends, and Neil with more of Uncle Jim's colleagues from the police. A policeman I don't recognize walks over to us.

"I just wanted to extend my deepest condolences," he tells Aunt Grace. "And to let you know we're doing all we can to find that monster. He'll be back behind bars soon."

"Thank you," she says quietly. "I hope so."

The policeman smiles at me and Millie, and I force a smile back, feeling unbearably guilty, sitting here on the front pew at Poppy's funeral. Guilty for lying to Aunt Grace about where I've been, guilty for lying to Christian about the real reason I'm here now, and guilty for protecting the very person everyone else is searching for.

I try to shut all of this out as I watch the rest of our family take their seats. Uncle Doug clasps the arm of ancient Great-Aunt Mary as she hobbles down the aisle, while Aunt Harriet flutters behind, dabbing her eyes, followed by a flock of various second cousins I don't know very well. Then I spot Vix and Kenny sliding into a row at the back, and I smile. I really don't know what I'd have done without them these past few days.

Soon the church is full, and the organ strikes up a slow, haunting rendition of Coldplay's "Yellow." Then the doors open and I gasp as the coffin appears.

I stare at it, transfixed, as six uniformed police officers carry it slowly down the aisle.

It seems impossible that Poppy's inside. It doesn't look big enough. How can that box possibly contain her? She never sat still—she was always running, dancing, laughing. . . .

The coffin blurs and I wipe at my eyes. The organist finishes with a flourish and the vicar approaches the lectern.

"Today we have come together to celebrate the life of an extraordinary young woman, Poppy Willoughby-White. It's a tribute to her how full this church is today." He sweeps his arms out, smiling at us all. "Poppy was special to all of us, whether as a pupil, a neighbor, a friend . . ."

I glance at her school friends, huddled together, heads on each other's shoulders, sobbing silently.

"A niece, a granddaughter, a cousin, a sister, or a daughter."

I squeeze Millie close as Aunt Grace tightens her grip on my hand. My throat swells.

"And she will be sorely missed."

I stare at my feet, blinking quickly.

"Poppy was only with us a short while, but—"

Suddenly the vicar is interrupted by a commotion outside. The stained-glass windows flash like lightning as the photographers' cameras go crazy, and everyone stares and mutters to each other.

Everyone but Aunt Grace, whose gaze remains intently fixed on the vicar, as if the slightest movement will shatter her to pieces. I follow her cue and don't turn.

He clears his throat. "But . . . but she achieved a lot in her—"

A loud clank echoes through the church as the latch is lifted from outside, and the vicar purses his lips tightly as the church doors creak open. A hush sweeps through the congregation; then, finally, Aunt Grace turns. Her face blanches in shock and she drops her hymnbook with a clatter.

I look round quickly—and my jaw hits the floor.

"Daddy—you're back!" Millie springs from my lap, bounds down

the aisle, and leaps into her father's arms, her face brighter than the sun. He engulfs her in a tight hug, his ginger beard buried in her golden curls as she clings to him, their mutual joy and love written on every part of their bodies.

Finally. My heart swells as I smile through the tears streaming down my face. *Finally something good.*

Escorted by a prison guard, Uncle Jim carries Millie back to the front pew, where he kisses Aunt Grace's cheek, then hugs me, his eyes filled with tears.

I squeeze him tight, unable to believe he's here—*he's really here!* He looks so different. The beard's new, but it's more than that. He's like a ghost of himself, like someone's stripped away the erect shoulders and proud chin that used to betray the fact that he was a policeman even when he wasn't in uniform, to leave a smaller, hunched, tired husk of a man.

It breaks my heart. He's the real victim in all of this. Not only was his daughter killed right in front of him in his own house, but he was locked up for trying to protect her. My stomach knits itself in knots at the injustice of it as he sits down next to Aunt Grace, clasping her hand tightly, Millie still clinging to him like a monkey. She doesn't know where he's been, of course—Aunt Grace felt she was too young to tell her the truth when it all happened, so she thinks Uncle Jim's been away working. Which means she won't realize that he's not back to stay . . .

As the vicar continues the prison guard slides into the pew behind us, and Poppy's friends and relatives take turns to read poems and tributes, sharing their memories of her with us all.

Then the vicar calls my name and I freeze. I totally forgot I'd promised to do a tribute. Aunt Grace squeezes my hand as he asks for me again, and slowly I rise from my seat, my heart pounding as I approach the lectern.

I look out at them all, this sea of faces staring at me, and my throat seizes up. I can't do this—I don't know what to say.

Then Millie sneezes and I look down at her, her big brown eyes watching me intently. I look at Uncle Jim, holding it together so well in spite of everything, and Aunt Grace, her eyes clear and green. She smiles at me, nods, and somehow words form on my lips.

"This is surreal." I gaze around at the crowded church. "It doesn't feel real. Every day I see something, laugh at something, and think 'I must tell Poppy about that.' But I can't." I blink quickly. "It's hard to imagine how the world can still be turning, how everyone's still going about their lives—when Poppy isn't."

I swallow hard, willing myself not to cry.

"Growing up we were inseparable." I smile. "Two peas in a pod. But then I went away to boarding school for sixth form, and . . . and it made me realize the huge difference she made to my life. How her infectious laughter tickled your insides, how her smile warmed you down to your toes, how she always brightened every single moment you were with her. I've spent so much time away from her that now I keep forgetting she's really gone. Before, I always knew she was still there, somewhere, that I could still talk to her whenever I wanted, even if I couldn't always see her . . . and I like to think that, in a way, that's still true." I blink fiercely and shake my head. "I wish I'd spent more time with her, treasured every second. Poppy's like—*was* like a sister to me. She was my best friend. . . ."

It's no use. The tears gush through my words and the congregation blurs before me as I clutch the lectern to keep from crumpling to the floor. I close my eyes, and when I open them again Uncle Jim is by my side. He hugs me close, his strong arms holding me together as he always has, then kisses my head, his bristly beard scratching my scalp like a toothbrush as the prison guard looks on.

Uncle Jim clears his throat. "Friends." He smiles. "Thank you so much for coming here today to remember my Poppy." His voice cracks. "But let's remember her not as a victim, but as the girl she was. Joyful. Cheeky. So, so funny . . ." He laughs hoarsely. "My princess. My angel." He swallows hard. "But now she is a true angel. And I know she would be incredibly touched by all your kind words, your beautiful flowers, your being here at all. Thank you. From the bottom of my heart. Thank you."

He squeezes my shoulders and leads me back to my pew. As I sit down Aunt Grace's cool hand finds mine and holds it tight.

As the organ strikes up again the six men from before approach the coffin, but Uncle Jim turns and looks at the prison guard, who nods. They both get up and slowly walk towards the coffin, and instantly one of the policemen steps aside to let Uncle Jim take his place. He stares sadly at his daughter's coffin for a long moment, stroking his hand slowly over the smooth wood. Then, taking a deep breath, they all lift it onto their shoulders.

We follow them outside, the bright sunlight blinding after the cool darkness of the church, but this time I don't wear my sunglasses. We trudge slowly through the graveyard, a great black snake, till finally we reach the gaping hole. It's all I can look at, all I can focus on as the vicar says the final prayers. The neat, straight sides slice deep into the soil, their dark walls plunging down, down, as they lower Poppy's coffin into the ground.

As I take my turn to sprinkle a handful of earth into her grave a million memories flood my head and hot tears streak down my face. I can't believe she's really gone. Forever. That these memories . . . are all I have left.

Goodbye, my beautiful Poppy, I tell her silently as the last crumbs of soil drop from my fingers. *I love you so much. Sweet, sweet dreams.*

I screw my eyes shut tight, take a deep breath, then finally force myself to turn away, to let her go.

Numbly, I follow the trail of mourners as they slowly, quietly, make their way out of the graveyard, lost in my thoughts, my memories.

Suddenly an angry cry breaks the peace.

I turn, startled, to spot an Asian woman with a stroller talking heatedly with one of Uncle Jim's colleagues, who's blocking her way to the grave. I frown, then edge closer.

"I don't know how you've got the *nerve* to show your face here," he growls at her.

"I only wish to pay my respects," she insists.

"Respects?" he scoffs. "If you had any respect, you wouldn't have come—now sod off!"

Her brown eyes darken. "I have as much right to be here as you."

"You have no rights." He steps closer to her, menacingly. "Not here. You've caused enough pain already. Now. Clear. Off."

Who is she? I've never seen her before in my life.

The woman meets his gaze for a moment, her eyes glistening.

"I'm sorry. I meant no harm," she mumbles. "Please put this on her grave for me." She hands the policeman a white rose, then turns her stroller and hurries away.

He watches her go, glares at the flower for a moment, then flings it carelessly to the ground, stamps on it, and turns his back on her.

What's going on? First Aunt Grace told Amir to leave; now this woman's been warned off. . . . Why aren't they welcome?

Carefully, I make my way around the crowd of mourners and pick up the rose. I brush the dirt from its soft velvety petals, then look round for the woman and I spot her kneeling by another grave, a few meters away.

As I approach I realize she is talking quietly—to the child? Or the grave? A twig cracks beneath my foot and she twists round sharply.

"Sorry," I say quickly. "I didn't mean to startle you."

"What do you want?" she snaps, her eyes filled with tears. "Aren't I even allowed to visit my own family now?"

"Yes . . . I . . . I'm sorry, I just . . . you dropped this." I hold the rose out to her awkwardly.

She looks at it for a moment, then sighs. "I didn't mean any harm."

"I know," I tell her. "It's just it's a difficult day. I'm sure he didn't mean it."

"Thank you." She sighs. "But I'm pretty sure he did." She turns back to the gravestone, rearranging the flowers at its base, and it's only then that I notice the name inscribed on it.

Tariq Khan.

The breath catches in my throat.

Tariq. Poppy's killer.

I glance at the woman.

"You're . . . you're Tariq's . . ." What? Sister? Cousin?

"Fiancée." She sighs, fingering a diamond ring that sparkles in the sunlight. She turns to me. "Sabina Mir. I'm sorry if my being here offends you. But, as you say, today's a difficult day. For everyone. I'm so sorry about Poppy."

My stomach hardens. She's *sorry?*

"I've been praying for her, always hoping she'd pull through."

I bet. "So Tariq wouldn't be remembered as a murderer?" I ask, a sharp edge to my voice.

"No." She looks at me, her eyes clear. "So she could finally tell everyone the truth."

I blink.

"Tariq didn't do this. I know it. My Tariq would never hurt anyone, especially a woman—a girl." She sighs. "She was a lovely girl."

"You *knew* Poppy?" I say, surprised.

She shrugs. "Not really. Not properly. I only met her a couple of times—with Leo."

288

Of course! Christian told me about Sabina! She's the one who introduced him to Tariq in the first place—she knows Christian was friends with Poppy and why he was really there that night.

"But I wish we'd never met," Sabina says. "Then none of this would've happened."

I frown. "How do you mean?"

She looks up. "It's my fault he was there that day. I asked Tariq to give Leo and Poppy a lift to the train station. Leo didn't have a car and they wanted to go to Glastonbury—"

I nod eagerly—her story matches Christian's. . . .

"And I . . ." Sabina sighs. "I wanted Tariq out of the house."

"You'd had an argument?" I ask. *Was that why he attacked Poppy, because he was already angry?*

"No," she laughs. "No, far from it. I wanted to cook him a special meal—a surprise. I wanted everything to be perfect when I told him." She glances at the sleeping baby in the stroller, her dark eyes glittering with tears. "He never knew he was going to be a dad. And now Ash will never know his father."

I stare at her, then at the little boy, snoring softly as he clutches his teddy bear against his tanned cheek. Tariq's son. Despite myself, my heart aches for them. I know how terrible it is to lose a parent.

But that doesn't mean Tariq was innocent.

"What makes you think Tariq didn't do it?" I ask. "You weren't there."

"I *knew* Tariq. Almost as well as I know myself." Sabina smiles. "Sometimes it doesn't matter what the evidence says, what the world says, if you know something to be true in your heart. And I do."

"But it doesn't make sense," I argue. "If Tariq didn't attack Poppy—"

"He didn't!" she says firmly.

"Then who did?" I demand. "How did she end up with a fractured skull?"

She looks away. "I don't know." She shakes her head. "It pains me to even think it, but if anyone hurt Poppy, it had to be Leo."

I freeze.

"Maybe it was an accident." Sabina shrugs. "Or maybe they had an argument—a lovers' tiff?"

My skin tightens. Christian was Poppy's *boyfriend*? I'd never thought of them like that—boyfriend and girlfriend. And then suddenly I remember something Joe said when he thought I was Christian's girlfriend: *Better luck with this one.* My hearts sinks. Could it be true . . . ? They were going away together, after all, and she was attacked in her bedroom. . . .

"No." I shake my head vehemently as bile swims in my stomach. "No, he wasn't even there—he texted Tariq to say he was running late!"

"He could've sent that text from anywhere." Sabina meets my gaze evenly. "He could've already been inside the house, buying time, trying to keep Tariq away till he'd figured out what to do." She looks away. "Only he didn't expect Poppy's dad to come home early, did he?"

I stare at her, my head reeling, all my evidence crumbling to ashes at her words.

"But—but then why was Tariq in the house at all?" I demand. "Why did he break in? They found his fingerprints and blood on the broken glass!"

"Tariq was waiting outside the house," Sabina replies calmly. "He would've seen Poppy's dad come home and heard the fight, so he must've broken in to try to intervene. He was like that—he always tried to keep the peace."

"But then why would Poppy's dad attack *Tariq*?"

Sabina's eyes narrow. "Of course he'd attack the Asian guy first."

"*What?*" I stare at her. "Uncle Jim isn't *racist!*"

"So he's your uncle." She nods bitterly. "Well, no one likes to believe the worst of the ones they love, but his neighbors *heard* him shouting racist abuse."

"I . . . He was upset!" I protest. "His daughter had been attacked—he was yelling every insult under the sun! It was the heat of the moment!"

"Well, the jury didn't think so," Sabina counters. "Why do you think he got such a long jail sentence?"

"What do you mean?" I frown. "Because he was charged with manslaughter."

She raises an eyebrow. "Defending his own daughter in his own house? Every jury understands parental instincts." She shakes her head. "What they couldn't understand were Tariq's handcuffed wrists, the racial abuse, the fact that he was stabbed in the *back*." She looks away, tears spilling down her cheeks. "Tariq didn't even have a weapon. He couldn't even defend himself."

"He didn't *need* a weapon!" I counter angrily. "He bashed Poppy's head against her bedpost! Uncle Jim stabbed him in the back to try to stop him killing her, and he used handcuffs to stop him getting away. It was defense!"

"It wasn't *defense*! Your uncle didn't call an ambulance, did he? He didn't try to save Tariq's *life* once he'd stabbed him and cuffed him up—he just sat there and watched him die!"

"Lou, there you are!" Kenny cries, rushing up to me, Vix on his heels. He glances at Sabina uncertainly. "Everyone else has gone back to the house, but I said I'd bring you—are you ready?"

"Yes, go back to your precious uncle," Sabina spits at me. "*He's* the murderer, not Tariq, yet he gets let off with manslaughter. Five years. *Five years* for taking away my little boy's father!" Her eyes blaze. "And the whole country's on his side. He's a bloody *hero*! While my *innocent* Tariq's remembered as a killer! Ash will have to

291

live with that his whole life." Tears splinter her words. "That's not fair. That's not justice."

Vix and Kenny glance at each other awkwardly, but my gaze falls on the sleeping child and I try to swallow my anger.

"It's not fair," I agree. "Ash is innocent. But Tariq wasn't— He *killed* Poppy."

"No, he *didn't*!" Sabina says angrily.

"No one likes to believe the worst of the ones they love," I repeat back to her. "But you can't *know* Tariq's innocent, Sabina—you weren't there."

"Neither were you!" she says hotly. "And both the people who *were* there have blood on their hands—they can't be trusted. Leo even went on the run from the police *the very day* Poppy died," she says bitterly. "You think that's a *coincidence*?"

I stare at her. "What do you mean?"

"I mean Leo can't afford for anyone to find out the truth—not now that Poppy's dead," Sabina says grimly. "Now that it's murder."

THIRTY-ONE

"Wow," Vix says as I fill her and Kenny in on the rest of my confrontation with Sabina on the drive back to my house. "I did *not* see that coming."

"But it's not true!" I protest. "Christian *couldn't* have attacked Poppy—he wouldn't!"

"No way," Vix agrees.

"But why would *Tariq* attack Poppy?" Kenny asks. "He didn't even know her, he had no weapon, and now we know he had a loving fiancée cooking him dinner at home. Plus he knew that Leo was on his way to the house and could arrive at any time. It just doesn't make sense."

"But if Tariq didn't attack Poppy . . ." Vix hesitates.

"It had to be Leo," Kenny says grimly. "He was her boyfriend, after all."

I shake my head. "I can't believe it."

"That he was Poppy's boyfriend, or that he killed her?" Kenny asks, looking across at me in the passenger seat beside him.

"Both," I say miserably.

"Maybe it was an accident?" Vix suggests gently. "Maybe Poppy fell and hit her head and Christian was about to call an ambulance when your uncle came home and—"

"No!" I insist. "No, what about the text he sent to Tariq? Christian didn't even arrive till later."

"But Sabina was right—he could've sent that text from *inside* the house," Kenny argues. "He could've been there all along. It doesn't prove anything."

"So where was Christian while Tariq was being attacked?" Vix frowns. "Hiding somewhere?"

"No," Kenny says, his eyes flicking to the rearview mirror as we reach a junction. "Hiding evidence."

"What?" I frown. "What evidence?"

"Lou, you can't bash someone's brain in without getting your hands dirty."

I flinch.

"Oh my God, Lou," Vix says suddenly. "Poppy's bag!"

"But there wasn't anything incriminating in there," I argue, turning in my seat to face her. "It was just jewelry and music and clothes—"

"*Bloodstained* clothes," Vix corrects, wide-eyed. "Lou, what if it's *Poppy's* blood?"

A shiver runs down my spine.

"*That's* why he hid it!" Kenny cries suddenly. "That's why he *didn't* give Poppy's bag to the police—why he withheld evidence."

"But then why would he tell *me* about it?" I counter. "Why wouldn't he just keep it safely hidden away?"

"It's like Sabina said." Kenny looks across at me. "He can't afford for anyone to discover the truth. Not now that Poppy's dead."

"Then why on earth would he send me to *fetch* it?" I protest. "It doesn't make any sense!"

"Actually . . . it makes perfect sense," Vix says slowly, her face grim. "Lou, maybe he didn't want you to *uncover* evidence. What if he's using you to *destroy* it!"

I swallow. "What?"

"Poppy's phone didn't prove his innocence, did it?" Vix says quickly. "It proved his *guilt*!"

I stare at her.

"'I'm coming to get you'? That text was a threat, Lou—*that's* why he asked you to find it."

"And that's why he told you to *delete* it," Kenny adds. "It proves he hurt Poppy—and that it wasn't an accident."

"No!" My mind spins. "No, Christian wouldn't *deliberately* hurt anyone!"

"Lou," Kenny says gently. "Look at your throat."

A chill runs down my spine as I remember the blade pressing against my neck, his iron grip hurting my arms as I pretended to be Christian's hostage. It had seemed awfully real. . . .

"It all makes sense!" Kenny cries. "Leo's grandad has just died, which means his allotment's no longer a safe hiding place—he might have been worried about a new owner finding Poppy's bag with the bloodstained T-shirt and her *phone* . . . and maybe her diary. . . ."

My breath catches. *The USB necklace.*

"And if the police got hold of that kind of evidence, they could use it to convict him of murder," Vix says quietly.

"He couldn't let that happen," Kenny says quickly. "But he couldn't retrieve Poppy's bag *himself* either—it's right in the middle of his old neighborhood—he wouldn't have lasted five minutes if anyone recognized him. So he sent you." Kenny covers my hand with his as we stop at traffic lights. "He *used* you, Lou."

"No." My voice comes out hoarse, hesitant. "He cares about me."

"Like he cared about Poppy?" Kenny asks.

I snatch my hand away as my eyes fill with tears.

"He used you to get Poppy's bag so he can destroy any remaining evidence, *and* to delete his incriminating text message, *and* to escape from the police," Kenny continues. "And it worked, too."

I close my eyes, feeling sick as I remember how Christian desperately grabbed Poppy's bag before fleeing from the police, how worried he was when her phone wasn't in there—how *relieved* when I'd answered it. Would he have ever contacted me again if I hadn't got Poppy's phone? If I didn't have something he needed?

Of course not. Kenny's right. He was just using me all along.

"How could I be so *stupid*?" I cry, angry tears scorching my eyes. "Me, of all people! I *knew* what he'd done—I tracked him down to get revenge for Poppy and I let him con me!" I shake my head, my insides churning with guilt and shame and humiliation as the events of the last few days whirl wildly in my head. "All this time I've been feeling *guilty* for lying to *him*! I can't believe he convinced me he was *innocent,* that he—" I break off, unable to say the words. *That I was starting to think he loved me—that I was falling for him . . .*

I screw my eyes shut against the tears stinging inside. "I'm such an *idiot*!"

"It's not your fault, Titch," Kenny says gently. "He's a con man, after all. He's good at deceiving people."

"He had me fooled too." Vix squeezes my shoulder.

"But not you, Kenny," I realize. "You never trusted him. Why?"

"Guess I'm just smarter than you guys." He smiles wryly, his eyes fixed on the road ahead.

"Yeah, whatever!" Vix scoffs.

"I can't believe he was using me this whole time," I say numbly. "He used me to get away with murder . . . and I let him."

"Hey," Kenny says. "He hasn't gotten away yet."

"What do you mean?"

"The USB necklace," Vix interjects, catching Kenny's train of thought. "Christian still thinks you're looking for the code at Poppy's house, right? Which means he'll call you again."

Kenny nods.

"And when he does"—I take a deep breath—"this time I'll be ready."

"Oh, sweetheart!" Aunt Harriet flings open the car door when we arrive at the house. "Oh, you poor love, you're all red and puffy—here you go." She pulls a manky tissue from her sleeve before I can protest.

"Allow me." Kenny winks, passing me a small pack of Kleenex.

"Oh, what a gentleman," Aunt Harriet simpers. "And so handsome and clever too. You've found a keeper there, Lulu—we had a lovely chat this morning, didn't we, Kenny?"

"Well, *I* certainly did." Kenny beams. "But I was worried I bored you."

"Bored me?" Aunt Harriet laughs. "Pah! I could listen to you all day!"

"I'll leave you to it, then." I smile, extracting myself quickly.

"I think Kenny's found a fan," Vix comments, following me as I pull on my sunglasses and head through the side gate. "You should have seen him earlier, schmoozing away."

I smile. "He's a star."

"I guess the ability to charm women, think on your feet, and lie convincingly comes in handy sometimes," Vix says, a note of bitterness in her voice.

"And it can also be heartbreaking," I add, slipping my arm through hers. We've both been victims of *that*.

The garden is scattered with people catching the last of the day's sun, sitting in plastic chairs on the lawn, and standing in groups on the patio. I duck my head and try to thread my way through them to find Aunt Grace, when suddenly a man steps backwards, treading heavily on my foot.

"I'm so sorry!" he cries, catching my arm as I stumble. "Are you all right?"

I stare up at his dirty-blond hair and those dark brown eyes and my heart pounds painfully. *It's the man from Joe's flat!* I'm sure it is. The man who cut the sheets, who chased us in the car—who burned down Christian's house.

"You okay, love?" He frowns.

Sweat beads on my forehead. Does he recognize me? But I've cut and dyed my hair since Joe's flat, and he couldn't have seen me clearly in the car chase, could he? And thank God I'm wearing sunglasses!

"Lulu? Are you okay?"

My head snaps round the group to find Neil looking at me, concerned.

"Hope this dope didn't break your toes—Jonno weighs a ton!"

Confusion spikes in my veins. Neil *knows* the thug? He's *friends* with him? Christian said the police must've leaked his location to the vigilantes—but it never crossed my mind that *Neil* could be involved! Not my kind, caring, funny godfather *Neil . . .* ?

But he was in Sheffield just before the arson attack, I remember, and all he could talk about was the flaws in the justice system. . . . *It makes me sick that innocent, decent, good people like Jim rot in jail, while the guilty live it up, walk free,* get new identities . . . *it's not right. Ever.* That's *why I'm really here.*

I feel dizzy. What if *Neil's* behind the whole thing?

"Lulu?" He frowns. "Somebody grab a chair for her, will you?"

"Lou, are you all right?" Vix asks.

"No!" I turn quickly. "I just . . . I need to—"

"Lulu, sweetheart, are you okay?" Aunt Grace hurries out of the house. She slips her arm protectively around my shoulders. "Come on, let's go and get a cuppa, eh?"

Gratefully, I follow her into the kitchen, where we find Uncle Doug boiling the kettle.

"Is there enough for three more?" Aunt Grace asks as Vix gets me a chair.

"Of course!" He smiles at me. "You look like you need some TLC."

"What?" I look up sharply.

"Tea, a good listener, and choccie biccies."

My skin prickles as Vix's eyes meet mine. *That's* where Christian got the phrase from—Poppy. I *knew* it sounded familiar—Uncle Doug used to say it whenever we went round to visit—I just couldn't place it till now.

"Biscuit?" Uncle Doug offers me the packet.

"Actually, no, I—" I stand up. "I think I might just . . . go and lie down, if that's okay?"

"Of course," Aunt Grace says, squeezing my shoulder. "Let me know if you need anything. And, Lulu? Your tribute was so lovely today. Thank you."

I smile quickly, then slip into the hall, ducking my head as I edge past the other mourners and head upstairs to my bedroom, desperate to be alone. But as I pass Poppy's room I stop. The door is ajar, and I can't help but peer inside.

Everything is exactly as she left it, frozen in time. Her Beatles duvet and matching sheets, her fluffy rabbit slippers, even her photo calendar still hangs on June of last year, the following months bare of photos and full of empty squares where Poppy's life should have been.

"It's blank!" Poppy had laughed in surprise when Uncle Jim gave her the calendar for Christmas two years ago.

"I know." He'd grinned. "That's because you have to fill it up with all your happiest moments of this year—and we don't know what they'll be yet."

"But, Dad, I don't have a camera!"

299

"Oh, yes you do!" He held up a shiny present.

Poppy's shrieks of delight were deafening as she unwrapped the digital camera, then threw herself at Aunt Grace and Uncle Jim, hugging them tight and thanking them a million times.

I step closer to the calendar, drawn to the photo—Millie's birthday picnic. Uncle Jim and Aunt Grace beam at the camera, their eyes sparkling in the sunshine while Millie balances precariously on my shoulders, her laughing face covered in chocolate as she tries to burst the bubbles I'm blowing.

Beneath us, Poppy's shadow stretches across the picnic rug, giving us all a thumbs-up as she takes the picture. I gaze at the shadow, feeling unbearably sad that she wasn't in the photo with us. That she never will be again. I look back at our laughing faces, so joyful, so carefree.

Uncle Jim was right—we were all blissfully oblivious to what the future had in store.

I'd come home from boarding school just for the day, I remember, for Millie's birthday. Poppy had begged me to stay for the whole weekend, to have a kind of slumber party catch-up that evening, but I didn't—I had to rush back to school for some reason. I can't even remember why. If only I'd known that was the last time I'd ever see her awake, alive.

My eyes trail sadly down, past her noticeboard full of photos and invitations to parties and events she never went to, past her beloved guitar, to her bedside table, the lid of the favorite perfume spray lying carelessly beside its bottle, waiting for her to return. I sink down on her bed, lift the bottle to my nose, close my eyes—and instantly she's with me. *Poppy.* I remember her sitting here with me on her bed giggling about the new shoes she'd just splurged on, how she'd be broke for months, but they were *so* worth it. "After all," she'd said, her eyes sparkling, "a girl only gets one prom—and I intend to make the most of it!"

I smile. But when I open my eyes she's gone. I spot the shoes, gleaming beside her wardrobe. Still waiting. Still unworn. She never got her one prom.

Yes, everything is exactly how she left it. Almost.

Her bedside lamp and computer are missing—smashed in the struggle—and her moon and stars rug has moved. It used to be in the center of the room, but now it's right beside her bed, under my feet. Tentatively, I lift up the nearest corner with my toe.

It's still there. The dark reddish-brown stain that wouldn't come out of the wood, however much Aunt Grace scrubbed, tears gushing from her eyes, her knuckles red and raw. I let the rug drop, shuddering as I imagine Poppy sitting right here that afternoon, completely unaware of what was about to happen.

Someone knocks on the front door, and as I glance outside to see yet more mourners arriving it suddenly hits me like a sucker-punch: *It couldn't have been Tariq—it could never have been Tariq!*

The front door is directly below Poppy's bedroom—so when Tariq broke in she would have *heard* him, then *seen* him downstairs—so why didn't she run to the door, or the landing, or lock herself in her en suite bathroom? Why would she just sit here, *waiting* for him?

The answer stares me in the face. Because, while Tariq may have broken in afterwards, Poppy's killer didn't have to. She was expecting him, waiting for him, trusting him.

After all, he was her boyfriend. . . .

My skin crawls as I remember Christian's hands on me, his lips on mine.

Did he touch you in the same way, Poppy? Make you feel the way I felt?

A tear rolls slowly down my cheek.

Did you love him too?

I brush it away roughly.

301

But you wouldn't have even been here if it wasn't for me.

I close my eyes.

I'm so sorry, Poppy.

"Lulu?"

My eyes fly open. Millie is clinging to the doorframe, her blond fringe flopping in front of her wide brown eyes as she stares at me.

"Hey, munchkin." I smile, holding out my arms. She scampers into the room and crawls onto my lap, wrapping her arms tightly round my neck.

"You okay?" I whisper into her hair. She smells of strawberries.

She nods, then whispers back. "Are you hiding?"

"No."

Yes.

"I'm just remembering Poppy, and all the happy times we had together." I point to the calendar. "Remember your birthday party?"

She frowns, then shakes her head.

"You must do." I smile. "Poppy made the cake herself—just for you!"

She stares at the photo, then shakes her head again sadly. "I don't remember." Her chin drops to her chest, her hair falling down over her face, and I have to strain to hear her whisper.

"I don't remember her."

Her bottom lip juts out and breaks my heart.

Millie was only three when it happened, after all. It's over a quarter of her life ago. She must only really remember Poppy being in hospital.

I hug her tight. "Poppy loved you so much," I whisper. "She always read you all your favorite stories—especially *Don't Get Dirty, Gerty!* You used to want that one over and over and over again!"

"It's my favorite." Millie smiles.

"I know, and even though you asked for it a thousand times,

Poppy never got tired of reading it to you, and she always did the best voices."

"She did?"

I nod. "You know, when Poppy discovered she was going to be a big sister she was so excited, because she'd finally have someone to take care of, someone to read bedtime stories to, someone to love and cuddle and play with. She even tried to knit you a cardigan—she spent hours and *hours* on it—but she got the stitch sizes wrong, so it was enormous! See!" I nod at Poppy's giant teddy bear on her bed, wearing the oversized garment.

Millie stares at me, then giggles. "It's ginormous!"

"I know!" I laugh. "Poppy said that you might grow into it someday, so she asked Big Bear to keep it safe for you."

Millie reaches out and gently strokes the soft woolen sleeve.

"Shall we see if it fits now?" I reach over and tug the cardigan off the teddy bear and wrap it round Millie. She sticks her arms through the sleeves, but it still dwarfs her. She giggles.

"It's far too big!"

"Oh dear! Shall we put it back on Big Bear?"

"No," she says, snuggling into the soft wool, pulling it close around her. "Not yet."

I stroke Millie's hair as I cuddle her tight. "She loved playing with you. Hide-and-seek, and tea parties and shops—you had such fun! She was the kindest, most loving big sister anyone could ever hope for." I kiss Millie's head. "She always said the day you were born was the best day of her life."

Suddenly my breath catches. *Millie's birthday*. The best day of her life . . . 17 June. 17.06. That could be Poppy's passcode, couldn't it . . . ?

"What are you two up to?" I look up to see Uncle Jim leaning in the corridor, smiling.

303

"Daddy!" Millie runs over and leaps into his arms, while the prison guard lingers awkwardly in the doorway.

"Hello, princess." Uncle Jim grins, rubbing his nose against hers in an eskimo kiss. He looks around the room and sighs.

"We left it all here, waiting for her, for when she woke up," he says sadly, carrying Millie further into the room. "Her posters, her photographs, even her Beatles bedding." He smiles, smoothing the duvet gently with his long fingers. "I hoped that one day everything would be back to normal. I'd be back home, and she'd be back home, and we'd all be together again. A family." His hand stops moving and he just stares at the bed. "But now she'll never come back."

I don't know what to say. What do you say to a man who's just lost his beloved daughter? Who's been jailed for trying to protect her? Who's only home for a few hours for her funeral?

I place my hand over his, and he looks down at me, his huge eyes deep brown pools of sorrow.

"Will you tuck me in tonight, Daddy?" Millie asks.

"I'd love to, princess." He kisses her nose, then takes my hand, but as he sits down on the bed the rug slides beneath his feet, revealing the bloodstain.

Uncle Jim stiffens.

"The stain wouldn't come out," I tell him quietly. "We've tried everything."

"Some stains don't." He sighs. "Besides, however you try to get rid of it, or cover it up, I'd still see it. It's burned into my mind. I'll always know it's there—that one slip, one shift of the rug beneath my feet will reveal its ugliness for all to see."

Silently, I nudge the rug back over the mark.

"I'll never forget what happened here," he says heavily, closing his eyes and resting his chin on Millie's head. "Not for the rest of my life."

I squeeze his hand. It must be so much worse for him—he was here, he saw Poppy lying unconscious—he tried to save her . . . but he couldn't.

"Mummy!" Millie cries and I look up to see Aunt Grace, pale in the doorway.

"So this is where you're all hiding." She smiles weakly.

"We're playing hide-and-seek, like me and Poppy did." Millie grins and I smile.

"That sounds like a good idea," Aunt Grace says. "I swear I don't know half of the people in my living room."

"Come and sit with us," Millie says.

"Oh, I'm not sure if there's room," she says.

"There's always room for my girls." Uncle Jim shifts over and pats the bed next to him. "Come on, Grace."

She hesitates.

"Group hug, Mummy!" Millie cries, stretching out her chubby arms.

Aunt Grace smiles at her, then sits down gingerly on the very edge of the bed, her face troubled. Haunted by bad memories, I guess.

"It's so good to bè home," Uncle Jim sighs, squeezing us all tight. "It's been far too long." I smile as I hug him close. It's been far, *far* too long.

Suddenly the tune of "Yellow Submarine" breaks the silence and my clutch bag vibrates violently.

Aunt Grace freezes. "Isn't that Poppy's—"

"Poppy's ring tone, yes," I say quickly, standing up and hurrying towards the door. "We both got the same one."

"Best friends, huh?" Uncle Jim smiles.

"That's right." I flash him a swift smile. "Best friends. Excuse me."

I hurry down the corridor into the bathroom and lock the door before I pull Poppy's phone out and answer the call.

"Lou!" Christian cries. "Thank goodness! When you took so long to pick up I was worried something had happened to you."

"Like what?" I ask warily.

"Like you'd been arrested for snooping around a stranger's house or something!"

Oh, *that*.

"I'm fine," I whisper. "But I can't really talk right now."

"Of course. Sorry!" he apologizes. "I was just worried."

I soften.

"Did you get into Poppy's house? Did you find anything? The passcode?" he asks urgently.

Of course—*that's* what he's worried about.

"I think so," I tell him. "There are a few possibilities."

"Brilliant! What are they?"

I hesitate. If I tell him now, he can open the USB files—but what will he find? More evidence to destroy?

"Sorry. You said you can't talk," he sighs, misreading my hesitation.

"Let's meet later," I say suddenly. "Do it together."

"Okay. Can you come to the Internet café—A Byte to Eat, in Dartford—at five-thirty?"

"See you then."

"Great," Christian says, sounding relieved. "We're in this together, after all."

I hang up quickly as an icy chill shivers down my spine.

THIRTY-TWO

As I step nervously into the dingy Internet café I straighten my shoulders, trying desperately to look less anxious than I feel. There's a girl busily tapping on her phone behind the counter, but as I look around I realize there's only one customer—an old man round the corner from the desk, tucked almost out of view.

Shit. I sigh heavily. Christian didn't come. He's done a runner. Something in my voice must've spooked him, scared him off.

Frustration battles with relief inside me. Now I'll never have to face him again, but I'll never know what was on the memory stick either, or what really happened that night—though the very fact that he's not here speaks volumes.

"There you are, sweetheart!" the old man calls across at me and the girl at the counter looks up. "You're late!"

"What?" I turn. "No, I—" He doffs his cap and winks, and my jaw drops. *Christian!* "I mean, sorry, yes—I got held up." I hurry over.

He replaces his hat and smiles as I round the corner, out of sight of the girl. I barely recognize him now his hair's dyed gray beneath his flat cap, and he's dressed head to toe in tweed.

"Aren't you a sight for sore eyes?" He stands up to hug me, but I stiffen involuntarily.

"Sorry, do I reek?" He cringes, misreading my discomfort. "The clothes are from a charity shop, so they're a bit old."

"No—it's fine," I say hastily. "They're . . . nice."

"You're such a bad liar." He grins and I feel my cheeks flush.

"So let's try some of the possible passcodes," I say quickly.

"Great!" he says eagerly, pulling the USB necklace from his pocket and stabbing it into the computer.

This is it. *Now or never.*

I slip into the swivel chair and try a few different possibilities as Christian leans over my shoulder, his breath hot on my neck. Then finally, slowly, I type in Millie's birthday.

Immediately the files pop open.

"Yes!" Christian's eyes widen as he leans forward. I frown. He looks *excited,* not *nervous.*

I scroll through the files, looking for anything that could be a diary.

"Shit," Christian mutters as we reach the bottom of the list. "Nothing."

I don't understand. It *has* to be on here. I scan the list again carefully, then desperately perform a file search on *Leo, Glastonbury, tickets,* and *festival.* But there are no results.

"So that's it, then," Christian sighs. "No evidence."

My skin prickles. No evidence to exonerate him or no evidence he's lying? What would he have done if he'd found the diary and it disproved his story? Destroyed it? But he could have destroyed the USB stick anyway if he thought it would incriminate him—so why did he want to meet up with me, if not to try to prove his innocence?

"Bollocks," Christian sighs. "What about Poppy's phone? You bring it? Did you delete my text?"

The penny drops. So *that's* what he really came for—the phone. Of course. I've got the one piece of evidence the police could still use against him—besides the bloodstained T-shirt he's probably already destroyed.

I pretend to check my pockets. "Shit! I must've left it at the hotel—sorry!" I lie. There's no way I'm handing it over.

"Hotel?"

"Yeah—I can't pick up my car till tomorrow, so I checked into a Premier Inn on the other side of town," I bluff, hoping he won't want to risk coming all that way to get it.

"But you *have* deleted my text?" Christian asks anxiously.

"Of course!" I smile, lying through my teeth.

"At least that's something," he sighs. "I can't believe I phrased it like that—my one piece of evidence! And now no diary . . ." He sighs heavily. "That's it. It's over."

I look at him carefully. "What did you think would be in Poppy's diary?"

"I don't know. Some *mention* of me, at least, to prove I wasn't some stranger, proof that she knew me, that I was her friend."

"Her boyfriend?" I ask quietly, staring at the screen.

"What? No!" He swivels my chair to face him. "No, Lou—where's that come from?"

I shrug.

"I was just Poppy's friend, nothing more," he promises. "Just mates."

Sabina and Joe's words burn my ears. "But Joe said—"

"Joe doesn't have any female friends," Christian interrupts. "He thinks all girls who are friends are girlfriends—which is probably why he hasn't got any female friends."

"But you were going away together too. . . ."

"Well, yes—but not like *that*." He sighs. "Poppy seemed like she was going through a rough time, she wanted to get away—to go to Glastonbury—and she asked me to go with her for some company, because we liked the same kind of music. That's all."

"That's all?"

He lifts my chin with his finger.

"That's all. I swear," he says earnestly. "We were just mates."

I nod, surprised at the relief flooding my heart. *But what difference does it make?* my head argues. He could still have killed her. He could still be lying.

"So what now?" I whisper, watching him closely.

"Now . . . I don't have a choice. I have to disappear. If the police find me, they'll send me back to prison." He looks at me, his eyes filled with sorrow. "I can never see you again."

He strokes my hair from my cheek and my heart races despite myself.

"Thank you, Lou," he whispers.

"For what?" I ask.

"For everything." He smiles, those beautiful eyes deep in mine. "For trying. For a few wonderful days of hope. For believing in me."

He kisses me then, his lips so soft, so warm, my heart thrumming so loudly it's impossible to remember why I should pull away.

He couldn't have killed Poppy, he just *couldn't*! Every part of my being refuses to believe it. What was it Sabina said? *Sometimes it doesn't matter what the evidence says, what the world says, if you know something to be true in your heart.*

And I do. Christian didn't kill Poppy. He couldn't have. I've never been more absolutely sure of anything.

I trace his jawline with my fingertips, his high cheekbones, the prickly stubble, then gaze into those blue eyes that I could easily drown in, so bright, so clear.

"We'll find proof of your innocence," I promise, tears blurring my vision. "We will. We'll be together."

He pulls me into his arms and my heart aches as I inhale his familiar musky, foresty scent, memorizing the feel of his body against mine, my mind filled with dread. *What if we never find any evidence to exonerate him, never discover what truly happened?*

310

I hold Christian tighter, unable to let go. If I do, I might never see him again. Never know if he's safe or in danger, dead or alive. I squeeze my eyes shut, wishing with all my heart that this moment could last forever.

"I love you," I whisper, surprising myself with my own feelings.

He kisses my hair. "I love you too."

Suddenly he freezes in my arms and my eyes fly open as DI Goldsmith and two other policemen burst through the front door. "They must have followed you!" Christian cries, his eyes flying to the counter as another three officers rush in from the back entrance.

There's nowhere to run to, nowhere to hide.

"Leo Niles, you're surrounded," DI Goldsmith warns. "Now step forward with your hands up."

Christian sighs and pulls away, but I cling tighter. *Just one more minute.*

"Lou," he says gently. "Let go. It's okay." He kisses my cheek and finally, reluctantly, I let him slide from my arms.

Tears streak down my face as I watch them handcuff him and lead him out of the café into the waiting police car.

I close my eyes.

He's gone. It's over. And it's my fault.

After all, I called them.

THIRTY-THREE

"Do you need a lift, love?" DI Goldsmith smiles as I watch the car containing Christian disappear from sight. "I owe you, after all. I wasn't sure you'd keep your word."

"No thanks." I turn away, unable to face him for a second longer, feeling sick at my betrayal. I'm Judas—right down to the kiss.

"So, Cindy, let's make a deal, shall we?" DI Goldsmith had said after the sergeant told him who I really was at the police station. "If you promise to call me next time Niles gets in touch, I won't make you miss your cousin's funeral."

I had no choice. It was a promise I made just so that I could make it to Poppy's funeral—and one that I never intended to keep—but after meeting Sabina and talking to Vix and Kenny, I'd been so sure that Christian was guilty, that this could be my last chance to catch him, to make sure justice was served. . . .

And if by some miracle he *was* telling the truth, if Poppy's diary proved it like he claimed, then I could show the police and clear Christian's name once and for all.

But there was no diary on the USB. And now he's gone.

What have I done? I trudge gloomily down a couple of side streets till finally I'm back at Kenny's waiting car.

"Lou, what happened?" Vix cries as I slide numbly into the back-seat. "Are you okay?"

I shake my head. I've never been less okay in my life.

"Oh, sweetie!" Vix jumps out of the car and climbs into the back to hug me close. "It's going to be all right."

"It's not!" I tell her miserably. "Christian's *innocent*!"

"*What?*" Vix's eyes widen.

"He's innocent—and I've just sent him back to prison!"

"Wait—you found evidence on the USB stick?" Vix asks. "Poppy's diary? Isn't that good news?"

"But, Lou," Kenny says as we drive away. "Even if it proves they were friends, it doesn't mean—"

"There was no diary!" I interrupt wretchedly. "No evidence at all. There wasn't anything!"

Vix and Kenny look at each other.

"Then how do you know he's innocent?" she says quietly.

"I just . . . *know*," I tell them desperately. "I know, in my heart."

Vix squeezes my hand, her eyes troubled.

"Your heart?" Kenny repeats incredulously. He stops at traffic lights and turns and stares at me. "Your *heart?*"

I nod.

"*That's* the compelling evidence that's convinced you Christian *didn't* kill Poppy? You know he's innocent *in your heart?*" He laughs bitterly. "Jeez, he's good. He didn't even have to *lie* to you this time. His good looks and charm did it all!"

"Kenny, that's not fair!" I cry.

"No, Lou. You think he's innocent because you *fancy* him. You've fallen for him *and* his lies! I thought you were smarter than that."

"Kenny, stop it!" Vix hugs me tight. "It's okay, Lou. If Christian is innocent, we'll prove it—and he'll be safer in prison than on the run."

"*Will* he?" I challenge. "You really trust the police, after everything that's happened?"

"Oh, please!" Kenny groans, pulling away fast as the lights change. "You still think there's a big police conspiracy against him?"

"Actually, yes," I say hotly. "Why else was Neil chatting to one of the thugs at the funeral?"

"Because, *as you said yourself,* it's likely some of the guys after Leo know your family!" Kenny says. "That's why they feel so strongly—they're trying to protect you!"

"Fine, but that doesn't explain how they found his house in Sheffield in the *first* place, does it?" I challenge. "The police were the only ones who knew where Christian was—they *must* have tipped them off!"

"They weren't the *only* ones," Kenny argues.

I roll my eyes. "Besides Christian."

"And you," he reminds me. "And me."

"Well, yes, but . . ." Kenny's eyes meet mine in the rearview mirror and suddenly my blood runs cold.

"You?" I say slowly. "*You* leaked Christian's location in Sheffield?"

He doesn't answer.

"Kenny!" Vix cries, horrified.

"Stop the car," I say.

"Lou—"

"Stop the car NOW!"

He swings over to the side of the road and I leap out.

"Where are you *going*?" Kenny calls, climbing out of the car and hurrying after me as I march down the street.

"Anywhere away from you!" I yell over my shoulder, my mind reeling. *Kenny* leaked Christian's location? All this time I thought it was the police! He *let* me think that—he *lied* to me!

"Lou, come back!" Vix cries, her heels clacking on the pavement behind me.

"Lou, it was for you!" Kenny yells. "Everything I've done is for *you!*"

I whirl round to face him. "For *me?*"

"I was worried about you," Kenny says. "You were getting in too deep, you were *dating Leo,* for God's sake—none of that was part of the original plan. I had to do *something!* I didn't know what he was capable of—what if he'd hurt you?"

"So you told violent thugs to set fire to Christian's *house?*"

"No!" he cries. "No, I just leaked his location on Twitter and Facebook. I didn't know Poppy had just died, that they'd react so strongly—I thought they'd just scare him and the police would move him somewhere else. Away from Sheffield. Away from you." He looks at me.

"You were jealous," Vix says quietly.

"What about Joe's flat?" I demand. "Did you leak *that* address too?"

"I had to!" Kenny protests.

"*Jesus,* Kenny!"

"You texted me asking for help!" he reminds me. "You said you were trapped—you were in *danger!*"

"So why didn't you just call the police?" I cry.

"I already had," Kenny insists. "I called them as soon as you stopped at the block of flats—I was tracking your signal—I told the police that you were missing, you weren't answering your phone and I thought you were with Leo, but I couldn't give them the flat number because the tracker can't distinguish multistory locations."

"And?"

"They told me you hadn't been missing long enough, that they'd had dozens of sightings of Leo, that Jonas Towers was a huge complex and they'd follow it up in due course, but as I hadn't actually *seen* him there it wasn't a priority. They said that as you were an adult I should call back after twenty-four hours.

"I panicked, Lou. We were still halfway to London—I was worried we wouldn't reach you in time—so I tweeted Leo's location again, saying that he had a hostage. Then when you texted with Joe's address they were already on-site, so I just updated them—it was the quickest way I could save you."

"*Save* me?" I stare at him. "You sent a dangerous mob to the flat, putting us both in danger—so you could *rescue* me?"

"No! I never meant for you to be in danger—that's why I told them you were a hostage and why I waited till you were safely at the allotments next time—" Kenny stops abruptly as he realizes his mistake.

"*Next* time?" I stare at him. "Oh my God, it was you who sent them to the Travelodge too!" I stare at him in horror. "Why would you *do* that?"

"You wouldn't listen!" Kenny protests. "Vix and I warned you Leo was a con man, but you didn't want to hear it, you wouldn't see sense, so I seized my opportunity while you were out. I couldn't rely on the police to turn up in time, and besides, they'd have just locked Leo up for the last few months of his burglary sentence. That's not what you wanted when we went into this—you wanted him to pay, to suffer, to live life looking over his shoulder, so I leaked his location once you were safely out of harm's way." He looks at Vix. "Once I *thought* you were out of harm's way."

I turn on Vix. "You *knew* about this? You were in on it? Keeping me out of the picture while Kenny went *psycho?*"

"No, Lou, I didn't know, I *swear!*" Vix cries.

"*I'm* a psycho?" Kenny yells. "You're the one who's fallen for the con man who killed Poppy!"

"He *didn't* kill Poppy!" I counter. "But those thugs nearly killed *him*—they could've killed me!"

"They wouldn't have *touched* you!"

"You don't know that, you don't know what they're capable of—they were violent vigilantes on a mission—they were out of control!"

"You're such a hypocrite!" Kenny cries. "*You're* a vigilante, remember? *You* were on a mission! You went to Sheffield with the specific intention of getting revenge."

"Not revenge," I argue. "Justice!"

"But you got sidetracked, distracted by a handsome face—it's pathetic! You let him flatter you, seduce you, *con* you into believing he's *innocent,* for God's sake! You completely forgot why you were really there—to make Leo pay, to watch him suffer. Everything that's happened is all because of you—it's what you *wanted*!"

"*No!*" I protest. "I never wanted Christian to get hurt!"

"No," Kenny says bitterly. "You wanted him to kiss you and hold you and tell you he loved you—"

"I wanted *justice!*"

"Well, it's the strangest justice *I've* ever seen!" Kenny yells. "Jumping into bed with your cousin's *killer!*"

Before I can stop myself I slap his face, hard.

Vix gasps as Kenny just stares at me, shocked.

Then he swallows, his voice deathly quiet. "The most tragic thing of all is that you're still brainwashed. Even now. Despite all the evidence that points to Leo being Poppy's *murderer*." He shakes his head. "You're the sick one, Titch."

Tears burn my eyes as I spin on my heel and run away, as far and as fast as I can.

Kenny's right; I *started* all this. If I'd never gone looking for Christian, if I'd never asked Kenny for help, Christian's location would still be secret, his house wouldn't have been attacked, he wouldn't have gone on the run, wouldn't be injured, and he wouldn't be back in jail now.

And he's innocent. I know it doesn't make sense—I know all the new evidence proves Tariq couldn't have done it, that it had to be Christian, but . . . but I just don't believe it. But how can I *prove* he's innocent, without any evidence?

What a complete and utter mess!

And I've only got myself to blame.

"Sweetheart! Thank goodness!" Aunt Grace opens the door and wraps herself round me like a warm blanket as the taxi pulls off. "Are you all right? Detective Goldsmith called and told us what happened."

"You're a brave girl," Uncle Jim adds, stepping forward and enveloping me in his arms. "What happened? How did you manage to find Niles when the entire police force couldn't?"

I hesitate. How can I explain? They think Christian's a monster, that he hurt Poppy, so how can I tell them I protected him—that he's innocent? How can I explain that once you get to know him he's the sweetest, kindest, gentlest guy in the world?

"I don't want to talk about it," I mumble.

"Of course you don't, sweetheart." Aunt Grace squeezes my hand.

"I'm just glad he's not out there anymore," Uncle Jim adds. "That he's safe behind bars."

"Me too," I say honestly. *Safe* behind bars. I hope so.

"Do you want something to eat?" Aunt Grace asks. "You must be starving. We've heaps of sandwiches left."

"No, I'm fine, thank you. Just tired. Do you mind if I go and lie down?"

"Of course, sweetie." Aunt Grace smiles. "Millie will be thrilled you're home—it might cheer her up a bit."

I frown. "What's wrong with Millie?"

"I have to go back in half an hour," Uncle Jim sighs, glancing at the prison officer sipping tea on the sofa. "The justice system is only compassionate up to a point. Millie's not taking it well. She's hidden my shoes."

I smile sadly. "Where is she now?"

"In bed, waiting for me to tuck her in," Uncle Jim says.

"Already?" I say. "It's only six-thirty."

"I know, but she was desperate for me to tell her a bedtime story before I go, and it had to be *Don't Get Dirty, Gerty!* for some reason—it's taken me ages to find it!" He holds up the picture book with the messy polar bear beaming on the cover.

Hide-and-seek and *Don't Get Dirty, Gerty!* I smile as I follow him upstairs. He's putting such a brave face on everything, when all the while he must be dreading that terrible return to jail after such a brief time at home. I sigh as I glance back down at Aunt Grace, so gaunt after burying her eldest daughter, and now she has to say goodbye to her husband all over again.

As Uncle Jim enters Millie's room I head to my own.

"Princess! What's wrong? Why are you crying?" His words stop me in my tracks and my eyes fly to Millie's open door.

"You were a-ages and I th-thought you'd g-gone away again!" I hear Millie whimper. "W-without saying g-goodbye!"

"Oh, sweetheart, I promised I'd read you a story first, didn't I? I don't break my promises, princess," he says softly. "Now, let's see what that naughty Gerty's up to, shall we? *Gerty was very excited. She was going to Jenny's party that afternoon. . . .*" He begins the familiar tale, his voice filled with forced brightness. "Isn't that exciting?"

"Mm-hmm." She sniffles and my heart aches.

Poor Millie. What a rough time she's had—losing a sister she can barely remember, now getting her daddy back for just a few short hours, knowing he'll be snatched away again any moment.

I slump into my room and close the door. It hurts when you lose someone you love after so short a time. *Especially when there's nothing you can do about it.*

I plunge my hands into my pockets miserably. Suddenly my eyes fly open.

Maybe there *is* something I can do. I hurry over to my old desktop computer, pull the USB necklace from my pocket, and plug it in.

It's worth a try, I reason. It might all be homework and photos and stuff, but by some miracle there might actually be *something—anything*—proving Christian's innocence, and I'm going to bloody well search every single document till I'm sure.

I type in the passcode and a whole bunch of files pop onto the screen. I painstakingly open each one and scroll through it carefully. Essays, coursework, photos . . . Then, suddenly, a document opens filled with different PIN numbers and passwords.

I glance at the file name: *Cryptology.* Nice.

I scan the list of passwords quickly. Online banking, email, Facebook, blog, Twitter, Movie-Memories . . . I frown. I've never heard of Movie-Memories. I open a webpage and type it into the browser and instantly a website opens: *Movie-Memories—the secure way to share your video diary with family and friends.*

I stare at the screen. A video diary?

I glance back at the password document and quickly type Poppy's password and user name into the login box. A list of dates and times scrolls down in front of me, each with a frozen thumbnail of Poppy looking into the camera beside them.

I click on one at random and my heart leaps as Poppy springs to life, grinning at the camera, wearing a paper party hat and blowing a plastic whistle.

"I can't believe I'm sixteen!" she squeals, her eyes shining excitedly. "I'm old enough to smoke—legally—but ugh!" She screws up her nose and I smile. "Old enough to get married—scary!" She pulls a horrified face. "Old enough to play the lottery . . ." She waves a pink ticket at the webcam. "Who knows, by the time anyone sees this I might be a multimillionaire! What a cool birthday *that* would be!"

I grin. She looks so happy.

"Well, it's already pretty damn cool actually, as I got some in*credible* prezzies! Look at these!" She hoists her leg in the air to show off a brown leather knee-high boot. "Four-inch heels!" she squeals. "I don't have to be a midget anymore!"

I laugh out loud. Poppy was always paranoid about her height and I was always jealous she was so petite and delicate.

"And look what Lulu got me!" She holds up a shiny MP3 player. "*And* she filled it with all my favorite songs—I have my very own sound track! How cool is *that*? Do I have the best cousin in the world or what? Thanks, Lulu!" She blows a kiss at the camera and I beam.

"I feel like the luckiest girl in the world." She smiles straight at the camera. "I wonder where I'll be in another sixteen years? *What* I'll be? What are you now, Poppy Willoughby-White?" She taps the screen. "A dropout? A housewife? Or did you finally fulfill your life-long ambition of playing lead guitar in a band? Of course, if I win the lottery tonight, none of that will matter! The life of a multimillionaire would suit me very nicely, thank you very much—and I could start my own band! Now excuse me, darlings, but my presence is required in the kitchen to eat vast quantities of birthday cake!" She blows another kiss at the camera, then reaches forward and clicks the webcam off.

I stare at the screen. *The luckiest girl in the world* . . . My heart aches for her. She would've made a wonderful guitarist. A wonderful anything, if she'd had the chance.

I scan the list of diary entries till I find the last one, dated 24 June—the day she was attacked! Quickly, I click the link.

"So this is going to be my last entry for a couple of days." Poppy smiles. "Because I am going to . . ." She beats a drumroll on her desk. "Glastonbury! Whoop, whoop! I just hope it doesn't flood this year, as Wellies *so* aren't a good look on me. *Why* hasn't someone designed Wellies with wedges? Hello?" She rolls her eyes. "Actually, I wouldn't have time to chat at all except Leo's running late. Again. *Typical!*"

I stare at the screen in disbelief—this is it—proof! Evidence that Christian was telling the truth. Poppy *was* going away with him, they *were* friends, and this proves it—from her own lips!

"I wish he'd hurry up, though." She checks her watch anxiously. "I can't wait to get away. Mum and Millie have gone to Gran's for the weekend, and—"

Suddenly there's a faint noise in the background and Poppy glances out of the window. Then her face falls. From further inside the house I hear a door slam; then heavy footsteps stomp up the stairs.

Shit. This is it.

I stare intently at the screen, watching, waiting, my breath tight in my chest, my heart pounding.

But is it Tariq—or Christian?

Poppy hurriedly fumbles with the computer mouse, the keyboard, the webcam—then suddenly her bedroom door bangs open, making us both jump. A man stands in the doorway, his face red with rage, and my jaw drops as all the feeling seeps from my body.

It's Uncle Jim.

THIRTY-FOUR

I stare at the screen, my breath trapped in my lungs.

"Poppy," Uncle Jim pants. "You're here."

But what's *he* doing there? My head spins crazily. It doesn't make sense—he's not meant to be here yet—he said he got home later. Why would he *lie*?

"Poppy. Sweetheart. What's your bag doing by the front door?" He stares at her, his eyes dark, his breath heavy.

Poppy squirms. "I—"

"You going somewhere, angel?" He steps towards her, his words slurring together. "You running away?"

"No . . . no, I was just—"

"Liar!" I flinch as he knocks a stack of DVDs crashing to the floor. Christian was right—Uncle Jim's completely wasted. I've never seen him like this. But *why*? Why would he get trashed that afternoon, when he hardly ever even drinks?

"You were just going to sneak off behind my back?" he yells, his voice cracking. "You were going to leave me?!"

"No, Daddy, I'm sorry, please—" Poppy begs.

"You don't love me," he slurs, shaking his head. "Yerown father." He turns away.

"I do!" Poppy protests, racing after him, grabbing his arm. "Daddy, I do!"

"Just—do what you want. Leave me alone." He shrugs her off, but she clings to him.

"Daddy, please!"

"Gerroff me!" He tries to shake her loose.

"Daddy—"

"*Get off me!*" he bellows, shoving her hard. My heart stops as she smacks the back of her head on the bedpost, smashing her bedside lamp as she crumples to the floor.

My blood runs cold in my veins, my eyes wide, disbelieving.

Uncle Jim killed Poppy.

I feel sick as I stare at her unmoving body. *Call an ambulance!* I want to scream at him. *Help her—do something!*

But he just staggers backwards, his hands covering his face as he groans miserably.

I can hear someone shouting in the background; then there's the sound of frenzied knocking, but Uncle Jim doesn't seem to notice. He hasn't even realized Poppy's hurt.

"Shit, I'm sorry." His shoulders slump as he crouches down and gingerly picks up the broken pieces of her lamp. "It was your favorite— Shit! Ouch!" He winces suddenly and sucks his thumb. "Bloody glass!" He grabs a pair of scissors from Poppy's desk and begins carefully prying the shards of glass from his thumb. "I'm sorry, angel, it's just—I can't do this!" He begins to sob. "I can't pick up the pieces—I can't fix it! I can't fix this and it hurts so much." Tears gush through his words and he buries his face in his hands. "Please don't go, Poppy—I need you. Please?"

But Poppy doesn't reply.

There's a sound like shattering glass in the background. The downstairs window.

"Please, Poppy." Uncle Jim turns to her, but she doesn't move. A pool of dark blood seeps from her head.

"Poppy?" His tone changes in an instant as he scrambles to her side. My heart beats fast as tears fill my eyes, praying for the impossible, yet already knowing there's no hope.

"Poppy, baby, are you okay?" He strokes her face, blood covering his hands. "Oh God, no. *Poppy!* Poppy, answer me, angel. Wake up!"

Suddenly her bedroom door flies open and an Asian man rushes in.

Tariq.

"I'm sorry to intrude, but I heard a commotion and— Oh my God!" He stares at Poppy's bleeding body. "Have you called an ambulance? What happened?" He pulls his mobile phone from his pocket.

"Who are you?" Uncle Jim lurches to his feet, grabbing Tariq's shirt and pushing him against the wall, his mobile clattering to the floor. "What are you doing here?"

Tariq stares at him. "I'm Tariq—Tariq Khan—I came to pick up Poppy, but—"

"You came to pick her up?" Uncle Jim frowns.

"Yes, but—"

"You! *You* did this!"

"What? No!"

"You were going to take her away!" Uncle Jim rages, tears streaking his cheeks. "You're the reason she was going! *That's why we fought!*"

"No, I—"

"How *dare* you!" Uncle Jim screams at him. "How dare you come into my house! How dare you try to take my daughter away from me! Thieving Paki scum—you're all the same!"

"What?"

"Look at her—*look* what you made me *do!*" He points at Poppy and Tariq seizes his chance, squirming from Uncle Jim's grip, but he's not fast enough.

Uncle Jim whips round to grab him and the blades of the scissors plunge into Tariq's back. He screams in agony.

"Shit!" Uncle Jim's eyes widen, the blades gleaming in his shaking hand. "I didn't mean—"

"Help!" Tariq yells, running for the door. "Help! Somebody!"

"No! Stop!" Uncle Jim cries, lunging after Tariq and knocking him over. Tariq cries out again as his head smacks against the floor.

"Calm down!" Uncle Jim hisses. "It was an accident! I'm sorry!"

Tariq moans and closes his eyes.

"Shit!" Uncle Jim panics. "Shit! Shit! *Shit!* This is your fault! Look what you've done!" Tears gush from his face as he pulls out a pair of handcuffs. "Just stay here and calm down while I . . . while I work out what to do."

He snaps the handcuffs round Tariq's wrist, but he doesn't react.

"Shit!" Uncle Jim stares from Tariq's unmoving body to Poppy's for a long moment, sobbing and running shaky hands through his hair, his expression wild, desperate, panicked. He picks up the bloodstained scissors and stares at them in horror.

Suddenly my heart jumps as Christian appears in the bedroom doorway behind him.

Run! I want to scream. *Run away now!*

"Poppy, are you ready? Oh my God!" Christian grabs Uncle Jim's arm and he whips round, startled. The scissors graze Christian's chest as he springs backwards.

He stares at Uncle Jim in terror, then darts back through the bedroom door, Poppy's pink rucksack bouncing on his back.

Uncle Jim moves to follow, then stops, drops the scissors, and covers his face with his hands as he screams with misery.

I flinch involuntarily as he reels towards the webcam and collapses against Poppy's desk, sending books and pens scattering to the floor. Then suddenly the video jolts and abruptly blacks out.

I stare at the blank screen, feeling clammy, cold, sick with horror. Uncle Jim did this. Uncle Jim did all of this.

Suddenly I notice a second face reflected back at me from the black screen, and twist quickly to see a shadowy figure standing in the doorway.

Uncle Jim.

THIRTY-FIVE

"Lulu, I—" Uncle Jim takes a step closer and I spring from the computer chair, back away.

"You did this," I say quietly, my eyes wide.

"Lu, please—"

"You killed Poppy!"

In one swift move he's next to me, his hand pressed tight over my mouth. I struggle against him, squirming and kicking as he pins me with his huge arm.

"Please," he begs. "Please, Lulu, just listen. I'll let go, just please, hear me out."

I scowl at him, but I'm not going anywhere—he's too strong. Reluctantly, I nod.

Tentatively, he moves his hand away from my mouth. I'm tempted to scream, but something in his eyes stops me. He looks even more terrified than I am. Aunt Grace and Millie are nearby, after all. A single scream and they'd come running. Not to mention the prison officer.

"Thank you," he says, his breath heavy. "Thank you."

I glare at him, rub my jaw. "You hurt me."

"I'm sorry," he says. "I'm so sorry, I didn't mean to. I just wanted— I need a chance to explain."

"Poppy's video diary seems pretty explanatory to me," I say

coldly. "You killed her. And you killed Tariq." Tears stream down my cheeks. "You're a murderer."

"No!" he cries, his eyes filled with pain. "No, it was an accident!"

"You handcuffed him to the bed!" I argue. "Then you told everyone *he* attacked Poppy—that it was a burglary gone wrong!"

He hangs his head, covers his face with his hands. "Oh God . . ."

"I bet you thought you'd got away with it too, when he died, and Poppy fell into a coma—when there was no one left to tell the truth. What a lucky escape!"

"No!" His head snaps up. "No, I'd . . . I'd give anything, *anything* . . ." He screws his eyes shut, his voice dropping to a whimper. "I'd give anything to have her back—anything at all."

"Maybe you shouldn't have killed her, then," I counter.

"Lulu." He looks up at me, his face lined with grief. "It was an accident—you have to believe me—I never meant to . . ." He shakes his head wretchedly. "I'd been out drinking—too much— but it had been such a rough day. Grace had gone and I—I needed one." He sighs miserably. "More than one. Then I came home and I found Poppy's bag packed by the door and I just—I don't know what happened—I felt so hurt, so angry. I wasn't thinking, I just snapped. I couldn't let her go—I had to stop her—I don't even remember what happened. One minute we were arguing, the next—" He breaks off abruptly, his face ashen, like he's about to throw up.

"You pushed her," I tell him. "You pushed her and she smacked her head on the bedpost."

He nods, tears streaking his cheeks as his face crumples. "I couldn't wake her up. She wouldn't answer—wouldn't move." He snatches a breath. "She was dead—I thought she was dead. . . ."

"But you couldn't be sure!" I protest. "Why didn't you call an ambulance? They might have been able to save her!"

"I know!" he sobs. "Don't you think I've reproached myself for that a million times? I wasn't *thinking* straight—I'd had too much to drink. I was stupid. And I thought she was already dead." He covers his face with his hands and curls over like a child.

"And Tariq?"

"He came from nowhere!" Uncle Jim's face grows wild. "He was going to call the police! I couldn't let him call them, they wouldn't understand—I had to stop him!"

"So you stabbed him."

"I didn't mean to!" he protests. "I just meant to grab him, but the scissors were still in my hand. . . . It was an accident." He shakes his head. "But then I couldn't let him go—I had to explain!"

"So you handcuffed him to the bed."

He nods. "I panicked. I had to stop him, that's all. That's all I could think about—*I have to stop him!* I never meant . . ." His words disolve into sobs. "That poor boy. That poor, poor boy."

I close my eyes, but I can still see the terrible expression on Tariq's face, the blood staining his clothes.

"Then suddenly another boy was there."

I open my eyes. *Christian.*

"I didn't even hear him come in—he just grabbed my arm, startled me, and as I spun round I . . ." He blinks quickly as tears gush down his face. "I don't know what happened, but suddenly he was bleeding too. Then he ran—ran out the door and I . . ." Uncle Jim shakes his head heavily. "I didn't know what to do."

I swallow hard. "Why didn't you tell the police the truth?"

"I . . . I couldn't. I couldn't even speak, function—I just sat there in that room of horror, just staring at what I'd done, unable to believe it was real. It was a nightmare. I *wish* it was a nightmare." He closes his eyes. "It's haunted my dreams every single night, reliving that scene, praying that when I wake up it will all disappear, that I'll have a second chance, that Poppy'll still be here, still be alive." Tears flood his words. "But she never will. She'll never come back. Because of me. I killed her—my baby girl, my angel. . . ."

I shake my head. "But how could you—how could you let Tariq and Leo take the blame?"

"How could I tell Grace what I'd done?" he asks in return, his red-rimmed eyes wide. "She was destroyed by what happened. How could I tell her it was me who hurt Poppy? How could I tell you, or Millie? Everyone was already hurting so much, how could I make it worse?" He swallows hard. "They could lock me up for the rest of my life, and I wouldn't care. I've lost my daughter. And knowing she's gone, knowing that it's all my fault"—his voice cracks—"that's worse than any prison sentence. But to lose all of you too? It'd kill me."

I bite my lip.

"The police—my old team, Harry Goldsmith—they drew their own conclusions, and I was too numb at first to think about what had really happened. And then it was just easier to go along with it. Tariq was—was already dead. There was nothing I could do to help him," he says wretchedly. "And Leo—I tried to make sure Leo got a lighter sentence, told them he only arrived afterwards, that I couldn't be sure he was involved."

I look up. He'd tried to *help* Leo?

"I had no idea how badly the press would react, the backlash there'd be towards him. I'm so glad he's safely back in jail. Those vigilantes are terrifying."

I stare at him. He was *worried* about Leo?

"Do you know, a guy actually came up to me this afternoon after the funeral and told me he was the one who set fire to Leo's house and chased him back to London?"

"What?" I stare at him.

"He looked so pleased with himself as well. Proud. Like he expected me to *thank* him or something," he says bitterly. "It's horrible. Disgusting. *Vigilantism.* For some people it's nothing to do with right and wrong, it's just an excuse—an outlet for their own pent-up anger and mindless violence. I didn't even know him that well! He was a mate of Neil's, apparently."

Figures, I think bitterly. That's why they were so chummy in the garden. Neil probably knew all about the attacks too—if he wasn't involved himself. After all, he was in Sheffield that weekend. . . .

"But that didn't stop Neil arresting him when I told him what had happened, though he looked heartbroken to do it."

I look up, startled.

"He's a straight arrow, Neil. Honest to a fault. Always has been, ever since he was a boy at school." Uncle Jim looks at me. "That's why your mum chose him as your godfather. It's one of the reasons I—I couldn't tell him the truth about what I'd done." Uncle Jim sighs. "He's my best mate. It would have ripped him in two."

Hot shame burns through me as Neil's words suddenly echo in my ears: *If you're innocent, you should go free, if you break the law, you should pay the price, end of.*

How could I have suspected him—my own godfather?

But then I've just discovered my own uncle killed my cousin.

"Believe me, Lulu, there is *nothing* I'd love more than to erase that day, to take everything back. But I can't. And I have to live with that, every day of my life." He takes a ragged breath, and I realize that his words echo Christian's: *You can't change the past, however much you'd like to. That's the biggest tragedy of all.*

"But *I* can change. And I have. I'm not that man anymore, sweetheart. I swear." Uncle Jim looks up at me, his eyes wide, beseeching. "And I'm so grateful to get a second chance. At life. At fatherhood, with Millie. My sweet little Millie Milkshake. With my wonderful wife. With you." He squeezes my hand.

I look away.

"My family is everything to me, Lulu." His voice quavers. "That's why—that's why I could never tell them." He swallows hard. "That's why I'm asking you—*begging* you." He presses my hand to his heart as his eyes search mine desperately, his voice a whisper. "Please. *Please* don't tell them."

I stare at him, my pulse racing, my head a tangle of emotions. Horror, confusion, scorn, grief—even pity. Tears tumble down my cheeks as I hesitate.

"Jim? It's time to go." There's a light knock at the door and Aunt Grace peers in. Her eyes widen. "What's happened? Are you all right?"

He swallows hard. "Just . . . saying goodbye." He sniffs as he wipes his eyes roughly. "It's always harder than you imagine."

She smiles sadly, nods. Uncle Jim pulls me close, his breath hot and damp against my ear.

"I love you," he whispers. "Take care of them for me."

Numbly, I watch him slowly walk downstairs to say his last goodbyes. He holds Aunt Grace in his arms like she's the most fragile, precious thing in the world, then kisses her tenderly, a tear trickling down his cheek.

"You can't go."

We all turn to see Millie padding down the stairs.

"You can't go with no shoes," she tells him stubbornly. "And they're lost!"

Uncle Jim pulls her gently into his arms, wrapping himself round her entire body.

"You look after them for me," he tells her. "I know I can count on you, right?"

She nods solemnly, and a lump forms in my throat as they rub noses—an Eskimo kiss—before he finally disentangles himself from her clinging arms and gives her to Aunt Grace.

He forces a watery smile, blows us all a kiss, then joins the officer at the door and walks slowly out into the dark, his bare feet gleaming in the pale moonlight.

THIRTY-SIX

"Are you all right?"

I jump as Aunt Grace touches my shoulder. I didn't even notice her come into Poppy's room behind me.

"Yes—yes, I'm fine," I say quickly.

She strokes my hair. "You were a million miles away."

I wish. Everywhere I look I see horrible images—Christian fleeing down the stairs, Poppy smacking her head on her bedpost, Uncle Jim stabbing Tariq . . .

"I called the hospital," Aunt Grace says. "There's still no change—she's still stable. I was going to go up tonight, but . . . Millie's in bed and it's been a really long day, so I thought we could all head up there together in the morning?"

"What?" I blink. "Where?"

"Sheffield." She frowns, touches my forehead. "Are you sure you're okay? You're really pale."

"I'm fine!" I stand up quickly. "That sounds fine. I just need to— Can I borrow your car?" I need to get out of this house or I'll explode.

"Of course," she says, her eyes troubled. "Or I could drive you somewhere, if you like?"

"I'm fine." I smile. "Really. It's just been a tough day and I could do with some fresh air, clear my head. I'll be back later," I tell her, unsure if it's true or not.

"Okay." She nods, handing me the keys.

"Thanks." I move to pass her, but she catches my arm.

"Take care, okay?" she says, her clear eyes deep in mine. "I love you." She kisses my forehead, her lips cool, soft, and I close my eyes, savoring the moment, wondering if she'll still feel the same way about me for much longer.

She finally lets me go and I leave, shivering as the night breeze billows through my hair, the cloudless sky looming like a black hole above me.

I slam the car door behind me and instantly my thoughts crowd into the tight space, my head a tangled tornado of terror and confusion as that horrific scene plays and replays over and over again in my mind. I lean against the steering wheel and shut my eyes, but the colors are brighter than ever, the terrible *thunk* as Poppy's head collides with the bedpost pounding in my head, leaving me sick and shaking.

I open my eyes and start the engine quickly, desperate to leave, to get as far away from this place as possible while I decide what to do with the crucial piece of evidence burning a hole in my pocket.

This is it, I realize wretchedly. This is what I wanted—the evidence that will clear Christian's name once and for all . . . but at what cost?

I think of Aunt Grace, and Millie—they've suffered so much already, how could they possibly survive the truth? The knowledge that the man who ripped their lives apart, who killed their beloved Poppy, is not some faceless stranger, some monster it's easy to hate, but her own father?

It would utterly destroy them.

I'm not that man anymore, Uncle Jim promised. But then, he's not the man everyone thinks he is either. At the moment he's a hero. A loving father, serving time for trying to protect his defenseless daughter.

It's an ocean away from the truth: a drunk father who killed his own child.

But it was an accident! my heart entreats. I know Uncle Jim. His family is *everything* to him, and absolutely nothing in this world could hurt him as much as losing them—and to know that it was his fault? That's the worst torture of all. Poppy was the light of his life—his angel—and she's gone. He'll hate himself forever. But does he really deserve to lose Aunt Grace and Millie too?

How could I do that to him? *Me,* of all people? He's my uncle. More than that—he's been like a *father* to me. He took me in when I had no one, welcomed me into his family, his home. I owe him everything. So how can I be the one to take it all away from him? Who am I to make that decision, anyway? I'm not God, I'm not the police, I'm his *niece,* for God's sake—where are my loyalties?

Suddenly the tune of "Yellow Submarine" fills the car and I freeze.

Christian.

A car horn blares behind me and I realize I've just jumped a red light. I slam on the brakes and swerve to the side of the road quickly, my head pounding madly as the traffic rushes past, my fingers fumbling for Poppy's phone.

I pull it from my pocket and stare at it as it hums merrily in my hand, ripping my heart in two.

How can I even *consider* hiding the truth from Christian? He's suffered for so long, he's done nothing wrong—how can I hold the key to his freedom and not give it to him?

But he's already in jail, a voice inside my head argues. He's already served almost half his sentence . . . and at least he's safe now. Now I know the police didn't leak his location.

But what will happen to him? Will he have to stay in prison for the rest of his sentence? Or longer, as punishment for breaking his curfew?

But he only had a few days of his curfew left—that has to count for something, doesn't it? And his house was torched; he had no choice but to miss his curfew—though he should've gone straight to the police. . . .

And when he finally does get out of prison, what then? Will he just disappear again—another new identity, another new life? Will the people that want to hurt him ever forget . . . ?

The police will protect him, the voice soothes. The public backlash is peaking at the moment because Poppy just died—by the time he gets out it'll be old news, they'll have forgotten. And he's only convicted for burglary, after all. Not murder, like Uncle Jim could be . . .

The phone flashes brightly in the dark car, demanding a decision. My fingers trembling, I press Answer.

"Louise?"

My heart sinks like an anchor.

"Hi."

"Thank goodness—I was about to give up!"

I kick myself mentally.

"Christian, how are you—aren't you in prison?" I frown.

"Yes, but I'm allowed one phone call—I nearly went crazy when you took so long to pick up! Was there anything on the USB stick?" he asks, his voice so full of hope it breaks my heart. "Tell me you found something—a mention of me—anything?"

I screw my eyes closed.

"No." I force the lie out, everything inside me feeling ugly and toxic. "Nothing useful. Just coursework and stuff."

He sighs heavily, and I hear every ounce of hope bleed out of him.

"Right," he says, his voice barely audible. "That's it, then."

The truth swells painfully in my chest, struggling to burst out of me. I'm longing to tell him I've found the evidence that he's innocent, that he's free, that we can be together. . . .

"I love you," he whispers, and tears stream unstoppably down my face. I've never felt so miserable, so utterly wretched, in my whole life.

"Listen, I've got to go," he says quietly. "But I just wanted to say thank you. From the bottom of my heart. You've been incredible, Louise. More than I ever deserved. And I'm sorry, for everything. For all the trouble I've caused you. The danger I've put you in. But I want to ask one more favor."

I hold my breath. *Anything.*

"Forget about me. Move on."

"What? No—Christian—"

"We can't be together," he argues. "When I get out I'll need another new identity—they could send me anywhere—and I . . . I can't ever see you again."

"Christian—"

"No, Lou. I can't put you at risk again. It's too dangerous, too hard."

I struggle to control myself as sobs swell in my throat.

"I really hope you have a wonderful life. I know you will. You deserve it." His voice cracks. "You're amazing, Louise Shepherd, and I love you. I'll always love you."

"I love you too," I whisper, the first true words I've spoken since I answered the phone.

"Goodbye," he whispers, his voice husky.

I try to form the word on my lips, but I can't. *I can't do this,* can't lose him, can't let him take the blame. I take a deep breath. "Christian—"

The phone goes dead in my hand, the dial tone flatlining in my ear.

He's gone.

Forever.

THIRTY-SEVEN

What have I done?

I stare at the phone, dead in my hand, and burst into tears.

What is the right thing to do? What would Poppy do? If she'd woken up and remembered everything, would she have kept quiet to protect her father? Or would she have told the truth? What would she want *me* to do?

I screw my eyes shut as the world blurs around me, but all I see are Poppy's frightened face, Uncle Jim's desperate eyes, and Christian's sad smile.

Whatever I do, someone I love gets hurt—so how can I *choose*?

I can't. I can't do this alone. I can't possibly make this decision by myself . . . but who can I talk to? I can't tell Christian, can't tell Aunt Grace; I can't tell Neil because he's a policeman and his moral code would make him use the evidence whether I want him to or not, and after what happened with Kenny, can I really trust Vix?

No. This is a family problem now—it's not just about truth and lies anymore. It's more complicated than that.

There's only one person I can talk to, I realize suddenly. Only one person I can tell.

I open my eyes, start the car and drive, just drive for hours, till finally I pull into the car park and race through the entrance, not stopping till I'm by her side.

She's still asleep, she probably can't even hear me, but she's here.

I collapse into a chair and Gran lies there silently, hooked up to machines, as I sob my heart out, pouring my story into the hospital bedclothes, hoping against hope that some of her infinite wisdom will seep into me in return.

"How can doing the right thing be so complicated?" I moan. "If only there was a way to protect *everyone*—some way of vindicating Christian without pointing the finger at Uncle Jim. . . ." I rack my brains, turning the USB necklace over and over in my hand.

"Maybe—maybe I could edit Poppy's video diary so that it cuts out before Uncle Jim comes home? Then it'll prove that Poppy and Leo were friends—prove that he was telling the truth . . ." I suggest hopefully.

Gran frowns in her sleep.

"But what about the text message he sent Tariq?" I sigh. "That doesn't look good—it connects them.

"How can I *choose*? How can I decide what to do, who to hurt, when I'm so involved, so biased? Should I sell out my uncle to save my boyfriend, or let Christian take the blame to protect Uncle Jim? How can I make the right choice when it's all mixed up with my own feelings?" I scrunch the sheets up in my fists, my thoughts hopelessly tangled.

"And it doesn't just affect Christian or Tariq or Uncle Jim," I sigh miserably. "It'll hurt their families just as much. Uncle Jim said he wouldn't have cared about telling the truth and going to prison— but he couldn't bear what it would do to his family. And what about Sabina and her baby? They deserve justice too." I think of the gorgeous little boy with his chubby cheeks and long eyelashes—so innocent. "It would be so easy to lay all the blame on a dead man—but he has family too. And they're suffering for what he did. What people *think* he did. But he didn't. He was innocent—he tried to *help* Poppy, and for that he died.

"And Christian . . ." My voice cracks. "All Christian wants is his old life back. His family. His mum. His dad." I think of the sad-eyed shadow of a man hiding from his memories in his allotment shed and my heart twists painfully. "I haven't just robbed him of a few months' freedom, after all. I've taken away his safety, his family—his whole life!" I shake my head.

"But if I tell the truth . . ." I screw my eyes closed. "What about Aunt Grace, and little Millie? You should've seen their faces when they had to say goodbye to him again, Gran." Tears streak through my words. "How could I do that to them? Betray my own family like that—and for what? Doesn't Uncle Jim deserve a second chance?

"But what if it happens again?" My heart sinks. "You should have seen him, Gran, he was really drunk—out of control. I've never seen him like that, not for years and years—since he punched that wall. I don't know what happened, *why* he'd been drinking— he said he'd just had a rough day—but, Gran, if he can slip once . . . what if it happens again? What if he hurts someone else—hurts Millie?" My insides twist at the thought, my head whirling so hard and so fast and so painfully it takes me a moment to feel Gran squeezing my hand, her pale green eyes shining up at me, her lips moving silently.

"Gran! You're awake!" I cry, relief thrilling through me. "Nurse!"

I move to get up, but Gran grips my hand tighter, holding me there, her lips still moving. I lean closer, her breath gentle on my cheek, her voice the softest whisper.

"You know what you have to do."

I look at her, her eyes so clear, so wise.

"Gran?"

She squeezes my hand.

"Is everything okay in here?" A nurse pops her head into the room. "Mrs. Brown! Good of you to join us!"

As the nurse fusses around Gran she holds my gaze and I swallow hard. She's right. *I know exactly what I have to do.*

But somehow it doesn't make me feel any better at all.

THIRTY-EIGHT

"Are you sure about this?" Vix asks me the following day as I stare out of the window at the students below milling about outside the halls of residence, laughing and gossiping without a care in the world. How I envy them.

"Last chance to change your mind," Vix says.

I bite my lip, feeling like I'm poised on the edge of a precipice. I've been changing and rechanging my mind all day, and all last night, stewing over what's the right thing to do, trying to filter through all the possible consequences and ramifications.

Finally I sigh heavily. "I'm sure."

"Okay." She squeezes my shoulder. "You're doing the right thing, you know?"

I turn. "Thanks, Vix. For doing this. For coming all the way back here. For everything."

She smiles, then gives me a hug. "What're friends for?"

I hold her tight and suddenly realize she's the only friend I have left.

"Did Kenny come back with you?" I ask.

"No, he's . . . not coming back," she says quietly. "He's dropping out of uni—said he's going to go to Oxford next year instead."

"I'm sorry, Vix," I say gently. "I know you really liked him."

"Oh no, that ship sailed last week." She smiles. "I don't pursue guys who obviously aren't interested in me—that's not my style. Besides, Matt keeps calling, and sending me all these really cute texts."

"Good." I smile. If I never see Kenny again, it'll be too soon. "I still can't believe he told the vigilantes about Christian. Why would he *do* that?"

"You really don't know?" Vix raises an eyebrow.

"Oh, I know he said he thought it was what I wanted, but I *never* intended Christian to get hurt, and he knew that, so why would he tip off the vigilantes after he'd come all the way to Sheffield to help me *harass* Christian? It doesn't make sense. I could have tipped them off myself, but the whole plan was to be *subtle*. I don't get it."

"You actually don't, do you?"

"What?"

"He's in love with you, Lou." Vix sighs.

I blink. *"What?"*

"You think Kenny followed you all this way just to help you out with Christian? He turned down *Oxford,* for God's sake."

"I know, but—"

"It was an *excuse,* Lou. Kenny was telling the truth on your birthday—he only came to Sheffield Uni because he thought he might have a chance with you."

I frown, remembering the look on his face when he'd told Vix he was in love with me outside Christian's house, how impressed I'd been by how believable he was. *Because he was telling the truth . . . ?*

"Yes, he wanted to help you," Vix continues. "Your campaign against Christian is what brought you together in the first place, after all—it's what you had in common, and it gave him a reason to spend time with you. A shared secret. A *bond. Partners in crime.*

"But then you started having feelings for Christian, and *that* wasn't part of his plan at *all,* so he decided to pull the plug, get rid of Christian once and for all. And then, I guess, everything just snowballed. Love can really mess with your head, you know?"

Love can really mess with your head. . . .

Her words haunt me as I try to get to sleep that night, images of Uncle Jim and Christian filling my mind. My decision would have been so much easier if I didn't love them both—if it was all happening to strangers. If I'd never met Sabina and Ash, it would be so tempting to just leave the blame on Tariq. If Uncle Jim wasn't my uncle, I would've told the police the truth in a heartbeat. And if I'd never met Christian . . .

My throat swells painfully.

If I'd never gone looking for Christian, I'd never have found out the truth, never *fallen* for him, and everything would have been a *million* times simpler. But it's true—right and wrong seem to get all muddled up when your own feelings are involved.

So who am I to judge Kenny, really? After all, I'm the one who hatched this whole wretched plan in the first place.

I toss and turn for hours, till finally it begins to get light and I give up on sleep. I huddle in my duvet, watching the sun rise into a clear blue sky, and wonder how in the world some things can be so simple, so pure, so beautiful. Nothing seems simple anymore. Everything we do, every decision we make has a million unforeseeable consequences, all tangled together. My head throbs, heavy with guilt, with fatigue, helpless to do anything but watch the new day dawn.

I've done my bit now. It's over.

It's only just begun.

The shadows slip slowly behind bins and lampposts and phone booths, hiding as the sun stretches searching scarlet fingers down every street, across every rooftop, as bright and unforgiving as the truth, hunting out the murky lies. But some shadows always remain.

What's that saying? *Red sky in the morning: Shepherd's warning . . .*

My skin prickles, wondering just what this day has in store once this moment's over, once the sun's high in the sky and people repopulate the streets, turn on their televisions, read their papers. . . .

A noise at the door startles me, and I turn to see a newspaper being pushed beneath it into my room. I look over at it for a long moment, my heart pounding with dread. Then I close my eyes and lie down, drained of every last ounce of energy.

It's done now. There's no undoing it.

I only hope I did the right thing. *If such a thing even exists.*

I stay in bed all morning, trying to block out the dawning day, to put off the inevitable for as long as physically possible, praying for the blissful oblivion of sleep. I turn Poppy's phone off and ignore Vix when she knocks on the door, reluctant to face her. To face anyone. Ever.

But I have to.

It's nearly one o'clock by the time I finally force myself to stagger outside, the low winter sun blinding, judging me like a spotlight as I hide behind my sunglasses and climb into Aunt Grace's car.

The radio blares on as I start the ignition and I flick it off quickly, anxious to preserve the silence, the peace, for just a little while longer.

I duck my head as I hurry past the television in the hospital waiting area, and make a beeline for the little gift shop, where I choose some beautiful yellow roses for Gran. But as I turn to the counter to pay there they are:

WILLOUGHBY-WHITE: COP COVER-UP?

WHO REALLY KILLED POPPY?

KILLER COPPER SHOCKER!

My heart sinks as I read the headlines, each carefully designed to ignite the maximum public outrage and hatred.

But what did I expect?

Guiltily, I remember the stacks of cuttings about Christian I'd hungrily collected, each one adding fuel to the fire of my anger and determination to get justice as I eagerly believed every word—not only believed them, but acted on them. Kenny was right; the media is scarily powerful.

I think of the violent vigilantes and feel sick.

I scan the rest of the papers in the rack. They're all jumping on the bandwagon too, spinning more and more salacious headlines. All except one, which has the exclusive:

LEO NILES INNOCENT—THE PROOF!
by Victoria Keeley

She finally got her big break.

I knew Vix would do a great job—she's the only person I could really trust to tell the whole truth, and to keep the focus on Christian, rather than gleefully dragging Uncle Jim's name through the mud like everyone else.

His bearded face stares mournfully out at me—a photo from the funeral—and my insides constrict. What must he be feeling this morning? Fear? Guilt?

Betrayal.

I pay for the roses, then hurry to Gran's ward to find her tucking into macaroni and cheese while watching the lunchtime news.

Her face lights up when she sees me.

"Gran!" I kiss her cheek. "You're looking so much better!"

"Good afternoon, darling!" She beams.

"Is it?" I sigh, glancing at the TV, which is replaying footage from early this morning: Uncle Jim's lawyer outside our house, giving a statement confirming that new evidence has been discovered against Sergeant Willoughby-White but that nothing has yet been proven.

The gathered reporters pelt him with questions, but all I can focus on is the pale face watching from the bedroom window.

Aunt Grace.

"What have I done?" I crumple into a chair.

"You did what you had to do," Gran reassures me. "Sweetheart, this isn't your fault, none of it is. Doing the right thing is rarely easy."

"But *was* it the right thing?" I say miserably.

"Darling, you had no choice," Gran says gently. "Even accidents have consequences that must be faced, and innocent people were suffering."

"But innocent people are *still* suffering," I argue. "Look at Aunt Grace. Think of Millie."

"Think of Sabina and her baby." Gran nods at the TV and I drag my eyes to the screen. A delighted Sabina is beaming at the camera, cuddling Ash, who keeps reaching for her dangling earrings.

"I'm just relieved that the truth is finally out," she says, her dark eyes shining proudly. "That my son can grow up knowing his father was a hero, not a criminal."

"A hero indeed," the reporter comments to camera. "For new evidence shows Tariq Khan entered the property *after* Poppy was attacked and was killed while trying to call for help. Here's what DI Goldsmith had to say about the matter earlier today." The image changes to show the same reporter outside the police station this morning.

"DI Goldsmith, how could you have got this case so wrong?" He points a microphone at the detective, who has aged a decade overnight.

"The footage has yet to be verified," he mutters. "But it does appear that the case may have been more complex than we thought. The justice system is not infallible."

"Did it have anything to do with Sergeant Willoughby-White's position in the police force? Did the police conceal evidence?"

"Absolutely not." The inspector glowers. "This evidence has only just come to light."

"In that case, why do you think this new proof was given to the press, rather than the police?"

The inspector glares into the camera. "No comment."

Of course, after Kenny's confession that he tipped off the vigilantes, I had no real reason to doubt the police, to believe that they were biased, or any proof that they ever knew about Poppy's phone—perhaps they did lie, but then maybe when Christian told them about the text and they said they didn't find it, they meant they couldn't find Poppy's *phone,* not just the text? It could easily have all just been a big misunderstanding—there was no irrefutable reason to believe that I couldn't trust them with this crucial evidence against a former member of their team. . . .

But Vix wasn't sure the webcam footage would be admissible in court anyway, and it could take ages to get it authenticated, and I wanted Christian to be exonerated as soon as possible, if only in the minds of the public and—more importantly—the vigilantes. That way, even if he has to spend the rest of his sentence in jail, when he gets out he will be safe, vindicated, and able to go back home to his family.

"Breaking news just in," the reporter says suddenly. "Following the leaked webcam footage, Sergeant Willoughby-White has *confessed* that he was responsible for his daughter's death."

I look up, startled. *Uncle Jim confessed?*

"His account of what he claims was a tragic drunken accident corresponds exactly with the scene as depicted in the webcam video.

Additionally, he has admitted that Leo Niles was Poppy's friend—and that he knew Leo had arrived that evening to visit Poppy, not burgle the house."

My jaw drops.

"There can be no more room for doubt," the reporter says. "Sergeant Willoughby-White has confessed his guilt and exonerated Leo Niles."

I can't believe it. I stare numbly at the screen, trying to take it all in.

I should be happy. This is what I wanted. The webcam footage might not have been enough to exonerate Christian, but this . . . this has to be. Uncle Jim told the truth about Poppy . . . but he lied about knowing Christian. One final White lie so an innocent man would go free, so he'd be safe.

He did the right thing. In the end.

And now he's lost everything.

"I think I'll go and grab a coffee," I say, feeling queasy. "Do you want anything, Gran?"

"No, thank you, but, sweetheart?" I turn as she smiles. "What you did took great courage. I'm proud of you."

I smile weakly as I push through the door, but once I've rounded the corner I deflate against the wall.

Proud? I've never felt less proud of anything in my life.

I close my eyes. Over the last few weeks I've betrayed everyone I love. Uncle Jim, Aunt Grace, Millie, Poppy, Christian . . .

Their faces float in front of me till I can't bear it. I open my eyes, but Christian's still there, walking towards me.

"Christian!" I gasp. "What are you— How?"

"They released me!" He beams, a beautiful smile filling his face, and for the first time since I've met him it reaches his eyes, which sparkle with happiness.

"You're free?"

"Well, officially I'm on license till my appeal can be scheduled, but there's no arguing with a confession! Did you see the news just now?"

I nod.

"I saw it on the TV in the waiting room as I came through—it's incredible!" He grins. "Of course, that would never have happened without that video evidence—have you seen that too?"

"Yes." I nod. "I've seen it."

He looks at me for a moment, his eyes shining. "It was on the USB stick, wasn't it?"

I nod again. "The password for the website was, anyway."

"And you found it." He grins at me. "I *knew* you must have been behind this—the timing was just too much of a coincidence. You didn't give up on me—even though I told you to. You're amazing." He throws his arms around me and hugs me so tight I think I'll burst. "Thank you. Thank you so much—you've given me my life back!"

The sheer joy in his voice lifts my heart and for the first time since I discovered the truth I find myself smiling too.

This was the right thing to do. Christian's free. He deserves to be free. He's innocent, he's done nothing wrong, and now he has his life back. I did what I had to do. What I always intended to do. I've achieved justice.

Just not at all in the way I expected.

"Joe drove me up here," he says, grinning. "It turns out that it wasn't him who betrayed me—I can't believe I ever suspected him! My lawyer says my location was leaked on Twitter, and Joe doesn't even own a *computer*—he's a complete technophobe! So it *must've* been the police!"

My smile slips.

"Thank God you took your evidence to the papers instead—

352

now everyone knows the truth! It's a miracle! *You're* a miracle!" He squeezes me again. "You have to come and meet my mum. You should have heard her on the phone, Lou, she's beside herself—she doesn't know whether to laugh or cry. *I* don't know whether to laugh or cry!" He laughs. "She can't wait to meet you. She's baking you a cake! Triple chocolate fudge!"

I laugh. "She wants to meet me?"

"Of course! I've told her all about you, my guardian angel."

I shift uncomfortably.

"How did you know I was here?" I ask him.

"I didn't—but when you didn't answer Poppy's mobile I rang the hospital to check on your gran and they told me her granddaughter had prompted a huge recovery. How's she doing? Is she up for visitors?"

"Yes, she's much better"—I smile—"thanks to you."

"Great—can I see her?" He moves past me.

"Actually, Christian, wait!" I hurry after him—*she could still give away my identity!*

But as I round the corner I find Christian frozen outside Gran's door, staring through the window.

"She's with someone. . . ."

"Who?" I follow his gaze to see Aunt Grace sobbing into Gran's arms, and my breath catches.

"Who's that?" He frowns. "She looks familiar. . . ."

"My . . . um . . ." My heart beats wildly as I panic.

"Wait. I know her. She's . . . she's Poppy's mother. . . ." Christian peers closer. "She was on the news this morning."

I hold my breath.

"But what's she doing here?" He looks at me, confused. "How does she know your gran?"

"Christian, I—" I can't think of a single thing to say.

"Oh, Mum!" Aunt Grace wails loudly. "How did this happen?"

My heart plummets at the despair in her voice—and the shock streaking across Christian's face.

"Mum?" He stares at me. "But . . ."

I shrink before him helplessly as his confusion turns to shock, then terrible dawning realization.

"You're Poppy's *cousin?*"

Pinned to the spot, I nod fearfully.

He staggers backwards, as if I'm a stranger. Which I suppose I am.

"You . . ." He struggles for words, his eyes wild. "Did you know who I was all along?"

I hesitate, then nod miserably.

"So you . . . you *lied* to me." He stares at me. "You lied about everything!"

I reach for him. "Christian—"

"Don't touch me!" He snatches his arm away, his jaw set. "I don't know you at all." He turns away.

"Wait!" I cry. "Wait—Christian!"

"Leave me alone!" he snaps.

"No—Christian—please, listen!" I hurry after him.

"I was right, wasn't I?" he says bitterly, walking faster. "Our meeting wasn't an accident. Only it wasn't fate that orchestrated it all, was it? It was you!"

"Christian!"

"Our meeting, our relationship . . . it was all just a sham!" Tears flash in his eyes.

"Please!" I beg, "Listen to me!"

"How did you find me?" He stops suddenly. "How did you know where I was, when it was a secret from the whole world?"

"I—" I falter. "I hacked into the police computers to access your files."

His expression darkens. "You mean *Kenny* did?"

I swallow anxiously, nod.

"Jesus, Lou, how long have you been planning this? Since boarding school?"

I nod again miserably.

"Why?" he snaps, his eyes ice-blue. "Why couldn't you just leave me alone? Let me try to start again, have a second chance?"

"Because . . ." I hesitate.

"Well?" he demands.

"Because you destroyed my family!" I cry, tears flooding my eyes. "Poppy was in a coma, my uncle was in jail, my aunt was in pieces, and my little cousin Millie can't even remember her own sister!" My throat swells painfully. "Why *should* you get to start again when we couldn't? You'd destroyed our whole lives!"

He looks at me, a faint, sad understanding in his eyes.

"But it wasn't me," he says quietly.

"I know that now," I say, tears tumbling down my cheeks. "But everyone said you were involved—Tariq was dead, Uncle Jim was in jail, and you were free—*free!* The papers were full of it—it wasn't fair, it wasn't right—you deserved to be punished!"

"Punished?" He frowns, then suddenly he stares at me. "*You? You're* behind the prank calls? The missing keys? The break-in?" He stares at me incredulously. "Bloody hell! Did you start the fire too?"

"*No!*" I stare at him. "No, how could you *think* that?"

"I don't know what to think anymore! I don't know you at all, or what you're capable of."

"I never wanted to hurt you!" I insist. "Just—I just wanted to scare you."

"Well, it worked. Do you know how worried I was about my family—their safety? I was terrified! How could you *do* that?"

I stare at my feet, my cheeks burning. "I'm sorry."

"You're *sorry?*" he snaps. "Because of you I broke my bloody curfew. Because of you I risked *everything!*"

I close my eyes.

"And for what?" he demands. "I thought you were different. I thought you believed in me." He strides on down the corridor.

"I do!" I insist, running to keep up. "I *do* believe in you—I proved your innocence, didn't I?"

"But you nearly didn't!" he counters bitterly. "I asked you outright if there was any evidence on that USB stick and you said no. 'No, Christian, there's nothing there. *Nothing useful,*'" he mocks. "That's the key word, isn't it? *Useful.* Useful to you. Useful to your family."

"I betrayed my family to save you!"

"You told the *truth!*" he corrects. "But you weren't going to, were you? You were ready to sell me down the river to save your uncle. Your child-abusing, murdering, racist uncle!"

"You don't *know* him!" I protest.

"No," he says coldly. "I don't know *you.*"

"You do!" I insist desperately. "Christian, please!"

"Why did you change your mind, then?" He turns suddenly. "Why did you decide to tell the truth after all?"

"I . . ." I falter. "I did it for you . . ."

His eyes narrow skeptically.

"And Sabina and Ash—and Millie . . ."

His expression clears. "Of course." He nods. "You were worried he'd do it again. To Millie. You did it for her."

"And for you!" I insist. "I couldn't bear to ruin your life, to never see you again!"

"So it was our sham relationship you wanted to save? What did you think would happen? That you'd clear my name and we'd run off together to some happy-ever-after? Me eternally grateful and

356

you—whoever you are—lying your head off every single day we're together?"

I stare at him helplessly.

"I thought you were the only person in the world I could trust," he says quietly, his eyes deep in mine. "But you've told me more lies than anyone else I know—from the moment we met. You've lied about absolutely everything."

"Not everything!" I protest, grabbing his hand. "I didn't lie about my feelings. I love you."

"Why should I believe you?" He stares at me coldly. "How can I ever believe anything you say?"

He rips his hand away and storms out through the hospital doors. They hiss at me as they slide shut, leaving me facing my own miserable reflection as he walks out of my life forever.

He's right. All this time I was worried about him lying to me, using me, tricking me. And all along it was me doing the lying. The using. The tricking. He's been nothing but honest, and I've told nothing but lies.

I close my eyes, unable to look at myself a moment longer.

THIRTY-NINE

"Lulu?"

The voice is so quiet that I can almost pretend I didn't hear it, that my heart plummeted another fifty feet for no reason at all.

"Lulu, can I talk to you?"

I sigh heavily and turn round to face yet another person whose life I've just single-handedly destroyed. Aunt Grace looks like a shadow, her face blotchy and pale, dark circles ringing her desolate eyes.

"Shall we sit in the car?" she says, drifting past me through the sliding doors. "It's more private."

I follow her outside, unlock her car, and slide numbly into the passenger seat. The car door slams behind me, sealing me inside with my guilt, with the consequences of my actions.

Aunt Grace slips silently into the driver's seat.

"Aunt Grace, I'm so sorry," I blurt. "I wasn't going to tell anyone, but . . ." I falter. "But I didn't feel I had a *choice*—there were other people involved, other innocent people were suffering— But you've been so good to me, you and Uncle Jim, and I feel so terrible—"

"Darling girl." The touch of her cool hand on mine stops me, midsentence. "I'm not angry with you."

Slowly, I look up at her, her face pale, gaunt.

"I'm angry with *him*. I'm angry with myself. I should never have

358

left Poppy there when . . . when I left Jim." She blinks quickly. "When we separated."

I stare at her. *"What?"*

"Things between us . . . hadn't been good for a while." She sighs. "We were both so busy, we hardly saw each other. We drifted apart, I suppose."

I frown. Since when? Why didn't I know about this? How could I have been completely unaware?

But then I remember Poppy's Skype call. *The atmosphere at home's been terrible since you left—they're doing my head in. Mum's always at her cookery class, and Dad's working too hard. . . .*

"I suppose I didn't really notice at first—the house was always so full of laughter and fun with you and Poppy—and then Millie came along and surprised us all, and it was like starting all over again, a wonderful whirlwind of giggles and nappies. But then . . ." Aunt Grace falters. "Then with you off at boarding school and Poppy in the library all the time studying for her exams, and Millie starting at play group, I . . . suddenly had more time on my hands. When Jim and I found ourselves alone together—for the first time in years—I suddenly realized we didn't really have very much to say to each other. And then I started going to a cookery class and I . . . I met someone."

"What?" I stare at her. "Who?"

"It doesn't matter." She shrugs. "It's over."

"Amir," I say, remembering the tender look in his eyes as he gazed at Aunt Grace at the house. Her cookery instructor.

She nods. "He just made me feel so . . . alive again." She smiles sadly. "I didn't even realize what I was missing out on till we met. It was love, Lulu. True love."

Aunt Grace *cheated* on Uncle Jim?

"We didn't act on our feelings." Her cheeks color. "I couldn't betray Jim like that, but I didn't know *what* to do. I wanted . . . I needed some space to think things through, clear my head. I arranged to stay at Mum's that weekend. I took Millie too and had asked Poppy to come, but she wanted to stay at home for some reason. I guess now we know that it was because she was planning to go to Glastonbury.

"But then Jim found out about Amir." Aunt Grace pales. "He read a text on my phone that lunchtime, and challenged me about it in front of Millie. . . ." She snatches a ragged breath. "We had the most terrible row. He accused me of cheating on him, of breaking up our family. It was awful!"

So *that's* why Uncle Jim overreacted when Tariq arrived. *Thieving Paki scum—you're all the same!* He thought Tariq was taking Poppy away from him, just as Amir had taken Aunt Grace.

"I should've waited for Poppy to come home, told her what was happening," Aunt Grace sobs. "But Jim was shouting and Millie was crying—I couldn't stay in that house. I had to leave." She shakes her head. "I called Poppy over and over on her mobile, left messages begging her to call me back. But she never did—I don't know if she even got them."

I remember Aunt Grace's unread texts on Poppy's phone, and how happy Poppy had seemed on the webcam. *She never knew.*

"It's *my* fault Jim got drunk!" Aunt Grace dissolves in tears. "It's my fault he flew off the handle when he saw she'd packed her bags, and it's my fault she's—"

I throw my arms around her as she shakes uncontrollably, her whole body trembling and cold.

"I felt so guilty. I thought what happened was my punishment." Tears streak her face. "And then I thought Jim was such a hero, that he'd gone to prison for trying to save our Poppy—I felt I owed him a second chance at our marriage, at our family. But truthfully, I've been so worried about his return."

I nod slowly. "And now?"

She shakes her head. "We can't go back. Especially now."

I swallow hard as I try to take it all in.

"What will you tell Millie?" I ask quietly.

"The truth," Aunt Grace says, her eyes clear. "When she's old enough. There's no point pretending." She sighs. "There's been far too much of that already."

"I'm so sorry," I tell her. "I wish I'd never found out—"

"No," she says, catching my hand. "I'm glad you did. I'd rather know the truth, however terrible. It's the only way we can really deal with what's happened, the only way we can try to move on." Tears splinter her words and I squeeze her hand tightly.

Move on . . . It seems so impossible at the moment. The rug's been pulled out from under our feet yet again, and it'll take time for things to settle down, to adjust to our new life. Without Poppy. Without Uncle Jim . . .

"We will get through this," I promise, remembering Gran's words. "One day at a time. Together. *Everything will be okay.*"

I wrap my arms tightly around Aunt Grace, pulling her close and stroking her hair, as she's comforted me so many times before, hoping with all my heart it's true.

Eight Months Later

"Ready?" Aunt Grace asks as I step into the blinding June sunlight.

I take a deep breath. "As I'll ever be."

The truth is, I didn't even want to wake up this morning, didn't want to come here, didn't want to remember what date it was. But Aunt Grace was determined.

"It's important," she said. "We can't undo what happened, but we shouldn't try to forget that day two years ago either. It changed all our lives."

Two years. I can't believe it's really been two years.

It feels like just yesterday.

It feels like a lifetime.

I gaze around the sunny graveyard as I follow Aunt Grace, Gran, and Millie down the winding pathway. It's changed so much since the day we buried Poppy. Then, the ground was shrouded in damp dead leaves, but now it is carpeted with pretty flowers coming into bloom, a sign of new life, new beginnings . . . new hope.

"Let's play hide-and-seek!" Millie cries.

"I . . ." I hesitate. I'm not really in the mood for games, and it *is* a graveyard.

"What a wonderful idea!" Gran smiles. "Let's hide together and wait for someone to find us!"

"Okay!" Millie beams.

"Poppy was always *wonderful* at hide-and-seek," I hear Gran say as they wander off, hand in hand.

"I know!" Millie grins. "That's why I want to play it!"

I smile as she skips through the leafy shadows, the dappled sunlight dancing over her golden hair.

"She's come through this better than anyone." Aunt Grace smiles. "Thanks to you."

I shake my head. "I haven't done anything."

"You've been here for her," she argues, wrapping her arm around my shoulders. "For both of us. I don't know what we'd have done without you."

"You've always been there for me," I counter. "I owe you everything."

"You don't owe me a thing—you're family." She kisses my head. "But I still feel bad about you dropping out of uni."

"I'll start again in September." I shrug. "And hopefully I'll get better grades now that I've retaken my A levels!"

"You should—you've worked so hard. I'm so proud of you." She beams. "And . . . and thank you for your support with Amir too. I know it must be weird, now that we've started seeing each other again. It probably seems really quick."

"You've waited months." I smile. "Over a year, really. And Amir's lovely. He's great with Millie, he adores you, and life's short." I squeeze her tight. "You need to do what makes you happy, be with *people* who make you happy. You never know . . . when they'll be gone."

I think of Poppy and Uncle Jim . . . Just two years ago I completely took them both for granted, two of the people I love most in the whole world—forgetting to call them back, letting months go by between visits. I was so wrapped up with myself and my own new life at boarding school, I had no idea what was going on back home, no clue things weren't right between Aunt Grace and Uncle Jim, was oblivious that Poppy had met a new guy in the art gallery. . . . If I'd just made more of an effort, been more attentive, more involved, then perhaps . . . I sigh. Christian was right, you can't change the past.

But you can learn from it.

That's why, wherever I end up studying in September, I'm not going to make the same mistake again. I'm going to stay in touch as much as possible, like I am with Uncle Jim. It hasn't been easy. I was scared to visit him at first. Terrified he wouldn't want to see me, that he'd hate me, even, after my terrible betrayal. But before I could say a single word he just wrapped his huge arms around me and hugged me so hard my insides crumbled. When we finally parted both our faces were streaked with tears.

"I'm so sorry, Lulu," he sighed, his eyes shining. "You did the right thing—what I should have done a long time ago. I'm sorry I didn't. I'm sorry I lied about it. And I'm—I'm so sorry for what I did."

"I know." I nodded. Then we hugged again until the warden made us part.

A few visits later, I brought Millie with me. Aunt Grace still didn't feel up to facing Uncle Jim, but she decided Millie was now old enough to visit him, and that it was important that she should have her father in her life.

"He's still her daddy, and she needs him," Aunt Grace told me. "And he needs her. Whatever he's done, he doesn't deserve to lose both his daughters."

We'd all been anxious about how she'd cope, seeing him in prison, but she just squealed with delight and jumped into his arms as Uncle Jim's face exploded with joy. Then we spent the whole hour playing together in the children's area, reading stories and painting pictures.

We've been to see him every two weeks since then. Occasionally Aunt Grace comes too, and I write to him as often as I can. He needs our support now more than ever, since the country's turned against him, the tabloids demonizing him for what happened, just like they originally did with Christian.

But Uncle Jim's no more a demon than Christian appeared to be. He's human. He's made mistakes. And God knows, he's paying for them. He'll be tortured with the guilt and heartache of killing his beloved Poppy for the rest of his life. The rest of the country should just mind their own business.

Suddenly Aunt Grace stops walking, and I look up, surprised. I follow her gaze to see a woman kneeling by a grave, with a stroller.

Sabina.

I swallow hard. It's the first time I've seen her since Poppy's funeral, but of *course* she'd be here today—it's the day Tariq died, after all. I watch as she slowly stands up, turns—then freezes when she spots us.

Before I can say anything, Aunt Grace hurries towards her.

"My dear girl, can you ever forgive me?" she asks, taking her hand.

Sabina's eyes widen.

"You've been through so much, suffered such a great loss." She turns to Tariq's headstone. "He was a very brave young man, and I'm sorry that it's taken so long for that to be recognized." She gestures to the bouquet in her hand. "May I?"

Sabina nods, and Aunt Grace bends down to gently place a white carnation on Tariq's grave. She takes a deep breath and touches the headstone gingerly.

"I'm so very sorry for what happened," she sighs, shaking her head. "For everything . . ." Her voice cracks.

Sabina stares at her for a moment, then steps forward and places her hand on Aunt Grace's shoulder.

"It's not your fault," she says quietly. "You didn't know. None of us knew what really happened."

Aunt Grace shakes her head wretchedly. "But I *should* have known—he was my husband, she was my *daughter*."

"Yes. She was your daughter. Your child," Sabina says, glancing at Ash. "And I'm so very, very sorry for your loss."

Aunt Grace looks up at her, her eyes full.

"She was a lovely girl," Sabina tells her. "She was too young to die."

Aunt Grace nods. "So was Tariq."

"He was." Sabina sighs. "But now at least the world knows the truth about him, who he *really* was." She looks at me. "Leo told me what you did. Thank you. It must've been really hard."

I nod. "Doing the right thing often is."

She smiles sadly. "It never stopped Tariq."

"He was a true hero," Aunt Grace tells her. "You should be very proud."

"I am." Sabina smiles. "We both are, aren't we, Ash?"

"Well, hello, Ash!" Aunt Grace smiles, bending over his stroller and shaking the toddler's hand. "How lovely to meet you. What a handsome young man!"

Ash grins at Aunt Grace, then pulls his blanket over his face.

"He's a bit shy," Sabina laughs and I marvel at how much she's changed since the funeral—how much younger she seems, her face falling naturally into a smile, her eyes bright. Happy.

"Can I . . ." Sabina hesitates. "I mean, would you mind giving Poppy a flower—from me?" She picks out a beautiful pink bloom from Tariq's grave and offers it to Aunt Grace.

Aunt Grace looks at it for a moment, then shakes her head, wraps her arm around Sabina's shoulders. "We'll go together."

I smile as I follow them along the path to Poppy's grave. They're free. Free from guilt, from persecution, from the shadow of Tariq's alleged crime. The truth has set them free, and now Sabina and Ash can finally live their lives in peace.

And so can Christian. Wherever he is. He's a free man. No longer Christian Webb. No longer a criminal. No longer a jailbird.

I watch a flock of birds scatter into the air as we approach, swooping through the boundless blue sky. What an odd term— *jailbird*. If there's one creature that should never be caged, it's a bird. I watch them flutter and soar, chirping and singing, my heart lifting as they fly far, far away, disappearing into the distance.

I may never see him again, but at least that's his choice now. He's free to do whatever he wants.

And I'm glad. I know I did the right thing.

"Well, I never," Sabina says suddenly. "Isn't that a sight for sore eyes? *Leo!*"

My heart stops.

Slowly, unable to breathe, I turn and drag my gaze across the graveyard, goose bumps breaking out down my arms.

His hair is back to his natural blond, and cropped short, making him look younger than he did before, but as those piercing blue eyes meet mine it's like the last eight months just melt away.

Christian.

Before I can read his expression, his gaze flicks to Sabina as she laughs and rushes over to him. Aunt Grace follows, but my feet are rooted to the ground.

I watch him embrace Sabina warmly and my heart aches—I'm desperate to run to him, but terrified of rejection.

Slowly, he releases her and bends to gently lay down a bouquet of flowers.

At Poppy's grave.

My heart plummets. Of course. *Poppy.* He's come to see Poppy. Not me.

"You found us!" Millie cries, rushing at Aunt Grace as Gran

walks out from behind a tree. They all gather round Poppy's grave, but I can't move, can't join them.

I stare at my feet, trying to make myself invisible. He has every right to hate me. And whatever I do, I don't want to make things worse.

Suddenly there's a sound of someone clearing their throat and I look up, startled.

"Not interrupting anything, am I?" he asks, eyebrows raised.

"No . . . no, sorry, I—I just . . . ," I stammer, looking away quickly. "Sorry, I didn't expect you to be here. Sorry." I stare at my feet.

"Lou, look at me."

But I can't. I can't face him after all I've done.

"I thought I might find you here today," he says quietly.

He did?

"I went to your house a while ago."

Really? Hesitantly, I allow myself to look up a little. I stare at his trainers. "We moved," I say. "There were . . . too many memories."

He nods. "I tried your halls too."

He went all the way to *Sheffield*? My gaze drifts up to his knees.

"I . . . dropped out," I explain. "I decided to resit my A levels instead, and apply somewhere closer to home. Make a fresh start."

"Seems like everyone is," he comments. "Vix too. I couldn't find her in Sheffield either, but then I saw her byline in the paper. She's doing really well."

I smile. "She is."

"She owes you a lot," he says, stepping closer. "We both do."

My heart beats harder.

"I'm an idiot, Lou. You gave me my life back and gave me a future worth living, and how did I repay you?"

My eyes travel slowly up to his stomach.

368

"Because of you, now everyone knows the truth. Not just about me, but Tariq too." He looks over at Aunt Grace and Sabina chatting to Gran, while Millie and Ash race each other between the trees, giggling.

"You did this. You told the truth. That's all I ever wanted." He turns to me. "Till now. Till you."

I dare to raise my gaze to his chest, my heart racing.

"Let's have our own fresh start," he suggests. "No more lies." He holds out his hand and finally, nervously, I look up and meet his gaze.

"Hello." He smiles, those blue eyes sparkling at me. "I'm Leo."

"Hi." I smile back, his hand warm in mine as I shake it tentatively. I take a deep breath, hesitate. *The truth.*

"I'm Lucinda."

His eyes widen for a moment, then he laughs, a rich, warm sound, and shakes his head in disbelief.

"Well, it's nice to meet you at last, Lucinda." He grins, pulling me closer. "Truly."

And as his lips meet mine and the last of our lies are scattered to the wind, finally, wonderfully, it's just me and him.

Acknowledgments

Huge thanks . . .

To my wonderful editors, Jane Griffiths, Michelle Poploff, Amy Black, Venetia Gosling, and Rebecca Short, for believing in me and my characters, and without whom this tale—and my life—would be a very different story.

To my brilliant agent and lovely friend, Jenny Savill, and all at the fantastic Andrew Nurnberg Associates for your incredible warmth, faith, support, and guidance.

To Guido Liguori, for so very generously sharing his wisdom, advice, and expertise.

To all my uni mates, especially Andy, Lander, Steve, Nick, Mach, and Sean, who not only made my time in Sheffield so memorable but became friends for life.

To all my author friends at The Edge and SCBWI, for their much-valued insights, good humor, and encouragement.

To Chris, for his endless support and love through this roller-coaster of a dream, for not going crazy when I became a hermit, and for keeping me sane, making me laugh, and doing the washing up when it wasn't his turn.

And finally to my incredible family, who are a constant—and much treasured—source of love, laughter, and inspiration.

Thank you all, from the bottom of my heart.

About the Author

KATIE DALE loves nothing more than creating characters—both on the page and onstage. She studied English literature at Sheffield University and spent a year at the University of North Carolina at Chapel Hill, followed by a crazy year at drama school, a summer with a national Shakespeare tour, and eight months backpacking through Southeast Asia. Her debut novel, *Someone Else's Life,* was a winner of the Undiscovered Voices competition run by the Society of Children's Book Writers and Illustrators British Isles. She is busily working on a variety of projects, from novels to picture books, while occasionally treading the boards as a princess, zombie, or fairy when she has time. She lives in England.